CASHMERE RUIN

GROZA BRATVA
BOOK 2

NICOLE FOX

CASHMERE RUIN

GROZA BRATVA DUET BOOK 2

My baby's here.

Her father's not.

And if I have it my way, we'll never see him again.

Because Matvey Groza stomped my heart to smithereens.

It went pretty much like this:

ME: "I love you."

HIM: "I'm marrying someone else."

I'm paraphrasing, but not by much.

Because some facts are undeniable.

Matvey got me pregnant. FACT.

I'm just now starting labor. FACT.

But Matvey is nowhere to be found. FACT.

Because he's busy getting married...

To the other woman he knocked up. FACT.

He said there's more at play than I could understand, but what's so hard to understand about that?

He swore he'd be there for me, and he's not.

He said he loved me, but he doesn't.

So I'm taking our baby and I'm running.

Let him try to catch us if he can.

CASHMERE RUIN is Book 2 of the Groza Bratva duet. The story begins in Book 1, **CASHMERE CRUELTY**.

PROLOGUE: MATVEY

I step through the woods in dead silence.

Yuri is covering my left flank, Grisha my right. With a single gesture from me, they spread out, circling the edge of the forest. The moon is high, but the trees swallow it whole, hiding it from sight. Behind the clouds, the stars are blind. There is no light to guide the way.

Only me.

I send my men into a wide arc around the perimeter. Then, with my gun drawn, I advance alone.

It's better this way. This is what suits me best. Me, myself, and the cold bite of steel in my hands.

I don't need to be betrayed twice tonight.

I make my way into the heart of the woods. Slowly, without stepping on a single branch. There are sentinels everywhere around here—it's a good thing they're as dumb as they look.

Finally, I spot it: a cabin in the distance. The windows are lit, a faint yellow seeping into the black and green around it.

Almost there. Just a few more seconds, and you'll find her.

Just a few more seconds, and she'll be in your hands again.

I listen in. Muffled conversation comes my way, but I can't make out a sound. No matter. This will all end quickly.

With my back to the cabin wall, I breathe in deep. I count back from *three, two, one…*

Then I kick down the cabin door and I see her. The mother of my child. The woman who disappeared from my life on my wedding day.

And the witch who took my daughter from me.

"April."

I want to demand explanations. Want to get up in her face and bellow with rage. I want to fucking howl.

But right now, all the anger I've nursed over these long weeks apart is knocked back. Right now, as I stare at the woman who ruined my life, I'm forced to swallow my fury.

Because there's another man in the room.

And he's pointing a gun at April's head.

I train my eyes on the shiny barrel. "Let her go," I snarl, my own weapon raised and ready to strike.

The man in the shadows chuckles. I can't see his face like this, nothing past a sharp chin. Only the cold glint of steel in one hand…

And the pink bundle cradled in the other.

Half-asleep, the baby coos weakly. I take in its little face: the shape of its nose, the curve of its tiny mouth, the color of its sparse hair.

There's no mistaking who it belongs to: it's April's, through and through.

Which means...

"Give me my daughter!" I roar.

But once again, the man simply laughs. There's something in his laughter that makes my skin crawl—something fucking creepy.

And fucking familiar, too.

It can't be, I tell myself, forcing my grip not to waver. *It's too early for this. We're not ready yet.*

I can't face him *now.*

As if reading my mind, the man steps out of the shadows. Slow, at his leisure—as if taking a stroll in the goddamn park.

And then, when he comes in full view, my worst fear is confirmed. When he smiles that horrifying smile, teeth gleaming like fangs, I know there's no one else this can be.

Only one person.

"You."

1

APRIL

24 HOURS EARLIER

"Concierge, how can I help you?"

Looping the phone lanyard around my neck like the noose it is, I start folding the towels. Though "folding" is a strong word. An even stronger word? "Towels." A dirty kitchen rug would be less of a health code violation than whatever passes for cleaning implements around here. One more round in Mrs. Tanner's germ-breeding excuse for a washing machine, and they'll end up developing a conscience.

Oh, well. At least that means somebody would have one in this place. I don't think my current bosses ever had that problem—certainly not Mrs. Tanner.

Or a soul, for that matter. You'd have better luck scanning for ghosts.

Though I would advise against waving around a blacklight. Some things are better left unseen.

"Bedbugs, you say?" I ask the caller as I pile up the clean laundry. Again, strong word. "Oh, those aren't *bugs*, ma'am, not really. If anything, I'd say they're bed*features*. Ever heard of a cat hotel? It's a bit like that."

Ms. Room 104 yells into my brain. It's an ear-splitting screech, a cross between a banshee and a dial-up modem. Nothing I haven't heard before. Ms. Tanner isn't big on what we'd call "customer service."

"A one-star review?" I try my best to gasp, but all I can manage is a yawn. "How terrible. So sorry your experience hasn't been up to standard. Tell you what: I can recommend a good place to eat. I swear to you, the wontons are to *die* for."

I take the clean(ish) sheets up to the third floor and start my final round of cleaning. If it can even be called that. With how quick Mrs. Tanner expects me to be, it's a miracle I manage to wash anything at all.

Probably because they weren't expecting you to actually do it, I realize with a shudder.

I vacuum the carpets (if they can even be called that), strip the beds (again, if they can even be called that), mend a couple of mysterious holes in the sheets (again—), and so on. All the while, the customer keeps yelling my ear off.

Just another Tuesday, really.

"Oh, you—you want *me* to go die?" I blurt out as I empty the bin. I always try not to look, but it's like watching a train wreck: you don't want to see it, but you also kind of do. "That's not very nice, ma'am. If you didn't like Chinese, you could've just said so."

Then I check under the pillows for drugs.

Not for me, of course. It's just that the local cartel seems particularly fond of hiding things inside pillowcases, especially if said things are expensive. And against the law. I suppose a motel in the middle of nowhere does make for an ideal storage space.

But I don't want that kind of trouble here.

I'm done with gang activity. And this may be a short-term, shitty gig, but I don't want anything jeopardizing it.

For now, at least, I need it.

I need a shitty boss like Mrs. Tanner, willing to turn a blind eye in exchange for me beavering away. As long as I don't kick up a fuss, or turn up my nose at the—ahem—bed*features* crawling all around the place, she'll let me keep my relatively clean room, my anonymity, and my hard-won freedom by not mentioning me to the authorities.

Or the newborn in my room.

That's the crux of the matter, really. That's the reason I don't want to get involved with anything dangerous—with any*one* dangerous—again.

Because it's not just about me anymore.

After finishing my rounds, I drag myself back to my room. "Exhausted" doesn't even begin to cover how I feel. But the second I lay eyes on the bundle by the window, everything melts away.

As if sensing my presence, the baby stirs. She lets out a whine, grabby hands reaching up into the air.

I cross the room and make my way to the crib. "Hush," I whisper, taking her in my arms. "Mommy's got you, Nugget."

I smile to myself. It's hard to remember sometimes that it's not her name anymore. Hasn't been for almost four weeks.

It's still a good nickname, though.

She gurgles against my chest, demanding dinner.

"I swear," I shake my head as I oblige, "sometimes, you're just like your father."

As Nugget latches on, I let my mind wander. I try my hardest not to think of him. Every day, from the moment the sun rises to its last blink over the trees, I dive into my work and try to forget him.

But sometimes… sometimes, I let myself remember.

"Matvey…" I breathe into the silence, too quiet for anyone to hear.

I wonder if he'd like her. If he'd look at her with the same cold gaze he did me that last time we saw each other, or if he'd let himself thaw. If he'd be warm with her as he once was with me.

I wonder if he'd smile.

It's pointless, I scold myself. *You've already made your choice.*

I don't regret what I did. It was the only play I had left. The only thing that would let my child grow up free from the shackles I've struggled against all my life.

I had to break the cycle. I had to break *free*.

Even if it meant breaking free from him.

"Seriously? You're already sleeping again?" I let out a laugh.

In my arms, Nugget coos tiredly. She's a real sleepyhead—a dream baby, honestly. Just as cozy as she was in my belly, though I have no idea where she gets it from. Certainly not from me.

Certainly not from her dad, either.

Just as I'm pushing away the thought of Matvey again, there's a knock on the door. A series of knocks, in fact, delivered with extreme precision.

"Come in!"

The door opens. The heavenly smell of takeout wafts in, making my stomach growl. "Can we please change the knock? I can't stress how unsafe this is."

"Hey!" I protest. "What do you have against *Shave and a Haircut*? It's a classic."

"And that's exactly why it will be anyone's first guess. It's not a secret knock if the junkie down the road can do it."

"Bold of you to assume the junkies *stay* down the road," I mutter.

"You picked this castle, princess, not me."

"Fair." I make grabby hands at the takeout bags. "Now, gimme. Mommy's hungry."

Wordlessly, Yuri hands them over.

Yuri. If anyone had told me two weeks ago that this would happen, I would've asked them where they kept the good stuff. Or not—what with the pregnancy and all—but still.

Instead, here we are.

"He hasn't stopped searching, you know," Yuri mutters around a mouthful of kung pao chicken. "He sent out another party today, not too far from here."

"But not here?" I venture.

"But not here."

Of course he hasn't. All this time, Yuri's been covering for me —overseeing the search, steering people away from the motel.

There's no way I would've made it four weeks under Matvey's radar otherwise.

"How is he?" I ask, unable to keep my mouth shut.

"How do you think?" Yuri snaps, but without any real bite. If anything, he just seems sad. "He's torn up inside, April. Hasn't slept a wink since it happened. Since..." He lets the sentence hang in the air, unfinished.

"Since you helped me run," I finish for him.

I regret those words immediately. Yuri's face tightens, darkens. His eyes fill with pain, with a thousand conflicting feelings at once.

"Why did you?" I finally ask. "Help me run?"

I remember it like it was yesterday: the hospital, the birth, the pain. The blood on the sheets and the phone in my hand.

"Yuri. It's me. I need your help."

It takes a while for him to speak. When he finally does, his voice is tight, too. "Matvey wasn't..." He hesitates. "He wasn't his best self back then. I can only imagine what that meant for you."

He told me he'd lock me up in a cage and never let another man near me, I almost spit, but I manage to stop myself. Even if Matvey said those things, I can't imagine he fully meant them. Or that he meant them the way I took them. And if he did...

Either way, Yuri doesn't need to hear it.

"He married Petra," I say instead. "He has a legitimate heir on the way. He didn't need me. Didn't need *us.*"

"Maybe he did," Yuri mutters, expression unreadable. "Maybe he needed you more than ever. Maybe he still does."

I don't reply to that.

It's pointless anyway: I made my choice. I *left.* There's no coming back from that.

Not with someone like Matvey Groza.

"Wanna hold her?" I ask instead.

It's one of the best moments of the day—getting to drop my baby in Yuri's arms. Watching his face go white and red at the same time, like he has no idea where his hands even go.

But he's been learning. "She really likes you," I say.

Yuri winces. "She likes everyone. She just wants something warm to snuggle into."

I watch his gruff face slip into a smile and I melt. *He looks so much like Matvey.*

"You're going to be a great dad one day, you know?"

Yuri chokes on his next bite.

I can't help it then—I laugh. I laugh with all I have. Things might be rough now. They might even be terrible. I'm at the lowest I've ever been, with no one to talk to but my daughter's spiritually teenaged uncle, and yet…

And yet, somehow, I think it'll be okay.

No, *I know i*t will be okay.

Because I'll make damn sure of it.

2

MATVEY

"Nice of you to join us, brother."

At the sound of my voice, the rest of the *vory* turn as one to the conference room's door. Sarcasm drips thick from my tone, but Yuri takes it without a word. He lowers his gaze, gives a quick bow of apology, and rushes to take his place at my side, not once dropping the beaten dog aura.

At least he has the decency to look sorry.

I can't say I'm fond of his newfound habit of his— disappearing into thin air at a moment's notice. Being late to meetings, late to summons, when we both know perfectly well the difference a split second can make in a crisis.

When you're Bratva, you don't get the luxury of being late.

Or of not being there at all.

"Anybody care to catch up my second?"

A few uncomfortable glances are exchanged. Gora clears his throat, while Ipatiy shuffles on his chair, opening and closing his mouth like the world's fattest goldfish, neither one sure if it's their turn to speak.

Finally, Ivan rises. "The updates are few." His clear voice echoes in the conference room. "We've ruled out the last of the neighboring states. So far, the search has been fruitless."

Quick, concise, to the point.

And most of all, merciless.

One month. It's been one whole month since my child—my *daughter*—was spirited away by her mother. Without a sign, without a word. Only a shitty letter goodbye.

I keep replaying the contents in my head: April's accusations, her reasons, her traumas.

Excuses, all of it.

That's what I keep telling myself, at least. If April truly felt that way, she would've said something. *Should've* said something.

What if she tried, though?

I silence that annoying voice at the back of my head. *Trying* isn't good enough. It isn't a good enough excuse to take my daughter away from me.

You left her out of the blue, that stubborn voice presses on. *You told her you loved her, then went to marry another woman. You let her think Petra was pregnant with* your *child.*

You didn't trust her with the truth. So what did you think was going to happen?

"Expand the search," I order. "Get as far as the West Coast if you have to. I want them found, and I want them found now."

Stanislav clears his throat. "*Moy pakhan...* if I may, there's still the matter of the D.C. deal to fix…"

"Did I fucking stutter?" I snarl. "I said *now*. Everything else can and will goddamn wait."

"But—"

"This meeting is adjourned." With that, I storm out of the conference room.

Yuri and Grisha hurry after me. "Motya—"

"Don't you 'Motya' me. Where the fuck have you been?"

Yuri reels back as if slapped. Grisha moves discreetly to shut the door to my office as my brother stammers out a weak, "I…"

Out of the corner of my eye, I see Grisha shake his head in disbelief. "This isn't looking good for you, Yurochka. You realize that, I hope?"

"Shut up," Yuri growls.

"Sneaking here and there, always late to everything. If I didn't know any better, I'd think you had something to hide."

I slam my palm on my desk. "Quit yapping, both of you."

I don't appreciate Grisha's tone, or his accusations. Truth be told, I've been fed up with him for a while.

But Yuri isn't making it easy to defend him. "You will explain yourself, brother," I say. "Because if you can't—"

"I was in Jersey."

Grisha's eyes go wide. I suspect mine do, too.

I take in the full implications of his words. Then, without glancing away from my brother's face, "Grisha, leave us."

"Pardon?"

"Leave us," I repeat. "Now."

A moment's hesitation. "Yes, *pakhan.*"

The door opens and closes. Just like that, we're alone.

"You've been looking for her."

He doesn't deny it.

"*Blyat'*, brother," I sigh.

Leave it to goddamn Yuri to go above and beyond the call of duty and act like a thief about it. I rub my temples. All of a sudden, exhaustion overcomes me. "Sit with me."

Yuri takes the chair across from me. I rest my elbows on the desk, head propped up in my hands. It's at times like these that the lack of sleep finally comes knocking. "I've been putting too much pressure on you."

"No!" Yuri denies quickly. "You haven't, Matvey. It's understandable that you'd be..." He bites his lip, looking for the right words.

"A lunatic?" I venture.

"In a hurry," he rephrases diplomatically. "To get this settled as soon as possible."

"So? Did you find them in Jersey?"

Yuri goes quiet. That's all the answer I needed.

"Fucking figured," I mutter. "It's your third sweep. If you were going to find them there, by now, you would have."

If possible, Yuri's face darkens even more. I reach for the glass cabinet behind my back. I take a bottle of bourbon and two glasses, then pour.

"Drink," I command.

Then I knock back mine.

The alcohol burns a path down my throat. It's not enough to ground me, but at least it dulls the senses. Mutes the noise of my ever-spinning mind.

Then I remember the last time I had this drink with her.

Neat, right?

"I have another job for you," I tell Yuri.

He looks up at me from his glass, still untouched. "Anything."

"I need you to tail Grisha."

His eyes go wide. "Grisha? Why?"

"Just following a hunch."

"You don't think he's involved, do you?" When I don't answer, Yuri pales. "Matvey, you can't possibly—"

"Think," I hiss. "There's no way she could've disappeared on her own. Not when she'd just given birth, and with a baby in tow at that."

"But Grisha's loyal to you."

"Is he?" I rise and start to pace. "He was the only one who knew where she was. He'd been arguing with me all week about my choices, about how I treated—" I grit my teeth. Even now, I can't bring myself to say her name out loud. "He was unhappy with me. And maybe he was a little too happy with her."

"Matvey, this is crazy," Yuri protests. "Grisha never showed any interest in—"

"Then how?!" I roar. "He had the means and opportunity. He had plenty of motive, too, even if he didn't care for her like that."

Or did he? Just the thought is enough to send my blood boiling: my third-in-command, setting his sights on *my* woman. The mother of *my* child.

How much time together did they have? How much time did I leave them with? With the excuse of standing guard, or being invited in for tea, or—

"Motya, this is insane." Yuri springs up, taking me by the shoulders. "He may be an asshole and a half, but he'd never betray you like that. I've never seen him so much as ogle the waitresses at Hedoneros, let alone think he'd steal Ap—"

"Do not say her fucking name!"

Yuri backs off, hands up in surrender. "Fine," he concedes. "But you have to know this is madness. You're chasing shadows."

"Better than chasing nothing at all."

I don't know what my brother sees on my face then. Whatever it is, it must be enough to make him reconsider. "Alright, look," he says, "I'll tail him. I'll do it. But Matvey, I won't find anything. She…" A pause. "Maybe she just needs time. Maybe she'll come back on her own."

"'Maybe' isn't good enough."

I force myself to calm down. Count back from ten, or whatever it is normal people do. Not like I'd fucking know.

Finally, I exhale and turn around.

"Do it, brother." I place both hands on his shoulders. "Follow that *mudak* and call me the second he steps one toe out of line. Right now, you're the only one I can trust."

Yuri swallows thickly. "Yes, Motya."

"Find them. Bring them home to me."

There's a flash of hesitation. "I'll do my best," he promises.

Finally, I allow myself a smile. The shadow of one, but that's already a small miracle. "I know you will."

Then I go back out to search some more.

3

APRIL

In this new life of mine, I sleep like the dead. Because being a new mother is exhausting and because, frankly, Mrs. Tanner works me like a greyhound. Unless Nugget starts crying or the building is on fire, I don't even twitch.

Which is why, when I wake up to absolute silence, I just know that something's wrong.

I don't hold my breath. Instead, I pretend I'm still deep asleep, coaching the rise and fall of my chest. Inwardly, I'm freaking out, but I force myself to swallow it down. *Don't you go into hysterics now, Flowers. If you start screaming your head off, there's a non-zero chance it'll get your head* blown *off.*

That's when I hear it: a creak in the floorboards.

I was never a big fan of firearms. Call me delicate, but I just don't like the idea of something made specifically to kill.

But when Yuri offered me his spare gun, I took it.

Now, I'm glad I did. I wait for the creaking to reveal the

intruder's position, all the while forcing my breaths not to speed up.

Then I act.

I whip the gun out from under my pillow and aim. "Get out or I shoot."

It's too dark to see much, but by the single ray of moonlight in the room, I see the intruder put his hands up. But the gesture is too slow for fear. Somehow, it feels mocking.

"I just want to talk," a male voice says, not at all concerned.

It sends a chill down my spine—that unfazed tone. So utterly out of place. "So talk, and then get out."

When the intruder speaks next, I can practically hear the smile in his voice. "I've been wanting to meet you for a long time, Ms. Flowers," he says. "I must compliment you on your getaway. It must have been far from easy, shaking off the infamous Matvey Groza."

"I don't know what you're talking about."

"No? Let's see if I can jog your memory: Bratva *pakhan*, all-around dangerous guy… and of course, your baby's daddy dearest."

The second he mentions my child, I freeze. I throw a quick glance at the crib, still safely tucked on my side of the room. But it won't be safe for much longer—not with this man standing between us and the door.

Who is he? I can't help but ask myself. *Why does he know us? Why does he know* Matvey?

And most importantly… *What does he want?*

"Oh, the tricks our hearts can play on us. The allure of the bad boy, right?" he jokes. "Absolutely irresistible. No wonder a good girl like you got roped in."

"I hope you didn't come all this way just to tell me how badly I need therapy. Believe me, I'm aware."

A sonorous chuckle. "And she's funny, too! All the more reason that sourpuss doesn't deserve you. You're wasted on him, my dear."

"And let me guess: I should pick you instead?"

"You flatter me," the intruder demurs. "But I'm afraid I'm old enough to be your father."

Another chill, this time stronger. Whoever this man is, he isn't half as harmless as he pretends to be. All the jokes, the façade—it's just another one of his weapons.

Just like the gun in his grip.

It's so dark, I almost didn't notice it. If the clouds hadn't shifted and let the moon pick out the glint of steel concealed in his hand, perhaps I never would have. Not until it was too late.

But he keeps pretending not to have it, so I keep pretending not to see it. "Then I'm afraid I fail to see the point of our conversation."

"On the contrary, Ms. Flowers: I believe we can help each other."

Buy time. Whatever happens, just buy time. "How?" I ask, using my free hand to reach for my phone under the covers.

"Let's see," he hums. "First off, you need protection. After all, you've got a bone to pick with the most dangerous man in New York."

"I don't have a bone to pick with him."

"Then he has a bone to pick with you," the man rephrases. "A baby-shaped one, I'd say. Surely you've heard of the search parties?"

Of course I've heard of the search parties. All this time, Matvey has done nothing but look for his daughter. For us.

"What do you think is going to happen when he finds you?" he asks, voice dropping to a hiss. For the first time since this conversation started, there isn't a trace of humor in his words. "What do you think he's going to do to the woman who beat him at his own game? To the illegitimate heir he never wanted? … Are you laughing, Ms. Flowers?"

I can't help it: I am. It's a sudden, bursting sound that catches even me by surprise. Because certainly this man can't be suggesting what I think he is.

Matvey, wanting to *harm* us?

I'd sooner accept the ocean going dry.

He may be an asshole. He may have promised me the world and thrown me away like a broken doll right after. He may be unfit to raise my child, to build the home she deserves.

But I know he'd never hurt us. *Never.*

Not on purpose, at least.

"I don't need your protection."

That's when I make my worst mistake: I forget.

I forget about the phone under the covers. I forget about the weapon in the stranger's hands. Most of all, I forget to keep my emotions in check.

I forget and cock my gun.

"Get out," I spit.

It's a misstep. I should have kept him talking and bought enough time to text Yuri. But now, it's too late.

The shadows around me grow, multiply: men, a dozen of them. Where did they come from? *When?*

That's when I realize: I had it wrong all along.

I wasn't the one distracting him.

He was the one distracting *me*.

"What a shame," the man sighs. "I was hoping you'd do this of your own free will. Oh, well." He makes a single gesture in the dark, and all at once, the figures loom closer.

That's when I turn to my last card: begging.

"Stop!" I blurt out. "Please. We don't want any trouble."

"Then you shouldn't have gotten involved with Matvey Groza."

The men descend on me. I see it play out as if in slow motion: a thousand shadows, falling upon me as one.

I decide to pull the trigger, but again, I'm too late.

My finger twitches, but before I can even squeeze it all the way down, the gun is slapped out of my grip.

As the back of someone's hand descends at the base of my neck, one last thought crosses my mind.

My baby.

I reach for her.

But darkness takes me first.

4

MATVEY

I'm startled awake by someone shaking my arm. "Matvey," my brother's voice calls, "wake up. Something's happened."

I pull myself up and check my watch: 2:33 A.M.

"It's the dead of fucking night," I snarl. My head's pounding with a hangover; it hasn't been an hour since I've actually managed to fall asleep. "This better be good."

"It's about April."

I freeze. "You found her?"

That's when I finally take stock of Yuri's appearance: his mussed hair, his trembling hands. His eyes, wide with panic.

"Brother, what's wrong?"

I'm terrified. For the first time since that day at the hospital, I remember what fear tastes like.

Yuri swallows. "There's something I have to tell you."

Then he speaks.

～

"Yuri. It's me. I need your help."

I got her call at the wedding. Petra was off entertaining guests, and I'd lost sight of you in the crowd. I figured she was calling me because she couldn't reach you, so I started looking for you.

But then she asked me to come alone.

She gave me a hospital's name. That's the kind of thing no one wants to hear on a phone call. So I got there as soon as I could.

That's when I saw them.

April, in her hospital bed, holding a bundle in her arms. I was so happy for her—for you both. I got closer to see the baby; I wanted to know if she looked like you.

Then April said, "I need you to help me hide."

At first, I didn't understand. I couldn't understand. Why would April want to get away? Why would she want to hide your kid from you?

Then she told me.

She told me about what had happened between you two. That you told her you'd marry Petra and refused to explain yourself. That she was pregnant with your legitimate heir.

You can imagine how I felt then.

I was so selfish, Matvey. I asked you to keep that secret; to marry Petra so she could be safe. So that my child could be safe.

I wasn't thinking of April when I did.

But now, she was staring at me, begging me to understand. Begging me to help *her.*

So I did.

I brought her the discharge papers. I walked her to the car. I held her up the whole way there, watching her grit her teeth against the pain.

Then I took her to the penthouse. I helped her pack a getaway bag. I got the baby's things, all the stuff she'd need on the run. I watched April write that letter.

I don't know what I was thinking, Motya. Only that the guilt was tearing me apart. The guilt of ruining her life. The guilt of ruining yours.

When I took them away, I didn't think it would be forever.

I thought April just needed a little time. A little space. To think, to heal. But the days turned into weeks.

I saw you fall apart. I saw you turn the city upside down looking for them, then the state, then the country. I saw you stop sleeping. I saw you start drinking.

But I couldn't tell you where she was. I'd made her a promise. After forcing you to keep yours, how could I break mine?

I still thought she'd come around one day.

I hid her in a motel. Every time you ordered to sweep the area, I made sure it was me who handled it. I brought her food, clothes, medicine. I gave her a gun to keep herself safe.

I tried to give her money, but she wouldn't take it. "You've already done so much," she'd tell me. I wanted to scream.

I don't expect you to forgive me. I don't expect you to tell me I did the right thing. Hell, I don't expect you to ever speak to me again after this.

But can you at least understand why I did it?

I don't let Yuri get one more word out.

I slam him into a wall, hard. "You traitor," I spit into his face.

"I'm sorry" is all Yuri says.

I clench my hands around his throat, trembling with rage. "You're sorry?" I snarl. "You took my child away from me, and now, you're fucking *sorry*?"

"I didn't know what else to do," he croaks, voice shaking. "It was my fault. What was I supposed to do?"

"You were supposed to *come to me!*" I roar. "You were supposed to *tell me!*"

Yuri's throat bobs up and down. I can feel the motion around my hands, can feel the rabbit-quick pulse of his blood against mine. *Traitor, traitor, traitor.* "You didn't see her in that room, Matvey."

"Damn right I fucking didn't!"

"She needed to leave. She needed to get away—"

"Shut up!" I bellow, making my grip tighter, tighter, *tighter*. "You don't get to talk about her! You don't get to—"

"She was scared!" he yells. "She was scared of *you!*"

That stops me in my tracks. *Scared.* Is that how I made her feel? Scared of talking to me, of seeing me? Scared of letting me raise her baby?

Your baby, the possessive voice inside me growls. *That was your baby, too.*

"You can hate me afterward," Yuri chokes with the last of his voice. "She's in danger now. They took her. They took both of them."

My blood freezes.

April's in danger. My child is in danger.

The second it sinks in, I drop Yuri to the ground. It doesn't matter how badly I want to beat his face to a pulp. How badly I want to take revenge on the brother who betrayed me. Who betrayed his own blood.

Right now, only one thing matters. "Where?" I demand.

"I'll take you," Yuri gasps, clutching at the red imprint of my hands.

"Not a fucking chance."

"It's in the middle of nowhere," he protests. "I don't need to drive, but let me guide you there."

"I said—"

"Please," Yuri begs. "Just… trust me."

A part of me wants to keep arguing. I'm dying to punch the answers out of this man I once called my brother. This man who now dares speak to me about trust.

But time is ticking, and we've already wasted far too much of it.

"So be it," I reply icily.

"Thank y—"

"But it's the last time I do."

With that, I grab my phone and dial. "Grisha. Meet me at my loft. It's an emergency."

Then I train my cold gaze on Yuri. "Well?" I demand, voice filled with spite. "Lead the way, *brother*."

5

APRIL

When I open my eyes again, I don't recognize my surroundings.

I'm no longer in my ratty motel room, that's for sure. Not with these hand-carved wooden walls, the decorative antiques peppered tastefully on expensive furniture—Mrs. Tanner would have pawned it all in a heartbeat.

And then there's the rustic air of the place, more forest-y and way less *"I can make all your dreams come true for ten bucks an hour, if you don't mind the smell."*

That's when it dawns on me: *This is a cabin.*

And then: *I'm not dead.*

I stir on the couch, a sharp pain stabbing through the back of my head. "Ow," I mutter.

"Apologies. My men can be a bit rough."

I sit up immediately. *That voice.* After what happened at the motel, I'd recognize it anywhere. "You."

"Me," the man agrees with a smile.

"Where's my baby?" I scan the room for her, but I don't see her anywhere. Panic sets in. "What did you do to my baby?!" I start screaming.

The man holds up a hand. "I assure you, Ms. Flowers, your baby's perfectly fine."

"I want to see her!" I rise from the couch. The lingering effects of the head blow make me sway, but I don't care. I could be crawling on my hands and feet, and I wouldn't goddamn care. "Let me see my baby!"

My baby. That's all that matters to me.

With a sigh, the man turns. He scoops up something from behind him. I couldn't see it before, but now, I do: it's a crib. A wooden one, like they used to make decades ago.

And inside…

"Give her to me," I snarl. "Give her to me right now."

The man tuts. He picks up my baby and holds her in his arms. She goes willingly—gently. And how could she not? She isn't even a month old; all she's ever known is kindness. And if there's one thing wolves in sheep's clothing have got going for them, it's feeling warm to the touch. "I'm afraid I can't do that yet, Ms. Flowers. After all, we still need to talk."

"Then talk."

Despite the urgency in my voice—or perhaps because of it— the man takes his time. He brushes his fingers along the line of the baby's nose, then plays with her tiny hands. Nugget's quiet in his hold, her sleepy coos fading quickly. "I have to confess, April: I'm almost jealous. Mine was never as easy to settle."

"That's still Ms. Flowers to you."

He makes a winding gesture with his free hand, as if amending his words. "Ms. Flowers, then. Nevertheless, you're a very lucky woman."

"She's a very smart girl."

He gives a slow hum. "Like her mother, perhaps."

Smart or not, I'm not stupid enough to miss the blatant threat. *Do as I say, and I just might let you live.* "You still aren't talking," I point out.

"My apologies. Let me start over," he clears his throat. "My name is Carmine."

I notice he pronounces it as *Car-mee-neh.* It's not a common name, not by a long shot; I'm unsure how you'd even spell it.

But then, as if reading my thoughts, he adds, "Ah, but I know that's a little bit tricky to say for you Americans. Feel free to call me 'Carmine,' like the color. I always did like red, after all."

I don't give a rat's ass what you like, motherfucker.

"Charmed," I deadpan.

For the first time since we met, I let myself take in his appearance: tall, reasonably built, with salt-and-pepper hair and a swanky black suit. His eyes are coffee-dark, pupils nearly invisible, and his hands are filled with rings of the gaudiest gold-and-gemstone variety. He practically smells like money.

And danger, a part of me adds.

It's so weird. This man couldn't be more different than

Matvey: the way he speaks, the way he acts—it all screams *slimeball*.

And yet, something also feels familiar.

But before I can put my finger on what, Carmine speaks again.

"You can't outrun Matvey forever, you know. Sooner or later, he's going to catch up to you. And then who knows what will happen?" he says casually. "It pains my heart to think about it."

"Maybe it's a coronary," I suggest.

He gives a warm laugh. "Such a spitfire. I get what Matvey saw in you."

"You know nothing about Matvey," I snap.

He sends me a look then—something briefly cold. Like the icy prick of an unexpected raindrop. "Oh, but I *do*."

The moment passes. When he speaks to me next, he's jovial again, as if nothing happened at all. But I know I didn't imagine it—the chill down my spine is proof.

"Anyway," he continues, "you can't think too highly of him. I mean, you're on the run, aren't you? Surely you're not dying to see him again. You must know what he does to his enemies."

I've never once doubted that Matvey would never hurt me. Ever since I got to know him, truly know him, I understood: however sharp his fangs may be, he would never turn them on me.

But Carmine's words are sinking deeper than I'd like. Without even realizing it, I've already started to feel it: fear.

Stop it, I scold myself. *It's not Matvey you're scared of.*

That's when it dawns on me: he's doing it again. Playing mind games, leading me in circles. It's how he got me last time.

I can't let it happen again.

"And what would you suggest?" I ask.

"That we join forces to destroy him."

I almost let myself get carried away again. Almost hurl at him all the choice words crowding my head.

Me, destroy Matvey?

I'd sooner destroy myself.

But I don't tell him that. This time, I have to be smart.

"Go on," I say.

"He has your ear," Carmine continues. "Right now, he's only angry with you because he thinks you left voluntarily. What if we spun him a tale?"

As he speaks, I start looking around the room for something to fight with. A weapon, a toothpick, anything. The more I see of this place, the more it looks exactly like the cabin serial killers use to turn lost hikers into hamburgers. Slightly less than reassuring.

"What kind of tale?" I ask, pretending to consider his offer.

"A beautiful tale." Carmine grins. "A tale of love and loss. You didn't leave that hospital on your own, you see—you were taken. Once he welcomes you back, all you'll have to do is keep me informed: what he does, who he sees, where he goes."

"Mm. And who's the villain of this story?"

"Yours truly, of course."

The room really is chock-full of trinkets. Antique teacups, tribal masks, glass animals: everything you'd find in an old couple's home, right next to the postcards from Normandy.

But nothing you could stab a man with.

It's strange: before today, I never seriously considered killing anyone. The mere thought would have made me sick to my stomach.

But with my baby in his arms, it's all I can feel: the urge to fucking *maim*. I'd gut him like a fish to stop him from harming so much as a hair on my daughter's head.

"He'd never buy it," I say, starting to pace around the room for better access to other potential weapons. "I didn't do this alone, you know. If my partner decided to talk..."

A sculpted elephant, a Moai statuette, a tiny glass fish...

"What, that blond delivery boy of yours?" Carmine laughs. "He won't talk. And even if he did, there are ways to keep people silent."

Crap. Did I just accidentally put out a hit on Yuri? "You seem awfully confident."

"Let's just say Yuri's no stranger to me, either."

That gives me pause. Someone who knows both Matvey and Yuri; someone I've never heard them mention by name, but who seems to be intimately acquainted with them. Enough to act condescending about them.

A Latvian fishscale vase, a Bastet paperweight, a queen bobblehead...

"I don't want him hurt. He's been kind to me."

"I have no beef with the little one," Carmine assures me. "Only the big boss."

There.

A stylographic pen, antique. And a really sharp one at that. "Just him? You won't hurt anybody else? Not even the wife?"

"Would you like me to hurt the wife?"

The mere thought sends a chill down my spine. I may despise Petra with all my heart right now, but homicide still feels a bit much. "No. She's pregnant."

"Then let's hope it's a girl."

I shudder so hard I nearly drop the pen. That cheerful voice, spewing such bloodcurdling threats—it's almost too much.

He doesn't just want to kill Matvey—he wants to end him. Wants to sever his line by any means necessary.

For once, I'm grateful for old white men and their weird fixations on male heirs. It might be the only reason my kid is still breathing after all. Three cheers for misogyny, everyone!

I stash the pen behind my back and pretend to consider the offer a bit more. "What do I get in return?"

"Safety, for one thing," Carmine starts to list off. "The Groza Bratva will be off your back for good. I'll also make sure you're properly compensated."

"Compensated how?"

"However you need." He shrugs. "Money. Apartments. New identities to settle far from here. Have you seen school tuition fees lately? Let me tell you, raising a child has never been more expensive. Especially in this economy."

"You don't have to tell me that," I mumble. It's not the first time I've looked into the yawning chasm of my future as a single mother and shuddered at the horrors waiting for me there.

Carmine looks pleased. "So? Can I count on your support?"

The pen is heavy in my grip. But I can't turn back now. Not with my baby still in the evil clutches of Smiley McCreepy here. "Shall we shake on it?"

This is it, April.

"Sure, why not?"

Whatever you do, do not miss.

I start walking. Carmine stays where he is, clearly used to having people come to him. God, I hope he doesn't expect me to kiss his gazillion rings. I'd die of old age.

Carmine offers me his hand—not to kiss, thank the stars— and I put forth mine. The free one, the one that isn't about to commit the gravest sin of all.

But is there any sin we wouldn't commit for our kids?

As soon as his hand is in mine, I strike. I hold the pen like a dagger and descend, aiming for the tender spot between neck and shoulder.

But Carmine doesn't even flinch. With a flick of his wrist, he twists mine and rids himself of my handshake.

Then he bats the pen away.

I watch my last hope fly through the air, cluttering to the ground on the other side of the room. As soon as it hits the floorboards, it snaps in half.

"Pity," Carmine sighs. "I quite liked that one."

I make a grab for my baby, but his grip is steel.

She starts crying then, a loud piercing wail. Honestly, I'm tempted to do the same.

I'm fucked. Completely, royally fucked.

"You should've taken my deal, Ms. Flowers," Carmine tuts, fishing for something behind him. "We could've been partners."

Then he points a gun at my head.

I know without question that I'm about to die.

"Any last words?" he asks.

"Yes," I blurt out. "Please don't hurt my baby."

Something flashes through Carmine's eyes then. Something that might almost be pity. "I won't. She's far too important."

I let out a sigh of relief. Whatever reasons he may have, whatever plans—he won't harm her. He won't harm my daughter.

"I'm sorry," I whisper, tears rolling fat down my cheeks. "I'm so sorry, M—"

Then the door bursts open.

Carmine turns.

So do I.

And Matvey's eyes meet mine.

6

APRIL

"You."

Matvey's voice is ice-cold. He spits that word at Carmine like a poisonous dart, but all the while, he keeps his eyes on *me*.

And those aren't cold at all.

They're burning.

God, I missed him. That's all I can think of. I'm standing between two dangerous men, in the crossfire of two deadly weapons, and all I can think of is three words.

I.

Missed.

Him.

Then Carmine breaks the spell. "Me," he agrees wickedly, his false smirk finally peeling away to reveal the snake beneath. "How nice to see you again, s—"

"Take your filthy gun off my woman," Matvey cuts him off, "and your filthy hands off my daughter."

I realize that I've never seen him like this. To me, Matvey was always "the man"—whether passionate, cold, or indifferent, he was always "off-the-clock." It's the first time I'm getting to see this side of him: the ruthless, bloodthirsty, stone-hearted other half of the equation.

The *pakhan.*

But Carmine isn't intimidated in the slightest. "I'm afraid I can't do that, *Matik.*"

It's like a switch has been flipped. At the sound of that name, Matvey's face goes white, then red with rage. "Don't you dare call me that."

"Or what?"

"Or I'll put a bullet in your fucking skull."

Carmine tuts. Then, without warning, he starts rocking our child in the crook of his arm. "How cute, no? Babies. Such miracles. And how fragile, too."

"If you fucking touch her—"

"They usually like me, you know," he bulldozes over Matvey's words. "So their parents are always asking me, 'Do you wanna hold 'em?' and shoving them right into my arms. And I'm always terrified. I keep thinking, *'Oh, dear... What if I drop them?'*"

Suddenly, Carmine's fake smile is drained of all warmth. His threat is so clear, it's all I can do not to scream.

But I force myself to pull it together. "That's anxiety, I hear," I quip back.

He seems pleasantly surprised by my remark. As if delighted to find out he can keep playing. "Perhaps it is! I'm anxious that way. So why don't you drop the gun, Matik, before my grip falters?"

I see Matvey grit his teeth in frustration, gun still raised.

"Matvey." I try to keep my voice from shaking. "Please."

A flicker of hesitation passes through his eyes.

"Come on, Matik," Carmine presses. "You don't want to scare your woman off again, do you?"

"She's not so easily scared."

"Mm. Then why did she run?"

Game, set, match.

For a long moment, I'm certain Matvey will lower his gun; and though I've just been begging him to do it, suddenly, I'm not so sure he should. Carmine said he wouldn't harm the baby, but that was before Matvey burst in. What if he no longer needs her, either?

"Because I was an idiot."

His words jolt me out of my thoughts.

Again, Matvey's gun is trained on Carmine, but his eyes are on me alone. "I was an idiot," he repeats. "I lied to her. I could've told her the truth from the start, but I didn't. I just kept lying and lying until she couldn't take it anymore. I was the lowest of the low. And for that, I'm sorry."

I can't believe my ears. All I've ever wanted Matvey to say to me, he's saying here and now, with just one piece missing.

I don't love her. I love you.

"So you forgive her?" Carmine asks, incredulous.

"No."

That single word chills me to the bone.

"What she did was unforgivable," Matvey continues, the fire in his eyes hardening to ice. "She lied to me, too. If Yuri hadn't come clean to save her ass, she would've kept lying. She is also the lowest of the low."

I finally stop hearing Matvey's words. Because, while my self-loathing would want nothing more than to stab me with them, it's time I started *listening*.

Matvey's never been a man of many words, but he's repeated himself twice now.

Lying and lying. Lowest of the low.

Lying low.

"Do you get it, April?" he presses, something desperate in his eyes. "*Can* you get it?"

I raise my head. "Yes."

Then it happens.

I drop myself down to the floor. The second I do, Matvey's gun fires.

Carmine howls, dropping the baby.

But I'm ready to catch her. Because Matvey told me this part, too.

Do you get it? Can you get it?

"I got you," I whisper to my child. "I got you, baby girl."

Then I duck under the desk.

I check my baby from head to toe: she's perfect, unharmed. Crying, but whole. "Thank God," I sob.

Behind us, bullets are flying every which way. I feel one lodge in the front panel of the desk, right where my left buttock would've been. Thank God for mahogany.

I cover Nugget's ears. "It's okay, baby. Daddy's gonna be okay."

I say it for her benefit as much as mine. Whatever our differences, whatever our problems...

Please, Matvey, don't get hurt.

I know the universe hears me. I know, because in the next second, Matvey's voice rises in a howl of pain.

"MATVEY!"

I dart out from behind the desk.

Matvey's sprawled on the floor, back against the wall, hand covering his shoulder. Blood is gushing out rapidly, staining his shirt and darkening his suit jacket.

Carmine stands by the door, one arm equally bloodied. "It appears we're tied."

"We're not. My men have the area surrounded. Yuri and Grisha are already on their way."

"Yuri?!" Carmine cackles. "After all he's done, you still trust him?"

"He's still my brother," Matvey grits. "He's still my blood. And I would never betray my blood."

"... I see," Carmine comments. "'Never' is a bold word, Matik."

"*Never,*" he snarls in defiance.

Then he raises his gun and shoots again.

But Carmine is already at the door, easily taking cover against the outer cabin wall. The bullet lodges between the boards. Matvey swallows another cry of pain.

I put down the baby and rush to check the wound. "Keep still," I order. I almost don't hear Carmine's parting words.

"I look forward to playing with you again," he yells from the door, "... *son.*"

Then he flees into the night.

7

APRIL

My hand stops midair. "'Son'?"

Matvey doesn't say anything. He doesn't need to say anything. One look at his face tells me all I need to know.

Carmine is Matvey's father.

"Matvey!" Yuri storms in, followed by a panting Grisha. "Are you hurt?!" Then he sees the blood. His face pales. "Motya..."

He makes to move closer, but Matvey stops him with a glare. "He's still nearby," he growls. "Go, both of you."

"But Matvey...!"

"I said *go*!"

"He's fine," I add, taking pity on Yuri. "It's just a flesh wound. I'll patch him up."

"You will do no such thing."

"Yes, I will."

"I said—"

"How many fingers am I holding up?"

Matvey's gaze grows in and out of focus. He's lost so much blood, he can't even tell *which* finger I'm holding up. And that should be an easy one. "Fine," he grumbles eventually. "Do what you must."

Only then does Yuri finally start heading out.

At the door, though, Matvey stops him. "Yura... it's him."

Yuri doesn't say anything to that. He simply stops, a heartbeat and a half, before obeying his *pakhan*'s orders and fleeing into the night after Carmine.

No—after *their father*.

Then the cabin turns silent.

Matvey's gaze wanders around the room. Mine isn't any steadier. After all that's gone down, we're left with nothing to say to each other.

Again.

"You shouldn't be so hard on him." Anything to break this wretched silence.

"I'll be as hard on my brother as I like," he growls back.

"It's my fault he did what he did. I put him in an impossible position."

"Believe me—I know."

It's the way he spits out those words, filled with venom and contempt, that finally makes me snap. "Did you even mean a word of what you said? Or was it all just coded language?"

Matvey stays silent. *I was an idiot. I'm sorry.*

No, *I* was the idiot. For ever believing him again.

"Take off your jacket and shirt," I sigh.

Matvey gives me a cold glare. "I don't need your help."

"Yeah, you do. So either take them off or bleed to death." Then, because he might actually pick the latter, I add, "I won't have you holding your daughter with blood all over you."

At those words, he finally seems to remember the reason he's here. Because at this point, it sure as hell isn't for me. "Where is she?"

I grab her from my other side. With the bullet wound, it's all Matvey can do to wait for me to place her in his arms. I don't make him wait long.

As soon as he's stripped bare to the waist, I give her to him. My daughter. *His* daughter.

The second I do, I feel faint.

Because all my mistakes hit me like a freight train.

His eyes light up. Every single muscle softens on his face, lips parting into an expression of pure wonder. It's like he's realizing it for the first time: *I have a daughter. This is my daughter.*

And I'm the one who took her from him.

What was I thinking?

If I had my way, I would have kept her from him forever. Kept her safe with me, where I knew she would be happy. That's what I've been telling myself over and over: she would be happy with *me*.

But how could I truly know that? How can I still think that, when her father is looking at her like she's the most beautiful thing he's ever seen?

"Hello, little one," he breathes.

For the longest time, he says nothing else. Only stares into the eyes of his daughter.

I swallow my guilt and take the opportunity to get up and look for what I need. I grab a bottle of whiskey from the liquor cabinet. If there's a good thing about murder cabins in the woods, it's that there's always a liquor cabinet. Then I grab my sewing kit.

When Matvey sees me come back with the supplies, he frowns. "Where did you even get that?"

"Thank Carmine. He saw fit to kidnap my bag, too." I pour a generous amount of whiskey on the needle and thread, then hand it to Matvey. "Here. Sterilize the—"

But he's already halfway through the bottle.

" … wound. Never mind."

Wordlessly, I grab another.

As I give Matvey's shoulder a booze bath, he keeps the baby safely tucked in his other arm. Not a single drop touches her, of alcohol or otherwise. In moments, she's already fallen asleep.

He's perfect with her, I think with another stab of guilt. *They're perfect together.*

"You can put her down, you know," I tell him. "She sleeps like the dead."

"I'm not leaving her."

"This is gonna hurt."

"I said I'm not leaving her."

Guilt stabs me harder.

I pick up my tweezers and force my hands not to shake. Or my voice. "Fine. Have it your way."

I don't offer him something to bite down on. He doesn't ask for it. "Check for an exit wound," he barks instead.

"Already did. It's there."

With that, we fall back into silence.

After I'm done picking out the debris, I let my hands follow the familiar planes of Matvey's back—the taut muscles, the sturdy bones. I've touched this place so many times: hugging, caressing, holding on for dear life as I shattered around him. I didn't need an excuse then.

Certainly not a life-or-death one.

"Hold still."

"I *am* still."

"You're shifting. The scar's gonna come out all jagged."

"Why does that even matter?" he snaps.

I hesitate, needle in the air. "You have beautiful skin," I settle on. The truth, for once. "It'd be a shame to have it marred."

To have it marred because of me.

He doesn't say anything in return.

But he does eventually put our daughter back down. I watch his fingers clench around the fabric of his pants, teeth gritted against the pain and dizziness. I don't say anything, either.

But as my fingers skate around the wound, I feel Matvey's pulse quicken.

"Are you okay?" I ask.

I wonder if he's feeling it, too—what *I'm* feeling. The chemistry between us, sparking back to life with a single touch. Or maybe it really is just pain, and I'm imagining things again. Like I imagined everything between us.

But Matvey refuses to give me a straight answer. "I'm fine."

"You're breathing harder."

"I said I'm fine."

More silence. *Silence, silence, silence.* Is that all that's left of us? Is that all I can have? Is that all I deserve?

"April?" Matvey asks suddenly. "Are you… crying?"

Only then do I realize he's right.

And then I can't do it anymore. I can't keep it in any longer. "I hate this," I finally blurt out. "I hate us. What we've become."

"April—" Matvey tries to turn his head, but I steer it back around.

"Keep still," I whisper.

A beat goes by in silence. Then: "Talk to me."

"*Talk* to you?" I snap. "All I've ever done is try to talk to you! But no, you won't tell me a single thing. You shut yourself away in your silence and leave me alone with my mind. Do you have any idea what that feels like? Being at the mercy of your worst thoughts, doubting every little thing? Wondering what you did to make it happen?"

"You didn't do anything," Matvey cuts in. "Marrying Petra was my choice. It had nothing to do with you."

"Then why didn't you just tell me that?" I cry out. "Why didn't you tell me anything?"

I barely manage to tie off the suture. I'm crying so hard, I can't see straight. It's like the floodgates have finally reopened, every ugly thing ready to rush back out.

"I'm going crazy here, Matvey," I whisper with the last of my voice. "I don't know what's real anymore, and it's driving me crazy. *You're* driving me crazy."

I don't expect him to answer. I've given up on it—figuring out what goes on in Matvey's head.

Then, when I've finally lost all hope, Matvey speaks. "I meant it."

"What?"

"I meant what I said earlier: I'm sorry. I didn't tell you the truth."

It takes me a moment to realize I haven't imagined it. "About which part?" I sniffle. "The part where you said you didn't want anyone else? That there was nothing between you and Petra? Or that you loved me?"

I could go on, but this time, it's me who falls silent.

Because, all of a sudden, I catch a small tremor in Matvey's frame. No, not a tremor: a dizzy spell. *He's lost too much blood*, I realize. *He's going to pass out.*

I jump back in front of him, holding him still. "Matvey!"

"The… the… b-baby…"

I frown. "She's right here. She's okay."

"No, the baby. Petra's baby." With the last shred of focus, he looks straight at me. "I lied to you."

"Now isn't the time—"

"It isn't mine."

I blink. "What?"

"Petra's baby. It was… never mine."

That's the last thing he says to me.

Then he blacks out.

8

MATVEY

I wake up with a pounding headache and a throbbing shoulder.

It takes me a moment to remember that this isn't just another hangover. That I didn't empty the liquor cabinet again—though I sure as fuck smell like it. But no, it wasn't the drinking that did me in this time. It was...

I spring up and a voice calls out, "Easy. You'll pull your stitches."

April.

After all this searching, it doesn't feel real. I wonder if it's a fever dream—God knows I've had enough of those over the past few weeks. I blink in the dim light, feeling for April by my side, terrified I'll find nothing.

But then I feel her hand around mine. "How long was I out?" I rasp.

"Around five hours."

Five hours. That's the longest sleep I've had in a month. "The baby?"

"Out like a light."

She points to an open drawer behind her. I can't see much from here, only that it looks like every blanket I've ever owned has been put inside it as padding.

Makeshift crib. Smart. I shake that thought off. I shouldn't praise this woman, not even in my mind. Not for anything.

She took away my daughter. She took away my blood. And she put her in danger, too.

Carmine. I knew he'd make a move, but I wasn't expecting another so soon. Not after the D.C. deal mysteriously blew up.

Because, clearly, he had a hand in that, too.

And not just that. The kidnappers, the assassins—from the start, it was all him. I had my suspicions, but last night was proof.

All this time, my father was behind it all.

I prop myself up against the headboard. As my eyes adjust to the dark, I realize it must be near dawn. There's a pale ray of light filtering through the blinds, but it's weak. Faint.

Like April looks right now.

I take in her sunken face, the bags under her eyes. A month on the run isn't kind on the best of us, but I can't imagine it'd be anything less than harrowing for a new mother. When she left that hospital bed, her stitches weren't even dry.

And whose fault was that?

I want to say "hers," but something stops me.

"I'm going crazy here, Matvey. I don't know what's real anymore."

"Here," April interrupts my thoughts. "Drink."

Cool glass touches my lips. I want to refuse her coddling, but I'm parched. That's the only reason I accept it, I tell myself. The only reason I let April take care of me.

Silencing my thoughts, I open my mouth and drink.

It feels like the first sip of water I've had in forever. I don't stop until I've guzzled every last drop. "Grisha left some painkillers for you," she adds afterwards. "Do you want them?"

Yes. My shoulder is killing me. "Medication dulls my senses," I mutter.

"Uh, right. I'm gonna take that as a no."

There's a disappointed edge to her tone. It irks me—what the hell did I do *now*? "I said I'm fine."

"Actually, no, you didn't. You just gave me some bullshit, alpha male one-liner and weaseled your way out of saying what you really feel. Then again, I shouldn't be surprised."

"What do you want me to do, April?" I snarl. "You want me to say it hurts? Fine: it hurts like a goddamn bitch. Happy now?"

"Yes!" she snarls right back. "Because at least I know what you're thinking!"

"What was I supposed to be thinking? 'Oh, gee, I'm so happy my father came all the way from D.C. to put a bullet in me'?!"

"How should I know? You don't tell me anything! And when you do, you lie."

"I never—" I start.

"Do not!" April cuts me off, standing up in a rage. "Do *not* tell me you never lied to me, Matvey Groza, because I swear to God, I will swap your painkillers with gummy bears and pour Everclear right on your stitches."

"I never—"

"Never told me you loved Petra?" she spits. "Never told me her baby was yours? Newsflash, Matvey: you didn't have to. You came home, you told me you were marrying her, and you damn well knew you didn't have to say anything else."

"I—"

"You knew. You fucking knew. At least respect me enough to admit that."

I want to reject April's words with all my heart. I want to scream loud enough to wake up the entire building, *That's not true.*

But I can't.

Because it is.

I let her connect the dots all while knowing exactly what picture she was drawing in her head. I let her think the wedding was of my own free will so that I wouldn't have to explain why it wasn't. I let her think the baby was mine so that I wouldn't have to explain that it wasn't—so that I wouldn't have to tell her *whose* it was.

I may not have lied to her face. But I might as well have.

"You won't tell me a single thing. You shut yourself away in your silence and leave me alone with my mind. Do you have any idea what that feels like?"

I don't. Silence is the one thing I never had to fight. Silence means bullets aren't flying; it means storms aren't coming. It means that, at least for as long as that silence lasts, that no one's getting hurt.

It was never my enemy.

But that doesn't mean it's not April's.

"Tell me I'm wrong," she rasps. "Tell me that, or finally tell me the truth."

So I do.

I tell her everything.

I tell her about going back to my apartment that morning. About finding Petra there. About how I almost shot the woman on sight.

Then I tell her what she told me. *I'm pregnant.*

It's not easy at first, getting it out in the open. Every word I say gets stuck in my throat on the way out, like it knows it's a secret. Like it knows I'm not supposed to share it.

I wonder what would have happened if I'd done this before. What pain we might've avoided. What blood might've been left unspilled.

"It was the only way," I add in a whispered croak. "The only way to keep the three of them safe. I had to claim the baby as mine. There's no telling what Vlad would've done otherwise. And Yuri… he didn't want anyone to know. In case word got back to Vlad."

April listens without a word. She listens until the very end.

It's unnerving—why isn't she saying anything? The irony isn't lost on me: Silence finally hurts.

But eventually, April speaks. "Did he ask you not to tell me?"

I hesitate. "He asked me not to tell anyone."

"Right. But he didn't ask you not to tell *me.*"

I'm starting to get irritated again. What's with the sophism here? He said *no one*—what's the goddamn difference?

"I tried to tell you," I insist. "The day before the wedding—"

"Which was a whole week later," she objects. "Why not tell me from the start?"

I want to say, *Because my brother asked*, but I can't even get the words out. After all these lies, I can't bring myself to say another one.

Because in truth, it was never about Yuri.

I could've asked him to keep April in the loop—hell, I could've demanded it. I was holding all the cards; I had no reason to compromise.

But then that voice said...

Can you trust her?

I'm trying to find a better way to say it. A way that doesn't make me sound like a complete asshole.

But April's had her share of silences, so it's only fair that she's gotten good at reading them. "Right," she mumbles, stealing the words right out of my mouth. "I'm not blood. Got it."

"I never chose Petra over you," I point out. "I never loved her, April. I—"

Say it. Just fucking say it.

"You loved *me?*" April fills in, but there's something off with her tone. Something dark and bitter. "No, Matvey. That's just another lie."

It's like a dagger to the heart. I clench the covers and rise, ignoring the biting agony in my shoulder. "How would you fucking know?!" I roar. "How would you know what I felt?"

"Because if you love someone, you trust them!" she yells into my face. "And if you can't trust someone…"

That's when I notice the tears in her eyes.

"Then you don't love them," she rasps. "Not really."

I feel my rage rise. Every time I'm near this woman, I swear, it's like I can't control myself anymore. It all goes right out of the fucking window. "I was right, though, wasn't I?" I say. "You couldn't be trusted. Tell me, April: did you think of 'trust' when you *kidnapped my goddamn daughter*?!"

She reels back as if slapped. "I…"

That's when a noise snaps us both out of it.

No, not a noise: *crying.*

"Oh, no." April rushes to the drawer. "No, no, no, shh. Hush now, sweet thing. Mommy's got you." She picks up the bundle of blankets and starts rocking it in her arms. "I'm sorry. I'm so sorry, May."

The breath catches in my lungs. For a long second, I forget how it goes. One beat, then another. " … 'May'?" I echo.

April turns to me, eyes suddenly wide. "Yeah. I… Sorry, I didn't ask you what names you liked. I just always thought, if I ever had a girl…"

She holds the bundle out to me. Her hands quiver.

With the utmost care, I take it. "It's fine." I shake my head. "It's a good name. It really... suits her."

May. My daughter's name is May.

I'm a father.

And speaking of fathers...

"Carmine was probably behind it all," I tell April, my face turning grim. "The kidnapping, the break-in. Until I deal with him, you're both back under my protection."

I don't leave her room to argue. Luckily, she doesn't. She may be a liar and a cheat, but from what I've seen...

From what I've seen, she's one hell of a mom.

"Okay," she says. "Until Carmine's dealt with."

"Until Carmine's dealt with," I agree.

It's a pact. We don't shake on it, but we don't need to.

Our baby seals it for both of us.

9

MATVEY

Minutes tick by, then hours.

By the time Yuri returns, the sun must have traveled all the way across the horizon, because the room has grown dark again.

Not that I've been keeping track. I was too busy watching something else.

"Matvey?"

I put a finger to my lips. "Quiet. She's asleep."

With a nod, Yuri walks around the currently occupied couch. "Must've been one hell of a night for April, too."

"I didn't mean her."

My brother reels back at my harsh tone. I watch his gaze linger on April out of the corner of my eye, one hand darting out to fix the blanket she burrowed herself into. "My bad."

I force myself not to bite it off at the wrist.

Silent, Yuri creeps closer. That's when he spots her: bundled up in blankets, tiny hands curled in tiny fists. Safe in my arms at last. *My daughter.*

"Oh. *Her.* Yeah, she's a real sleepyhead."

"Mm. Guess you'd know better than me."

Hurt flashes across my brother's face. "Mot—"

"Don't," I warn. "No more excuses."

Grimly, he nods. "I'm sorry."

"No, you're not."

"What?"

"You heard me." I force my voice into a low, even tone. "You're not sorry. Given the choice, you'd do it all again."

"You don't know that," he rasps.

"Yeah, I do—"

"—Motya—"

"—because I'd do the same, too."

For a second, Yuri looks stunned. Like he'd been expecting to be mauled by a wild wolf, only to get his hand licked instead. "You'd do… what?"

"Protect my blood."

I can tell my brother has no idea where I'm going with this. Truth be told, until a few hours ago, my own mind was a mystery to me. This past month… It was hell on earth. I had no time for clarity. No time to sit down and just think.

But with my daughter in my arms, it's all finally coming together.

"You didn't trust me."

"No, that's not—" Yuri starts.

But I cut him off. "You didn't trust me," I repeat, "because you saw I wasn't myself. With you or with anyone. And because of that, you lost faith in me."

Next to me, Yuri shakes his head once. "You were helping me. Of course I trusted you."

"No, you didn't. When you trust someone, you tell them the truth."

I watch my brother blink, utterly lost. "Are you feeling okay? Did you take something?"

"On the contrary, my shoulder's been killing me all day. I'm almost too lucid."

"Pain doesn't make you lucid," Yuri objects. "It just makes you hurt."

"Maybe," I concede. "Or maybe it helps put things into perspective."

In my arms, May stirs. She coos weakly, but doesn't crack her eyes open. I haven't even had a chance to check their color yet—she's that sleepy. No wonder she took ten-odd months to pop out. Dr. Allan had it right: she's one cozy baby.

"I haven't put her down once, you know," I confess. "Ever since I got her back. I just haven't been able to stop holding her. Not for one damn minute. Do you know why that is?"

"Why?" Yuri asks.

"Because I keep thinking that she'll disappear."

I see the words stab deep into my brother's heart. I don't feel guilty, though: pain can be good. Pain can help.

Pain can show us what truly matters.

"I find myself thinking, 'Maybe I'll get a glass of water.' Then I go to put her down, but I can't. Because what if she's gone by the time I come back?"

"You know why April did it," Yuri replies tightly. "Why *I* did it. It's not going to happen again, Matvey."

"'Again.' That's a funny word. It shouldn't have happened in the first place, Yuri."

"I know, and if I could go back—"

"We've been over this," I interrupt. "You'd do it all again, just like I would."

"That's what you meant?" Yuri asks me, incredulous. "You'd… lie to April again?"

"I would."

Even as I speak the words, something inside me howls. Something desperate to mend what's been broken. *Stop lying. Stop lying to yourself, to her, to—*

But there is no fixing this. Not after what April did.

Because, if I hadn't found them, I never would have seen my daughter again.

Yuri shakes his head frantically. "You don't mean that."

"All this time, I kept thinking, 'If only I'd told her the truth.' But do you want to know the real truth? I chose *you*, brother. And I was right. The second I crossed her, she took my child from me. Who knows what she would've done if I'd told her about *your* baby?"

"Nothing!" Yuri insists. "She would've done nothing. I was in the wrong for asking—"

"Hell, maybe she would've gone to Vlad herself."

"You know that's not—"

"Why do you keep defending her?!" I bellow.

I rein my voice back in just in time not to wake my kid. I couldn't give a shit about April's beauty sleep, but I see Yuri check on her and sigh with relief. *Both still out, then.*

It's that look incenses me more than anything. That look, and that pull on the blankets, and all those nights they must've spent plotting behind my back—

If I didn't have a literal newborn in my arms right now, I would've jumped him already.

But there's only one way to know the truth. Only one way to find out if I can ever trust my brother again. If I could ever trust my brother in the first place.

"I guess it is the oldest tale in the world," I murmur. "I married your girl, so now, you're going to fuck around with mine?"

"Matvey, what the hell are you talking about?!" he nearly screams.

"Or was it all those takeout dinners at the motel? Maybe you shared a dumpling once, and then something more—"

"*I love* Petra!" This time, he's the one who almost shouts. "I love Petra," Yuri repeats, out of breath. "And I couldn't bear the thought of losing the one I loved. So I went crazy and ended up costing you the one you loved. Worse, I ended up costing April. But she was innocent, Matvey. She had nothing to do with me or you. That's why I've been trying to help her. And I'm sorry, I really am, but if you keep suggesting that I'd ever cheat on Petra, I'm gonna have to ask you to put your baby down and step the fuck out with me, because I will not let you insult—"

"Your niece."

Yuri blinks. "What?"

"She's not just my baby. She's your niece, too."

With that, I finally hold her out.

Yuri looks more confused by the minute. "By 'putting her down,' I didn't mean give her to me—"

"I know. You meant 'put her down so I can punch you.'"

"So…?"

"So you don't need to punch me. I believe you." Then I add with a smirk, "Though I'd like to see you try, brother."

At first, Yuri hesitates. "Are you sure?"

I roll my eyes. "Quit pretending you haven't been holding her every chance you got. Besides, you need the practice."

"That's not what I mean. You… truly believe me?"

"Yura, Yura, Yura," I sigh. "If I really thought you'd been fucking my woman, do you think you'd still be standing on two legs?"

His face drains of all color. But that finally seems to convince him, because he leans in to take the bundle from my arms. "You trust me with her?" he asks in disbelief.

I watch him pick her up slowly. Carefully. "All these years you've stood by my side... don't think I didn't take notice. I know I can be kind of an asshole—"

"You can lose the 'kind of,'" Yuri mutters.

"—but I know you've always been in my corner," I continue, pretending not to hear him. *Cheeky brat.* "You may have fucked up this time, but I know that, in your own misguided way, you were doing this for me, too."

"I..."

"You got in too deep. Didn't understand what the fuck you were doing. And how could you? You're not a father yet."

"Matvey..."

"But you will be. And I'll be by your side for that, too."

Yuri's eyes are wet. Jesus Christ, could he be any more of a crybaby? "So you forgive me?" he croaks.

"This time, yes" I answer. "But there won't be a second, Yuri. If you ever lie to me again..."

He looks like he's choking on something. Words, maybe—or regrets. "Matvey, there's something I need to—"

"You don't need to say anything," I cut him off. "You're forgiven."

"But I—"

"After all, we're blood."

He stops. "That's... why you're forgiving me?" he stammers. "And why you won't forgive...?" Wisely, he doesn't say her name.

"That's right," I growl. "You're my family. She is not."

If I ever need proof of my credo, April is the living, breathing thing. The wolf in sheep's clothing who snuck past my defenses.

I won't let her take another bite out of my heart. Never again.

"Regardless, she's family to my daughter. Arrange for both of them to be moved back to the penthouse. I want them there asap."

"Right," Yuri mumbles. "Right, I'll… get on that."

I frown. "Are you feeling alright, brother? You didn't get shot out there in the woods, did you?"

"No, no, I just… I'm a bit overwhelmed, I guess. Need to take this all in." Then he hands me back my kid.

I shake my head and smile. My first real smile in a long, long time. "Go. Double the guard around the penthouse. Remind everyone you're still my number two."

With a nod, he stands up to carry out my orders.

"Oh, and brother?"

He turns back to me. "Yes…?"

"Never betray me again."

I watch his lips press into a tight, scared line. "Yes, *moy pakhan*."

Then he's out the door.

10

APRIL

I've only ever felt home in three places in my life.

One: the brownstone I shared with my grandmother. It's where I grew up—where I finally felt accepted for the first time. There, I could go to sleep with both eyes closed. I didn't even have to wonder if I'd be woken up by the sound of my mother yelling, or my father throwing furniture into the walls. Out of this world, right? What a luxury. What a privilege.

Two: my hole-in-the-wall with June. For my whole adult life, it's been my safe space: just me, her, and a shared bowl of mac-and-cheese on a ratty old couch. I don't know many people who would call it "heaven," but it was heaven to me.

Three: Matvey's penthouse.

It wasn't as immediate there, though. For the longest time, it felt like a prison. And then, towards the end, it turned back into a cage. A golden one, yeah, but find me a single prisoner who'd care about the color of their cell bars. Not me, that's for sure.

But for a while, in the middle days, it didn't feel like that.

It felt like *home*.

The penthouse is exactly as I remember it: the luxurious sofas, the sleek décor, the stunning floor-to-ceiling windows. The only significant change is the dinner table.

I run my hand along the surface of this new one. It's... colder. Steel and glass instead of sun-warmed wood. The corners are sharp, like I could cut my finger on them just by poking too hard.

We're gonna need to baby-proof these when May's older, I find myself thinking.

And then: *Wait. Are we still going to be here when she's older?*

Am I still going to be here?

I yank the emergency brakes on my train of thought. It's way too early to worry about that. To think about something as vague as the future.

Especially when I'm still trying to make sense of the present.

"Where do you want these?" Yuri wheezes from the heap of suitcases in the doorway.

Anywhere but here. "It's okay," I answer from the middle of the living room. "You can just leave them there. Do you want some water?"

It feels strange, acting like the lady of the house. Like this place is mine in any way that matters.

But maybe it's not the penthouse that's different. Maybe I'm just not the same person who walked out.

I take Yuri's wheezing for an affirmative and bring him some fluids. "Familiar, isn't it? This whole scene," I joke.

Yuri guzzles down the water and grins. "Kind of. Last time, it was toys."

"Mhmm. This time, it's just boring supplies."

"Nothing boring 'bout a stroller filled with diaper packs."

I hum in agreement. If I've learned anything in these past few weeks on the run, it's that newborns need a lot of interesting things. So interesting, in fact, they can cost you an arm and a leg and a plasma donation. "Last time, you had to haul everything inside on your own, too."

Yuri shrugs. "Last time was an apology from Matvey."

"And this time?"

His face dims. "This time, it's an apology, too," he mumbles.

An apology to *Matvey,* I read between the lines.

Guilt pierces my heart. I should be getting used to the feeling, shouldn't I? Being the worst thing that's ever happened to everybody. Instead, the pain just keeps getting worse.

"For what it's worth, I'm sorry, too," I say shyly. "I put you in an impossible position. I wasn't thinking about you, or what this would do to you, or to your relationship with Matvey. If anybody deserves an apology here, it's you."

I stroke my baby for courage as I speak. Nugget is a comforting weight in my arms—no, *May,* I remind myself. I'll need to get the hang of that. Can't keep calling her like food forever, can I?

But it brings back so many memories...

Next to me, Yuri shakes his head. "I put *you* in an impossible position. I don't know if... if Matvey told you yet, but I..."

I watch his face twist into an expression of pain. The petty part of me says I should let him stew a little longer. Unintentionally or not, he was the catalyst for my falling out with Matvey—the spark that lit the fire on our love. Afterwards, there was nothing left but ashes.

But the rest of me rebels against the thought: Yuri *helped* me. More than that, he was the only one who did. The one who had the most to lose.

And I can't watch him torture himself for one more second. "I know," I reassure him. "It's okay. I don't blame you at all."

"But it's not okay! I—"

"You protected your family," I cut him off. "You did what you had to do. And so did I."

Something flickers across his face then. Something like amusement. "You sound just like Matvey."

I act surprised. "Yeah? Imagine that."

There are other words, fighting to get out, but I lock them far away. Words Matvey said to me, and words he didn't.

Say to *me*, that is.

A piece of advice to all the *pakhans* out there: if you're going to argue with your brother, do it far away from the object of contention.

And maybe don't shout so loud.

"You'd lie to April again?"

"I would."

Last night, those words gutted me. For a hot second, I thought I'd never get back up. The regret I thought I saw in his eyes, the sadness—how long did it take for Matvey to rationalize his way out of it? A day? An hour? Or even less than that?

But I did get back up. Eventually. I dusted off my broken heart, picked up my baby, and got myself all the way back to my dear old cage.

If there's one thing parenthood taught me, it's to bleed in silence.

"Who knew it'd be this hard, huh?" I muse out loud. "Being parents?"

Yuri makes a choking noise in his throat. "I wouldn't... know about that."

Yeah, you do. You're a dad in the making already. "Plenty of time to figure it out, though, right?"

"I guess," he mumbles, uncomfortable the way only a new parent can be. He may be Matvey's brother, but I could swear I see myself in his eyes: that big, neon sign flashing the words *I Am Freaking TF Out* with every single blink. "It's going to be at least six more months, and Petra—" Yuri halts, looking guilty. "Sorry. I probably shouldn't mention her to you. Not after..."

"The wedding?" I list off the top of my head. "The forced heist? The hospital scare?"

"Don't forget the kidnapping at gunpoint," someone chimes in.

Our heads snap towards the door in unison. "Petya," Yuri murmurs. "You shouldn't…"

"—be here?" Petra fills in from the doorway. "Neither should she. I told you that motel was a shitty idea. Next time, leave the hiding to me."

Petra. I haven't seen her since that day at the Mallard. The day everything changed between us—and between me and Matvey.

Then everything changed again, and I thought it was her fault.

It's odd—for over a month, I've cursed this woman out in my nightmares, cursed the way she played me for a fool. The way I thought I'd let *myself* be played for a fool.

But none of that was real.

"April…" She's suddenly uncertain now that she's speaking directly to me. "Can we talk?"

A month ago, I would have used a few choice words to answer that question. Mostly creative suggestions on where a hypothetical backstabbing bitch could put—or possibly shove—her desire to talk to me.

Now, I find myself nodding once.

Petra turns to Yuri. "Give us a moment?"

"Of course," he says. "I'll go check in with the guard detail."

I watch in silence as Petra's hand brushes the air above Yuri's shoulder in an almost-touch. The way his voice softens in return. The way their eyes meet and don't, as if afraid someone might see too much.

If I wasn't holding a baby right now, I would smack myself right across the face. How in the hell could I have missed it? How could anyone have missed it?

When Yuri finally steps out, the tension becomes unbearable. It's so thick, I could dice it into sashimi.

Then Petra starts talking.

11

APRIL

A few months ago, I started throwing up in the mornings.

I didn't think anything of it then. Honestly, I figured it was just stress. With everything that was going on, how could I not be stressed?

I stopped eating breakfast. It didn't solve a thing.

Then I started gaining weight.

It wasn't anything outrageous, just a couple of pounds here and there, but it was weird. I was throwing up half my fluids every morning—how could I be gaining anything? Then again, maybe I was compensating. Maybe I was stress-eating too much during the rest of the day.

I tightened my belt. It didn't solve a thing.

When I started missing my period, I thought for sure it must be stress. Because what else could it be? All my life, doctors told me it was unlikely I'd get pregnant. Back then, I thought it a blessing. What child could possibly want me as their mother? What child could possibly want the life I had to offer?

Even still, I made an OBGYN appointment.

This time, something came of it.

It was the day after the heist, bright and early. I was still shaken up by what I'd done to you, feeling queasy from my morning sickness and from shame. The shame of hurting you—my first friend.

That's what you were to me, April: not just a friend, but the first. Lena and Julia are my knights, but you... you were the queen on the other side of the board. You had every reason to want to eat me whole.

Instead, you made a friend of me. You knew I was a killer and you didn't care. You knew I wanted you gone and you didn't fucking care.

How could I not think of you as a friend in return?

Yuri offered to take me to the appointment. I said no. I could take care of myself. It was probably nothing.

But then it wasn't nothing.

Yuri... I never meant for that to happen, either. For us to happen. With the alliance and the wedding plans and everything else our Bratvas had going on, the last thing I needed was a complication.

But love is never simple.

That's right: I fell in love. Feel free to laugh, but I did. I fell in love with my intended's brother. What a cliché, right? Wake up, Jane Austen, 'cause I have a new novel for you.

I could have handled being in love, though. I could have buried it in the same shallow grave my enemies shared back in Russia. I could have killed it in the snow.

But then he did the worst thing he could've done.

He loved me back.

He loved me first, actually. I could tell right away. He was respectful, distant—but he liked me. That's what I thought it was at the time: like. Not love. Another first I didn't see coming.

But it was never meant to go this far. To bring ruin to all our hopes and dreams.

They say a child is a blessing, regardless of the circumstances. Whoever "they" are, they never met Vlad.

I knew my father would kill me for this. That he'd bury me in the shallow grave of his enemies.

That he'd bury Yuri.

That he'd bury our child.

So I did the only thing I could think of: I turned to Matvey. I asked him to protect us. To protect us from everyone.

I'm sorry, April. If it's the last thing I get to say to you, I want it to be this: I'm sorry. I am so, so sorry.

I never meant to harm you. I never meant to harm your baby. I don't know what I was thinking the day of the heist—maybe I wasn't thinking at all. And afterwards? I just didn't want us to die.

I don't expect your forgiveness. I don't expect to ever be your friend again. If you want to get one good swing in, I'll even hold the baby for you.

But can you at least understand why I did it?

I made the mistake of not listening once. When Matvey tried

to tell me. Even if it was too little, too late, it might have saved something of us. Of the family we could have been.

So this time, I listen. This time, I let Petra get every single word out.

Then I give her my baby to hold.

"Oh, are you really going to—okay, wait, let me take out my contacts—April? April, what the hell are you doing?"

I wrap my arms around her. It's like trying to hug a jellyfish: all she does is squirm. "Shut up," I tell her. "Just shut up and take it."

For a few seconds, Petra stays frozen in shock. "That's not how you punch someone," she points out.

"I can't punch you, Petra."

An indignant huff. "What, because I'm pregnant?"

"Because I'd break my hand on that thick skull of yours. Now, shut up and let me hug you."

"… Why?" she whispers in the end.

And isn't that the question of the year: *Why?*

I could say it's because forgiveness is a virtue. Because Dominic sent me to Sunday school every week and some of it stuck. Or because I'm just that good of a person.

But the truth is, it's because I'm tired.

I can't hold another grudge. I just can't. It's exhausting, being angry with the people you love. It takes everything out of you. Matvey's already doing a stellar job of hollowing me out; I don't need to get any emptier.

And maybe I just want my friend back.

"That's for me to know and for you to wonder about forever," I answer with a sniffle.

"So it's torture you're choosing? Hell, we might make you Bratva yet," Petra sniffles back.

Jeez, look at us: tears, snot, and hormones. Such sexy ladies.

"Truth is, I really need a mannequin."

"I can do that. Just be warned, I've gained half a size."

"Oh, half a size. Boo-hoo, poor you."

We're separated by May protesting the lack of air.

"Sorry," I laugh, tickling my baby's cheek. "Don't like being squished, do you?"

Only then does Petra finally seem to realize what she's holding. "God, she's…"

"Beautiful? Perfect? Just like her mother?"

"A stink-bomb," she grimaces.

I take a whiff and realize she's right. Oh, well. "You get used to it."

Petra's eyes widen in terror. It's the most satisfying thing I've seen all day. "You most certainly do not."

"Guess we'll know soon enough, Mommy-To-Be."

We're interrupted by a panicked guard shouting: "Hey, all of you! You can't be—"

"April!"

Three voices converge at the entrance. Three voices I would recognize anywhere.

My family.

June is on me in seconds, followed by Corey and Rob. I barely glimpse Petra making a quick getaway—God, she really hates crowds, doesn't she?

And displays of affection. I swear, she's more terrified by hugs than firearms.

"What are you three doing here?" I balk.

"We were worried!" June yells.

"You disappeared for a month!" Corey scolds.

"I heard you left with stitches!"

"I heard you got shot at!"

"Where did you hear all that?!" I yelp.

From the doorway, another familiar figure emerges. "Apologies, Ms. Flowers." Grisha bows. "I took the liberty of updating your friends and bringing them here. I hope you won't mind."

"She sure as hell better not," Corey harrumphs.

"She has a lot of explaining to do," June adds sternly. "Falling off the face of the Earth like— Oh my God, is that your baby?!"

"Let me see! Let me see!"

"Meow."

I mouth a silent *Thank you* to Grisha over June's shoulder. Then: "Wait—who meowed?"

Rob raises his hands in protest. "Wasn't me."

Then I notice the carrier on the ground. "Is that... Mr. Buttons?!"

June grins. "Thought you could use a pick-me-up. Still no pets allowed here?"

"And no friends?" Corey asks with puppy eyes.

I think back to Matvey's draconian rules. *No visits, no guests, no nothing.*

Then I decide I don't give a damn.

"The rules have changed," I tell them. "Come on in. I want you all to meet someone." I hold out the bundle in my arms. "This... is May."

As the trio's eyes grow wet—June's especially—and my cat finally returns to me, sniffing suspiciously at the stink-bomb in my arms, all I can think of is one thing.

I still have a family after all.

12

MATVEY

I hate *I-told-you-so*'s.

No, more than that: I despise them. There isn't a single string of words more annoying than that, in the English language or in any other.

The fact that Grisha isn't saying them doesn't fucking help matters.

Because he's sure as fuck thinking them. I know it; he knows it; hell, even the goddamn hot dog man on the curb behind me knows it. If he had it tattooed on his face, it wouldn't change a thing—that's how obvious my third-in-command is being.

And the worst part is… he's right.

I doubted him. I had him followed by the same man who was pulling my leg the entire time. And when he tried to tell me —when he tried to point out Yuri's suspicious behaviors to me, or worse, my own failings—what did I do?

I bit his fucking head off. I pushed him out of the inner circle, accused him of being disloyal, even threatened him in the middle of the street. I did everything short of kicking him out.

And I was goddamn wrong.

He greets me next to the car, expression impassive. *"Moy pakhan."*

But all I hear is, *I told you so.*

"Grisha," I say back stiffly.

But all I want to say is, *Shut up. I know.*

We get into the car. Grisha merges into the rush hour New York City traffic. "I saw April at the penthouse," he mentions offhandedly. "She seemed glad to have her friends back."

I told you so. "Hm."

"I also saw Yuri there. He left with Petra soon after, though."

I told you so. "I see."

"I spoke with the *vory*, too. It appears this won't be a friendly meeting."

I told you so. "Grisha."

"Yes?" he asks innocently.

God fucking dammit. And they say wives are passive-aggressive. Whoever "they" are, they've never had Grisha Aldonin drive their car.

"... Thank you," I grit out. "For your continued loyalty."

Grisha's eyebrows arch skeptically in the rearview mirror. "I wouldn't dream of being anything but loyal."

I told you so. "And I appreciate that. What you've done so far… and what you'll continue to do."

"You sound confident that I will."

"Yeah, well, you haven't given me cause to be disappointed yet."

"'Yet.'"

I roll my eyes. "Can we drop the fucking act already?"

"What act?"

"Jesus fucking—alright, fine: I was wrong. Happy?"

For a moment, Grisha doesn't say anything. Then: "You know, you have the same uncanny ability your grandfather had."

"And that would be…?"

"Saying 'sorry' without actually speaking the word."

I snort. "Your father told you that?"

"He did. Several times." For the first time since the ride began, I glimpse the hint of Grisha's old smile in the mirror. "Must be a family talent."

Grisha's father. That's how I found him all those years ago. I wasn't looking for him—I was looking for Yakov Aldonin. My grandfather's second.

But he was dead already.

His son, however, was interested in what I had to say. He was the first to join my cause after Yuri. The first to *believe*.

He'd grown up watching his father kick ass. More than that, watching him protect his *pakhan* and being protected in return. That's what people looked for in a Bratva back then: a bond. A pack.

A brotherhood.

Lacking any parents or elders, Grisha took his role in that pack seriously. He was the lowest-ranked, but the oldest in age. I have no idea if he was always the mother hen type, but with us... Let's just say that, after we found him, we didn't have to raise ourselves anymore.

If I were a better man, I'd acknowledge how shitty I've been to him. As his *pakhan* and as his friend.

But I'm not a better man. Everything good I had in me has been turned to ashes along with my heart. If I ever had anything to give, it was for *her*.

Now, I'm empty.

Luckily, Grisha seems content with his lot. Has to be, really. How else would he have put up with me all these years otherwise?

"I hope this means you'll listen to me every now and then," he quips.

I bark out a laugh. "Now, where's the fun in that?"

"Not a friendly meeting" is the understatement of the year. As soon as I enter the office where the meeting is to take place, I can feel the temperature plunge. It's like dipping a toe into the Arctic.

Then it begins.

Once upon a time, my *vory* used to be terrified of me. I wasn't just respected—I was feared. That's the prerequisite of every *pakhan*: if you can't make your men fear for their lives at the slightest slip, you're just not cut out for the gig.

But now, my men are no longer mincing words. Worse than that, they're pushing back against me.

When the Solovyov half of the table joins in, I realize who's behind it all.

"I have to agree with the others," Vlad coughs and spittles all over the table. "Between the botched acquisition, losing track of your own newborn, and now, this mess with the Italians... let's just say there's been more than a few setbacks, son."

"Not to mention the business has been suffering." Ivan twists the knife. "Our partners and top clients have seen you decline every request to meet over the past four weeks. If they were feeling neglected before, now, they're outright scorned."

"'Scorned'?" Grisha laughs. "Forgive me, Ivan. I wasn't aware that our *pakhan* was supposed to treat his business partners as wives."

Ivan fires back, "If he treated them like his wife, he'd pretend they never existed at all."

I slam my palms on the table and rise. "Enough."

I didn't want Yuri here today—that's on me. I needed him elsewhere. But it's one less voice to speak in my favor on a shitty fucking day to be without advocates. If there's one thing I hate more than *I-told-you-so*'s, it's politics.

Petra could have helped, though. After all she's done to fuck up my life, I wouldn't even have to ask—she'd side with me in a heartbeat. If she was allowed to be here, she'd bring the Solovyovs around with a single glare.

But with her pregnancy so heavily publicized, it was the worst possible timing in the world to push for her promotion to *vor*, so she's not in this room, either. No, if I want to get anything done here today, I'll have to rely on the one person who never let me down.

Myself.

After my outburst, I look every single *vor* in the eye. Aside from Ivan, none of them dare hold my gaze, not even Vlad. That's the thing about packs: take their members one at a time, and they'll be nothing but lone wolves, ready to roll on their backs and whine pitifully at the first hint of an alpha's teeth.

So I bare my fangs. "While you squabble over minor setbacks and missed dinners, I've been hunting for our enemy. The one who botched our D.C. deal, who tried to kidnap my daughter *three times* and failed—and who now threatens the very existence of our organization."

Then I whip out a picture and toss it over to the center of the table.

The *vory* lean in like chickens over scattered grains. "Who is this man?" Stanislav asks.

"Carmine Bonaccorsi," I snarl.

The table falls silent.

"The Bonaccorsi family?" Vlad frowns. "As in, the Italian mafia in D.C.? What do they have to do with us?"

"Everything."

It's Ivan who steals the word right out of my mouth. But he spits it out with disdain, like he's just seen a bug crawl over his papers. "Is this what we've become then, Matvey? A personal vendetta you can't let go of?"

"No."

"Then—"

"This is what we've always been."

The *vory* fall quiet in unison. Ivan's lips press into a tight, white line. It's my turn to speak. Their turn to fucking listen.

"You of all people should know that, Ivan. You were there at the beginning. Since the first Groza Bratva, am I wrong?"

"I served your grandfather with pride," Ivan snarls. "He was a great man with a great vision."

"Yes. And he's dead."

I watch Ivan bristle at my words. *Good.* Let him lose his cool, for once. "How dare you—"

"No, the question is how dare *you*. All of you." I start walking around the table, circling. Right now, I want my men to feel like prey. To remember what it's like to be at the bottom of the food chain. "Let me make something perfectly clear: *I* brought the Groza Bratva back from the ashes. *I* gave it new life. *I* gave it a new purpose."

"And that purpose is revenge?" Ivan questions.

"The purpose is survival," I retort. "Unless you've forgotten what it was like back in Russia…?" I throw a wide glance around the table. "I know not all of you were there back then. On those grounds alone, I'll forgive you this time—so long as you never fucking forget again."

"But *pakhan*," Ipatiy tries to amend weakly, "we *are* surviving. More than that, we're thriving. Surely it's not worth it to pursue old grudges now?"

"'Old'?" I bark out a laugh. "Did you all forget I just found my kid two days ago? That those *mudaki* tried to murder her twice while she was still in the womb?"

"What does that have to do—?" Gora starts, but I cut him off.

"Everything!" I roar. "An attack against my blood is an attack against me. And an attack against me is an attack against *you*. Because, unless you've forgotten about this, too, I'm still your *pakhan*."

"So what do we do?" Ipatiy asks, panicked sweat dotting his forehead.

"We go to war."

This time, the silence is different. Half-terror, half-awe.

"We go to war," I repeat, loud enough to rally the troops, "and we fucking win. Unless some of you prefer to run?"

No one speaks another word. No one goddamn dares.

"Good. Dismissed."

As the *vory* file out one after the other, both Ivan and Vlad look back at me with something sharp in their eyes.

"You got them back under control," Grisha mutters once they're out.

"For now," I sigh. "I swear, this is a fucking mutiny in the making."

"They're testing the hierarchy." He shrugs. "Like wolves. Checking if their alpha's still up to the task."

"How do they do it?" I lean back in my chair, fucking exhausted. "The wolves?"

"Usually, they kill each other."

"Let's hope it doesn't come to that."

I let the silence fall, but we're both thinking the same answer to my unspoken question.

"Hope" isn't good enough.

13

MATVEY

One more thing about being *pakhan*: you have to be ready for everything.

It's a simple matter of survival. The quickest to prepare, adjust, predict—that's who comes out on top. It's true in the animal kingdom, and it's true for us, too.

After all, what's a man if not simply another kind of beast?

I wasn't ready to face Carmine, and it almost cost me everything. I wasn't ready for today's ambush, and I almost lost control of my Bratva.

But there's something else I'm unprepared for, and it's seeing April again.

No, not just *seeing* her—but having dinner with her. Like we used to do when we still meant something to each other.

You still can, whispers the voice of my own wretched weakness. *You still do.*

I rip its throat out and silence it.

I know that won't last forever. That ugly part of me has a tendency of roaring back to life when I least want it around, but it takes time. Time I can use to get my head on straight.

Time I can use to forget her.

You don't have to forget her, that hateful voice keeps hissing. *You can fix things. You can try again. You can apologi—*

On the elevator ride up to the penthouse, I kill my weakness over and over again. Because if there's one thing I'll never do, it's apologize to the woman who took my daughter from me. April betrayed me. Worse than that, she betrayed her own blood. That's unforgivable.

What about your *lies?* that voice still goads. *What about* your *betrayal? Are* those *forgivable?*

Then I step in and find something else I wasn't prepared for.

"Meow."

A goddamn cat.

"I see you've met Mr. Buttons," April acknowledges coolly.

"Mr. Buttons," I deadpan, staring at the offensive orange creature giving me the stink-eye from my carpet.

"That's right. June brought him back for me."

I vaguely remember this topic coming up when April first moved here. Back then, I blew her off with some bullshit about the hotel's pet policy. I was under the impression that she'd pop the baby out in a matter of days, we'd work out a living arrangement somewhere else, and that would be it.

I didn't think I was actually going to have to *deal* with the fucker.

"I see. How… hygienic."

As if on cue, the fluffy menace jumps into the crib. I watch him with disgust as he curls around my daughter's sleeping form and wraps his tail around her foot. Like he's setting up a fucking tripwire or something.

April blows me off with a wave. "Oh, please. He's up to date with all his shots. Besides, he's an excellent baby monitor."

"The geriatric cat with the eyepatch works security?" I frown.

"Hey! He wears it very well."

For a brief second, it feels just like old times: the jokes, the banter, the chemistry. Coming home to new shenanigans every day.

And then I remember: *She took my kid. She ran away. She betrayed me.*

It seems like April remembers, too, the same moment I do. She clears her throat, face clouding over. "Did you want something?"

I set my jaw. "As a matter of fact, yes."

Then I open the door and let in the food cart.

We watch in tense silence as a jittery waiter sets the table. It must be the most uncomfortable minute of his career, but frankly, I don't care. I pay my employees well enough—the least they can do is their fucking jobs.

He does. "Enjoy your dinner, sir, ma'am."

April gives a tight nod of acknowledgement.

Then we're alone again.

Well, not alone exactly. May is still snoozing in her crib, the cat curled up around her like a dragon with his treasure. Only, it's not *his* treasure.

It's mine.

"So you're still set on this?" April asks eventually. "Family dinner?"

"Yes."

"Why?"

I take my place at the table. "Sit."

"Matvey—"

"I said *sit.*"

After a beat, she obeys.

We dine in silence. I watch her push the food around on her plate, but I don't have a good excuse to force her to eat. After all, she's not carrying my child anymore.

She could still do that, that annoying voice whispers. *She could carry all your children if you'd just—*

"Are you going to stay here?" April breaks the silence. "At the penthouse?"

Like I'd ever let you out of my sight again. "Someone has to make sure our daughter doesn't disappear into thin air."

"I thought that's what the guards were for."

"The guards are there to protect her against Carmine."

"And you're here to protect her from me?" she fills in bitterly.

"Your words, not mine." I take in the hurt on her face. I try to pretend it doesn't touch me.

I fail.

After our torture of a meal, I pick up the baby from the crib, dodging a swipe from April's hellspawn of a cat. By contrast, May is pliant like a doll, only cooing in protest for a second before I place her against my chest, trading warmth for warmth.

When I go to put her back, my shoulder smarts with pain.

I head to the guest room. "Going to bed already?" April asks me.

See? She can't get rid of you fast enough.

"Yeah. Goodnight."

"Wait."

When I turn, April's face is a mask of concern. For a second, I'm stunned. "What?"

"Let me check your stitches first," she requests. "You haven't let anyone else see, have you?"

Something thick settles in my throat. Something dangerously close to a lump. "I'm fine."

"Please," she insists. "Just one look. I promise I'll be quick."

"So you can slip me a sedative and run?"

"So I can make sure our daughter still has a father in the morning, actually."

Her words catch me off-guard. Her eyes, shining with that familiar fire. "Fine." I drop back onto the couch.

April gathers her supplies and perches next to me. This time, she has a proper first-aid kit. "No whiskey?" I ask.

"Your liquor cabinet's locked."

I frown. "Since when?"

"Since Grisha locked it," she answers. "Didn't you order him to do that?"

I roll my eyes internally. *Goddamn Grisha.* "Must've forgotten," I mutter.

April starts to pull on my collar, then seems to think better of it. Her fingers brush my skin as they retreat, warm like embers. "Take off your shirt," she whispers in a choked voice.

The sensation lingers. I swallow around it, unbuttoning my shirt with careless movements. I don't care if it hurts—I want to get it over quickly.

No, I *need* to.

Once that part's done, April's hand comes back, fingertips ghosting over my skin. "Sit still," she murmurs, voice lower than before.

"Just get it over with."

She gives a small nod. "Alright."

Her touches are soft, measured. She follows the wound carefully, cleaning away the dirt, warding off the rot. I can't believe I'm letting her do this again—getting close to the most vulnerable parts of me.

But a *pakhan* can't afford to be vulnerable. Nor can he afford to fall back into the waiting arms of the siren who almost got him killed.

"So, Carmine…" She hesitates. "He's your dad?"

"He's not my anything. I just share his genes, that's all."

"That's ironic," she observes. "All you do is go on about 'blood this, blood that,' and now, it's just genes?"

"Family doesn't betray each other," I cut short. "Never."

April takes the blow. She accepts it gracefully, like she's always accepted everything: my moods, my orders, my desires.

Everything but your lies, that horrible voice whispers.

I shake it off. Whatever it has to say, I don't want to hear it. "What's it to you?" I demand.

She looses a pensive sigh. "Aside from the fact that it's just nice to know? It's..." She fumbles for words. "I don't know— weird? I never pegged you for half-Italian."

"I'm Russian," I growl back. "Whatever Carmine is has nothing to do with me."

"Good."

I frown. "'Good'?"

"Well, I always did like pineapple on pizza."

For a split second, I almost lose control of my face and smile.

Get it together. Remember who she is. "Hm."

"How d'you end up with an Italian mafia boss dad—sorry, gene-lender—anyway?"

"Aside from the fact that my mother had terrible taste in men?"

"Yeah, aside from that."

I take a moment to think. Not about what to say, but whether

I actually want to say it. April doesn't deserve my confessions —not after how she treated my last one.

But this isn't just about me. This concerns May's roots as well as mine.

And she's her daughter, too.

"His father wasn't particularly good at playing the mafia game. He got in a turf war with a rival family and lost. Instead of staying and fighting, Carmine joined the army and fled."

"Fled to Russia?"

"Bosnia, actually. He was deployed there first. Lasted a couple of months and then…" I grit my teeth. "Then the fucker deserted. Again."

"Seems like a real lionheart," she drawls.

You don't have to tell me that. "He spent the next few weeks on the run. Landed himself across the Russian border. My mom found him starving in the snow and took him in. Within a year, I was born."

"That…" April hesitates. "That doesn't sound like the start of a tragedy. It sounds…"

"Romantic?" I scoff. "Yeah, that's what my mom thought, too. But he wasn't the type to settle down. Or stay on the straight and narrow."

"Well, that's not you, either."

"No," I concede. "That's not me, either."

A long moment ticks by in silence. I almost managed to forget about April's hands on me, but now, it hits me twice as hard: her warmth, her scent, her everything.

"Alright. That's enough," I growl.

"Almost done. Just patching up."

Every touch, every breath—it's torture, pure and simple. I can feel her fingers working over my skin, her labored huffs breaking against my neck. Her knees, parted on either side of my back.

It would be so easy to turn our positions around. To nestle between those warm thighs until all I can feel is *her*. Until I can't fucking breathe. Until I'm where I belong.

Without warning, I lurch to standing. "I said that's *enough*."

April manages to tamp down the last corner of the gauze just before I'm out of reach. "Matvey?" she calls to me. "Wait—did I say something wrong?"

"I just need to sleep."

"Matvey, did I hurt you?"

More than you'll ever know.

14

APRIL

They say good things come in threes. Well, apparently, they're not the only ones. Bad things arrive in nasty little triplets, too.

"Legs a little wider, please."

Bad thing number one: moving back here.

Bad thing number two: yesterday's "dinner."

Bad thing number three—

"Like this?"

"Wider, April."

Dear God, please, let me be reborn as a yoga instructor. "I don't think they'll go any wider, Dr. Allan."

"Okay, don't sweat it. Just wanted to see how the healing was going."

I have no clue if this is Matvey's idea of a punishment or my own karma circling back to me with both middle fingers up, but it feels like retribution. Either his, or the universe's. Maybe both.

I throw a glance in Matvey's direction and find him resolutely turned the other way. *Thank God.* At least he isn't seeing this R-rated Cirque du Soleil audition of mine. "And...?"

"And you're very lucky. Everything appears to be in order."

"Oh, good—"

"—despite your every attempt to self-destruct."

I make what I hope is a pleading and adorable face. Lately, my puppy eyes have been failing me. "I was fine, I swear! I just wanted to go home and—"

"And never call again for a month?" she scolds me. "April, I nearly went to the police. The only reason I didn't was your husband talking me down."

"I'm sorry, Dr. Allan, I really—wait, my what?"

"Which is no excuse for your own recklessness, Mr. Groza," the doctor presses, raising her voice to make herself heard across the room. "You should've brought your wife in for at least a check-up! Who even leaves their hospital bed with fresh stitches? And a whole ten minutes after giving birth?!"

"First, I want to reiterate how sorry I am," I say. "Truly. Second—I'm no one's wife, thank you very much."

"Small mercies," Matvey mutters back, dripping sarcasm everywhere in a five-mile radius. Possibly on the baby in his arms, too.

"Well, uhh..." The doctor droops back uncomfortably, glancing from one "spouse" to the other in quick succession.

"Marital statuses aside, you were very lucky. Sure, the scar's looking a bit wonky—"

"That would be my fault," I interrupt. "A couple of stitches came out, so I had to put them back in myself."

"… As I was saying," Dr. Allan sighs, pretending I haven't spoken a word while presumably questioning if it's too late to switch to a less stressful career, like maybe skydiving, "despite your best efforts, nothing's broken. I'd give it a few more days to be sure, but you're pretty much back to prepartum condition. You can go back to doing everything you did before."

"Like lifting weights and signing up for yoga classes I'll never go to?"

"Yup."

"That's great, thank—"

"And sexual activity, too."

I blanch. "By 'sexual,' you mean…"

"The very same thing that got you into this." Dr. Allan smiles. "And hopefully back into *this*, if that's your wish. Weren't you telling me on our very first appointment that you wanted a big family?"

Suddenly, I understand what deer feel at the sight of headlights. My head snaps automatically towards Matvey, whose head seems to snap automatically towards me, and— wait, is he pissed off?

Is he pissed off that I can *use my body* again?

For some reason, that pisses *me* off. Big fucking time. So

what if I've got the green light to mess around? Surely he isn't expecting to ever get back into my, ahem, "good graces"?

"Don't worry, Doctor," I say with my biggest smile. "That will certainly not be a problem for the time being."

"If you say so." She shrugs. "I'll just leave you a fresh prescription for birth control, then."

"Oh, no, I didn't mean—"

But she's already writing.

On the other side of the room, Matvey's doing his best impression of a statue. Or maybe it's the three monkeys: *I do not see it, I do not hear it, I do not give a damn about it.*

Defeated, I accept the prescription slip. "Thanks, Doc."

"You're always very welcome."

After Dr. Allan leaves, I've barely pulled down my dress before Matvey's already shoving our baby back into my arms. In some respects, we really are just like any other couple.

Except that's where traditional behaviors end for us.

"Grisha, keep an eye on her," he calls into the hallway. "Make sure she doesn't leave."

I roll my eyes. "Gee, what now? I was just planning to go bar crawling."

"Without me?" a feminine voice calls from the hallway. "And here I thought we were friends again."

"Petra." Matvey's voice is ice. "I wasn't aware you had business here."

"Oh, you know how it is," she smiles sweetly. "Mommy Pilates got canceled. Thought I'd ditch the dolls and get some hands-on experience with the real thing. If that's okay with you, April?"

What does it say about me that I'm actually relieved to see her? "Sure. I think May needs changing anyway."

Petra's smile falters, but only for a moment. "Perfect."

Matvey frowns at our newfound friendliness. What, did he really think I'd blame the other woman?

"No leaving," he repeats to Grisha.

"Yes, *pakhan*."

Then he strides out.

For a moment, we just look between the three of us. "Are you... staying for the impromptu mommy class?" I ask.

To his credit, Grisha only pales a little. "I'm afraid I have prior commitments," he politely declines. "But you two have fun. If you need anything, I'll be right outside the door."

Then he makes himself scarce, too.

Just like that, we're alone. "Thanks for the assist," I exhale.

"Sure. How's the confinement going?"

"You know, I feel like I'm learning what being a single mother in a Middle Ages convent was like."

"Does that make Grisha a nun?"

I snort. "Let's not ask him that."

God, it's the most normal interaction I've had in ages. Again, what does that say about me?

"For the record…" Petra clears her throat. "I'm not helping you change that."

I find myself snickering. "You're gonna have to learn at some point, Mommy-In-Waiting."

"I'll have nannies for that."

I shake my head sadly. "You're actually freaking out about it, aren't you? Motherhood?"

I put May down in her crib and start moving around the kitchen to make tea. Petra leans against the back of the couch, inspecting her nails with a carefully casual air. "I don't know what you're talking about."

"Yeah, you do. All the lying awake at night, the sneaking suspicion that you should've splurged for therapy while you still had the chance."

"Therapy is for cheerleaders."

"… staring at the ceiling and wondering just how hard it's going to be…"

A shrug. "Can't be too hard if *you're* doing it."

"Ouch." I fake-stab myself. "Really hurt my feelings there, *Petya.*"

Ah-ha. I knew that nickname would be the ace up my sleeve. Her face burning like a stoplight is all the confirmation I needed. "Shut up."

"Why? It's so sweet."

"It's just Yuri being informal."

"Oh, is that what we're calling pet names now?"

Before I know it, the water's boiling. I pour us two cups and set some cookies in the middle of the table. "C'mon. Don't pretend you're not starving."

"I hate you," Petra mumbles around a mouthful. "You're just trying to fatten me up."

"And make you gain another half-size? Heaven forbid."

"You say that now, but I'd like to see you without your emergency living mannequi—WAH!"

My head snaps towards the sound. At first I think Petra's burned herself with the tea, but then I follow her line of sight straight into her lap and—

"Oh, you've met Buttons!"

"What is this thing?" Petra panics. "Why is it sniffing at me— *bozhe moy*, is that an eyepatch?!"

I try to hide my snickering, but fail. "Oh my God, your face."

"*My* face?" she balks. "How about *his* face?!"

"He's a Persian mix." I shrug. "That's just how they look."

"He looks like his mother had an affair with a pug and a weedeater, in that order."

I can't help it then: I laugh. Worse—I fall over the table and just honest-to-God *lose it.*

Petra watches me with her trademark RBF. "Ha-ha, very funny. Yuk it up."

"I can't…!"

"Your cat is a scurvy-riddled pirate, but somehow, *I'm* the ridiculous one."

"Help...! *Help...!*" It's a good handful of minutes before I manage to collect myself. "Sorry," I wheeze at last, drying literal tears from my eyes. "I think I needed that."

Petra's face softens then. Her manicured hand reaches for mine over the table, the other scratching idly behind Buttons's half-bitten ear. "April... how are you holding up, really?"

My first impulse is to deny: *Everything's fine. I'm okay. Just haven't been sleeping that well.*

But just thinking about it is exhausting. I'm so tired of it. Tired of lying, of hiding, of this web of deception we ended up weaving around each other.

For once, I just want truth.

"I have no idea," I answer honestly. "Last night, I finally slept in a real bed."

"That must've been nice."

"It was. There were no bedfeatures."

"Sorry, what?"

I ignore Petra's confusion and press on. "We had dinner in silence. Again."

"April..."

"He won't talk to me. Hell, he barely looks at me. We were so happy before, and now—" Suddenly, I realize what I'm saying. I gaze up and find Petra's eyes on mine, her expression crestfallen. "Sorry, I..."

"You don't have to apologize." She shakes her head. "Not in the slightest, April."

"It's not your fault," I blurt out. "I didn't want to make it out like…"

"It kind of is, though."

"No, I'm serious. I… I used to blame you," I mutter. "Blame you *and* him. But now, I know the truth."

"What truth is that?" she asks, coaxing my feelings out. My *true* feelings.

"I know that he lied to me," I rasp. "That he *chose* to."

"Maybe he didn't want to."

But I shake my head at that. "Petra, tell me honestly: when was the last time Matvey did something he didn't choose to do?"

That stumps her for a while. "He didn't want to get married," she answers finally. "I can tell you that with certainty."

"Right. But it was still his choice."

For a long moment, we're quiet. It's a different kind of silence—the kind that doesn't hurt, but only because there's nothing left to wound. Because everything's already out in the open, all the blood and guts.

Then I hear my own voice breaking it.

It's too quiet, though: barely a mumble. Petra frowns and leans in. "Sorry, what was that?"

"He said he'd do it all over again," I rasp out through a shaking voice. "Lying to me. Pushing me away."

"He can't have said that. No. No way. April, it's his biggest regret."

"I heard it with my own two ears. He hates me, Petra."

"He doesn't—"

"And he's right, isn't he?" I finally break. "I took his kid away. I did that. I knew how important she was to him, and I still…"

My words are cut off halfway. Before I realize it, there's something warm around me that wasn't there before.

Arms, holding me.

"Shut up, *koshka*."

"But…"

"Just shut up. You're hurting. Stop torturing yourself even more."

Buttons paws at my leg, as if agreeing with her. I've never felt more like an impostor—like a thief stealing love she doesn't deserve. "I…"

"When's the last time you cried, April?"

I try to answer… and then I realize that I don't know. I've teared up in fights. I've feared for my life and nearly cried there. But I can't remember when I last did *this*.

So I let it happen: I cry. I sob all over Petra's pristine white shirt and then some. I fall over the precipice of the breakdown I've been tiptoeing around all this time, these four weeks of nothing.

I cry until I have nothing left to give.

And then, just to be sure, I cry a little bit more.

15

APRIL

After a lunch of ice cream and pizza, I finally manage to convince Petra that it's safe to leave me alone. It's a hard sell, but if there's one thing I'm good at, it's crafting things people will buy.

She hasn't been out five minutes when someone else knocks on my door.

This time, I know exactly who it is.

"Charlie!" My brother wordlessly crushes me into the second hug of the day. "Jesus, have you grown taller?" I laugh. "It's like Jack and the freaking Beanstalk here, and you're both characters."

"Couple of inches," he preens. Then he starts looking around excitedly. "Where is she? Is she awake?"

Straight to the point. "You're in luck. You caught her in a rare moment of awareness."

"That makes it sound like she's in a coma, sis."

"Trust me, she'd be more awake if she was." I go pick up my bundle of joy. "May I, Mr. Buttons?"

My cat gives a slow blink of approval. *"Just don't keep her too long,"* he seems to be saying. *"My lady's schedule is full as it is."*

As soon as I put her in Charlie's arms, he starts beaming. I worry he's seconds away from holding his newborn niece up like Simba just so he can show her to the world. *Look, I'm an uncle now!*

"What's her name?" he asks with stars in his eyes.

I bite back a laugh. "May."

"May," he repeats, awed. "That's funny. It fits."

"Right? I'm a riot like that."

"So are you going to keep up the tradition? Next one is June and so on?"

I make a so-so gesture. "I think our June likes being the only one of her kind."

"Maybe Julius for July if it's a boy," he muses. "August also works. Oh, or Augustus! Did you know that's where those two months' names come from? Julius Caesar and Caesar Augustus?"

There he goes, my history buff baby bro. "I'll keep that in mind for the next Roman emperor I birth."

He gives a pensive hum. "Maybe Matvey will want to pick a Russian one. He… April, are you okay?"

I force myself to unfreeze. Charlie's words caught me like an ice bucket—I didn't see them coming at all. "Of course," I lie. "It's just… maybe it's too soon to think of other kids. I'm not sure Matvey will even want them."

Certainly not from me.

It's the same train of thought Dr. Allan's visit brought on: other kids. A big family. Matvey doesn't want me anymore; he's made that abundantly clear. But he also said...

You can't have someone else. Not now, not ever.

So where does that leave me?

"Oh," Charlie says, expression falling somewhat. "Right. Well, this one's probably a handful already. Ain't that right, Li'l M?"

I fail to suppress a snort. Leave it to Charlie to put a smile back on my face after such a grim tangent. "Is she getting her street name already?"

"Damn right she is. She's dope like that."

At that moment, another knock comes. "Am I interrupting?" calls a deep, familiar voice.

I beam at the sight of my boss in the hallway. Something very few employees can say, I'm sure. "Elias!"

The third hug of the day nearly makes me two-dimensional. "There's my employee of the month!"

"I thought I was your only employee."

Elias blows me off with a wave. "Details, details. Ohh, is that the little mannequin?"

I shake my head and laugh. "A perfect one. Barely moves at all."

He boops May on the nose while she's still wrapped up in her uncle's arms. "Don't say that too loud. Other moms might get jealous."

"I'll make sure she cries every now and then at the grocery store to even things out."

"Look," Charlie tells him, "she has freckles, too."

Elias squints playfully. "Is that right?"

I watch them from the door, tenderness filling my heart. Elias and Charlie are already familiar with each other, of course—what with my little brother kicking back at the shop on more than a few occasions. Basically whenever our mom went batshit, or when his dad...

Don't think about it. That's in the past for you. They can't hurt you anymore.

Charlie transfers the baby into Elias's arms, interrupting my train of thought. The old man grins down at her and lets her grab his gnarled finger with her tiny ones. She seems very curious about this new face in particular—probably because she's never seen such a long beard before. He lets her play with it, then turns to me with a smile. "She's perfect, you know."

"She kind of is, isn't she?" I murmur.

"You always did make the most beautiful things," Elias says, surprising me. "But this time you've truly outdone yourself, April. You made a miracle."

I can feel a lump forming in my throat, tears pooling at the corners of my eyes. I blink them away quickly; I will not go back to being a sobbing mess for the second time today.

"Thank you," I say sincerely.

Elias nods, eyes shining with tears of his own. God, look at us: a bunch of crybabies. May's eyes are literally the only dry ones in the room. "Uncle Charlie, can I leave her with you? I have something for your sister."

Charlie's only too happy to get his baby niece back. He starts playing peekaboo with her on the couch while Elias beckons me towards his suitcase. "As you requested," he says while opening it with a flourish.

I check out the contents: fabrics, notes, instructions. As my hands run across the materials, I feel something click into place, like I'm finally back in my element. "This is all this month's backlog?"

"This week's, actually."

I blanch. "Elias, did you at least hire a temp?"

"Nonsense," he pshaws. "Kids these days don't have the passion."

"In case you've forgotten, I'm 'kids these days,' too."

"You're the exception, my dear, not the rule. Maia was the same."

At the mention of my grandmother, I stop rummaging through the suitcase. "Yeah?" I rasp.

"One of a kind," Elias confirms. "And she worked too much, but you could never tell her that."

I find myself laughing. "I definitely remember that part. She was always hunched over some dress or another."

"Give your kid a few years—she'll be saying the same about you."

My smile fades a bit. For some reason, it's sad to think about —what May will think of me. I'm already failing her so much, between my focus on work and my drama with her dad…

The dad you tried to take her from, a nasty voice inside of me whispers. *Don't forget that.*

Something must show on my face, because I feel Elias's warm hand on my shoulder. "Sorry," I say quickly. "Just spaced out a bit."

"Mhmm," he hums, unconvinced. "You know, this all reminds me of a story."

"A story?"

"About your grandmother."

We settle at the table, just the two of us. Charlie's still on the couch, making faces at the baby while Mr. Buttons circles around them suspiciously.

"It was the day she brought you home," Elias continues. "The day she *really* brought you home. To stay."

"You were there?" I frown.

"You wouldn't remember. You were already asleep. Maia asked me to come over—I thought something had happened. I got there as fast as I could. When I did, she offered me a cup of tea."

"That's her, alright."

"Sure was." He laughs with me. "You'd passed out on the couch after crying yourself to sleep. You had this checkered blanket over you; it dwarfed you. That night, Maia confessed she didn't want to give you back."

"What? I thought my parents agreed that it was…"

"They did," he amends quickly. "The *next* day, when she asked them. But she hadn't asked yet. She knew she wanted to keep you, but she was... scared."

Scared? That doesn't sound like my grandma. Maia was smart, confident, funny... and stronger than anyone I'd ever known. She feared nothing.

"Of what?" I ask.

"Of failing you."

On the other side of the room, Charlie laughs out loud. Whatever he's doing, it makes May laugh, too.

"Failing me?" I blink. "Elias, she *saved* me."

"But she didn't know that yet," he replies. "She didn't know she could. You have to remember that Maia was never actually a mother. She was a stepmom first, and you know how that went."

I give a grim nod. "My dad hated her."

"Mhmm."

Suddenly, the proverbial lightbulb goes off in my head. "Wait—is that what she was afraid of? That I'd hate her, too?"

I can't believe this. Maia was the first good thing to happen to me: she was my family. Not by blood, but by choice. And she thought...?

As if reading my thoughts, Elias gives me a reassuring smile. "It's hard to understand what she was feeling back then. She wanted to be your grandmother so badly, but she had no idea if she could actually pull it off."

"Because she'd never done it before," I fill in.

"Mhmm. Just like you've never done it before."

It feels... indulgent, to let myself follow this train of thought. To let myself be comforted by the idea of Maia. She might have been scared, but she never...

She never took you away from a parent she thought was bad for you? She never did her best, however flawed?

I shake my head. However tempting these ideas are, I can't let them get to me. I can't let myself off the hook.

After all, what I did was unforgivable.

Still, I appreciate Elias's intentions. Most of all, I appreciate that he told me something new about my grandmother. It makes me feel closer to her. Like maybe my story with her isn't over yet, even if I can no longer reach her.

"Thank you," I tell him. "I needed that."

We play with the baby some more, then Elias offers to drive Charlie home.

"I'll visit again soon," my brother promises. Whether to me or May, I'm not so sure anymore. I might've slipped down a spot on the totem pole of his favorites.

"We'll be waiting for you, Uncle Chuck." I hug them both goodbye, then walk them to the door.

"Oh, almost forgot," Elias says with a snap of his fingers. "Did you ever enter that contest? I believe the deadline's closing in."

The contest. With everything that's been happening, it slipped my mind completely. The fashion competition—the one with a full ride at the Mallard Institute as grand prize. "Actually, I don't... I'm not sure that I'll make it."

"I can take some work from your hands," he offers. "In fact, I'd have taken it all off your hands, but..."

I shake my head. "It's fine. I insisted. Besides, it's good to keep busy. Helps keep my mind off things."

Off Matvey, specifically.

"You should do it," Charlie joins in. "You'd win, Apes. I know you would."

I ruffle Charlie's hair. "You think I hung the moon in the sky."

"I think you should do whatever makes you happy."

Goddammit, tear ducts. Working overtime today. "I'll think about it," I promise them both.

As I wave them off in the hallway, those words keep spinning in my mind: *Whatever makes you happy.*

If only I deserved to be.

16

MATVEY

It takes me the entire drive home to calm down.

I can't help it. The second the doctor uttered those words, I saw red. *Back to prepartum condition. Sexual activity.*

Like *hell* am I letting that happen.

It's a dark, vicious spiral of thoughts, and it just keeps getting darker as I slam the door to the loft closed and reach for something stronger than coffee. At least *this* liquor cabinet is still mine to use, thank you very much.

"Unbelievable," I mutter to myself. "Un-fucking-believable."

I try to steer my mind back to business, but it just won't quit. I just keep remembering our fight before she left, that cursed day where I did my worst to push her away. That I'd get rid of her, that I didn't owe her anything, that I—

And if I want somebody else to move in, you won't stand in my way, either?

That was the one concession I couldn't make: another man. Another fucking man, putting his hands on her.

April Flowers is *mine*.

But you didn't want her, whispers that sadistic little voice in my head. *You rejected her to her face, then threatened to force her to die alone. And you still wonder why she left?*

"Shut up," I growl into the silence.

But it does nothing. The voice prattles on. *You didn't have the balls to go all the way. You cut her out, then locked her up. What else did you expect? That she'd obey you?*

"Shut up."

That she'd stay with you? That she'd love you?

"I SAID SHUT THE FUCK UP!"

I throw the glass across the room. Shards go flying everywhere: the couch, the table, the bed. The liquor trickles down from the wall to the carpet, spreading like blood.

"... Motya?"

Only when I hear *that* voice do I snap out of it. "Yuri."

My brother rushes to my side. "Who were you talking to?" he asks, eyes filled with concern.

I hate it. I hate being looked at that way. "No one."

"'No one'? Matvey, you were yelling. I heard you from the street. If it's about one of the *vory*—"

"It's not about the goddamn *vory*."

I have no idea what Yuri sees in my eyes. These days, I barely recognize myself in the mirror. But whatever it is, it's enough to make him back off with his hands up. "Okay, okay," he says. "I just came by to... I can come back later."

"No. Tell me now."

He swallows, as if hesitating to speak. As if afraid this madman that's taken his brother's place will wring his neck again for uttering one wrong word. "It's about the D.C. deal," he rasps eventually.

My ears perk up. "Talk."

"I found something, I think," Yuri stammers out. "In the paperwork." He reaches for the files in his bag but fumbles, scattering sheets everywhere.

Jesus fucking Christ. If I didn't know any better, I'd say I was staring at a kid caught with his entire arm down the cookie jar, not my Bratva-hardened brother. Am I really that scary now? "Leave that. Just tell me."

Yuri gives a shaky nod. "You know how we thought it was Carmine? Given, you know..."

The kidnapping and timely appearance in our territory. "Go on."

"Well, here's the thing..." He wrings his hands and the papers with them. "It's not. Or rather... it's not *just* him. It can't be."

I snatch the files from his grip and spread them out on the table. "Show me."

"See here, here... and here?" He points at a few underlined pieces of data. "This is the *vory*'s login records around the time of the acquisition. As you know, they're technically nominal, but..."

"But the lazy sons of bitches just use whatever computer's

already on when they need it," I fill in. "Grisha already told me. Well?"

"Well, the timing's suspicious. See how the timestamps match here?" He points to another stack of papers.

No, not papers: *emails.* "Where did you get these?"

"From the database of the company that ended up acquiring the building. Look how the exchanges happened just after the logins. It's too perfect, Matvey."

It is. Either I'm looking at the weirdest coincidence in the world, or...

"We have a mole," I realize. "All this time, we've had a mole in our ranks."

Yuri gives a grim nod. "It's likely that someone has been feeding Carmine information. Someone from the inner circle."

I sift through the papers again. There are notes in the margins, scattered thoughts here and there, as if Yuri really took his time with it. His handwriting looks more rushed than usual, less rounded, though still familiar somehow.

He must have spent many late nights on this. It's really good work.

I almost tell him that. But then I remember he's still on thin ice. Praise is the last thing he deserves.

"Who else knows?"

"Just us."

This is a real fucking headache. I just promised the *vory* a war, and now, I have to stop everything. To stall at the worst possible time.

But I can't risk losing with Carmine. And with an unknown variable in our midst, it's anyone's guess how exposed we'll be. He's the kind of man who can turn a breadcrumb into a mountain of ammo—who knows what he can do with a *spy*?

"Good," I tell Yuri. "Let's keep this between us."

"I think that's for the best—"

"Except for Grisha. I want him looped in."

Yuri's face falls. "Grisha? Why?"

"Because he's proven reliable," I snap, irritated at being questioned. "And loyal. Something harder and harder to find these days."

Those words make him flinch. "But..." He fumbles for a reason to object. "But he's not blood," he says finally.

It doesn't matter, I almost reply. Then I come back to my senses. "I want him looped in," I repeat. "Don't make me say it again."

Yuri swallows. "Yes, *pakhan.*"

A mole. I never thought anyone would have the guts to try, given what I do to my enemies. But there it is: a spy—no, a *traitor.* Another betrayal waiting in the wings.

Join the fucking club.

17

MATVEY

"You could at least try to smile," Petra hisses at me through perfect rows of teeth, whitened just for the occasion.

The cameras flash. "I'm not in the mood, Petra."

"Really?" she coos back, eyes still fixed on the crowd of reporters. "And here I thought we were doing this for fun."

I force the corners of my lips to twitch. "Yeah? And yet we both know you love this."

"Posing for a bunch of sweaty guys in suspenders?"

"Being the center of attention."

Just my luck: I learn about a mole in my organization and instead of being free to deal with it, what do I get?

A fucking photo op. With Petra.

When the vultures with Nikons have eaten their fill, we head into the venue. Jupiter Hotels is inaugurating their newest location—which of course means media time. I hate this part of my job more than any other, but at least it's contained to grand openings.

Besides, it's my *day* job. And as someone so kindly pointed out to me recently, I haven't been great at keeping my cover.

"This is *your* hotel, Matvey," Petra whispers to me as she keeps smiling and waving at the crowd like the goddamn Queen of England. "No one's paying attention to me."

"Everyone's paying attention to you." I smile back—or at least try to. "You're the new Mrs. Groza. People will be wondering what you did to finally lock me down."

"Aside from getting pregnant by your brother?" she asks, words just low enough for me to hear. "I'd like to think it was my charming personality."

"That's a good one. Almost made me laugh for real."

"Laugh all you want." She winks at a particularly interested photographer. No doubt that one's going to be all over Page Six tomorrow. "We both know you aren't winning any contests in that department."

"Guilty as charged."

"Especially with how you're treating your *actual* Mrs. Groza."

I freeze mid-wave. "You don't know what you're talking about."

"Don't I?" She grins as we take the elevator to the terrace. "Then I guess I just spent forty minutes drying the eyes of the cleaning lady. My mistake."

Those words send a pang straight to my chest, but I force myself to ignore it. My shoulder isn't healed yet; some pain is to be expected, especially with all the waving. "Whatever lies she's selling you—"

"She isn't selling me anything, Matvey. She's a wreck."

I finally find my smile. It's not a pleasant one. "Right, right. Remind me again whose fault that was."

Yours, answers the nagging voice inside my head. *All fucking yours.*

Petra scoffs. "You're impossible. She made a mistake, Matvey. She didn't kill anyone."

"Like that means anything to you or me."

"It means something to her. Right now, you're treating her like a war criminal."

"What she did was a crime."

"Now, who's spewing words that mean nothing to us?"

Finally, the cursed ride ends. We step out onto the terrace, where Petra is quick to plaster her winning smile back on. Hopefully, the facial paralysis will keep her from talking.

It's a short-lived hope. "If you're going to blame someone, blame me. I'm the one who forced you into a shotgun wedding."

"Bold of you to assume I don't blame you," I reply.

"But you talk to me. You're okay working with me, even joking with me. To April, you won't say a single word."

"'Okay' is a strong word."

"I'm still breathing, though, aren't I?"

Cameras flash in unison. I try to keep my eyes from squinting, but it's nearly impossible; the barrage of lights is merciless. I swear, if those camera shutters were any louder, I'd think I was being shot at. "I think we both know that wasn't my first choice."

"Petra! Show off your ring!"

My blushing bride does as instructed. She flashes the photographers another charming wink, giving the papers a shot to fight over until the sun rises. "But it *was* your choice. Keeping me alive, and then marrying me."

"A choice you're already making me regret."

"Oh, please. As if you haven't been regretting it from the second you had to break the news to April."

My hard-won smile falters. "Careful," I growl. "I'm not above hitting a lady."

Petra laughs like I just whispered something funny in her ear. "Yes, you are. Besides, I'm carrying your *blood*, remember?"

As if I could ever fucking forget. "If I were you, I'd keep my nephew in there for as long as possible. The second he's out, I just might lose my patience."

"Who says it's a 'he'?"

"He, she, they, it—whatever the case, it's the only thing keeping you safe right now. Don't forget that."

Petra's smile finally dims. "See, Matvey, this is your problem: you can't go two seconds without pushing someone away. As soon as they get too close, your hackles go up."

This time, it's my turn to bark out a laugh. "You? Close to me?"

"I'm close to your brother, which is close enough. You know I'm not going anywhere." Then, just for a second, her eyes turn sharp. "And neither is April."

Petra's words have the same nasty habit as her throwing knives: they stick the landing. Try as I might, I just can't shake them off.

"This has nothing to do with April," I snarl under my breath.

"*Au contraire*—it has *everything* to do with April."

Once downstairs, we're swept up by the reporters. We give our interviews. We pose some more. We don't say another word to each other.

And all the way throughout the event, Petra's words stick into me like a thousand knives.

18

APRIL

The idea of the contest keeps lingering in my brain. Personally, I blame it on Elias's art of persuasion. That man could sell shades to a polar bear.

"How about this one?" I ask, holding up a design sketch.

Charlie's face scrunches up. "It kind of looks like the Liberty Bell."

I slump against the couch, defeated. "Forget it. I'm not doing it."

"Yes, you are." He drops down to the floor next to me. "You've got this, Apes. You've always been great at this."

"Moping on the floor?"

"Sewing," he corrects. "Fixing, creating. Remember when I was a kid?"

"Implying you're not still a kid."

"Okay, first of all, I'm fifteen. Second, don't change the

subject. You know those sweaters I had? With the long sleeves?"

"The ones that were constantly falling apart?"

"Bingo." Charlie nods. "If it weren't for you, I would've had to go to school looking like Swiss cheese. You're the one who patched them all up. Hell, the only one who even noticed."

"It was nothing," I protest in a miserable mumble.

"You did it *in a single night*, Apes. You were worried Mom would get mad if she found out and wouldn't let you finish the others."

"To be fair, she did get mad when she found out."

"A whole six months later, and only because she caught you doing it again. Otherwise, she never would've seen it."

I have to suppress a shiver at the memory. I may be an adult now, but Eleanor's banshee screams will stay with me until the day I croak. "Your point?"

"My point is that you're good at this. Better than that—you're *great*." He boops May on the nose as he says it. Because of course there's only one place for her to be whenever Uncle Charlie's around: nestled inside his giant kangaroo pouch. Where do they even sell sweatshirts like that? And *why*? "You're an amazing seamstress."

"Now, you're just trying to extort a pizza out of me."

"If I was trying to do that, I'd also add in how you're an amazing mom. So… you're an amazing mom."

I make a face at that. Compliments are already like cold medicine to me—you take them because you have to—but being called a good mom of all things…

It just doesn't feel right.

Nor the seamstress part, if these sketches are anything to go by.

"If I fold on the pizza, will you stop?"

"Nope," he replies, popping the *p*. Then he starts sifting through the mess of papers on the floor. "See this one? And this one?"

I squint at the sketches he picked out. "I don't know. They just feel... old."

"Vintage, maybe?"

"No, like, really old. Great-grandma's closet old."

"I don't think great-grandmas had V-necks, Apes."

And if *that* isn't the kind of image no one wants in their brain... "You know what I mean," I sigh. "They're... tired. Nothing we haven't seen already."

"So try again," he encourages me. "You'll come up with something."

Something else for the shredder's lunch, maybe.

God, why am I getting so testy about this? When I started sketching, I told myself it was just a way to pass the time; that I wasn't actually going to enter the contest. After all, I have a newborn to care for. I have responsibilities.

And I certainly don't have the talent. So why bother?

I gather up my sketches, wishing the penthouse somehow had a fireplace. Alas, into the shredder they go. "Let's just do something else, alright? How about that movie you wanted to see?"

"It's not a movie," Charlie says with a trademark eye roll. *Seriously, teenagers.* "It's an art documentary."

"Since when are you into art documentaries?"

He shrugs. "Just exploring my options."

I shake my head with a smile. Sometimes, I forget that not everyone knows what they want to do in life by their seventh birthday. This, at least, has always been easy for me: there was never anything but clothes in my head. Nothing but fixing broken things, or turning scraps of plain fabric into something beautiful.

But Charlie's at that age when you start wondering. *Exploring*, like he said. Last year, it was video games; six months ago, it was pro skating. A week from now, it'll be something else entirely.

I envy him. You forget how wide open the world can seem sometimes. How vast. How beautiful.

"Alright. Put it on."

As we settle on the couch, I pick up May from his pouch. Buttons takes advantage of the transition to trot close, ever vigilant. "How about you, Nugget? Wanna watch a movie with your uncle?"

May makes a cooing noise.

"I'll take that as a yes."

As the movie—sorry, *art documentary*—begins, I sneak glances at my baby's enraptured face. Only, she doesn't seem to care about the TV at all: instead, she's looking at *us*. Me, Charlie, her dashing defender Mr. Buttons. As if we're the only movie worth watching.

I make a face at her and watch her erupt in giggles.

Will she have this phase, too, one day? Will she come to breakfast in full gothic gear at fifteen and roll her eyes at anybody who questions her? Will she want to go to death metal concerts one weekend and archaeological museums the next?

Will her dad let her go?

I force myself to stop there. It's a good day today. No sense in ruining it with complicated thoughts.

For once, I just want to lose myself in the moment.

The documentary seems to be all about Bernini. I almost nod off once or twice, but my cat slaps me awake. Like, honest-to-God *slaps.* I have no idea where he got that habit, but I suspect June may have something to do with it. That's the way she wakes me up when I start dozing at the height of a romcom.

The way she used *to wake you up*, whispers the voice inside my head, sharp as a dart.

Right. That's not my life anymore. Not the mornings spent fighting with the water heater, and not the evenings spent curled up on the couch with snacks of dubious origin and a bossy cat in both our laps. The bickering, the banter, the food fights.

The *laughter.*

So much for staying in the moment.

I snap myself out of it one more time, determined to enjoy the documentary. Or at least not fall asleep during it. That's when something catches my eye on the screen: a statue of two figures intertwined, a man and a woman, her arms stretched to the heavens as if trying to escape. I squint at the odd shape of her fingers, trying to make out what's wrong with them. Because they almost look like...

"Laurel," Charlie answers my unspoken question. "Those are laurel leaves. She's turning into a tree."

"Why?" I frown.

"It's a Greek myth," he explains. "*Apollo and Daphne*."

"Oh, so it's not just art, history, video games, and skating? You're also a mythology buff now?" I tease.

"Bite me," he retorts, but he's laughing. "I had a Percy Jackson phase in fourth grade. Pestered Mom for a library card every other day until she gave in."

"Seriously? How did I miss that?"

As soon as the words come out of my mouth, I realize: *fourth grade*. Charlie must have been around nine, which means I was just turning eighteen then. It was when...

When you left your parents and never looked back.

God, what is it with my brain today? Why do I keep knocking myself down on purpose? And why am I wondering if May will leave me, too?

You know she will. She'll see how unhappy you are and find someplace else to be. Another home. Another family.

"Look," Charlie snaps me out of it. "They're about to explain it."

I push my nasty internal monologue away and shift my attention to the screen.

"'... no longer able to escape Apollo's pursuit, Daphne prays to her father to save her. Bernini's sculpture captures the moment of her metamorphosis: her fingers elongate into branches; her toes root into the ground; her body becomes enveloped in a thick layer of bark. There is desperation in her final stand, but also a combined and conflicting sense of yearning. While it is Apollo who yearns to trap her into his arms, Daphne who yearns to be freed. Ironically, it is only by losing her freedom completely that she finally manages to save herself, becoming truly free. Bernini's craftsmanship in this piece...'"

Without thinking, I place May in Charlie's arms and pick up my sketchbook. "Apes...?" he asks.

I don't answer.

I don't know how long I stay like that, tracing my pencil across the paper like a woman possessed. All I know is that the world disappears. For one, blissful moment, there isn't a single thought in my head that isn't, *Draw. Make something good.*

When I finally come up for air, there's a finished dress project in front of me.

Charlie pauses the documentary, then leans over to gawk. "Sis, this is..."

Embroidered lace for the corset. Tulle for the skirt. Chantilly lace for the details. "Do you think this could work?" I ask, suddenly uncertain.

But Charlie beams at me. "Are you kidding me? This is *the* sh—"

"No swearing!" I jump up to cover May's ears.

"Apes, she's one month old. She has no idea what it means."

"You don't know that. She could be a prodigy."

"And if you don't submit this, I'll put on Kanye West right now. Good luck covering her ears then."

Now, *that's* a threat. "Fine, fine!" I give in. "I'll… consider making it. Maybe."

"*Let's have a toast for the douche—*"

"Okay, I'll make it! Happy?"

"Very." Charlie grins.

For the first time in forever, I feel that familiar itch come back to my hands: the itch to *work.* To make something out of nothing. "Then… would you mind staying a little longer to watch her?" I ask.

My brother beams. "Throw in that pizza you were talking about and you've got a deal."

"Only if we get pineapple."

As I start moving around the room, that tickling frenzy already taking me over, my thoughts finally grow quiet. For the first time today, I feel like I can breathe. Like I don't have to worry about tomorrow.

Which is, of course, when the doorbell rings.

"Grisha?" I frown as I answer. "Is something going on?"

"Not at all," he reassures me. "I was just given this for you."

He holds it out formally, all butler-like. And that's fine, because this is Grisha we're talking about, right? Except that in his hands is an oval, golden plate. And on top of that…

"A sealed envelope," I mutter.

"Very old-fashioned," Grisha comments, not without a little admiration.

"Does it say who's it from?" It's a stupid question. Deep within, I already know.

I take the envelope and rip off the wax seal. Charlie hovers close, having sensed something's wrong. "April? Is that…"

You are hereby invited for afternoon tea at the Flowers Mansion,
13 West 10th Street. Time and details on the back.

"From my dad," I confirm. "And that's not all."

"What else?" Charlie frowns, concern suddenly on his face.

"It's…" I try to find the words, but they fail me. All I have is questions.

Why this? Why now?

And most importantly…

How does he know?

"It's addressed to me," I swallow thickly, "and…"

How does he know about her?

"… and to May."

19

MATVEY

By the time dinner comes along, I still haven't managed to shake off Petra's words.

It's death by a thousand cuts: I keep replaying that conversation in my head, feeling the pain of every jab all over again. Worst of all, I'm starting to wonder if she's right.

But you talk to me. You're okay working with me, even joking with me. To April, you won't say a single word.

I don't care what delusions Petra harbors about being "close" to me now; if she's seeing unicorns, that's for her to deal with, not me. But there is one fact here that even I can't keep denying, no matter how hard I try.

The anger I feel.

With Petra, I'm annoyed. I'm pissed that she keeps getting in my way, whether through stubbornness or stupidity. Every time she opens her goddamn mouth, I'm supremely fucking irritated.

But I'm not furious anymore.

And it's not because I forgave her. Forgiveness is for those you care about. The truth is, I just don't give a shit about Petra.

But it's different with April.

Because...

You know why. All this time, you've known how you really feel.

No. I have to stop thinking like this. Letting a lunatic's words get to me isn't going to make me feel any saner. Besides, what the fuck would it matter if they were true?

April kidnapped my child. She discarded me. She threw away everything we had like it was nothing.

Only because you threw it away first.

"Matvey?" April's voice snaps me out of my thoughts. "Are you okay?"

"Mm" is all I have to offer.

I keep eating my food in silence. I focus on my plate. I do everything in my power to take my mind off the bane of my existence, even as she's sitting right across from me.

But clearly, April has other plans. "You know, something came in the mail for me today," she starts again.

"Mm."

"An invitation."

I don't know how else to signal that I don't give a shit. That I don't want to fucking *hear* it. Her voice, her thoughts—I want it all as far away from me as possible.

"Mm."

"I…" She fiddles with her napkin, drawing my eyes to her chest. To her blouse a size too small that leaves nothing to the imagination. "I was just wondering if— I mean, if you'd want—"

"No."

April flinches. "No? You haven't even heard…"

"I don't want to hear it," I snap. "I don't want to hear a single word from you. I don't care what you have to say unless it's about the baby you fucking stole from me. Are we understood?"

It's like a metamorphosis takes place: April shifts from meek and timid to the picture of fury. A hare turned mama bear. "'Are we understood'?" she echoes with disdain as she stands. "Are you kidding me? The baby I *stole* from you? How about you get off that high horse of yours, then come back down to earth and talk to me like a human being?"

"Like that's not exactly what happened," I grit, knocking my chair to the floor as I rise to meet her.

"No," she roars back, "it's not! I'll tell you what happened: you *married someone else.* You let me think you'd knocked up another woman, then started treating me like garbage. *That's* what happened."

With every word she spits, every venomous dart aimed at my throat, she steps closer. She strides around the table and glares at me, fury made flesh, the fire in her eyes blazing brighter than a star. A supernova ready to burn planets to the ground.

I step forward, too, the same rage coursing through my veins. "And you think that justifies what you did?" I snarl, forcing her back against the floor-to-ceiling window. "Taking *my daughter*—"

"I took her from a monster!" she screams, loud enough for the entire penthouse to hear. "I took her from a man who didn't care about her anymore, who had a *better child* coming!"

"There was never another child!" I roar.

"And I didn't KNOW THAT!"

She's so close I can feel her breath on mine, ragged and panting. Her screams split my ears in half, but I don't have the patience to de-escalate; instead, I just raise my voice louder. "SO WHAT?!"

"So I did what was best for her! I did what was best for both of us!"

"And that was getting away from me?!"

"YES!"

We're both panting now, yelling into each other's space. Our hands are balled into fists at our sides, April's knuckles so white they almost disappear. From the window, the night lights frame her like a vision: a vengeful goddess come to drag me down to hell.

"You told me you wanted no one else. You told me you wanted me. You said..." She keeps listing off my sins, one after the other, voice shattering at the edges like glass, stained and broken and—

Beautiful. Beautiful above all else.

"What else?" I rasp.

"You told me you wanted to live with me," she croaks.

"What else?"

"That you were going to get your things and move in with me."

"What *else*?"

"You told me that you *loved—*"

I kiss her.

It's the last fucking straw: I take April's face in my hands and claim her lips with mine, swallowing the rest of her words. Swallowing *everything*.

If I could, I would eat her whole.

I can feel April struggle against me, her hands curling in the fabric of my shirt before finally giving in. But when she kisses back, it isn't a surrender—it's a declaration of war.

"I hate you," she gasps into my mouth.

I rip her blouse at the seams. "Say it again."

"I hate you."

"*Again.*"

"I hate you," she hisses as I bite into her neck, half-pleasure, half-pain. As I hoist her up and press her naked back against the cold glass, tearing the rest of her clothes right off her body. "I hate you, I hate you, I—*ahh!*"

I plunge my fingers into her, making her scream.

It's barely even sex: it's too brutal to be called that. It's a fight by a different name. It's nothing like we've ever done before, and at the same time, it's exactly what I've been craving all along.

Because the truth is, I could've never stayed away.

Not from her.

"I hate you," I snarl in return, knuckles-deep inside her. "I *hate* you, April Flowers."

I bite into her full breasts without a single thought for how tender they must be, how sore after nursing day in, day out. April keens, taken by surprise. "Ahh, s-stop that, they might...!"

Sweetness fills my mouth, but I don't stop. "Mine," I growl, swallowing everything she gives me. Everything that belongs to her, and therefore belongs to me. *"Mine."*

"Matvey," she gasps, nails sunk into my back for purchase. *"Matvey—"*

I keep scissoring her open without mercy, without an ounce of restraint. I fuck into her like an animal, with three fingers all at once, because who does she think she is? This woman who stabbed me in the back, who betrayed me in the worst possible way, a way I've only ever tasted once at the hands of my own blood—*Who the hell does she think she is?*

And why can't I stop wanting her?

"Blyat'," I growl into her neck, cock pressing hard between her thighs. "Fuck, April."

"Say my name," she splutters as she writhes. "Say it, say my— *ahh—!*"

I don't give her what she wants. I don't call her name again. Not as I fuck her senseless against the window, on display for the entire city at our feet, and not when she comes over and over under my thrusts. Even as she squeezes my cock into a vise grip for orgasm after orgasm, I refuse to call for her.

But inside, it's all I'm calling for.

April. The woman who will be the death of me.

The woman who already is.

20

APRIL

After that, it's a landslide.

We can't keep our hands off each other. Like, we literally can't. The second we're in the same room, that spark we've worked so hard to deny flares up hotter and brighter than ever. It's exhausting. It's terrifying.

And it's sexy as all hell.

"I hate you," I gasp into Matvey's ear as he hoists me up on the table.

"Not as much as I hate you," Matvey growls back, clearing the table with one fell swoop of his arm, food and plate shards scattering everywhere on the floor.

Needless to say, these activities aren't exactly confined to the dining area. There isn't a spot in the penthouse that we haven't—*ahem*—re-christened. So far, we've made improper use of the couch, the carpet, the shower, all four walls, and the washing machine. Yes, while it was on.

The one thing we haven't touched is the bed. *Our* bed. The bed where we exchanged so many promises.

It's not something we've talked about. Lately, if there's one thing we *aren't* doing, it's speaking. Hell, I haven't even managed to bring up Dominic's invitation again. The heights of our conversation so far have been scathing exchanges of insults, often without clothes on. But is it really so bad that we're letting our bodies do the talking for us?

Yes! yells the last scrap of my self-awareness. *You need to clear the air, not heat it up!*

If only it was that simple.

One night, I haven't tucked May into bed for five full minutes before I feel his hands on me. Rough hands, treating me like a ragdoll. "Turn around," he snarls, so close to my ear I can feel the vibrations against my skin.

I do as I'm told. "Like this?" I breathe.

He doesn't give me a reply. But soon enough, I feel one of his hands slide under my dress, the other tight around my throat. "Don't move," he growls, then rips my panties off with a single yank.

I try to stay still, I really do. But the sting of the elastic band snapping around my hips makes me yelp out loud, and his grip on my neck only grows tighter in return. A punishment for disobeying.

Then he bends me over.

He spears me open without a second of prep. "Matvey," I choke, vision swimming with pleasure as he fucks me senseless over the counter. "Matvey, I'm gonna—"

But he doesn't care what I'm gonna do. He doesn't care if I come, doesn't care if I don't, doesn't care how long or short it takes for me to fall apart. Doesn't care if it *hurts*.

But it hurts so good that I don't care, either.

Here's the thing: back when I was pregnant, we never had a chance to be this careless. To test the limits of my body and throw caution to the wind. But now, there's no child inside me, no precious cargo to be mindful of, and Matvey *hates* me. Enough to bend and break me.

What I didn't expect is how good it would feel to be broken.

"You're a sadist," I pant when he knocks me down to my knees; when he fists my hair and *yanks*, stuffing my mouth too full to speak.

"You're a witch," he snarls back, all animal. He slams himself all the way to the back of my throat and I wish to God it didn't make my thighs tremble like it does. "A lying, cheating vixen."

Other times, the position is reversed: he sinks down on me like a predator and locks my wrists into place, forcing me to stay. Forcing me to *take it.* He plunges his boiling hot tongue inside me and suddenly, I understand what it's like to be prey. To be devoured bit by bit, until nothing's left but bones.

I lose count of the orgasms. Frankly, I don't even try to keep track. I knew it would be impossible going in.

Because Matvey may hate me, but he still loves my body.

It's a furious kind of worship, like cursing at an altar. He fucks my pussy raw and acts like *I'm* the one ruining him. But I don't have any otherworldly powers. All I have is a streak of bad decisions, and I'm not even sure we're breaking it here.

But at least this bad decision isn't mine alone.

"Ow! *Suka*, that hurt!"

I snap out of my thoughts. "Sorry!" I quickly pull my pin back. "Sorry, I was just…"

"Lost in thought?" Petra huffs, arms crossed like the world's angriest mannequin. "Yeah, I noticed."

I cringe. How many of these thoughts have been showing on my face? "My bad."

"Quit apologizing. If you want to make it up to me, spill."

"It's nothing!" I lie. *When in doubt, always deny.* "I just haven't been sleeping well, that's all."

"Uh-huh. And has my husband been helping with that?"

Straight to the point. "You know, I feel like a homewrecker when you say it like that."

Then I catch Petra's smirk and realize: I haven't denied her accusations.

Goddammit, April. You had one job! "I mean…!"

"Save it, Flowers. We all know what you meant. Right, Pirate Cat?"

As if on cue, Mr. Buttons peeks out from May's crib to make a judgmental face. To be fair, that's just his face most of the time, but still.

"Traitor," I mutter.

"So?" Petra demands. "Have you guys kissed and made up?"

Kissed? Pretty much everywhere but on the cheek. But the rest? "I don't know about the 'made up' part," I confess.

She frowns. "What does that even mean? You're just having hate sex all over the furniture?" I must blush to the tip of my ears, because Petra's face instantly grows horrified. "Ew, ew, ew! I did *not* want to know that!"

"Then don't ask!" I blush harder. "And keep still, or I'll have to start over!"

That threat seems to have the desired effect. "Fine. But I still don't get it. When I told him to treat you better, I didn't mean go back to being fuck buddies. Or is it fuck enemies now?"

"Wait a second—you told him *what*?"

"To be fair, I just pointed out that he was being more of an asshole to you than to me. I have no idea why he decided to make it about sex."

"Maybe he didn't," I try. "Maybe it just… happened."

"Maybe. But he still could've thrown in an apology."

I force myself not to speak the words crowding my head: *He's right not to. I don't deserve it.* "It's complicated," I sigh instead.

"'Complicated,'" Petra scoffs. "Can't relate."

"I'm sorry, Mrs. 'Accidentally Got Myself Pregnant By My Fiancé's Brother'? What is it you can't relate to?"

"That's *situationally* complicated," she objects. "Everything else is pretty straightforward, really."

"Is this where you confess to me that you and Yuri are secretly a super vanilla couple?"

God, it's so weird to be thinking of them like that. The images alone make me wish I could scrub my brain with bath salts.

"Nope," Petra says proudly. It's already more than I wanted to know, but that's on me. By now, I should know better than to ask questions I don't want the answers to. "It's just... he brings me breakfast in bed."

I almost poke her with another pin. "I'm sorry, what?"

Suddenly, it's Petra's turn to flush strawberry red. "I'm just saying—he takes care of me. He likes being around me. He... *loves* me." She says that last part like it's something incomprehensible. "And because he loves me, he acts like it."

"Rub it in a little more, why don't you?"

"I wasn't trying to 'rub it in,'" she air-quotes. "Just explaining what I meant."

"Funnily enough, I'm still missing that part."

She rolls her eyes like I'm a toddler. "If Matvey hates you, why is he still with you? And if he loves you, why hasn't he forgiven you?"

For a long time, I just stare at the fabric in my hands. If I'm being honest, I've been trying to wrap my head around that exact same question.

But then again, I'm the same, aren't I? I *hate* him. I hate his stupid face and his stupid Bratva and his stupid talk of "blood, blood, blood."

And then his hands are on me, and I just can't *think.*

Like I said: it's complicated.

"Can we talk about something simpler? Like the meaning of the universe?"

"Sure. How about the concept behind this dress?" Petra suggests, frowning down hard at my work-in-progress creation. "Why am I covered in leaves? Is this an Adam and Eve situation?"

"Apollo and Daphne," I correct. "Charlie gave me the idea."

"As in, your teenage brother Charlie?"

"Apparently, he's really into mythology. Go figure."

Petra hums in surprise. "Guess you really can't judge a book by its cover. I would've pegged him for a skater boy."

"He *is* a skater boy. And a Bernini fan."

"The duality of man." Petra's eyes stray towards her shoulder strap, now peppered with placeholder paper leaves. Ideally, those will become embroidery. Just as soon as I can catch a break from this hem, that is. "I remember this myth," she muses. "Apollo tried to rape Daphne, right? She didn't want to break her vows, so she turned into a tree."

"Takes 'no means no' to a whole new level, right?"

"I mean, yes," she concedes, "but it's not all about that. Not really. It's a story about sacrifice."

Now, I'm stumped. "Sacrifice?"

Petra nods. "When Apollo starts chasing her, Daphne's forced into a choice: she can either submit or resist. But both options come at a cost."

"Her integrity or her freedom."

"Sure, but then there's the irony: to break free of Apollo, she has to renounce her freedom completely."

"And if she submits to his will, then she isn't truly free," I realize. "So you're saying that's the big theme here? What it truly means to be free?"

"In part."

I frown. "I still don't get it. Where's the sacrifice?"

For a moment, Petra hesitates, as if handpicking her words. "Daphne's choice isn't just between freedom and captivity," she finally says. "It's between staying in a world that could hurt her or separating herself from it. Living with scars or running away."

"Before anything can touch you," I murmur. "She paid the ultimate price for a life without pain."

"Exactly. Until it was barely a life anymore. So that's the question: what's truly important to you? How much are you willing to sacrifice, and for what?"

I turn over the myth a little more in my head. Petra's explanation has opened up new interpretations. Shades of gray I hadn't considered before. "So it's not about the abuse? Not really?"

"I mean, there's that, too, but come on. This was ancient Greece. Have you ever read what Zeus got up to?"

"Suddenly, I'm not sure I want to know."

As I get back to work, Petra's words keep swirling in my mind. About Daphne's story—and about sacrifice. About the price you're willing to pay.

Then I think of Matvey. Of our nights of fire and brimstone, and then our days of ice and snow. And I can't help but wonder...

What price am I willing to pay?

21

APRIL

The Flowers mansion isn't as big as I remember.

It's *bigger*.

I get out of the car with May in my arms, Grisha holding the door for me. My eyes wander across the huge courtyard, struggling to take it all in. Even after all these years, this place still makes me feel uneasy. A stranger in a strange land.

I never felt at home here. Hell, I never thought I'd be back here, where nothing holds a single good memory. Where there's trauma waiting behind every door.

But then the invitation came, and I couldn't say no. If there's even a small chance that my father wants to make things right with me, that he wants to be a part of May's life... Then I have to give him that chance.

Doesn't make it fun, though.

"Here we go," I mutter.

"Will you require assistance?" asks Grisha.

I shake my head and smile. "Thanks, but I think I'll be okay."

"Big place for someone to visit on their own," he observes. "You might get lost."

On my own. It's weird, hearing it from someone else's mouth: how alone I am. "True. We had a few gardeners that never returned. They say it's the south hedge—swallows them whole."

"That sounds frightening. Shall I call Matvey, then?"

Matvey. Just the thought of him makes my heartbeat freeze. I tried to tell him so many times… that this was coming, that I wasn't ready, that I didn't want to do this alone.

But he never listened.

"It's fine," I reassure Grisha. "We'll do fine."

He acquiesces with a small bow. "I'll be right outside."

Then, with my baby swaddled to my chest, I take a deep breath and step through the gates.

"Wonderful to see you again, Miss April. May I take your coat?"

In the Flowers mansion, you can't go two steps without encountering staff of some kind or other. When I was a kid, it was just the cook and maid, but after Grandma passed away, the ranks filled up considerably: a butler, a footman, a dedicated laundry maid, an army of nannies. It's like Regency England crashed into the Upper East Side through a rift in space and time. Any minute now, I'm half-expecting to run into the Duke of Hastings.

"Thanks, Jonathan."

My coat is kidnapped to the guest wardrobe. I hold onto my bag: diapers aside, it still has my sketches. If Dominic forgets I'm here—as he usually does—at least I'll have something to do while Grisha brings the horse-drawn carriage around.

"Someone will be with you shortly," Jonathan says.

"Mhmm." I know better than most what "shortly" means around here. Just making it from the dining room to the closest bathroom is enough of a trek to give you bladder rupture.

With that in mind, I sit.

I notice May looking around with curious little eyes. Everything must seem so sparkly to her: the immaculate floors, the hanging chandelier, the gold buttons on the staff's uniforms. If Matvey's place screams "money," this mansion takes it up a notch, broadcasting one word only: opulence.

Another reason my father and grandmother didn't see eye to eye.

Back when I used to live with Maia, we never splurged on such luxuries. Not because she didn't have the money, but because we didn't need anything more than we had. Our little brownstone made us happy, and we made each other happy. That was enough. What nest egg Maia had left, she was keeping safe for the future—hers and mine.

But now, Maia's gone, and my future is a golden handrail on a staircase.

"Shh," I hum to soothe May's sudden fussing. Sometimes, I think she's almost too attuned to the emotions of the people around her. "It's okay. Maybe he's forgotten about us. Maybe we can go home soon."

The words haven't been out of my mouth for five seconds before a rumbling voice calls my name from the top of the stairs. "April."

My head snaps up. *He's here.*

And he isn't alone. "April, dear. How long it's been!"

Nora.

Arm in arm, the couple descends the curving staircase. They're the picture of elegance and grace, their steps small and measured. As they make their way down, Nora's manicured hand delicately follows the line of the handrail, her luscious ebony skin jutting out against the gold.

"Hi," I squeak. "Dominic. Nora."

"You look well," Dominic offers blandly. He puts his hand forth for a handshake, like he's greeting a business partner instead of a daughter. No, a business *associate*—one that's new to the scene and also several steps below him.

I give him a lukewarm handshake. "You, too."

Nora's smile curves into a crescent. "And this must be baby May!"

She reaches to take her from my arms without so much as asking. May gives a wail like a tiny banshee, curling up tighter against me. Luckily, the swaddle keeps Nora's grabby hands from yanking her out, too secure to give even an inch. Thirty seconds into this disaster and I'm already glad I took this precaution.

"Sorry. She gets shy with strangers."

Nora recovers quickly. She drops her hands and gives a sickly-sweet smile. Funnily enough, it doesn't reach her eyes. "Maybe later."

How about maybe never. "So, you wanted to see me?"

"Right!" She claps her hands together. "How rude of us. Darling, why don't you show her into the drawing room?"

With a noncommittal grunt, Dominic starts walking. Nora's arm hooks into mine, her sharp nails digging half-moons into my skin as she kindly leads the way. You know, like I haven't lived here most of my life.

After what feels like an unnecessarily long walk to the gallows, we reach the drawing room. Yes, the actual drawing room. I look around for Elizabeth Bennet, but she seems to have missed this particular invitation. Lucky her. "Look, I can't stay long, so—"

"But you just got here!" Nora gasps. "And the girls were so looking forward to seeing you! Isn't that right, girls?"

Suddenly, I hear it: giggles.

My blood freezes. It's like that scene in *The Shining*, but worse, because at least the protagonist there didn't have childhood trauma about twins. And these twins? I bet there isn't a ghost out there they couldn't scare back into the grave.

"Hi, Kate, Diana."

More giggles. "Hi, April," they chirp in unison. I swear to God, it's like they practiced this.

"Is that your baby?" Kate asks.

"She's paler than you," Diana remarks.

"Her hair is lighter."

"And shorter. No pigtails."

"Why aren't *you* wearing pigtails anymore, April?"

"Yeah, we liked them."

"Liked them lots."

"Like" is an understatement. I don't think I've spent a single day here without one twin hanging on either pigtail, tugging like their lives depended on it. It's one of the reasons I don't wear my hair like that anymore: no hairstyle is worth getting scalped for.

I suppress a shiver and force myself to smile. "Yeah, I know."

"Girls, give our sister a breath. Don't you see she's tired?"

If my blood froze before, the sound of that voice turns my veins into pure ice.

A new face saunters up from the hallway. Regrettably, it isn't new to me.

"Hi, Anne. You've… grown."

She shoots me a winning smile, the carbon copy of her mother's. "So have you," she says, eyes wandering eloquently down to my hips.

Bitch. Of Nora's litter of three, only one is the actual spawn of the devil. Sure, Kate and Diana might enjoy pulling wings off of butterflies, but there's always someone behind them egging them on, musing out loud, "I wonder what they look like without…?"

Well, that someone is Anne.

"Aww," she coos, lowering her head to look at May. It gives me chills *and* goosebumps. On top of that, there's a glint in her eyes that I really don't like. "Did you see that, Kay, Dee? It's like a little doll!" she squeals. "Why don't we wake it up and see if it's real?"

It's like a queen snapping her fingers: one second, the twins are keeping their distance, and the next they're on me—on *us*. Trying to yank my baby out of my arms like it's a toy.

"Stop!" I yelp, shielding her with both hands. "You'll—"

"*WAHH!*" As if on cue, May starts screaming bloody murder. She's always such a quiet kid, so it stuns me to hear her like this: distraught to the point of tears.

"Oops." Anne smirks, poking her on the cheek. "Guess it *is* real."

That smirk. I've been away for so long, I almost forgot what it looked like—Anna's innate cruelty.

Or maybe it's not innate. Maybe it's exactly the kind of virtue her mother wanted her to learn.

"Please, just—don't touch her. She doesn't like it."

"Oh my."

"Did we do something wrong?"

"So *sorry*, April."

"Here," Anne cuts through the twins' apologies—if they can even be called that. "I'll make it up to you. How about I take your bag?"

"Actually, it's fine—*ah!*"

The instant Anne gets ahold of the strap, she yanks with all her might. My bag breaks open, spilling pens and baby supplies all over the floor.

And sketches. Lots and lots of sketches.

"Give those back!" I yell at the twins, who are now running around the room throwing my sketchbook's pages in the air. "I need them for work!"

"Are you okay, April? You sound tense," Anne croons. "It's not a big deal, right? They're just drawings."

"Indeed," Nora comments with a self-satisfied smile. "I dare say, you may be overreacting a bit."

Overreacting? I'm barely reacting. In fact, I'm using up all my self-control *not* to react. "It's work product," I lie. "I can't share it."

It's not a complete lie, though. Those are my sketches for the contest. Technically, it's *my* work product—no NDAs signed whatsoever—but it still makes me uncomfortable to see it in my half-sisters' hands. To see anything of value in their hands, especially if it's of value to me.

Another reason I'm glad for this swaddle. If they'd had their way, that would be my baby right now, being tossed from one set of arms to another. I can't even bring myself to think about it.

I gather up as many papers as I can and stuff them hurriedly in my bag. "If there's nothing else—"

"Nonsense!" Nora tuts. "You're staying for tea, aren't you?"

I glance in Dominic's direction. "I am?"

Dominic looks between her and me. As always, it's an easy choice: *Whatever the missus wants.* "Of course. Clarissa, if you'd be so kind."

A maid appears out of nowhere, bows, then hurries out the room again. I stash my bag in a corner and spend the next five minutes soothing my crying baby, taking deep breaths that are for me as much as they are for her. I keep doing that right up until the tea cart comes in.

This is going to be a long afternoon.

22

APRIL

"Are you still working at that quaint little shop?"

"Did you get a C-section?"

"Ohh! Can I see the scar?"

"Where's the father?"

The barrage of questions makes the teacups tremble on their plates. It's like that scene in *Jurassic Park*, but worse, because at least for the people in the movie, there's just *one* sharp-toothed reptile they have to deal with.

Me? I've got two on either side.

"Yes, I'm still working with *Mr. Turner*," I answer Nora with a tight smile before turning to the twins. "No, I didn't get a C-section, so there are no scars to be seen."

"Bummer," Kate says.

"I wish I could've been there," Diana sighs.

"And the father?" Anne presses with her usual smirk. "Who is he? Why isn't he here?"

My smile grows tighter. "He's a businessman. He's busy."

It's a half-truth, but it's all I can offer. I can't very well say, *I tried to tell him and he kept finding better uses for my mouth*, can I?

"A businessman," Nora echoes with interest. "What kind of business?"

The kind that feeds cemeteries. "He owns a hotel chain. Actually, he's the CEO as well."

"The CEO," Diana coos.

"Sounds expensive," Kate giggles.

"It's just like a fairytale," Anne sighs dreamily. "Isn't that right, Mother?"

"Yes, it is quite... hard to believe."

I have to play that line back in my head three times. Because either I'm going deaf, or Nora just went there. "As in, I made it up?"

"Dear, dear!" Nora laughs nervously. "No need to be so defensive, April. We were just... wondering, that's all."

"Speak for yourself." Anne flips her hair back. "I was calling it romantic."

That burst of attitude seems to catch Nora off-guard. "I see."

It's so good to watch, I almost feel a burst of affection for my estranged hellbeast of a sister. "Thank you, Anne."

"So where's the ring?"

I freeze. "Where's the… what?"

"Your wedding ring," Anne drawls. "Or at least an engagement one? Where is it? I'd think a CEO has money for that."

"The ring? I…" Suddenly, the words won't come. I'm fumbling for no good reason, four pairs of hungry eyes on mine. Well, five, but Dominic's stare is fixed on his teacup, as if I'm not even there. "I…"

"It's okay," Anne says, all conspiratorial. She draws close on the sofa and takes hold of my hand. "You're just not that kind of couple, right?"

There's something in the way she says it that makes my heart sink. "What kind of couple would that be?" I ask, cold sweat running down my back. Because suddenly, all I can think about is *those kinds of couples*: the kind that wasn't careful or the kind that doesn't care; the kind that has no money or the kind where it changes hands every night, always in the same direction.

And then the one that terrifies me most of all: *the kind that doesn't love each other*.

Anne seems taken aback by my question, but after a beat, she shrugs it off. "Just, like, not traditional. That's all I meant."

"Right," I echo. "We definitely aren't that."

"Does he have a name?" Kate asks. "Your boo?"

"Yeah, does he?" Diane echoes.

"He does." I smile politely. "Excuse me."

I put my cup down without having taken a single sip and rise from the plush sofa. "Where are you going?" Nora asks, scandalized.

"To feed my daughter," I reply. "Unless you'd rather I do it here?"

My threat seems to have the desired effect. "No need," she mutters, scrunching up her face like a disgusted bunny. One would think she'd be used to it, having done it three times, but who knows—maybe she had nannies for that, too. "Use the side room."

I don't go into the side room. Instead, I veer all the way to the left, looking for the one place that will ease this sense of suffocation in my chest: the balcony.

Looking out onto the view I'm so familiar with, I feel like I can finally breathe. Still, even this little haven doesn't hold a single pleasant memory.

Hello, darkness, my old friend.

I lean against the railing, May safely snuggled in my arms. "Can you believe this, Nugget?" I murmur. "First, your father doesn't exist; then, he's some lowlife. Just pick one already."

My baby coos in vague agreement. She isn't a fan of perceiving the world in normal circumstances, so I can only imagine what this is doing to her. Probably putting her off social gatherings forever. I can hardly blame her.

"Sorry." I press my lips against her wonderful little forehead. "I had to try. I thought…"

Thought what? a part of me mocks. *That they'd welcome you back with open arms? That they'd finally treat you as one of their own? That they'd treat your kid as one of their own?*

That they'd changed?

Yes. As ridiculous as that sounds… yes, I did think that. Just for a second, but I did. I hoped that maybe, now that the girls were grown, they'd have developed some personality traits other than mockery and spite. That maybe they'd finally be able to see me for who I am, not for the person their witch of a mother taught them I was.

An outsider. A failure. A plaything.

And if not them, then at least…

As if on cue, a familiar voice drifts out onto the balcony. "April? Are you still… *feeding?*"

The sheer level of discomfort in that word is enough to make me laugh, though it doesn't last long. "I'm decent, if that's what you're asking."

With an uneasy nod, Dominic steps out to join me.

For a beat, there's silence. He glances from one corner of the balcony to the next, as if looking for something to say and then realizing he has to find that elsewhere. Maybe somewhere closer to the heart than the charcoal grill. "Chilly out here, isn't it?"

"It's okay, Dad. You don't have to force yourself."

"Mm."

It wasn't like this all the time. Between us, I mean. When I was little, I remember him taking care of me: I remember car rides, packed lunches, checking homework. I even remember games—nothing outrageously funny, but it was funny to me. It was *fun.*

Because he was my dad.

But then there were the fights with Mom. The screamed insults that stopped at nothing, not even a daughter's desperate cries. I remember his anger as he threw every single one of Eleanor's faults back into her face: the short temper, the drinking, the mistake daughter.

If you couldn't raise a kid, you should never have had one.

Then Nora came along, and I didn't even get the screams anymore. Only silence.

Sometimes, that hurt worse.

I remember standing in the hallway one night when I wasn't feeling well. I wanted to ask my dad if I could sleep in his bed. He used to let me do that when I was smaller. I knew he had a new baby, but maybe...

And then I heard Nora through the door. Her soft, honey-sweet voice, pouring poison as if it were wine.

You have a new family now. You need to forget your old one.

I waited for my dad to say something. To tell her that it didn't matter if he had a second family—his first daughter could still be a part of it. That families don't get swapped out for better ones: they *grow*. Together.

But he didn't say a thing.

I never came to his door again.

"Why did you call me here?" I finally ask. "Was it just to relive the good old times? Because let me tell you, they weren't so good for me."

Dominic hesitates. It's not unusual to see him uncomfortable, but this is... odd. A clash with that aristocratic "man of the house" image he's spent so long cultivating.

Maybe that's why he doesn't like having me around: I bring him back. His true self, the person he was before. The one who thought you could change a person by putting a ring on their finger, even if that person was a pregnant, alcoholic disaster. "There's something I want to discuss with you."

Now, *that* perks my ears. "What—did I come into another inheritance you want to steal? Or did you suddenly grow a conscience?"

He sets his face into his trademark stern look of disapproval, but doesn't say anything.

"Wait, you're not dying, are you?" I ask, ready to feel horrible.

But luckily, he shakes his head. "Nothing of the sort. I want to offer you something."

Then he pulls something out of his pocket. It takes me a second to realize what it is, but once I do... "Your checkbook?"

"Mm."

"Wow," I deadpan. "Maybe you really have grown a conscience."

The truth is, I simply can't believe what I'm seeing. If I'm reading the situation correctly—and I don't think there are many other ways to read it—my father is about to offer me money. My estranged, distant, *loaded* father.

And I won't lie: I could use it. After all, I can't rely on the goodness of Matvey's heart forever. Elias pays me well, but this is New York City: even breathing in the wrong neighborhood can set you back an arm and a leg.

With some money of my own, I could look after myself. I could look after May. I could...

Finally achieve your dreams, says a hopeful little voice at the back of my mind.

And even I can't—even if it's just a gesture…

Maybe he still cares about me.

I watch my dad scribble down a sum. Then he hands me the check. I read it and nearly faint: *one hundred thousand dollars.*

I count the zeroes just in case I read wrong. Then I reread it again. Finally, once I'm certain I'm not hallucinating or miscounting, I ask, half-joking and half-terrified, "What's the catch?"

Say nothing, I beg as my question hangs in the air. *Say nothing and let me have this. Better yet, say you're sorry. Say it's a present for your granddaughter. Say you want to be a part of her life; that you want to be a part of* my *life again.*

Say you're still my father.

But that's not what he says.

That's not even close.

"You know you're not fit for this, April. Being a mother."

I feel the air being sucked out of me. Like I've been punched in the gut with a knuckle duster. "I'm not fit for being a mother?" I tremble, full of outrage. "*I'm* not fit?"

Even though I've just heard it with my own two ears, part of me still hopes I'm mistaken. That I made it all up in my head, everything in the past five minutes, money included.

But I haven't. This is the cold, hard truth of Dominic Flowers: everything he gives, he gives with strings attached.

"You know I'm right. You're too much like…" He grimaces. "Like *her*."

"Say her name," I snap. "Eleanor. Your ex-wife. Say it, Dominic. Stop pretending we weren't real."

May starts stirring in my arms, upset all over again. But there's nothing I can do, because I'm upset. And my kid's heart is already bigger than my father's.

"See?" He points at her as if he was waiting for exactly that. An excuse to confirm his theory. "You're just proving my point. You're too immature."

"So this is what?" I hiss, slapping the check down on the railing. "A bribe? A price tag for my daughter? Do you even hear yourself right now?"

"We just want the best for her," he replies. "You can't give her what we can, April. You know that."

"Because you stole it from me."

"Again with that story—"

"Yes, Dad, again with that story! You robbed me so your new wife could strut around in Cartier and YSL, and don't you dare deny it!"

"Nora will raise her right," he insists. "She will teach her discipline, respect. Things you clearly lack."

"Oh, so Nora put you up to this?"

"I didn't say that."

"But you did, Dad. You just did."

I can see the slow transformation on Dominic's face taking place—a Daphne in reverse. His wooden expression turns heated, back to flesh and bulging veins. The Dominic I remember. "So what? So what if this is Nora's idea, huh? She owes you nothing. You're not even family to her and she's willing to give you this—and now, you don't want it?"

"She owes me nothing? She owes me *half a million dollars.*"

"So this is greed then? Fine!" He picks up his cursed checkbook again and jots down another sum, this time much larger. "Now, will you see reason?"

Then he shoves it in my hands.

Against my better judgment, I read it. I know there's no price that could possibly talk me into this, but my eyes still gravitate towards the number.

Half a million.

Just like that, in my hands, ready to change my life.

Of course they can offer that now: what Nora didn't flush down the drain of Coco Chanel handbags, Dominic invested. No doubt, that sum has tripled by now, with more to come in the future.

But it still doesn't make sense. Whether it's chump change to them now or not, it's still money. Money they're willing to give me—and for what? Another stray kid to pitter-patter around in their spotless halls?

"She didn't even want me here," I say. "She didn't want me, so why…"

It comes together slowly, then all at once. Like a grim, horrifying puzzle, every dirty piece finally falls into place: the cruel pranks, the bullying, the twins yanking my baby out of my arms. Anne's aggressive attitude when she talked back to her mother, the kind she would usually reserve for *me.*

Why aren't you wearing pigtails anymore?

"They're rebelling," I realize. "They're teenagers now. They don't have an outlet anymore, so they're turning against you. And you can't handle that."

"How dare you…!"

"But it's true, isn't it?"

Dominic stiffens. His gaze starts to wander, everywhere but towards my eyes.

That's all the proof I need.

"You want another plaything." Each word I'm saying sounds less real than the one before it. "You turned your daughters into monsters, and now, you can't control them."

"Careful," he hisses. "Or else the offer's off the table."

"You know what you can do with your offer?" I spit. "With your dirty, stolen bribe?"

Then I do something I never thought I'd do.

I tear it up.

I tear up half a million dollars.

Dominic looks at me like I've finally gone mad. Mad like my mother, the mistake he could never forget. My existence alone made sure of that. "Have you lost your damn mind?"

"Actually, I think I've finally found it again."

"Listen—"

"No, you listen," I interrupt. "You *all* listen."

They crawl out of the woodwork like worms: Kate, Diana,

Anne… and behind them, Nora. Eavesdropping, all of them. Like I knew they would be.

Nora's face twists. "April, quit this tantrum this instant. Your daughter—"

"My daughter is not for sale."

"Lower your voice!" Dominic snarls. "The neighbors will—"

"I don't care if they hear me all the way to Staten fucking Island."

"Staten Island?" Nora blinks. "What's that got to do…?"

"I never told him I was pregnant," I explain icily. "I never told anyone he knew—except for one person. So tell me, Nora: how do *you* think he knew?"

Watching Nora's perfect mask fall to pieces is the first good thing that's happened since I stepped foot here. "You said you weren't talking to her," she splutters at Dominic, all grace lost. "You…!"

"Oh, believe me," I snort. "If I know Eleanor, they're doing a lot more than talking."

"Dad?" Diana demands.

"Is this true?" Kate asks.

Only Anne stays silent. Even as all hell breaks loose on the respectable Flowers balcony, Anne doesn't say a single word.

Until she does.

"It doesn't change anything, you know."

I blink. "What?"

"I said it doesn't change anything," she repeats. For once, her smile is gone. "You're still a failure. You'll fail as a mother, too."

Silence falls around us. It's like the world has gone still on my behalf: only me, my sister, and the frozen blood in my veins.

Failure.

"I bet it wouldn't even take much to get custody," she muses. "Any judge would see we're the better option. So just take the money, hm, sweetheart?"

"That's right." Dominic regains his composure with a haughty sniffle. "I'm sorry you thought this was a negotiation, April. It's not. Either you take what we're offering, or we'll just take her."

"I see."

"I'm glad you underst—"

"Then try."

Dominic blinks. "What was that?"

"I said, *Try*," I repeat. "Try taking my daughter and see what the fuck happens."

All this time, I've had one thought hammering at the back of my head—a single, pressing regret. *If only Matvey were here.*

But now, I'm fed up with it. I'm tired of waiting for someone to save me. For someone to care about me.

If Matvey isn't here to pull the trigger, I'll just do it for both of us.

"'See what happens'?" Nora echoes. "Nothing will happen, April. You have no resources, no family—"

"I have a boyfriend," I exhale softly.

"Right," Anne smirks. "The 'CEO.'"

"Yes. And the head of the Groza Bratva."

Dominic's face falls. Nora's, too. The twins just look confused, but Anne…

She's heard of them. She knows what I'm talking about.

"You're lying," she hisses.

"Then by all means, test me. Better yet, test *him*. Like I said: see what happens." I circle the herd of Flowers devil spawn with measured steps, then calmly stop in front of my father. My *blood*, like Matvey would say. "But if you ever try to take my child again, I won't grace you with a warning."

"You're threatening us?" Dominic stammers. "Your own family?"

"You're not my family," I reply. "None of you. So stay the fuck away from my daughter."

I elbow my way past the little crowd of four, ramming straight into Nora's side. "You're making a big mistake," she warns.

I don't spare her a single glance. "Enjoy the monsters you created."

Then I show myself out.

23

MATVEY

I come home to an unexpected noise: crying.

It shouldn't be that unexpected. With a baby at home, silence should be rarer, but May's something else—and I'm not saying that just because she's mine.

In all the time I've known her, I've never seen her cry without reason. If she's tired, she sleeps; if she's hungry, she sends the cat to get us; if she's dirty, she makes a disgruntled noise I've only ever heard come from geriatric pugs. The one time she burst into tears out of nowhere was back at my apartment, when I was having a shouting match with her mother.

Her mother. That's a different story.

I've fallen back into old, bad habits: the second I see her, I can't keep my hands to myself. Goddamn vixen has sunk her claws back into me, shredding my self-control into bloody ribbons. It's fucking Pavlovian—the second I ride up in that elevator, my cock starts throbbing like it's about to explode.

But tonight, something's different. Tonight, no claws greet me at the door.

"April."

No answer.

I make my way across the empty living room and follow the noise. Could the baby be sick? My protective instincts flare all at once, phone already in my hand to drag the doctor out of her office and through that door within the next five minutes.

But when I get to the bedroom, I realize my mistake: it wasn't May crying after all. She's safely in her crib, sound asleep, her little chest rising and falling and her tiny hands curled tightly around her blanket. No sign of the annoying security cat, either.

But on the bed, under a shaking mountain of blankets and pillows, something's still crying. "April...?"

April's head emerges from the nest. She seems startled to see me, like she hadn't even heard me come in. Judging by the darkness in the room, she must've been like this for a while, enough not to notice the sun setting.

"Go away," she sniffles.

"I beg your pardon?"

"You heard me. Go away."

"Last time I checked, this was still my place. Not yours."

She mutters something unintelligible in return.

"If you want me to catch that, you'll have to at least come up for air."

"I said, of course it's not mine!" she snaps. "Nothing is ever mine, is it? Not my future, not my life, not even my baby. There's always someone else in line."

"Your bab—what the hell are you talking about?"

"Forget it. You wouldn't understand."

"And what exactly am I supposed to understand?"

"I said, forget it," she mumbles. "Stay or leave; I don't care. Just don't bother me."

Then she burrows back into her fortress. I spot her accursed cat peeking from her arms, his one-eyed glare grumpier than ever. *Go away*, he seems to echo.

I could. I should. Whatever's going on here, it clearly has nothing to do with me. This woman took my kid from me and threw me away like I was nothing—why should I give a shit about her feelings?

Why should I give a shit about *her*?

Except you do.

"Get up."

"No."

"I said, get up."

"Why? So you can put me in a chair across from you and play house with a bunch of food I won't touch?"

"*April—*"

"So you can tell me what a horrible mother I am, too?!"

"SO I CAN MAKE SURE YOU'RE OKAY, GODDAMMIT!"

The outburst shocks her. That makes two of us.

"Get up," I repeat for the third time, my voice a weary, hollow husk of itself. "Get out of bed right now and let me look at you."

"… Why?" she murmurs back.

"Because I say so."

"But—"

"Now, April."

Slowly, something emerges from the covers. Like a broken butterfly from a cocoon, April comes to stand in front of me: unsteady legs, smeared makeup, puffy eyes a thousand shades of red. "Happy now?"

"Happy" is a universe away: I'm beside myself with fury. "Tell me who did this to you."

She rolls her eyes. "What does it matter?"

"It matters to me."

"Yeah, right."

I cross the distance between us in one long stride. "Tell me who's responsible for this, or I swear to God I'll find out myself. And then you won't get a say in what happens to them."

The threat at least is effective. Without a word, April snatches something from the bedside table and shoves it in my hands. "Here."

Then she drops back down on the bed.

Frowning, I unfold the crumpled piece of paper. It's almost too dark to see, and the pretentious cursive in which it's written doesn't make it any easier, but in the end, I manage to make out the words.

You are hereby invited for afternoon tea at the Flowers Mansion, 13 West 10th Street. Time and details on the back.

"This..." I stare at the letter in my hands. *The Flowers Mansion.* That must be...

"Dominic sent it," April explains. "Around a week ago. He wanted to see the baby."

A week. She's been holding on to this for a week, without breathing a single word to me about it. Another fucking lie for the pile. "And you *brought* her?!"

Anger bubbles back up into my throat, ready to be shouted: how dare she take my child anywhere without my permission again? What was she thinking? Why?

But then I see her.

I've never witnessed anything like this: April Flowers, drained of all life. Her hazel eyes find mine, exhausted, and she rasps, "He was my father. What choice did I have?"

He was *my father.* "Was"—past tense. Either something happened to the old bastard, or he did something himself.

Something that made even April cut him off for good.

And suddenly, it's like I've got a knife lodged between my ribs, cutting deeper and deeper with every breath. It's all I can think about: April and the baby, defenseless in a den of wolves, without a single soul to protect them. Without *me.*

"You went alone?"

"Grisha drove me."

"That's not what I asked."

"Then use your words, Matvey, because I'm too tired for games."

"You want my words?" I snap. "I'll use my words then: what the fuck were you thinking?"

"I was thinking I was going to see my father!" she yells back. "That he wanted to meet his granddaughter, not that he'd try to buy her off of me!"

I freeze. "'Buy'?"

"He offered me half a million dollars," April explains in a deadened monotone. "In exchange for full custody, if you can believe that."

I'm no stranger to bloodlust. My entire life is a quest for revenge, the bloodier the better. But right now, if I had Carmine and Dominic standing at opposite sides of the room and only one bullet, I'm not certain which one I'd shoot. All I know is where I'd aim: straight in the fucking crotch.

But there's another, more pressing question in my mind. One that's got nothing to do with hypotheticals and everything to do with the woman in front of me.

"What did you answer?"

April's eyes widen. "What?"

"Don't make me repeat myself. What did you fucking answer?"

It's like a switch has been flipped. One second, April's a shell of her former self, barely able to stand on her own two legs. And the next—

The next, she's fury incarnate.

"What did I answer?" she balks. "What did I fucking answer? You're really asking me that?"

I set my jaw. "You're evading the question."

"I'm—" She opens and closes her mouth like a goldfish, but it doesn't last long. The moment she gets her bearings, she springs up from the bed, crowding me against the wall. "I'm evading the question?!"

"If you won't answer, then—"

"NO, you asshole!" she shouts. "No, I didn't fucking sell my baby to a psychopath! But thanks for the vote of confidence."

"Oh, you want a vote of confidence now? Like I can trust you? Please. After everything you've done—"

The crack of her slap echoes in the room. I feel a tingle spread from my cheek. It's nothing more than that; my face hasn't even turned.

But April's face is red. And now, her hand is red, too.

"Everything I've done has been to protect her," she hisses. "Every step, every decision, every mistake. Everything I've sacrificed, I've sacrificed for her. And you're asking me if I would *sell* her? If I would get rid of her for a goddamn *check*?!"

"Then why didn't you tell me?!" I snarl back. "We could've gone together! We could've—"

"I fucking tried, you asshole!"

Suddenly, my words fail me. It's like the entire world has shifted on its axis, sending me ass-first into the concrete.

Because suddenly, I remember.

Something came in the mail for me today. An invitation.

She did tell me. She tried.

She tried, and I didn't listen.

It's humbling to say the least—being literally slapped in the face with your own worst mistakes. Realizing all at once you've been doing everything wrong, without a single chance for denial. "Apr—"

"Don't," she chokes out. "Don't you fucking dare apologize now. Not after what you said to me."

"April."

"I said, don't—"

"I'm sorry."

That annoying voice in my head—the one I bricked away in the ugliest corner of my mind—it's roaring now. Breaking out of its cage like a starving animal.

Because that's what I've been: a beast. Nothing but a miserable fucking beast.

"I'm sorry," I repeat, pulling her against me.

At first, she struggles. Her entire frame trembles as she fights me with the last of her strength. Then, finally, I feel her slump against my chest, a puppet with her strings cut.

"I hate you," she whispers.

"I deserve it."

"You weren't there for me. You're never there for me."

"I know."

"You never listen to me. Never."

It cuts so deep, I almost want to laugh. Because that's just it, isn't it? We never listen to each other. It's a vicious, rotten cycle, and we're still feeding it now.

I spent so long hating April for what she did to me. Not just for taking the baby or leaving, but for not giving me a chance in the first place. For not letting me explain.

When I tried, she threw my words back at me. But this past week, when she tried to tell me something important—what did I do? What did I do, if not the exact same thing?

"I'm sorry," I tell her again, even though it's hard. Even though a part of me still hurts like hell at the thought of that nightmarish month without my daughter. That wound has never stopped aching, but April's cut is fresher. And it's bleeding right now, in front of my eyes.

I can stop it. I have the power.

"I had to name-drop you," she cries harder against me. "You weren't there, so I had to pretend you were— I had to tell them you—"

The more I listen, the more one thought pushes its way to the forefront of my mind: *I want to kill Dominic Flowers.* I want to lay waste to his perfect little house and gut his perfect little pigs until they're nothing more than pieces of rotting meat. I want to pry their apologies out of them with a rusty set of pliers and then leave them there to suffer. To leave them like they left her.

But for once, I'm lucid enough to realize one thing: *That won't help anyone. That won't break the cycle.*

"You did the right thing," I murmur instead, lips pressed to the top of her head.

She scoffs. "You didn't even know what I said."

"I don't care. You protected her." *You protected both of you.*

"He told me I'm not fit to be a mother." She breaks down into sobs. "And Nora, and Anne, too—they all think that."

"Don't listen to them," I spit. "They have no idea what a good parent is supposed to look like."

"But you think that same thing," she sniffles. "You've told me. You do."

I hold her tighter. "No, April, I don't."

"Liar."

"I really don't."

"Liar, liar, *liar*—"

Slowly, I tip her head up and start kissing her tears away. It's nothing like the passion of the past few days.

This time, it's softer.

This time, it's gentler.

This time, it's real.

24

APRIL

I'm sorry.

I still can't believe it.

He apologized. Matvey Groza actually apologized. The man who's been tearing into me for weeks about my sins, my inadequacies, my mistakes—he *apologized*.

And then he *stayed*.

He slept in my bed, like old times. Held me until I stopped shaking and finally fell asleep. As I drifted off, I could feel his strong hands stroking through my hair, so familiar I wanted to start crying all over again.

Because I don't know when I'll lose it.

In the morning, he looks at me like he's on the fence. Like he's contemplating canceling all his plans just to keep watch over me for a few more hours.

"I can stay," he offers.

But I simply shake my head. "I have to work. You might as well go to work, too."

He doesn't fight it. He looks like he wants to, but he doesn't. For once, I'm treated to a sight I never thought I'd get: Matvey Groza, looking utterly unsure of what to do next.

In the end, he just nods. "I'll see you at dinner."

"Yeah. See you at dinner."

All morning long, I feel like a ghost. Like someone's taken an ice cream scooper to my insides and cleaned out the joint. I can sense this empty space inside of me, just growing and growing with every passing hour. It's not a new feeling, but it's never lasted through the night before.

What's worse, it keeps me from doing things. That's always been my trump card: immersing myself in work. But today, I keep messing up. I miss a stitch on Mrs. Kurt's skirt hem, use the wrong color for Ms. Fairfax's sleeve, even cut Mr. Boyd's pant legs half an inch too short.

And then there's May.

That sweet, calm kid I've grown to know and love is nowhere to be found today. From the second Matvey shuts the door behind his back, she's a sobbing mess, shrieking like I've never seen her do before. I try to change her, but she's clean. I try to feed her, but she won't latch. I try to play with her, to sing to her, to rock and hold her in a desperate attempt to lull her back to sleep.

But nothing works.

"What's wrong, May?" I try to keep my voice gentle. "What do you want? What can Mommy do for you?"

Shockingly, she doesn't answer.

It takes the entire morning just to settle her. When I finally put her down, I'm exhausted. Is this what it's like for everyone else? For people with colicky babies, fussy babies, difficult babies?

Maybe she isn't the problem, a voice in the back of my head whispers, sounding a lot like Anne. *Maybe it's you.*

… Yeah. Maybe.

In the end, I call in the cavalry.

"Who's a cute widdle girl?" June coos, making the kinds of faces that would give any kid nightmares. Except my kid, apparently. "Who's the cutest widdle girl in the whole wide world?"

May squeals with delight. It's like no one has ever made her play before—certainly not her exhausted mother with a store full of Gucci bags under her eyes. "She isn't being cute today. She's being a menace."

"Who's a cute widdle menace?" June amends, eliciting another squeal from my baby.

"Cute widdle traitor*" is more like it.*

I sigh and go back to work. "Thanks for rushing over. I don't know what was wrong with her. She just kept screaming."

"Welcome to parenthood, dear."

"Silly me. I thought I'd been doing that for two months already."

"That was honeymoon parenthood," she declares. "This is *real* parenthood, where babies scream for no reason and always have dirty diapers. Get used to it, Mommy."

Mommy. I don't know why the word jars against my ears, but it does, like tiny nails on a chalkboard. "Mm."

June switches to peekaboo. Mr. Buttons flicks his tail with disinterest. I get back to work on the Daphne dress. If I want to have anything to submit for the contest that isn't a pile of haphazardly sewn fabrics, I have to speed up the process.

Easier said than done. Not only is the piece ridiculously elaborate—*thanks, Past Me*—but also, my focus is all over the place. I'm so scattered, I have to redo the same leaf four times. And that's only so far.

"I'm sorry. You were probably busy, too…"

"Where's that coming from?" June laughs. "Of course I'm busy. That doesn't mean I can't make time for my two favorite girls in the world."

"Meow."

"*And* my favorite boy."

I shake my head at Mr. Buttons piping up. "Ruffian. He's been hiding under the couch all day. He loves playing babysitter until there's actual sitting to do."

"Really? I thought he'd be very good at sitting."

"Yeah, sitting *around*." I poke myself with a pin. *Crap.* Can't get blood on this ivory lace. "Band-Aids, Band-Aids, where did I put the Band-Aids…"

I throw the kitchen into chaos looking for the first-aid kit. When I finally find what I'm looking for, I slap one on without even disinfecting the spot. Can't waste time; need to get this done, need to...

A hand comes down on my wrist. "Are you okay?"

My head snaps back to June. "I— Of course. Why wouldn't I be?"

She doesn't answer my question. Instead, after a moment's pause, she asks another one. "How are things between you and Matvey?"

"How... what?"

June bites her lip, suddenly uneasy. "It's just—you don't seem happy. You used to be, but then... I guess I'm just asking if he's been treating you alright."

Can I answer for the past twelve hours alone? "It's... complicated."

She gives a tight nod. "I see."

"It's nothing bad, just—"

"Come back to the apartment."

I blink. "Sorry?"

"Come back," June repeats, scooting over to me on the floor. She takes my hands and fixes the Band-Aid as she goes, so natural I almost miss it. "I can handle a screaming baby. Hell, I'll handle an army of them. But I can't see you like this, Apes. I can't."

Come back. It's so tempting. Just for a second, I let myself think about it: walking back into my old apartment, getting my old life back. Without any of the luxury or the silences. I could talk Matvey into joint custody, let him put guards at the door for protection, whatever satisfies his need for control. I could—

And when Carmine comes for your best friend? Will it have been worth it?

I could never. I can't put June's life in danger. And it doesn't matter how bad of a mother I am—I can't put my baby in danger, either. Not again.

So I hug my best friend and shake my head. "Thanks. But it's nothing that serious. I'm just tired from work."

"Liar," June mumbles into my neck. "Fine. Have it your way. But I'll keep the door open."

"Please don't. The third-floor creep might take it as an invitation to dinner."

We laugh at that. God, it's good to be back like this: me, June, our cat. Tiny little Nugget, however riotous her mood may get. "Just promise you'll call if things get bad, okay?"

I nod. "I promise."

It's another lie, but it's the kindest one I've got.

25

MATVEY

Something's wrong with April.

After that night, it becomes more and more obvious. The faraway look, the one-syllable answers, the sluggish way she drags herself from bed to couch and couch to bed... All innocent brushstrokes on their own, but the picture they paint is far from reassuring.

If it were just that, I could ignore it. I could chalk it up to exhaustion. Hell, even to sheer hatred of me. After everything I did to her, I wouldn't expect anything less.

But then there's the baby.

Until a few days ago, May was her one source of joy. Even when I was acting my worst, I could see April's face change the second she picked her up: her frown smoothed over; her nervousness disappeared; her smile came back tenfold. It was the one thing that made me feel like I hadn't broken her, even when I didn't think I cared anymore—how happy she was with her daughter.

Now, it's like holding her own baby makes it worse. This vacant stare fills her eyes, like she can't even *see* our child in her arms. Like she's watching something else, somewhere far away from us.

Like she's not even there.

"Matvey?"

Grisha's voice snaps me out of my thoughts. "What?"

"I was just saying that I prepared those documents you requested." When my face doesn't show any recognition, Grisha frowns at my reflection in the rearview mirror. "You know, the logs? About the D.C. matter?"

Right. Those. "Good. I'll check them out in my office."

I try to make myself sound normal. Like I'm not being haunted by omens I don't understand. But I don't seem to be doing a very convincing job.

"Is everything okay?" my nosy driver pries. "With April and the baby?"

"Of course," I lie. It's my first instinct, even now: deny, deny, deny. "Why wouldn't it be?"

I watch Grisha hesitate in the mirror. It's unlike him. Whatever it is, I wish he'd just fucking come out with it instead of fishing for the most diplomatic words in the dictionary. "The other day, she was rather... distraught. I just hope that whatever happened at her father's house isn't weighing on her anymore."

At her father's house. When I wasn't there to protect her. Another one of my failings, the latest in a long line.

"Keep an eye on the place," I order him.

"Alright. How many eyes did you have in mind?"

"Just a couple of men will suffice."

"Understood. Do we want these men to be seen?"

He says it casually, like a comment about the weather, but I know what he's really asking me. A Bratva man isn't spotted unless the *pakhan* wants them to be.

So the real question is: *Do we want the Flowers family to know they're being watched?*

I can picture it in my head—Dominic peeking out the windows, being haunted by a black shape looming just beyond his pristine garden wall. *Hunted.* Nora, parting the curtains with her five-hundred-dollar manicure, telling her girls not to leave the house. And then April's lifelong bullies, quivering through the night, sleeping huddled together on the floor like the litter of spoiled brats they are.

It would be deserved. It would be righteous, and vengeance, and a goddamn treat to witness.

But it wouldn't help anyone. It wouldn't help April. On the contrary, it'd only make her life harder. And it doesn't matter how badly I want to avenge her—I can't be the one who keeps doing that to her.

Even if it costs me my reputation.

"No. Just surveillance."

I may be mistaken, but I think I catch Grisha's mouth doing something. Something that almost resembles a smile. "As you wish, sir."

≈

After five hours poring over the same fifty pages of logs, I start contemplating the surface of my desk. Specifically, how hard I could slam my forehead against it without breaking either thing.

"What a fucking mess," I mutter.

Across from me, Yuri sighs. "Yeah."

"This is a goddamn farce. What's the point of having a logging system if no one bothers to actually use it?"

"To be fair, your *vory* aren't exactly the freshest batch of Bratva men on the market," Grisha points out. "The youngest is Ipatiy, and even he's pushing fifty."

"That's no excuse for disobeying orders," I snap. "If they can surf porn on company hardware, they can damn well learn to use company software."

"There's a joke in there somewhere," Yuri says wryly.

"I should just punish them all," I sigh. "Grisha, how much would that set me back?"

"Executing all your *vory*?" He shrugs. "Oh, not that much. Only every single company they run. Ten billion or so?"

Figured. "Any progress on the surveillance tapes?"

Grisha slumps in his chair. An uncharacteristic display, but then again, none of us is at our best right now. Give us a street fight any day, but bureaucracy? I'd rather carve my own head out like a goddamn jack-o'-lantern. "Unfortunately, it was too long ago. That week's footage has been erased automatically."

"Perfect." I roll my eyes. "So we have nothing."

"I wouldn't say *nothing*," Grisha counters. "We have the names of the accounts that were used. It's worth considering that the mole might, in fact, have acted from their own computer."

"Seriously? You think they'd be that dumb?" Yuri scoffs. "Some mole that would be."

"Are you getting upset on the mole's behalf, Yurochka?" Grisha asks. "We haven't even established it's a smart mole yet. Only that, whoever they are, they're currently one step ahead of us."

"Is that your idea of good news?" I frown. "They're an idiot, but we're even bigger idiots, so that's why they're winning?"

"Glass half-full, Matvey."

"Why do you keep saying 'they'?" Yuri cuts in. "The *vory* are all men."

It's a good point, but Grisha starts tutting immediately. "Ah, but the *vory* are not the only ones with access. There's you and me, and of course, Matvey…"

"Thanks," I say dryly.

"And one more person."

It takes me a beat to realize who he means. Yuri must realize it at the same time as I do, because his face goes absolutely livid. "You fucking take that back," he snarls.

"No need to take it so personally." Grisha shrugs. "Just considering all options."

"Petra isn't an option! My—" He cuts himself off at the last second. "Our *pakhansha* isn't a suspect. She has no reason to hurt us."

"Really?" Grisha fires back, all cheer suddenly gone. "Did she tell you that herself? In that case, by all means, let's strike her from the list. Honor system is a fantastic way to run a Bratva."

"You goddamn piece of—"

"Enough!" I slam both palms on the desk. "Grisha's right. No one is off the suspect list, Yuri. Not even you and me."

"Not even— Are you hearing yourself right now?"

"The question is, are *you* hearing *me*?" I growl. "Don't forget, brother, that I am still your *pakhan*. And that you're in no position to be challenging me. Not after what you did." I lean in, voice dropping to a vicious whisper. "So remember your goddamn place."

Yuri's face drains. "Petra's done nothing wrong," he stammers back anyway. It's a testament to how much he cares—at least that, I can't begrudge him. Not all the way. "She's innocent."

"Then prove it," I tell him. "Bring me the mole and I won't have to keep looking."

Grisha has a point: no one is above suspicion. This isn't a court of law—this is the Bratva. And in this world, it's guilty until proven innocent.

"… Yes, *pakhan*."

I nod. Then, just as Yuri starts heading out the door, I stop him. "Oh, and brother?"

"What?"

I give him a pointed look. "Clock's ticking. Be quick, or I'll have to be."

I don't know if I believe Petra actually has a hand in this. After Yuri's one-eighty with the April situation, I can't be certain of anything.

But I do know one thing.

And that's the lengths we'll go for the people we love.

26

MATVEY

When I step back into the penthouse, I'm greeted by a shocking sight: Petra Solovyova, holding an actual baby. Specifically, *my* baby.

"Oh," she deadpans. "Look what the pirate cat dragged in."

Speak of the devil. After this afternoon's accusations, seeing her here feels like talking shit behind someone's back just to watch them pop up around the corner. Not that I give a damn.

"Petra," I greet back with a matching degree of enthusiasm. "Is there a reason you're holding my daughter like you're trying to find the perfect spot to pin her up on the wall?"

"Well, she *is* the picture of grace." She wrinkles her nose. "And… other things."

"Don't tell me you're scared of a dirty diaper."

"'Scared' is a strong word. Let's just say I'm not a fan."

"Like you're not a fan of spiders?"

"Eight legs and not a single pair of Louboutins?" she scoffs. "Right, like I'd ever trust that. Here, hold this."

"This" turns out to be my infant daughter. I tuck May into my arms and raise a skeptical eyebrow. "Skipping class? That's unlike you."

"I'm sure my nannies will have plenty of practice."

The second she sees me, May lights up like a tiny Christmas tree. If I ever needed an incentive to find the mole, one look at my girl would do it. They say Helen of Troy's face launched a thousand ships—now, I finally know how that's possible.

For this little face right here, I would launch a thousand more.

"Where's April?"

Petra jerks her head towards the master bathroom. "Taking a foam bath. Doctor's orders."

"A real doctor's or yours?"

"I don't see the difference."

My eyes wander back towards the bathroom door. I swallow the lump of worry in my throat and force out, "Is she…?"

"Alive?"

"I was going to say 'okay.'"

"Mm. I can say yes to one of them. The other, I'm not so sure."

And if that isn't reassuring… I try to curb my worry, but all it does is grow stronger. It seems to be the theme with April: anything I try to feel less of, I just end up feeling more.

I motion for Petra to follow me into the balcony. The walls may be thick here, but they certainly aren't soundproof. "I asked Grisha to keep an eye on her."

"Great job he's gonna do from outside the door," she drawls.

"I'd ask the same of you."

On the scale of hardest things I've ever done, this probably takes the cake: asking Petra Solovyova to help. Technically, I'm her *pakhan*—I could just order her to do this. I don't owe anyone a request, let alone a polite one.

But this is *my* failing. *My* responsibility. And I'm not going to push it on anybody else.

Petra's eyes crinkle with amusement. "Should I pinch myself? The great Matvey Groza, asking me for a *favor*? Wonders never cease."

I should've known she wasn't going to make this easy. "I'm not asking for free. I'll…" I scrunch up my face in disgust, feeling like I've just swallowed a fly and all its little winged family. Fuck, is this what humility tastes like? "… *owe* you."

"Hold up, let me record this. I'm gonna play it at your kid's eighteenth birthday party."

"Just cut the shit and say you'll do it."

She crosses her arms. "And why would I?"

It's the worst bluff she's ever pulled. "Because I know you care for her, too."

I watch her hesitate. It's always like this when her mask starts showing its cracks: you get a glimpse of the Petra beneath. Not the assassin, but the *human.* The raw, bleeding heart.

"In that case, I want something in return now."

I raise a skeptical eyebrow. "Not gonna wait until the worst possible moment to spring it on me?"

"That would be the smart thing, wouldn't it?" She sighs. "A year ago, I wouldn't even have questioned it. Do you ever wonder what happened? To make us dumb like this?"

"No."

"Because you already know?"

I don't reply. I have no desire to inflate her ego any more tonight, certainly not by telling her that she's right. That the four-letter creature that dulled her senses is the same beast that came after mine.

As if reading my mind, she finally speaks. "Yuri."

"Excuse me?"

"That's my favor. I want you to lay off your brother for a while."

I frown. *"That's* your ask? You want time off to honeymoon in Bora Bora?"

She shakes her head with a laugh. But there's a bitterness to it, like a piece of sweet candy gone sour. "I'm not talking about vacation days—though it certainly wouldn't hurt. I'm asking you to go easier on him. Lately, he's been… in a darker place than most."

For some reason, her words irk me. "Right, and you know this because…?"

"Because I have eyes, Matvey. That look you've been seeing on April's face? I've been seeing it on Yuri's every night since your fight." Her stare grows more distant, lost in the Manhattan skyline. "Maybe even before then."

"You talk as if I'm the monster in this story."

She shakes her head once. "Not a monster, no. But it still takes a toll."

"What does?"

"Loving you."

If this had been a week earlier, I would've torn into her. Denied, denied, denied, until my last furious breath. But that was then. Now, it's all I can do to put up half a fight.

"He betrayed me, Petra. He lied to me. He—"

"Don't you get tired?"

I blink. "Of what?"

"Of holding a grudge against the whole world."

For the first time in a long time, I'm stunned into silence.

I might've stood there forever if something didn't interrupt. "Matvey?"

The sound of that third voice turns both our heads. "April."

"I thought that was you. I heard…" She shakes her head. "Sorry. I didn't realize it had gotten so late."

"Nonsense." Petra smiles. "Did you follow the doctor's orders?"

"Yeah. Thanks for the advice." She turns to me. "Did you know Petra has a PhD in History?"

"No, she doesn—"

"Alright then!" Petra claps her hands loudly. "I'll be on my merry way. Get some sleep. Don't do anything I wouldn't approve of."

"Like going to church?"

"Always a riot to chat with you, husband." She gives April a small squeeze on the shoulder. "See you for alterations."

Then she sashays out the door.

Silence fills the empty space. April makes herself small by my side. Her eyes start wandering around the dark balcony, as if not knowing where to look.

"So, alterations?" I ask.

She nods reluctantly. "Petra's been helping me with a dress. It's for..." She shakes her head. "Forget it. It's nothing important."

She starts heading back in, but I stop her, my hand on hers. "April. Tell me what it's for."

"Why?"

"Because I want to know."

Because I want to learn everything I've spent my time trying not to see. Everything that makes you you.

Everything that makes me lo—

"It's just this contest. I won't win, so don't worry. Actually, I'm not even sure I'll turn in a piece after all."

"Show me."

April blinks. In the moonlight, her skin looks grayscale, almost like a statue. The kind of marble that can be made to look soft, but only after years of painstaking work. One stroke of the chisel at a time.

"Okay," she says finally. Then she leads me to a mannequin. Her fingers hesitate over the drape. "It's unfinished."

"I know."

"There's still much to do."

"April. Just show me."

The drape comes down.

I'm not an appreciator of fine arts. Frankly, I never had the time. And fashion—I don't understand it at all. I just buy whatever's expensive enough, anonymous enough, to get me through a day of pretending to be someone I'm not: a respectable CEO, a self-made billionaire. Sheep's clothing for the wolf within.

But even I can't ignore this. "It's…"

"It's bad, right?" She shakes her head. "You've probably seen hundreds of dresses that look like this. I don't know what I was thinking, I'll—"

"*April.*"

I put one hand on her shoulder, the other arm still cradling May. Like this, it's even clearer: she's ours. It's in her jet-black curly hair, in the line of her nose and the shape of her chin, in dark freckles and snow-blue eyes. Pieces of me and pieces of April, sewn together into something new.

April looks up at me, lost. "Yes?"

"I've never seen a dress like this before."

It's the truth. I say it plainly, without the awe it deserves, but I do say it. I'm too much of a heathen to sing praises—to even understand what praises should be sung. And it's never been my style to flatter, anyway.

But lately, I've been leaving too many of the right things unsaid. And I'm tired of only saying the wrong ones. I'm—

Aren't you tired of holding a grudge against the whole world?

Yes, Petra. Yes, I fucking am.

April smiles in response. But it's a smile that doesn't reach her eyes, too weak to go anywhere. "Thanks."

I try to kiss her, but she slips by. Like a ghost, or water, or a midnight mix of both.

All throughout dinner, she doesn't glance at May once.

"Sir?"

I keep seeing it in my mind: April's weak smile, her empty eyes.

"Sir...?"

It's worse than a gaping wound; worse than a bleeding bullet hole. At least then, I'd know how to handle it. But how do I handle *this*?

"*Pakhan*, are you listening...?"

How do I handle an evil I can't see?

"Matvey."

How do I fix it if I don't know where it's broken?

"*Motya*—"

Where *I* broke it?

"Maybe we should adjourn—"

"No. Enough."

I snap back to the present to the screech of a chair against the floor. *That's right. I was in a meeting.*

"Ivan," I say coldly.

Ivan's face is set, a mask of barely-concealed fury. "You've been neglecting your duties for far too long, Matvey."

I grit my teeth. "Have I now?"

"Yes. You're absent, distracted, and your priorities clearly lie elsewhere. I won't stand for it anymore."

All around the table, people start murmuring. My *vory*—and Vlad's, too. All finally turned against me. Just like everyone warned me would happen.

"Matvey Groza…" Ivan rumbles. "In the name of the code of honor, I challenge you to a duel."

27

MATVEY

I keep my composure. I don't even rise from my chair, just gaze into Ivan's eyes with a calm I don't feel. "Name your prize."

"Control of the Groza Bratva."

More whispering. Hushed, frantic. "Sit down, Ivan."

"No!" he barks. "I won't."

I clench my fist on the table. "Sit down now and I'll forget you spoke. I won't ask again."

"Are you saying you refuse the duel?"

It's like the room explodes: suddenly, no one is whispering anymore. It's so loud, it feels like being at the center of a beehive.

Did you hear that?

The pakhan's *refusing—*

Does that mean...?

I slam both palms on the table and stand. "Don't mistake my mercy for weakness. You are my oldest *vor*. You served my grandfather before me. That is the only reason I'm extending you this courtesy right now. So do yourself a favor and back off."

It's taking all my self-control to keep my anger in check. Of all the people I'd expect to be on my side—of all the people I'd expect to be loyal—

I never thought I'd have to watch my back from Ivan.

The others? Of fucking course. Those hungry jackals are waiting for nothing but a sign of weakness from me to seize my share of the spoils. If they could strip me of everything I've built in the past two decades, they wouldn't hesitate a goddamn second. From them, I'm always expecting a knife in the back.

But not from Ivan. Not from the man who stood next to my grandfather through every step of the first Groza Bratva, from the rise to the fall to the oblivion that followed. The oblivion that *I* then dragged us out of.

If he'd only come to me in private, we could've solved this without invoking the old laws. Hell, I might have even looped him in on the mole hunt. It would have been a risk, but a calculated one.

But he didn't come to you—he did this. *And now, there's no turning back.*

"No," he growls to my final mercy.

"Then at least give me a reason."

He scoffs. "You promised us change and you didn't bring it. You promised us war, but where is it? You ignored all my warnings, and now, you have the guts to demand reasons? To offer me mercy?"

Warnings? "I don't know what you're talking about."

"You know perfectly well what I'm talking about. Or did that whore fry your brain as well as your cock?"

The room falls silent. No one dares speak another word, the whispers dead. And something else, too, is dead beyond saving: my desire to give Ivan grace.

Criticizing me? Questioning my leadership? As if there isn't a *vor* every quarter who does that. It's the oldest power play in the world, but it can be handled. A disgruntled employee can always be put back in their place. I won't kill someone for speaking their mind to my face, no matter how out of line.

But the second you touch my family, you're done.

I clench my jaw. "As *pakhan* of the Groza Bratva, I accept your challenge."

Ivan doesn't seem surprised. "Good. We'll set a time and a place—"

"No. We'll do it here and now."

Everyone's stares are on me. Ivan's thrown, but it only takes him a second to recover. A second for his eyes to ice over again. "Fine. First blood."

"No."

A frown. "No?"

I walk to my weapons cabinet and pluck out a box. The smooth, lacquered black surface returns the reflection of a man barely holding back. A beast, howling against the constraints of its human-shaped cage.

I slam the box on the table and unlatch it. "Only one kind of duel is worth the name."

The *vory* crane their necks like a bunch of nosy swans. Across from me, Ivan is silent, eyes trailing along the edges of my weapons of choice.

Daggers.

"To the death, then?"

It's a message: *If you're going to stab me in the back, you'd best finish the job.* I don't give a shit about first blood and old laws: you want me gone, you make it happen. You want me sentenced, you swing the sword. You want to spit on my family's honor—

You deal with the fucking consequences.

My consequences.

"To the death," I confirm.

No one dares speak another word.

As the headquarters of the Groza Bratva, our offices aren't simply offices. And the top floor, the one reserved for the *vory* and the *pakhan*—

It is not, in fact, the top floor.

There's a code to the elevator. If certain buttons are punched in just right, it will take you to the ghost floor of the building. The *true* final floor, just under the rooftop.

And on that floor, there is a ring.

Most of the time, it's a training space. The *vory* aren't all exactly combat-oriented, but their men have to be. That's where they spar, bleed, and practice.

And that's where any disputes are settled.

"Are you sure about this?" Yuri asks, kneeling before me on the changing room floor. He's bandaging my hands before the fight, but I can't help noticing that his own are shaking. "Killing Ivan?"

By contrast, mine are perfectly still. "He left me no choice."

"Maybe you can still work it out. He can apologize formally for the insult, or…"

"Yura."

My brother looks up from his task. "Yes?"

"If I fall today, the Groza Bratva is yours."

His face goes as white as a sheet. "Don't say that. You'll win."

"I might not."

It's the truth: out of all the *vory* to duel, Ivan is the worst possible match for me. I fight with instinct and rage; he fights with calculations and a mind that's sharper than any blade. I'm strong, but he's older. I've got youth, but he's got experience.

And if that wasn't enough, he *knows* me. My moves, my tactics, everything.

After all, he was the one to train me.

I want to win. I am going into this to *win*. But I can't afford to be reckless. Not against Ivan.

And Yuri knows that, too. "Motya—"

"But if that happens, make no mistake: I'll take Ivan down with me. No matter what."

He shakes his head frantically. "Matvey, let me talk to him. Let me talk to you both. I think I know why he's so mad. I'll make things right. I'll—"

"No, you won't. Because this isn't your doing."

"Matvey, just listen. Please."

I squeeze both his shoulders. "I know I've been putting a lot on you lately. That was my mistake. I kept holding onto a grudge that didn't matter anymore, and for that, I'm sorry. I'm sorry it took me so long to see it."

His eyes are lucid now. Goddammit, what a crybaby brother I'm leaving in command. I'd better win this thing after all.

"You don't have to apologize," Yuri rasps. "You didn't do anything wrong."

"But I did. And you've been warning me this entire time."

Don't alienate the vory; *don't make them mad; don't lose them.* All along, Yuri's been pointing out my biggest blind spot: not my enemies, but my allies. The ones I should have kept closest.

"I didn't think it would come to this," he whispers.

"I know, brother."

I take off my *pakhan's* signet ring and drop it in Yuri's waiting palm. We don't speak another word—we don't need to. That one gesture says it all.

"What—" he calls after me as I start walking to the ring. "What should I tell April? If…?"

April. I've been trying not to think of that. If this truly goes south, I can't imagine that anyone would be angrier than her. I can almost hear her in my mind: *"Losing your life for a* Pacman *dispute? Are you kidding me?"*

Somehow, that makes me laugh. Even here, even now, April always manages to bring out the bright side of things. The bright side of *me.* Before her, I didn't think I had it—a part that wasn't darkness.

"Tell her to take care of our daughter."

Then I step into the ring.

28

MATVEY

Grisha's gaze sweeps over the crowd. It feels odd to have a referee for a duel to the death, but the old laws are clear: a neutral party must be present.

Despite being my third, no one would question Grisha's integrity. Beyond Ivan, he's the one with the strongest ties to the original Groza Bratva. After all, his father was Igor Groza's second. That's not something anybody here would take lightly, not even the newest recruits who haven't so much as stepped foot on the eternal snows across the ocean.

Ivan doesn't take it lightly, either. "Thank you for your service, Grisha."

He hasn't even grazed me and already, he's acting as the new pakhan.

"No thanks needed," Grisha replies stiffly. "I serve the Groza Bratva, now and always."

The subtle jab almost makes me laugh. If there's one thing Grisha's never liked, it's brown-nosers.

"Old rules?" I cut in.

Grisha nods. "One dagger each, no armor. Bandages are allowed, but only up to the elbow and the knee. No additional weapons and no shoes."

We take each other in. I don't know if today's Ivan is expecting any dirty tricks, but I learned to fight with honor. If he's still the same man who taught me, he'll fight with honor, too.

But is he? Would the old Ivan have challenged you like this?

Satisfied with our inspection, Grisha continues, "The duel ends when either participant stops breathing."

"Perhaps we should allow our *pakhan* to tap out," Ivan suggests. "Lately, he's shown a tendency to jump ship when things get bad, hasn't he?"

What the hell is he talking about? "Sounds like you're the one who wants the option," I retort. "Is your back acting up again? Don't worry; I won't stab you there. Someone taught me better than that."

Ivan's jaw sets. "If only."

It's like I'm missing a piece here, but there's no time to find out which one. Ivan made that call for the both of us.

I catch some commotion out of the corner of my eye: on the Solovyov side, someone is elbowing their way to the forefront.

Vlad's eyes and mine go wide at the same time. "Petra!" he cries out. "What are you doing here? This is no place for you."

"No place?" she scoffs. "When my own husband is dueling to the death? Was anyone even intending to tell me or was I supposed to find out from the evening news?"

Which raises a good point—*how* did she find out?

But no sooner do I ask myself that question than I realize I already know the answer.

Yuri. I swear, if I get out of this alive, I'm gonna kill him.

"Go home, Petra. You don't need to be here for this."

"He's right!" Vlad spits, the surreality of agreeing with me making his beady eyes bulge even more. "You can't be here in your condition!"

"It's a pregnancy, Dad, not scurvy."

"Regardless! A Bratva ring is not meant for women!"

He keeps prattling on, but his daughter ignores him and looks at me instead. "Matvey, please reconsider. Think of your family."

She words it very carefully. To the onlookers, there wouldn't be a doubt left that she's talking about herself and her baby. But we know differently.

"My family will be safe with you," I rasp.

With that, I turn my back on her.

I breathe in once, twice, three times. I feel the weight of the dagger in my hand, the balance of steel and brass. Soon, it will be bathed red. "Any last words?"

Ivan's face darkens. "You should have listened to me."

Then he charges.

I don't have time to think about anything else: not Grisha hopping out of the ring, not Yuri clinging to the ropes like lifelines. Not Petra, one hand on her minuscule baby bump and the other trembling around a throwing knife.

If I let myself get distracted, that's it. I'm dead.

Steel meets steel. We push against each other's guards and end up face-to-face, close enough that we can hear the other breathing. He tries to knee me in the gut, but I keep him at bay.

"What did that mean?" I demand.

"What are you talking about?"

"That I should've listened to you. What did that mean?"

Ivan clicks his tongue. He jumps back, putting distance between us, and I do the same.

Maybe he thinks I'm trying to distract him. I wonder when his opinion of me fell so low—when he started regarding me as this coward I've never been.

It's odd, me being on the defensive. Usually, a fight like this would go the other way—me assaulting, Ivan guarding, waiting for a weak point to exploit.

But he seems to have lost himself. He isn't fighting with his mind—he's fighting with his gut. For some reason, he's *angry.*

"Enough talking," he hisses, leg swinging forward to trip me up again. "I've said all I needed to you and yours. Time to end this."

He's angry. I can use that.

The next time he charges, I'm ready. I block his blow with

my arm, and when his knee tries to crash into my abdomen, I let it.

Then I stab into his thigh with all my might.

Ivan howls. He closes his eyes out of pain, just for a second, and that's when I act: I fling away my dagger and grab his with my bare hands. "Do you apologize?" I snarl. "Do you apologize to my family?"

Ivan's teeth grind together to hold back the pain.

Say yes, I beg him silently. *Die with honor. If you won't stay by my side, at least don't die as my enemy.*

He spits on the ring once. "Fuck you and your family. Damn you all to hell."

I twist his knife back to face him and plunge it into his chest.

Ivan's body crumples. He falls back on the ring and so do I, tipping forward alongside him, my hand tight around the hilt of his own dagger.

With his last breath, he whispers something into my ear.

Then his eyes glaze over.

I wait for ten seconds. Distantly, I hear Grisha count them off, but it's all drowned out by my heartbeat. Even now, the adrenaline won't stop pumping.

I yank the knife out and stand.

"Clean this up," I tell Grisha. "Yuri, drive me home."

～

For the longest time, I don't say anything. The car's

vibrations flow in and out of me, bringing my racing heart back under control.

"Should I drop you off at the loft or the penthouse?" Yuri asks. "Or I can do both if you want to clean up first—"

"Carmine."

He freezes. "What?"

"That's what Ivan said to me before he died: '*Carmine. Carmine is here.*'"

"Why would he say that?"

"Because he was the mole."

I watch Yuri's face falter in the rearview mirror. "That's impossible."

"It's not. He had access." Clearly, he had motive, too, but I'll be damned if I know what that is. He said so many things to me, but in the end, none of it made any sense. None but the last. "It was him, Yuri. It was him all along."

Carmine is here. A brag. *You might have killed me, but I still let the enemy in.*

Yuri doesn't speak right away. Ivan raised him as much as he raised me—he must still be processing the shock.

But eventually, even he has to accept reality. "It was Ivan," he says out loud, as if trying to make himself believe it. "Ivan was the mole."

"Mm." After what feels like eternity, I say, "The penthouse."

"What?"

"You asked where I wanted to go."

He blinks. "Oh… right. Penthouse, then? You're sure?"

"Yes." I've never been more sure of anything. "Bring me there. I want to be with my family."

When I finally step out of the elevator, I'm drained. All I want is to be with them: my woman, my child.

"April?" I call. The apartment is unusually dark, not even a single light on. *She's probably asleep.*

From memory alone, I make my way to the crib. "Hi. Sorry Daddy's so late today."

May coos, her hands outstretched towards me. She's pushier than usual, demanding a place in my arms. "Alright, alright. Come here, you."

"Meow."

I look down. "I don't have any more arms. Go bother April."

"*Mrowwr.*"

Great. The security cat's acting weird, too. I go to corral him, but—

"Get back here," I bark.

But he slips out onto the balcony.

Goddammit. If this mangy cat leaps from fifty floors chasing a butterfly, April will never let me hear the end of it. They say cats have nine lives, but I'm not sure how many this old bastard's got left.

I part the curtains. I step out into the balcony, eyes adjusting to the skyline. "I said get back—"

And then I see her.

April, sitting on the railing, her feet swinging over nothing.

29

APRIL

Is this how it feels to be treated like glass?

Ever since I came back from my dad's, it's like everyone I know made the unanimous decision to put me under surveillance: Grisha, Yuri, Petra, the damn hotel concierge. I'd suspect Matvey is behind it, except that June's doing it, too. And Corey, and Rob... Even Mr. Buttons isn't leaving me alone for a second. It's like they think they can't blow their noses without someone else picking up watch duty. Like they think I'll...

Break. Shatter. Be gone in the blink of an eye.

It's ridiculous. I'm a grown ass woman, not some puppy on a flier. I'm not going to rush out into traffic the minute someone leaves the door open, or follow some stranger home, or... whatever else they think I'll do. This isn't how these things happen. Surely it can't be that easy?

Disappearing from the world?

"I'm so sorry, April."

Petra's voice jolts me out of my thoughts. "What?"

"I said I have to go. Something came up with…" She shakes her head. "It's nothing. Don't worry about it."

"Are you sure?" Her expression looks so torn, I can't imagine it's *nothing.* "If you want to talk…"

"It's okay!" she answers, a little too quickly to be believable. "Seriously, it's fine. Just work drama. Don't stress yourself over it."

Don't stress yourself. Relax. Don't worry. If I had a quarter for every time I've heard these words in the past week, I'd be on my way to buying an island. "If you say so."

Petra plasters on a smile. It's cracking in a thousand different places, but I pretend I don't see it. Lately, it seems to be the polite thing to do—pretend the cracks aren't real. In others or in myself.

"I'll see you tomorrow?" she asks.

I return the same kind of smile: glass shot through with hairline fractures. "Sure."

Then I'm alone.

It's strange—ever since May was born, I never felt alone, not really. On my worst days at the motel, when Mrs. Tanner decided to drive me extra crazy and the phone wouldn't stop ringing for a second, all I had to do was walk back into my room. Back to her crib. I'd grab her little hand with two fingers, and sometimes, she'd squeeze back, giving me the strength to get through one more shift, one more day.

Now, I don't dare reach in.

It reminds me of the day I turned five. We went to Coney Island for my birthday, me and Maia, and I wandered off on my own to pet a dog I'd seen. I didn't ask the owner for permission like I'd been taught—I was too excited. The dog was small and fluffy, the kind that seemed incapable of harming anyone. But when I touched it, it snapped at me instantly.

I remember the sting of the bite, the irrational sense of betrayal. I remember thinking, *Why would it do that?*

Afterwards, I never tried to pet a dog again.

Maia tried to help me get over it. To explain what I'd done wrong, how to avoid having it happen again. One day, she invited a friend with a Maltese over for tea. I'd known that dog all my life, but I still cowered in my room, unable to touch it. When Maia insisted, I reluctantly put out my hand, but at the last possible second, I snatched it away again.

That's what it feels like now to pick up my daughter.

I hover at the edge of the crib like a ghost. May's staring at me, her big eyes all teary. She hasn't been crying outright, but it's like she's always at the brink of it.

I watch her reach for me. I don't reach back.

It's better if I don't reach back.

You're going to fuck it up. You're going to hurt her. You're going to ruin her.

Like you ruined everything else around you.

Without thinking, I step out for some air.

My friends... They all see me as a burden now. It's plain on their faces that they're terrified of leaving me alone. It's creating all sorts of trouble for them.

The other day, I made June late for a shift.

Today, I kept Petra from a work emergency.

Tomorrow, it might be Matvey who pays the price.

Matvey. I've spent so long waiting for him to forgive me, and now that he seems to be getting around to tolerating me again, I don't want it.

No—I don't *deserve* it.

Besides, it wouldn't last. He doesn't trust me. Without trust, there's nothing.

Certainly not love.

He was right, though, wasn't he? You took his daughter. You thought you could raise her better, but look at you now: you can't even touch her.

Some mom you're shaping up to be.

I put my hands on the railing. Mr. Buttons is rubbing insistently between my ankles, as if begging to be picked up. *Show me what's out there. Show me what you see.*

"I can't do that, silly," I laugh. "It's dangerous."

Then I climb over the railing.

It feels dreamlike. Maybe it is. Lately, it's been happening more and more: me falling asleep without realizing it, the real and the fake blurring behind my eyelids. If I was awake, I'd never do something like this, would I? I'm way too much of a coward for that.

I swing my feet and don't feel anything.

Right. A dream.

It's really pretty, the sight from here. I don't even think about what I'm doing—just that I want to see more of the city. More of the skyline and the night, of the lights and lit-up windows.

Glass. Like me.

When did I turn into that? Something dangerous and fragile that no one wants to touch? Something *invisible*?

I wonder if Daphne realized what was happening to her when she began to transform. I wonder if, at the last possible second, she tried to stop it.

I wonder if it hurt.

"April. *April.* Get down from there."

I snort. "What happened to 'hello'?"

"April, come back inside this instant." He's as bossy as ever, but his voice is unusually soft. Like he's scared of something.

For some reason, that makes me laugh. What could Matvey Groza possibly be scared of?

"Why? Afraid I'm gonna catch a chill?"

He'd raise her right. He'd raise May better than you could. A fearless father versus a coward mother. A more obvious choice, there has never been.

"That's not true," Matvey growls from somewhere behind me.

"What's not true?"

"You're not a coward."

Was I talking out loud? Ah, well. Maybe I was, maybe I wasn't. Dream logic and all. "I kind of am, though, aren't I?"

"April—"

"I ran," I cut him off, voice starting to crack. Like the glass I'm made of, this fragile thing I became. "I ran away from you. I could've faced you, but I ran. And I took your daughter."

"That's in the past," Matvey says.

"Is it?" I whisper. "Because you still haven't looked me in the eye."

Silence.

"I know why." I smile through the tears. It's kind of comforting—having all the answers at last. "It's because you hate me, isn't it? But you don't want to tell me that."

"That's not true."

"You're afraid I'll do something. To myself or to her."

"You'd *never* hurt her," he snarls. "Never."

"I already did. I took her from you."

"You brought her back."

"No. *You* did. And now, I'm just in the way."

"April, stop. Just—"

"Even now, you won't look me in the eye!" I cry out. "Why is everyone acting like this? *April, April*—can you all just forget me already? I get it: I'm a burden. I'm stupid and pathetic and I can't even be trusted with my own daughter. I can't even be trusted as a *partner.*"

"Come inside. We'll talk about this, just—come inside. Please."

Please. In all his life, I doubt Matvey ever said that to anyone. More evidence that I'm dreaming this up.

But that's alright. If this is a dream, then at least I can be honest.

"I suppose you weren't all that wrong, though. You couldn't trust me. Even my father couldn't trust me."

"Your father is scum," Matvey spits back. "Don't listen to a word he said. He's not worth it."

"And I am?" I laugh bitterly. "I wasn't even worth an explanation when you got married. I wasn't even worth an apology. Tell me, what exactly am I worth?"

"EVERYTHING!"

I open my eyes. The skyline blinks back, a bit hazier than reality, a bit sharper than a dream.

I almost fall, but Matvey's voice anchors me. "You're worth everything. I'm the one who's not worthy of you."

It's a dream. It's all a dream.

"You're lying."

"I'm not. For once, I'm not lying to you."

Could my mind be any crueler? Conjuring up Matvey like this, making him say things he'd never say? Things I've been waiting all my life for someone to say to me?

"When you took—" A sharp inhale. "When you took her away, I was furious, yes. But I understand now why you did it."

"No!" I shake my head. "You shouldn't. I—"

"Let me speak. Please."

Stunned, I obey.

"Back then, you weren't taking her away from a loving father —you were taking her away from your own fate. You've been treated as a second choice all your life, and then I treated you that way, too. You thought I'd do the same to her, didn't you? That's why you took her."

"And I was wrong! I should've talked to you."

"Yes," he admits, voice raw. "Yes, you should've talked to me. But I didn't make it easy, did I?"

"It doesn't matter."

"It does. If you thought I was a monster, it does. If you thought I'd be a monster to her—"

"But you wouldn't have been!" I say. "You're a great dad, Matvey. I see it every day."

"And you're a great mom."

"Stop that. You said you wouldn't lie to me."

"I'm not."

"But you are! You—"

"April!" he barks, but it's desperate. "You accused me of not listening to you once. You were right. But now, I want you to listen to me. I need you to listen to me."

Wordlessly, I nod.

"You made a choice," he rasps. "You made the only choice you thought you could make. You did what was best for your child. For *our* child. Even if it broke your heart to do it."

"How do you know that?" I murmur. "That it broke my heart?"

"Because it broke mine, too."

My breath hitches. The skyline blinks at me from afar, hazy one second and sharp the next, like a camera lens hunting for focus.

"You said there can't be love without trust," he presses on, taking a step towards the railing. "You're right. There can't be."

"So you never loved me?"

"No, April. I loved you from the start."

Please, don't let me wake up. If this is a dream, I don't want to wake up.

"From the second I saw you in that shop, I loved you. From the second I touched you the first time, kissed you the first time, I knew there would never be another."

I want it to be true. I want so bad for it to be true, it's killing me. "What about trust?"

"Trust doesn't come easy to me," he whispers. "When you have the kind of life I've had, you learn quickly that you can't trust anyone. You push fear out and harden your heart, but trust is the one thing that can still kill you. Trust is a weakness."

"That's why you didn't trust me?"

"No, April. That's why I refused to admit I already did."

Around the railing, my hands are shaking. "What?"

"I buried it," he confesses, one step closer to my turned back. "I didn't want to face it. But I did trust you, April. I trusted you more than anyone. And when the time came to choose between my blood and you... I got scared. Because I realized that, deep down, I'd already made my choice. So you're not the one who ran—I was. I ran away from the truth and from you. And I can never apologize enough for that."

This isn't real. This can't be real. "You chose me?"

"I will always choose you."

I try to blink away the tears, but it's useless. "You trust me?"

"I trust you."

"You love me?"

"I love you."

I can't stop shaking. I can't stop the tears from falling. I watch them drop into the void like rain and suddenly, it's like my body's paralyzed. Like every part of me is screaming, *This is real.*

"I understand if you don't want it," Matvey adds, sounding more pained than I've ever heard him. "If it's too little, too late, just tell me to go to hell. But right now, I need you to come down from there."

"Come down from...?"

It hits me all at once: where I am. What I'm doing. What I was about to do.

"Come back to me," Matvey rasps. "Come back to *us.*"

So I do.

I whirl around and *see them*: Matvey, May. My family. I reach for them.

And they reach back.

Matvey's hand seizes mine, his grip steel. Without a second's thought, he yanks me back from the railing, making me topple in his arms. May's little hands start searching for me immediately, gripping my clothes like they're never going to let go.

God. What did I almost do? "I'm—" I gasp. "I'm so sorry, Matvey, I didn't— I wasn't myself, I wasn't thinking; I—"

"Shh," he croons into my ear. "It's okay. You're safe now."

"I didn't want to do it," I cry helplessly. "I wouldn't— I'd never—"

I can feel his entire body tremble against mine. Is it rage? Fear? Passion? Somehow, it feels like all three at once. "Promise me, then. Never again."

I nod into the crook of his neck. "Never again."

Slowly, I let myself take it all in: the warmth of Matvey's arms, the soft cooing of my baby between us. What I almost lost for good.

Safe.

For the first time in months, it feels like the truth.

30

APRIL

I spend all night being cradled by those arms. I've never been held tighter in my life. Until now, no one's ever been afraid of losing me.

No one except Matvey.

But maybe that's not entirely fair. I do have people who care about me. And lately, all I've done is force them to walk on eggshells.

That needs to change.

Promise me. Never again.

When morning comes, I make good on that promise.

I call Dr. Allan and tell her what happened. I try not to focus on how anxious I've clearly made her—if I start feeling guilty now, there's no telling where my thoughts might lead me. Instead, I ask for one thing: a referral for a therapist.

I don't know if the process is usually so quick, but within the next twenty minutes, I'm being contacted by someone. In another hour, she's at the penthouse.

"Hello, April. I'm Dr. Knox. We spoke earlier on the phone."

She offers me her hand. I shake it. "Thanks for arranging this so fast. I really appreciate it."

"Nonsense. We're a bit like Batman, us therapists: if we didn't go where we're needed, then no one would need us at all." She winks for good measure, then lets me lead her into the living room.

Her sense of humor immediately puts me at ease, which is a miracle in and of itself. I was already picturing myself shaking through this whole ordeal. Like a Chihuahua at the vet or something.

When Matvey emerges from the bedroom, she shakes his hand, too. "Hello. Dr. Laurel Knox. I'm gonna be having a chat with your girlfriend. Would you mind letting us have the place for the next hour or so?"

I can practically see Matvey's hackles rising. "I'm not leaving her."

"I understand your concern. But I assure you, she'll be perfectly safe with me."

I can see he's about to start arguing again, so I step between them. "Matvey." I tug on his sleeve. "It's fine. Please, trust me."

A beat goes by. Two. "I don't like the thought of not being here for you."

"You are," I reassure him. "In fact, you're going to be helping me out by taking May on a stroll. How's that sound?"

"Like I'm being micromanaged."

"But is it working?" I crack a smile and hope it's a convincing one.

After a couple more seconds, Matvey finally relents. "Fine. But I'm leaving Grisha at the door."

"Okay."

"And I'm putting that thing on security detail."

I follow his line of sight to an unimpressed Mr. Buttons. "I don't think he'll mind."

Within a few minutes, they're out the door. "If there's anything—"

"I'll call you," I promise. "Now, go. It's a pity to stay cooped inside with such nice weather."

Matvey ignores my transparent attempt at bossing him around. Instead, he locks eyes with the doctor behind me. "Are you good at what you do?"

She smiles. "One of the best."

He gives her a tight nod. "See that you are."

Then he's out.

"I'm so sorry," I apologize to Dr. Knox. "He didn't mean anything by that; it's just—"

"How he is?" she laughs. "Don't worry, April, I'm used to being growled at by partners. Now, shall we?"

We sit down at the table, across from each other. "Not gonna make me lie down?" I joke.

"If you'd prefer that. But I get the sense that you've been doing a lot of that lately, haven't you?"

I think back to the blur of the past week: sleep, sleep, sleep. Short, fitful rests, and an eternity of staring at the ceiling to get them. "Yeah. I'm kind of over it."

"Thought so. How about we just have a chat then?"

I smile. It feels like the first genuine one in a long time. "I'll make tea."

Then, with a warm cup between my hands, I take a deep breath and do what I promised to do.

I tell her everything.

By the time I'm done, Dr. Knox has filled five pages of her notebook. "So?" I press. "Am I going crazy?"

She shrugs. "No more than the average person, believe me. That said, I do think I have an inkling of what's going on."

"As in, a diagnosis?"

"It's a bit early for that."

I slump. "Oh."

"Now, don't go getting all disappointed on me. These things take time."

"I just…" I force my frustration back down. "I don't want to be a burden. Or worse, a danger."

"A danger to whom?"

"Myself. My…" I breathe in sharply. "My b-baby."

Dr. Knox pushes her notebook aside. "Do you know what postpartum depression is, April?"

I blink. "I thought it was too early for a diagnosis."

"It is. But I did say I had an inkling." She crosses her legs and takes a sip of her now-cold tea. "So? Ever heard of it?"

"I... Yeah. My mom, she—she went through that. Not with Charlie, but..."

"With you," she fills in.

"Yeah. With me."

Another rapid scribble. "Tell me what you're thinking right now."

"What?"

"Just now, what were you thinking?"

"I guess..." I twist my hands in my lap. "'Figures.'"

"'Figures'?"

"Yeah. Like, sounds about right. That she'd get sick with me and not with him."

"So we're blaming ourselves then?"

I frown. "Kind of? Does it count as blaming yourself if it's the truth?"

"Do you blame your baby?"

"What?"

"For your postpartum. Do you blame your baby?"

It's a bombshell, one that I don't even know where to begin to unpack. A part of me suspects that that's the point—to get my rawest, most honest reaction—but I still find myself getting angry. "Of course not! I could never... Oh."

"That's right. '*Oh.*'"

Damn. She wasn't lying about being good, was she? "So, um. Postpartum. That's what I have?"

"I think it played a part—but honestly? I don't think it's the heart of it."

"How could it not be?" I ask. "I was fine before, and now, I..."

But were *you?* asks the little voice inside me. *Were you fine?*

Dr. Knox seems to be thinking the same. "Let's go a different way," she suggests. "Let's focus on last night for now."

That's when I realize something else. "People with postpartum, they hurt their babies, don't they? Or at least try to? So am I...?"

Am I a danger to my daughter?

For a second, Dr. Knox seems to be deep in thought. Then, without preambles, she asks, "When you climbed over that railing, did you take your baby with you?"

"No!" I yelp. "I—I'd never—" I stop dead in my tracks. "Never" doesn't apply here. After all, didn't I do something I thought I'd never do just last night? However hurtful, the question is fair. "No," I settle on, quieter. "No, I didn't."

"Did you think about taking your baby with you?"

I shake my head again. "No. I wasn't thinking of her at all. Not like that, at least. Just that... she'd be better off without me."

She gives me a warm, understanding smile. "Then you're not a danger to your baby."

I let out a breath I didn't know I'd been holding. "I'm not?"

"You're not."

"But then… how can I have postpartum?"

"Well, let's see." She starts flipping through her notes. "You said you felt alienated from her. 'Like you couldn't relate to her at all.' Is that correct?"

"… Yes."

"That's textbook postpartum depression for you."

"But why didn't I have it before?" I ask. "The first couple of months, I—I was fine."

Again, that voice: *Were you, though?*

This time, Dr. Knox takes a little longer to answer. "Sometimes, when we're in fast-paced situations, our mind takes a backseat. Instinct takes over. The more stressed we are, the more it holds us up, like a sort of survival mode. Think of a marionette on strings. Back at the motel, you didn't really have time to stop, did you?"

"I guess…?"

"Think of it like this: these past few years, what day of the week did you most often get sick?"

I don't even have to think about it. "Saturday. The weekend."

"Right, the weekend. Because that's when you could finally catch a break. So when you came back to the penthouse…"

"I wasn't in survival mode anymore," I fill in, stunned. "That's why it hit now? Because it couldn't hit before?"

"In part, yes," Dr. Knox says. "But I think your postpartum's the least of it. If it had been a severe case, survival mode wouldn't have mattered. You'd have gotten sick, period. Instead, you went through a depressive episode two months after giving birth, with only marginal symptoms of postpartum. They contributed, but they weren't the cause."

"So…?"

"So there was a trigger. And I think you know what that was."

Dominic. The thought bubbles up before I can stop it. That house. Those people.

As if reading my mind, Dr. Knox nods. "That's right. The visit to your father's house. That's when it all really started crashing down, right?"

"But that's got nothing to do with the baby," I protest.

"I agree. Because this isn't about your baby, April—it's about *you.*"

It's like the world has shifted under my feet. Suddenly, I'm knocked off-balance. "Me?"

"Yes. How you feel about yourself." The doctor uncrosses her legs, leaning closer on the table. "I'm going to ask you a question now, April, and I want you to answer honestly. Okay?"

"Okay."

"When did you first start thinking about going away?"

"I…" I mumble out. "You mean suicide?"

"No. I mean disappearing."

I frown. "Like a fantasy?"

"Yes. Exactly like a fantasy."

I force myself to go back in time. To years I'd rather forget. "When I was a kid, I used to imagine it. Just… not being there anymore. It was before Maia took me in."

"And after?"

A stab of guilt pierces me. "Afterwards, sometimes, I'd still feel it. An urge to just… leave. To not be…"

"A burden?"

I nod. "Yeah."

Finally, she snaps her notebook shut. "Here's what I think. You've been holding up against tremendous stress your entire life. You grew up in not one, not two, but *three* avoidant households. Living with your grandmother was your respite, but even that didn't last. Eventually, you were thrown back into it. Honestly, I wish you'd come to me years ago."

I blink back tears. "So it's too late? I'm fucked up now?"

"Not at all! I'm sorry—that didn't come out right. I just meant that you've been needing this for a long, long time."

Therapy. For some reason, it never crossed my mind. I thought the bad times were in the past. I handled that, so of course I could handle whatever else came along—right?

Apparently, wrong. So, so wrong.

"So I'm not a danger to my family?" I croak through unshed tears.

"Goodness, no. If anything, it's your old family that's a danger to you."

The relief almost crushes me. "I'm not a bad mother?"

"In my experience, bad mothers tend to think they're God's gift to their children. Instead, you're questioning yourself. That alone makes you a better mom than most."

It's pointless to try and hold back tears now. The dam's broken. "What now?" I rasp.

"Now, we make an appointment for next week. You're carrying a lot of guilt, April, and we need to work on that. Specifically, on how you see yourself. Because I can guarantee you, it's a hundred times worse than what others see in you."

I give her a wobbly nod. "Okay."

"Okay," she smiles. "Then let's make that appointment."

We figure out a schedule for the next couple of months. "Any homework for next time?" I joke, trying to lighten the mood.

To my surprise, Dr. Knox says yes. "One: keep bonding with your baby. You had a great relationship before all this—try to get it back. If she's as empathetic as you say, it's possible she might have picked up on your distress long before you did, and that's why she's been behaving oddly. Make her understand you're on your way to recovery."

"Okay," I whisper.

"Two: keep an eye on that boyfriend of yours. I understand he's trying to do better, but he's got a history of toxic behaviors. If any of that pops up again, call him out. Okay?"

"I will."

A smile. "Three: focus on positive, constructive activities. You're a designer and a seamstress, right? So go wild. Create for the sake of creating."

That catches me off-guard. "I... Okay. I'll do that."

"Good. Then I'll see you next week. Take care of yourself, April. We can't care for those around us unless we do that first."

After she's gone, it takes me a full ten minutes to process everything that's just happened. I feel drained, but in a strangely good way, like after the gym.

Still, it was a lot.

Once I've got my bearings, I text Matvey that it's okay to come back. No doubt, Grisha's already done it, but it's about more than that.

It's about trust.

Then, while I wait for Matvey to come home, my gaze falls to the covered Daphne dress.

Create. Doctor's orders.

I pull off the drape and get to work.

31

MATVEY

I almost lost her.

That's the thought that keeps pounding in my head. Not "my Bratva's in shambles," or "Ivan is dead." Because the truth is, none of that matters.

Not if I don't have *her*.

It was one hell of a wake-up call. I wish I hadn't needed it. I wish I'd been awake from the start, not so fucking blind. My flaws, my mistakes—they almost cost me everything.

They almost cost me April.

When that doctor told me to get out, I wanted to rip into her. After that night, I'd told myself nothing and no one could ever pry me away from my woman again.

And then April said, *Trust me.*

So I did.

It's the hardest thing I've ever done. Even now, it takes everything out of me and then some.

Trust. It means having no control, and I hate that. All this power, and what's it good for? What's the use if it can't protect the ones closest to me? If it leaves me so fucking *exposed*?

Every day, it takes everything out of me.

But I do it anyway.

Because she asked me to.

"And this is her favorite toy, so if she starts crying—"

"April," Elias's booming voice laughs, "relax. This isn't my first rodeo."

"Sorry," April sighs. "I'm just nervous. I've never really left her with anyone. Even with June or Petra, I was always in the next room, so…"

Elias pats her on the shoulder. If anybody else dared get so familiar, I'd be snapping the offending limb in half. That said, it's a little hard even for me to be jealous of an octogenarian. And besides, Elias isn't just her boss; he's her family.

"Go get your dress," he says in that thick New Orleans accent of his. "I'll keep the young lady occupied."

With an apprehensive nod, April disappears into the bedroom, leaving us alone.

Awkward silence reigns. For the first time, I find myself wishing May would throw a tantrum just to give me something to do. But whatever advice that therapist has been giving April, it's been working: the baby is significantly less nervous now.

Elias starts humming a tune under his breath. May giggles at the unexpected music. Even the cat seems somewhat relaxed around the old man.

I clear my throat. "You said this isn't your first rodeo. I assume that means you've had experience?"

"Mhmm. Three nephews and seven nieces."

"You have siblings, then?"

"Five. I was the eldest. Helped rear the whole bunch of 'em."

Five siblings. I can't even picture that. "April never mentioned it."

"Oh, don't hold it against her. They're all away now. I barely mention them myself. Canada, Sweden—all those cold places with much warmer policies."

"So you're alone." I cringe at myself. That didn't come out like I wanted.

But Elias doesn't seem offended. His eyes crinkle at the corners, the faint hint of a smile on his thin, cracked lips. "I have a very good apprentice."

It makes me uncomfortable—the warmth he says it with. Like he considers April a part of his family, too, just as she considers him a part of hers.

"That's why you suggested the contest?" I say, if only to change the subject.

"Well, yes. And because I believe she's made for bigger things than a quaint little tailor's shop."

"I don't get it." I blurt the words out without even thinking.

The old man's face doesn't change. "You don't think she can win?"

"I know she can win. What I don't understand is why she needs to."

"My boy! Surely you know the Mallard isn't cheap?"

"I'm not cheap, either. If she'd asked, I would've taken care of it."

"Ah, but it's not that simple, is it?" he tuts.

I frown. "Of course it is."

"For you, perhaps. But for April?" He shakes his head, but the smile stays on—fond and proud and just a little bit sad. "She's had to fight tooth and nail all her life. That's the only way she knows how to get things."

"But I'm here now," I counter.

"Yes, but for how long?"

The blow comes out of nowhere. What's worse, the old man still isn't showing a trace of ill intent towards me. Just a hint of a smile on his lips—and the truth. As sweet or bitter as it may be.

Once, I would've gotten angry. I would've raged and been outraged at the implication.

Now, I read between the lines.

"You think that's April's concern? That I won't stay?"

"I think no one's ever done that for her," he replies diplomatically. "And that, when you're used to everybody leaving, you stop considering the alternative. It's too painful to start hoping."

A stab of guilt, straight through my chest. "And if I paid for her tuition in full right now—would that show her? That I won't leave?"

He laughs. "My boy, what makes you think she wants you to do that? Anything worth having must be earned. And April's a fighter. So let her fight—and let her *win*."

I don't understand shit about clothes. I don't get fashion, or fabrics, or the fine details of design. But fighting for your place in the world? *Earning* it? That's the one thing I get.

The one thing I'll always respect, no matter what.

"I understand."

"You know something, son? I've no doubt you do."

Then April rushes back in. "Okay, I think I got everything. Remember, there's formula in the cupboard—"

"I think Elias can figure it out," I cut in.

She seems surprised by that. As if expecting I'd fight her more over this. "Right. Sorry. Thanks for doing this. I'm just—"

"Late," Elias chides. "You're late. Didn't you say submissions close at noon? You'd better hurry, or you'll have to go back tomorrow."

One glance at her phone and April's face grows horrified. "Oh my God. We have to go!"

Before following her out, I throw one last look at our daughter in Elias's arms.

A stranger. An interloper.

Try as I might, I can't bring myself to feel like that anymore.

We get there right before the gates close.

I walk in after April, who's now taking the stairs three at a time. Then, once we're finally at the front desk, I watch her deflate like a balloon. "I need, uh... to, uh, turn in..."

"Her piece for the contest," I fill in. "Here's the paperwork."

The woman at the desk blinks. If she finds the scene strange, however, she wisely keeps it to herself. "Sure, Ms....?"

"Flowers," April wheezes.

"Flowers-Le Blanc?" the clerk asks.

"No, just—wait, what?"

"Oh!" says the clerk. "Sorry, my mistake. I thought you might be related to—"

"No mistake," a girl's voice giggles from behind us. "She is, though it's hard to tell."

At the sound, April freezes.

"Now, now," another voice drawls, deeper and thicker with poison. "Don't be rude to your sister, Anne. Sorry—*half*-sister."

I don't even have to turn to know who it is, but I do anyway. I want to look them in the eye: the witches who almost pushed my woman over the edge of reason. Who tried to buy my child.

If looks could kill, there would be nothing of them left to bury.

"Nora," April greets tightly. "Anne."

They don't acknowledge me. Most likely, they think I'm some kind of driver. Last time they met, April used my name to threaten them—there's no way they'd be this casual if they'd realized who I was.

I don't let them in on it. Not yet.

"What a wonderful coincidence," Nora croons. "I trust you've been well? You left so abruptly last time."

"We didn't even get to say goodbye to little May," Anne pouts. "Speaking of, where is she?"

Somewhere you'll never get your dirty paws on her. My fists go tight at my sides, but I force myself to keep them there.

"Home," April replies flatly, more tactful than I could ever be.

"Alone?!" Anne gasps with the fakest concern I've ever heard.

"Of course not," snaps April. "She's well-cared for."

"No need to be so defensive," Nora purrs. "Dear Anne was simply worried. It's only fair, given... Well, no need to rehash." She puts on a plastic smile, the edges just sharp enough to cut. "We're here on a happy occasion."

Given what? I want to press. *How bad of a mother she has?*

See, this is why I fucking hate catfights. In the Bratva, if you've got something to say, you come out and say it. Maybe it earns you a punch in the face, maybe it earns you a bullet, but you still speak your mind clearly. You take responsibility.

Here, cowardice and backhanded jabs are the law of the land.

"Oh?" April says, pretending not to catch the insult. "And what's that?"

"Anne's entry for the contest, of course!"

I frown. That any of April's sisters should have followed in her footsteps is news to me.

Apparently, it's also news to her. "Anne's… what?"

With a slide of a manicured hand, Nora pushes the entry form across the desk. "Here. Did you get the dress delivery?"

"Of course, ma'am." The clerk smiles. "Right here."

And then she pulls it off the rack.

No fucking way.

Ivory lace. Embroidered leaves. A curving shape that turns bark-like halfway through. In all my life, I've only seen a dress like that once.

On *April's* mannequin.

My gaze turns to April immediately. I watch her face fall, her mouth opening and closing like a goldfish. "That's… that's my dress," she whispers once the clerk disappears in the back.

"What was that, dear?"

"I said that's *my* dress!" she snarls, all fury. "How dare you! How…"

"*Your* dress?" Nora laughs. "Perhaps you should calm down, April. Envy's not a good look on you."

"Is any look good on her?" Anne quips.

Fucking vipers. I force myself to breathe through my nose, count down from ten, though all that Zen shit that never helped anyone who was truly mad.

And by God, I am. Right now, it's taking all of my willpower to keep my fists where they are, let alone keep silent.

But I have to.

April's a fighter, Elias said. *So let her fight.*

"Envy?" she balks. Then, as if a lightbulb just went off, she turns to Anne. "My sketches. Back at the house, you saw my sketches."

"This should be good." Anne smirks viciously.

"You took pictures of them, didn't you?"

"Really? Did I also fake the moon landing, sister?"

"You...!" She grits her teeth. "How can you shamelessly cheat like this?"

"Oh, please. Don't be such a sore loser," Nora scolds. "So what if it looks like yours? People have similar ideas all the time."

Similar, my ass. It's a carbon fucking copy.

"Besides, it's the execution that counts, yes?" the wicked stepmother adds. "And I don't know about you, but I spare no expenses for my daughter. Right, dear?"

"We hired the best tailors," Anne grins. "A whole *équipe.* I think they did my design justice, don't you?"

"*My* design," April retorts. "At least when it's just us, you could have the guts to be honest. You didn't sketch out that dress—*I* did."

Something shifts on Anne's face then, soft features turning sharp and cunning. "Maybe. But I still turned it in first."

The clerk comes back. Nora makes a beeline for her, asking who the fuck knows what, and Anne doesn't waste any time going back to hiding behind her mother's skirts.

As soon as they're out of reach, I whisper to April, "Is that allowed? Making others do the dress for you?"

Reluctantly, she nods. "It's a design contest, not a tailoring one. Most entries here haven't been sewn by their designers."

"I see."

Then I take a step towards the counter.

"Wait!" April stops me. "Where are you going?"

"To tell the clerk," I answer. "She stole your piece. She deserves to be disqualified."

April shakes her head. "As much as I hate to admit it, she's right. She turned it in first."

"All done." Anne glides back towards us, Nora in tow. "What's wrong, April? Aren't you going to turn in your dress?"

That's it. I take an aggressive step forward, all good resolutions forgotten. There's only one urge in my veins now: to make these goddamn snakes *pay.*

Anne's demeanor changes instantly. She draws back, an instinctive fear telling her to get the fuck away from me. It's the first good idea she's had today.

"You little—" I start.

But April's hand settles firmly on my back. "No," she says. "It's not worth it. Let's go."

It takes everything in me to swallow back my rage— *everything.*

But I do.

Because I trust her.

~

In the car, a thousand worries crowd my mind. Last time she had to deal with these people, she ended up dangling over a railing. What's this going to do to her? After all the work she's put in to get back into a good place—for our daughter, for us...

"April, let me fix this."

She smiles at me. A warm, genuine smile. "Thanks," she says. "But this is my fight. Trust me."

So I do. Even if it's the hardest thing in the world, I do it for her.

Because I promised.

At the penthouse, I'm fully expecting April to make an emergency call to Dr. Knox. Instead, I watch her hug Elias, offer her thanks, tell him she'll call.

Then I watch her grab her sketchbook. "What are you doing?"

She looks up then: fierce, fired up, a fighter 'til the death. "I'm making another fucking dress."

Beautiful.

"Tell me how I can help," I say at once.

April's eyes light up. "Okay. I'm gonna need two things."

"Name them."

"One: if you could watch May for—"

"Done. Two?"

Her lips curve into a grin. "Two: I need to borrow your wife."

32

APRIL

Forty-eight hours. That's how long I have to come up with a new dress. No, not just "come up with": sketch, sew, and submit a new dress.

For the Daphne gown, it took weeks.

Now, I have two days.

"Unbelievable," Petra mutters under her breath, pacing up and down the room like an angry lioness. "Un-fucking-believable. The nerve of those *suki*. And you didn't shoot them?"

"I was asked not to," Matvey replies laconically.

"Well, I wasn't. Where do they live?"

"Guys," I call over, "I appreciate the sentiment, I really do. But can we think about this dress first?"

"Sorry," Petra sighs. "It's just so unfair. I saw how hard you worked on that other dress. Can you really make something else so soon?"

And if that isn't the million-dollar question… "I don't know. But I have to."

Matvey gives a grunt of approval. In his lap, May coos in what could be encouragement or a polite request for food. On the floor, Buttons chases a stolen ball of yarn.

I grab my fabrics off the floor and sigh. Petra isn't wrong. Make a high-concept piece in two days? Not even dear old Vivienne could have swung that. And I'm no Westwood girl. More than that, I'm a *working* girl. One who's been pushing off deadlines to this specific weekend.

"Goddammit," I curse.

I take another look at my sketches. There's lots of decent ideas there, but "decent" doesn't win contests. There's this one mermaid-inspired concept that I really like, but it would also involve hand-gluing about a trillion mother of pearl scales, something I have neither the budget nor the time nor the finger dexterity for.

Time and money. God, why does it all have to boil down to that?

Negative spiral. I shake my head and force myself to snap out of it. Dr. Knox has been very clear with me: when I get trapped in my own thoughts, I need to anchor myself to the present. The here and now, in the world outside my mind.

It doesn't come easy, but it comes easier than most days today. And honestly? I think I know why.

Because I'm *pissed.*

Anne stole my work. Nora helped her. They stole my future once, but they couldn't be happy with that. They had to do it again.

But I'll be damned if I let them.

I'm not seventeen anymore. I'm not a scared little girl with nowhere to go and no one to help. I'm a grown woman now. I'm a *mom.*

And I have a family.

If there's a silver lining to this entire situation, it's how good Matvey's been to me. He's been handling it so well. Letting Elias watch our daughter, keeping his cool in front of my wicked stepmother and stepsister, letting me fight my own battles. *Listening* to me. Trusting me.

With this Matvey by my side, I feel like I can take on the world.

Speaking of... "Any thoughts from the peanut gallery?" I ask hopefully.

...

...

...

Crickets.

"Come on!" I pout. "We're brainstorming. There's no such thing as a bad idea here."

I can practically feel Matvey's skepticism fill the air. "You want us to give you advice?"

"Why not? You both dress snazzy."

Matvey's eyebrow rises. "'Snazzy,'" he echoes.

"Yeah. You know, fancy. Sharp."

I detect a hint of amusement on his lips. "Well, in case it slipped your mind, I'll remind you I have tailors for that."

How could I ever forget? I give a discreet cough and quickly change the subject. "Petra, save me. I know you have a fashion sense somewhere."

"Sure." She shrugs. "How about steel?"

"See? That's exactly—sorry, what?"

"I don't know. It's durable. Interesting. It's—What are you laughing at?"

Behind us, Matvey gives an equally discreet cough. "Nothing. Why not chainmail?"

"Ha-ha. Very funny."

"With a nice helm to match. Thin eye slot so it can prevent arrows and spears from penetrating."

"Still think there's no such thing as bad ideas?" Petra deadpans.

"To be fair, chainmail dresses aren't that uncommon," I point out. "Some brides even wear them to their weddings. It's all about personality."

"Huh," she remarks. "Can't really see that. Much too restrictive. If you're attacked, you're gonna want to move fast."

"No sane person is expecting to be attacked at their wedding, Petra."

"Speak for yourself. *I* had a bulletproof vest underneath." She lets out a long, weary sigh. "It's really a pity. Your Daphne dress—now, *that* I could see as a wedding gown."

"I guess…" I frown. "I didn't really consider that. But it kind of works, doesn't it? It's full-ivory with a trumpet shape, and the corset's decorations are elaborate enough, so it wouldn't really look out of pl…" I trail off.

Petra looks at me funny. "April?"

"… place…"

"Matvey, I think your girlfriend's having a stroke."

Suddenly, I bolt upright. "That's it," I whisper to myself. "That's *it.*"

I make my way to my work closet and start yanking out pieces. Commissioned ones, half-finished ones, and among them…

There.

"I can't make something else from scratch. But maybe…"

Then I pick up the phone.

"April?" Petra rounds up on me. "Are you going to let us in on—"

"Hush."

From the other side of the room, I catch Matvey mouthing, "Let her work."

Again, I'm moved by it: Matvey's faith in me. His willingness to trust me, despite and because of all we went through. Together and apart.

"Hello?"

"Ms. Pierce?" I pipe up. "This is April, from Third Chance. I was hoping we could talk about your dress."

It's a long shot. If it goes wrong, I'll be sacked on the spot. Not even Elias could make excuses for me stealing a dress from a client.

Especially not a wedding dress.

"Another model?" she murmurs. "I don't know, April. I really liked what we settled on. Besides, I'm kind of on a budget, so I can't really splurge on a more expensive type…"

"I know, I know. I promise this won't affect the price. I just ask that you take a look."

"But…"

"Please, Ms. Pierce," I plead. "I'm sending you the picture right now. If you don't like it, you can pretend this conversation never happened. But I think this piece might be the answer."

It's not a lie: Ms. Pierce was looking for exactly this kind of model before the issue of budget came into play.

I wait on the phone, tense as a violin. With every second that ticks by, my anxiety grows. God, this was so unprofessional of me. What was I thinking? I need to apologize. Right now, before the client slams the phone in my face. "Actually, I'm so sorr—"

"I can… really have that?"

I blink. "What?"

"The dress. Can I really have that for the same price? It looks… I mean… Wow."

I can't believe my ears. "I—Yes. Yes, absolutely. And it's already in your size, so we would only have to make minor adjustments…"

The rest of the conversation flows easily. I can't get over how excited Ms. Pierce is about this dress. A dress that *I* made.

Whatever bitterness Anne's stunt had left in my mouth, it turns instantly sweet. By the time we get off the phone, my anxiety has melted. All I can feel is excitement.

"I take it you know what you're gonna do?" Matvey asks in my ear, coming up behind me.

I smile. For the first time since this whole thing began, I give a big, genuine smile. "Yeah. I do."

Then I unveil the dress.

Petra's eyes widen. "That's…"

Huge. Princess-y. A pure white bonbon. "My piece."

It's only half-done, but that's okay. For once, this is a good thing. I'm not going to make a princess dress anyway.

I'm going to make something *new*.

"Wanna put this on?"

Petra looks horrified. "Do I have a choice?"

I grin. "Not really."

Then I rip the skirt in half.

33

MATVEY

After the balcony incident, I've been wary of leaving April alone. I came so close to losing her—I don't even want to think about what it would be like to come home and find it empty a second time. Just me, May, and an endless void to fill.

And a cat that can't stand the sight of me, but that's a different story.

So when Vlad demanded another round of drinks with his son-in-law, I almost declined. I almost made up some work-related emergency—my legit business, because otherwise he'd know I was lying—and shut myself back in the penthouse, away from the chaos my Bratva has been lately.

But then April started working again.

This past day and a half, it's like someone lit a fire under her. Her wicked stepbitches have no idea what's going to hit them. For once, they actually did something useful with their lives, even if their intentions were far less than noble.

Of course, if April loses, I'll pay them a midnight visit to balance the scales.

The point is, I can't picture that happening. Not with how hard she's been working. And her eyes—it's like there's life again in there. Like there's *light* again in there.

That's the only reason I accepted Vlad's invite. Well, that and the fact that Petra's staying with her, even if she's currently mummified in a thousand layers of chiffon.

"You got this?" I ask Grisha before leaving.

My third looks at me with pleading eyes. In his arms, May starts pulling on his beard. "I believe I've got this," he says uncertainly.

Who would've thought? So Grisha's got a gap in his resume after all.

I clap him on the shoulder and make my way out to the car. Tonight, it's Yuri who drives me.

"How have things been at work?" I ask as we take off.

"Tense," he admits. "But no one's thinking of rebelling anymore. After Ivan…"

We let it hang in the air. Ivan's been the last in a long, painful streak of betrayals this year. Tonight, I'll ascertain if it's really over.

A scantily clad hostess leads us to our table. Since Vlad was the one who picked the place, it's only to be expected that it reflects his standards of class rather than mine.

When he sees me arrive, Vlad stumbles upright. "Son!"

I glance at the half-empty bottle of vodka on the table. "I see you started without me."

"Nonsense. We'll get more."

That's exactly what I'm worried about. "I hope you don't mind if my brother joins us."

"Of course not!" Vlad bellows. "But he'll have to loosen up, too."

"Sorry?" Yuri balks.

"Come on, you bastard, drink something!" Vlad drags him down to sit. "You aren't pregnant, too, are you, boy?"

"He's driving," I cut in. "No drinks for him."

Yuri shoots me a grateful look. By contrast, Vlad scrunches up his nose. "Kids these days. Back in my day, you didn't leave the house without a nice bottle of vodka to warm you up."

"Yeah, 'cause you had to sleep in the trenches," Yuri mumbles under his breath.

"What was that, son?"

"Nothing."

I bite my cheek. "Get to the point, Vlad. I know you didn't ask me here for the pleasure of my company."

"So paranoid," the old man sighs. "Always so paranoid. Very well."

He motions for us to sit. I take my place in front of him; Yuri remains standing at my side. I can practically feel his dislike for Vlad oozing out of him. My brother has many fine qualities, but subtlety isn't one of them.

Not that it matters. I'm the one who married his daughter. As far as Vlad knows, that's my baby in her belly.

Which means I'm the one who has to endure him.

"The *vory*, son... they're concerned."

"Oh?"

Vlad steeples his wrinkled fingers. "Yes. I'm afraid that nasty business with Ivan has left you looking a bit tyrant-like."

"I didn't realize I was running a group of Girl Scouts."

"My boy, you really should take this more seriously."

"And you should really stop calling me that."

He raises his hands in surrender. "Fine, *Matvey*. But my point stands. The *vory* are afraid of you."

"Good. That's the way it's supposed to be."

"If they respect you, yes. But even that's starting to falter."

"And I assume you have some pearls of wisdom on that front?"

Vlad smirks, oblivious to my sarcasm. "Of course I do. Anything for my dear daughter's husband."

I clench my fists under the table. "Let's hear it, then."

The old man downs another shot of vodka. His face is a ridiculous shade of red, but under the pink neon lights, I can't tell if he's really that drunk. For a while now, I've been wondering if Vladimir Solovyov is truly the fool he wants me to think he is.

He clears his throat before I can fully decide. "What you did to bring the Groza Bratva back from the grave—that was admirable. It earned you a reputation. But it also means you're lacking a type of security all other Bratvas have."

Oh, this should be good. "And that would be…?"

"A bloodline."

I frown. "My grandfather—"

"Is dead. Has been for many decades now. And your heir is still unborn."

Behind me, Yuri growls, "How dare you—"

I hold my hand up. "It's fine. Let him speak."

He backs off in surprise. Vlad takes the opportunity to pick up where he left off. "You don't have a bloodline behind you, Matvey. That's your weakness. All Bratvas are built upon one thing: history. Family. That's where leaders get their legitimacy. And you, Matvey—you have more skill than any *pakhan* out there. But you don't have a father to back you, and that hurts your position."

"Are you suggesting I make peace with Carmine?" The mere idea is enough to make me sick. With every second that goes by, it gets harder and harder to hold back my anger.

Vlad must sense that, because he hurries to clarify. "No, no. I wouldn't dare presume."

"Good. Then—"

"… but you could still do something else."

I scoff. "Let's hear it, then. Should I raise my grandfather from the grave?"

"No. You should appoint me."

For a second, I'm sure I must have misheard. "Say that again."

"Make me your *brigadir*," Vlad insists. "Do that and I'll keep your ranks in order. My men and yours."

"Last I checked, they were all *my* men."

"Then you should check again, because their loyalty is wavering."

I can't believe what I'm hearing. This is ludicrous. It's so absurd, I almost want to laugh. "What about your beloved bloodline? In case you haven't noticed, you still aren't my father."

"I'm your father-in-law. That's as close as it gets."

"And if I refuse?"

Something crosses Vlad's eyes then. Something frosty and sharp. "Then that's your prerogative," he says coldly. "But your men will keep scattering. And it won't be long before someone runs their mouth again and blows up another D.C. deal."

I freeze. "What?"

"It's about credibility," Vlad keeps prattling on. "And frankly, you've already screwed the pooch too many times, both figuratively and literally. Like that girl you keep—"

"That's enough." I rise from my seat.

Vlad scrunches up his face. "You can't go on pretending, man! You're married, but you're living with another woman and child. I'm not saying you can't have bastards, but most men have the sense to keep them far away from—"

"Vlad. Stop talking."

"Because you can't handle the truth?"

"Because if you say one more word, I'm gonna have to blow your brains out."

Vlad stiffens. Neon lights or not, I can see the color drain from his face plain as day. "Very well. I'll stop."

"Thank you for your advice, as always. Yuri, let's go."

I'm halfway down the hallway when I hear Vlad's voice calling after me. "So you'll consider it? My proposal?"

I bark out a laugh. "Go to bed, Vlad. You've had too much to drink."

Then I head out into the night.

As soon as we're out of earshot, I pull Yuri close. "Did you hear that?"

"Hear what?"

"He knows about the D.C. deal. That someone from the inside blew it."

Yuri blinks. "That's…"

"Something he shouldn't have known," I snarl. "Take the car. Tail him. I want to know if there's more."

"More what?"

"More moles."

My brother looks shocked. "You can't seriously be thinking about accusing Vlad. You'll lose the Solovyov support."

"I'm not going to accuse him. His slip might mean nothing."

It's true. Vlad's got a big mouth; he could've easily heard something and parroted it back to me. Or…

He could've been in league with Ivan.

Either way, I can't be taking chances. Not now. Not when I

have so much to protect. If I'm going to oust Vlad, I'm gonna need ironclad proof.

"Then isn't it better to let it go?" Yuri pleads. "If he finds out—"

"He won't find out," I interrupt. "I trust you."

Yuri's objections die on his tongue. "Motya..."

"I'll hail a cab. Keep me posted."

He gives me a short nod. "Yes, *pakhan.*"

Then he's off into the night.

By the time I make it home, it's already dark. But when I open the door, I find the lights on. "April...?"

Then I step into the living room.

It's a familiar scene: fabric lies scattered everywhere, like a bomb has gone off at Louis Vuitton. Shaking my head, I search for April amidst the chaos.

A bunch of tulle shifts. From underneath it, a human figure pops up. "Oh! You're back!"

Shaking my head, I pluck a piece of lace from her hair. "Where's Petra?"

"She went home. She said, and I quote, 'I'd rather die than see another ribbon.'"

"Sounds about right. Grisha?"

"In the guest room with the baby. Don't worry—he's watching me, too." She points to a nanny cam in the corner.

"I think May fell asleep on his lap, though. He probably can't get up. Or call for help."

"He's faced worse."

"Wanna go relieve him of his duties?" April grins. "I have a surprise, but I need to set it up."

"Oh?" I lean in close. "And am I going to like this surprise?"

She puts on a mysterious air. "We'll see."

I smirk and head to the guest bedroom. "You dead yet, old man?"

"Nearly." Grisha's voice is a terrified whisper.

"C'mon, I'll take her."

My third is all too happy to dump the hot potato back into my hands. "All yours, boss."

May stirs, but only for a moment. The second I put her down in her crib, she snuggles against her fluffy feline bodyguard and quickly goes back to snoozing.

"I didn't know she did that," Grisha comments, dejected.

"She's a baby, not a bomb. You're allowed to put her down."

"I'll make a note for next time. How did it go with Vlad?"

"Strange. I'll update you tomorrow. Go get some sleep."

To be fair, Grisha does look like a truck ran him over twice, but that's not the reason I'm dismissing him early. That wicked glint in April's eyes, her mischievous smile—I wanted to take her then and there. If he doesn't get lost in the next five seconds, I won't care that he's in the room at all.

Luckily, he seems too tired to argue. "Alright. Goodnight, boss."

When he leaves the room, I stay behind. I take a moment to watch my baby, sleeping peacefully in her crib.

Your heir is still unborn. Like fuck she is. I don't care what Vlad says—my bloodline is right here.

Just then, April peeks her head in the room. "All done. You can come look now."

I follow her out into the living room. She goes to stand next to her mannequin, covered by a long white sheet. She's wearing the biggest grin I've ever seen. "Ready? One, two… *three!*"

WHOOSH.

It takes me a second to understand what I'm looking at. There's a dress there, certainly, but there's also… more.

Guns, for one thing.

The mannequin's pose is nothing like I've seen in any shop's window: elbows bent, center of gravity low, one Kalashnikov in either hand. Like a bride ready to turn her wedding into a bloodbath.

"Are those real?" I ask.

"I don't think so? Petra lent them to me."

Definitely real, then. "Hm."

I walk around the piece, taking in the details. That pure white bonbon dress I saw two days ago has been transformed completely, ripped in a million different places. Around the waist, a sturdy black bodice. "This is…"

"Kevlar," April confirms. "Or rather, my take on that."

"Your take?"

"Yes! I've been thinking about this for a while now, actually. Since you…" She gestures awkwardly at her shoulder.

"Since I got shot?" I fill in.

"That, yes. Back then, your shirt was ruined, but your jacket could still be salvaged, yeah?" She starts walking around excitedly, her mile-a-minute mind struggling to get the words out all at once. "So I've been wondering: what if you'd been wearing a different jacket? One that was light, stylish, but bulletproof? Because vests don't really cover your shoulders, and anyway you're not always gonna be wearing one, but you know what you *are* gonna be wearing no matter what?"

"A suit jacket?" I guess.

She snaps her fingers. "Bingo. A suit jacket. So this vest is kind of like… an experiment? I was thinking, if you like it, I could try to do more with it. Like, make an actual suit. What do you think?"

I think you're amazing. I think you're beautiful, and smart like a whip, and way too fucking pure for me.

I think I… "Matvey, stop that!"

No can do. I already scooped her up.

I twirl her around and she laughs, over and over. I could listen to that forever—the sound of April laughing.

"I think," I finally answer, "that you've outdone yourself."

"Why, thank you. Can you put me down now?"

I bring my lips close to hers. "Not a fucking chance."

34

APRIL

When I go back to the front desk this time, it's with Petra in tow. Partly because Matvey couldn't come, and partly because the fake guns are really heavy and I needed the extra pair of hands.

"They *are* fake, right?" I whisper while we wait for the clerk.

"The leather straps? Of course. No cows were harmed."

"Actually, I meant—"

"Here we are!" the clerk smiles cheerfully. "Please fill these forms. I'll carry your dress to the back."

"I'll help," Petra says.

"Thank you, but there's no need—oh, wow, that's bulky. Haha. Wait, these aren't guns, are they?"

"Props," we assure her in unison.

I dot my *i*'s and cross my *t*'s on the application form. At this point in the race, I don't want anything to go wrong. Well, anything *else.*

I force myself not to think of the Daphne dress. What's done is done.

When I hand the form back to the clerk, she grins. "'The Bulletproof Bride.' Sounds like a winning piece."

I smile back. "Let's hope so."

Then I head to the Mallard lounge.

I sit down with Petra in one of the booths, feeling jittery all over. "You know, maybe coffee isn't the best—"

"I agree," she says. Then she turns to the waiter. "One coffee and a shot of tequila."

"*Petra!*"

"What? You can drink now."

"It's not even three in the afternoon!"

She waves me off. "It's night somewhere. Besides, you need to calm down or your heart's gonna burst. I'm not looking forward to explaining *that* to your boyfriend."

"Why is he only 'my boyfriend' when he's dangerous?" I mutter.

"'Cause I need him for the cameras when he's not. Sorry, *koshka.*"

"It's no trouble," I lie. The truth is, however fake their marriage is, a part of me still smarts at the thought. But it's necessary, and I'm not in the business of rekindling past strife. Water off a duck's back and all that. "Speaking of boyfriends, how's it going with yours?"

She sighs. "I have no idea."

"That's a weird response." I frown. "Is everything okay?"

"Kind of? I just…" Petra slumps in her seat. "I don't know. I feel like he's been distant lately."

"Distant as in, 'I'm just gonna go out and get some milk'?"

"I don't know, maybe?"

Our orders arrive. Petra starts sipping her coffee. I eye my tequila shot with suspicion. "C'mon, Petra. This is *Yuri* we're talking about! He's not gonna ghost you guys."

"It's just—he used to be so easy to talk to," she explains weakly. "And I don't talk to people. Like, ever."

"Y'know, I gathered that."

"But now, I can't even tell what's going through his head! It's like he's somewhere else, all the time. Like he's been… keeping something from me."

My frown deepens. This doesn't sound like the Yuri I know. Sure, he's been a little gloomier lately, but he and Matvey have also been fighting pretty hard.

A stab of guilt pierces me at the memory. They have been fighting alright—and I was the reason for it. "Want me to put out some feelers?" I offer. "If something's going on, Matvey might know."

"You'd do that?"

It's my fault to begin with. "Of course. But I make no promises."

For the first time since this conversation began, Petra smiles. It's small, but genuine. A rare sight to see. "That's already more than enough."

Her gratitude is making me uncomfortable. I've been trying to work on this with Dr. Knox—she says I have trouble accepting good things, that I'm only comfortable with giving —but it's an uphill battle. Especially when I'm being thanked undeservedly.

"And who knows!" I say, eager to lighten the mood. "Maybe he's just working up a proposal. You know, for when circumstances allow it."

Petra laughs. "Yeah, right."

"Better have a dress ready," I tease.

"It's funny. Of all the wedding dresses I've tried on in this past year, you know which one's convinced me the most?"

"Which one?"

"Yours."

It takes me a moment to figure out what she's talking about. "Oh! The Bulletproof Bride?" I give a nervous laugh. "To be fair, you were kind of my muse for that."

"Really? I'm not sure whether I should be flattered or offended."

I put on my best puppy eyes. "I'll lend it to you for free?"

"Fine," she huffs. "But I have one condition."

"Which one?"

She points at my tequila. "Chug."

～

"'One shot,' huh?"

I hide my face in Matvey's chest. I should've known it would end up like this. Tipsy April has absolutely no filters—and no shame.

Which is how I ended up jumping him the second I stumbled through the door. "Maybe it was two," I mumble against his skin.

"Mhmm."

"I'm serious!"

"I'm sure you are."

I roll on my side and pout. Unfortunately, I'm wrapped in blankets and nothing else, so it doesn't come across as particularly convincing. "Ask your wife. She'll tell you."

"She already told me. Texted me to give you plenty of water."

"Great. Now, I'm a houseplant."

Matvey pushes me on my back, rolling over on top of me. "You're mine," he rasps with that low voice of his, the one that never fails to send chills down my spine. "And I'd rather not talk about my wife when I have you like this."

I feel my body respond like it's the first time. I can't help it: whenever Matvey's this close, I turn sinfully greedy. "Yeah?"

"Yeah."

I bare my neck to his kisses. It's slow, deep—like being eaten whole one bite at a time. But before I can surrender completely, I remember. "Oh! I have to ask you something."

Matvey groans. "Right now?"

Yes. Otherwise, you'll make me forget. "I promise I'll be quick."

"Fine. Ask away."

"Did Yuri seem weird to you lately?"

He blinks, caught off-guard. "Where's this coming from?"

I bite my lip. I'm sure how much I'm allowed to say. Eventually, though, I cave. "Petra. I asked her how it was going with Yuri, and she mentioned he felt... distant. Like he's keeping something from her. Do you have any idea if there's anything going on?"

Matvey rolls off me, face suddenly conflicted. He seems to be struggling with himself—torn between speaking and keeping everything to himself.

But in the end, he caves, too. "You can't tell Petra what I'm about to tell you."

"Okay."

"It's about Vlad. I put Yuri on his tail. We think he might be working with the enemy."

I frown. "'Vlad'... That's her father?"

"Indeed. The devil himself."

I let it sink in. Petra's dad might be a mole, and Yuri's been tasked with finding out the truth. No wonder things might have turned awkward between them. I can only imagine what it must be like, not being able to tell the one you love the truth. Being forced to smile and nod, all the while knowing you have to work against them. Against their family.

"That's awful."

"It's less than ideal. Hopefully, there's nothing there."

I wrap my arms back around Matvey. "I'm glad you told me," I whisper.

A beat goes by. Two. "Of course," Matvey rasps. "No more secrets."

No more secrets.

"Which reminds me."

I tilt my head up. "Of what?"

Unexpectedly, Matvey smirks. "I have a job for you."

35

APRIL

The job, it turns out, is for the Groza Bratva.

I follow Matvey through the winding twists of the HQ's basement level. It feels weird to be here—like I'm snooping around somewhere I shouldn't.

At the same time, I've been invited here. Matvey invited me here. That alone fills my chest with warmth.

No more secrets, huh? I could get used to that. Being a part of Matvey's life—*all* of Matvey's life. Including the dark side.

Now, the only mystery left is what the heck I'm doing here.

When he opens the last door, I half-expect to be greeted by armed guards and crates of weapons, maybe piles of suspicious white bags in the corners... but there's none of that. Hell, there isn't even a speck of dust on the floor. Nothing like the spooky backroom I'd been expecting.

Instead, there's machinery. Lots of it.

Oh, and people.

"Mr. Groza!" A woman in a lab coat strides up to us, eyes brimming with excitement. "So glad you could make it."

Matvey shakes her hand. "And you. I've heard good things about your work, Professor Simmons."

"I'm flattered. And this must be Dr. Flowers!"

For a second, I jump. Is my father here? Why didn't anyone warn me?

And then I realize, *Oh. She's looking at* me. "Um, I'm actually not—"

But she's already shaking my hand. "It's an honor to meet you! When Mr. Groza talked to me about your project, I nearly lost my mind."

"In a good way, I hope?" I smile nervously.

"More than good. I've been begging the military for years to let me work on a project like this, but they wouldn't have it. I'm thrilled someone's finally thinking ahead."

"A project like…?"

"Nanofibers." She grins. "Truly, your vision is amazing. I can't wait to start."

I admit, my head's starting to spin. "Thank you. I— Uh, same, really."

"Great! I'll go get the others."

"Th-The others?"

But she's already running off.

"Excited, isn't she?" a new voice pipes up behind me.

I barely hold back a squeak.

"Lionel," Matvey greets. "Glad you could come aboard."

"After that check you offered me? I'd have jumped on the Titanic. This must be the mind behind the grind?"

Matvey nods towards me. "April, this is Dr. Reznikov. Lionel, meet…"

"The next big name in fashion," he fills in with a warm handshake. "Charmed."

I feel like I'm being spun around like a doll. "Um, pleasure's all mine?"

Dr. Reznikov doesn't seem to mind the question mark. "I've taken the liberty to run a few numbers. I hope you don't mind."

"N-Numbers?"

Out of the blue, he produces a tablet. *What the hell…?* "This is a list of materials split by cost, availability, and durability. I think the top five would integrate splendidly with Kevlar, but I didn't want to narrow it down too much, so I kept an open mind for alternative bases. Tincture shouldn't be a problem, but we might want to stick to black for the first few product runs."

"Uh-huh," I mumble as I nod along like a bobblehead.

"Then there's the matter of sizing. Of course, tailor-made is better, but we need to think about mass production as well. I put together a proposal based on large-scale export…"

I keep humming along to Dr. Reznikov's ideas, pretending I absolutely know what he's talking about. "I see. That's… interesting."

"Right? I respect creativity, of course, but a practical enterprise needs a practical mind as well. Don't you agree?"

"Right, we're all here!" Professor Simmons reappears out of nowhere, her smile somehow even brighter than it was before. "Oh, Lionel, won't you go get your team, too? So we can do a proper introduction?"

"Sure! Be right back."

As soon as the opportunity presents itself, I pull discreetly on Matvey's sleeve. "Uh, Matvey? A word?" Then I drag him to a secluded corner of the warehouse.

"What's wrong?" he asks.

"What am I doing here?"

I catch the hint of a smirk on his lips. "Leading, of course."

"Leading…?"

"Everything."

I throw my hands up in defeat. "Okay, look, you got me. I'll buy a consonant, I'll buy a vowel, I'll buy the whole damn alphabet. Now, can you please tell me what's going on?"

He must be satisfied with my begging, because he finally stops teasing. "We're here to make clothes."

"Clothes?" I frown.

"*Your* clothes. The bulletproof suits."

For a second, everything sways. "What?"

"I want you to bulletproof my Bratva. If you're interested, that is."

Suddenly, I'm overcome with the urge to pinch myself. Out of all the proposals a gal might expect, this certainly takes some kind of cake. Though what kind, I'm not sure. "That's… wow."

"Is that a good wow or a bad wow?"

"It's a great wow." Now that the initial shock is fading, I feel a smile slowly spread across my lips. "Seriously, I can't even… Why? How?"

He shrugs. "Your idea was good. I want to invest."

Invest. God, I can't wrap my head around this. The only investment anyone's ever made in me were bets for *Most Likely To Fall Over During Cheerleader Tryouts.* Needless to say, I won those guys some money.

"So Professor Simmons and the 'others'…"

"They're your R&D department," he explains, like it's the most obvious thing in the world. "You'll have full access to the facilities, complete control over the project, and round-the-clock assistance. And of course, you'll be paid."

Okay, now, I *really* have to pinch myself. "P-paid?" I stammer.

Without a word, Matvey hands me a folded piece of paper.

At first, I think I must be reading it wrong. Then I wonder if there isn't a mistake—an extra zero. Or three.

Then I pinch myself, hard.

Breathe, April. Just breathe. "Matvey, this is too much. I can't… If you needed help, you only had to ask. I would've gladly done this all for free."

"That's out of the question."

"But—"

"April." Two strong hands descend on my shoulders. I have no choice but to tilt my chin up and let myself get captured by those ice-blue eyes. "I'm not doing this for you. I'm doing this for my men. It's the right decision."

I force myself to swallow back tears. All my life, no one's valued me, and now…

Now, someone's asking me to do what I love. Someone *needs me* to do what I love, and they want to pay me handsomely for it.

"You don't need to hire me just because we're together, you know. If you want to take my idea and… and ask someone more skilled, I'll understand."

"Is that what you think this is?" Matvey asks, a trace of impatience in his words. "I'm not in the business of mindless nepotism, April. If I was, I'd be dead and buried."

"That's not what I meant!" I hurry to clarify. "It's just… Don't you want the best person for the job?"

"I do. And I've already got them."

This isn't real. This can't be real. "Matvey…"

His hand comes up to my cheek, catching a stray tear rolling down. "You don't have to do this," he says eventually. "You're allowed to say no, April. But I hope you won't. I hope you'll take this job, you'll take the money, and you'll take the opportunity to sign your name on your first line of clothing. I know it's not dresses and gowns, but…"

"No!" I shake my head. "No, it's perfect. I… I just can't…"

I stare at the number in my hands. The ridiculously high number. It's silly to worry about money now, with Matvey backing our family's every need, but it's hard to shake it off— the insecurity.

"It's still too much," I whisper.

"No, it's not. You're worth it."

You're worth it. How long have I waited for someone to say that to me? How many sleepless nights? How many Band-Aids? How many silent tears evaporating on a tulle hum?

"Why me?" I murmur as a last resort.

Matvey's lips twitch upwards. "Why not you?"

"… Okay. I'll do it."

His half-smile spreads into a full grin. "You'll lead the project?"

"I'll lead the project."

"You'll sign the line?"

"I'll sign the line."

"You'll take the money?"

I sigh, exasperated. "I still think it's a ridiculous amount."

"It's not. You should see what we spend on marketing." He shrugs. "Besides, I've already deducted room and board."

I blink. "I can't tell if you're joking."

"I'm not. I'm a businessman."

Unbelievable. I roll my eyes and finally blink back the tears. "Thanks. That actually makes me feel better about taking this."

"So that's a yes?"

I push myself up on my tiptoes. "Yes," I murmur against Matvey's lips. "Yes, Mr. Groza. I'll take your big, fat, shameless check."

I watch his pupils dilate. Black holes, eating away at the ice in his irises. "Good. Because I'm gonna run you ragged, Ms. Flowers."

"Is that so?"

"Mhmm. In fact..." He leads me into a side office and hoists me up on the desk. "I'm gonna start right now."

36

APRIL

Time starts flying. And I mean, like, *flying*. Hurtling towards the horizon at rocket speed, with a big, fat cloud in its wake.

Me? I'm just trying not to get left behind in the dust.

"How about we increase the percentage of Kevlar nanofibers?" Dr. Reznikov asks.

Professor Simmons frowns. "That's going to be tricky. Too much and the clothes won't be flexible enough for movement."

"Flexibility is a must," I stress. "We need to walk the line between 'suit' and 'suit of armor.' Try a wool mix—that should even it out. We'll figure out the spring/summer line later."

"On it," Professor Simmons says.

"I'll run the numbers." Dr. Reznikov grins. "Be on your desk by three, boss."

It takes me a full five minutes to realize he means me. *I'm* the boss.

Which leads to an awkward conversation with my *old* boss. "It just happened so fast," I mumble to Elias, filled with guilt.

Over the phone, he laughs. "Child, please. All I ever wanted was for you to get your big break. You think I'm gonna go sour on you now that it's finally happening?"

"It's just one project," I counter. "It might not lead anywhere. We're on a three-month timeline for a functioning prototype, so maybe afterwards…"

I could come back. The words are on the tip of my tongue, but I swallow them back. After all, can I even make that promise? Can I swear that I'll be back at Third Chance, that everything will go back to the way it used to be?

Part of me wants to. It's the part that spent so many years between those shelves—happy years, sad years. The part that knows nothing else.

But things change. And so much has changed already—me most of all.

"Then afterwards, we'll talk," Elias reassures me, as if he knows exactly what I'm thinking. What's holding me back from committing, one way or the other. "Now, I want you to do one thing and one thing only."

"Of course," I murmur. "Anything."

"Use up the rest of your maternity leave."

"Elias, I can't!" I protest. "This project's well-paid. I can't possibly keep collecting a paycheck when you still need to hire—"

"You can and you will." Elias's voice is amused, but inflexible. "Besides, I've already hired a temp. You can't change my mind, missy."

"But...!"

"No buts. All complaints can be sent to HR."

"You're HR!"

"Then your complaint has been received. Now, go change the world."

I roll my eyes fondly. "I'm just making clothes."

"'I'm just a tailor.' Do you know who said that?"

"I have a feeling you're about to tell me."

I hear laughter on the other end. "Gianni Versace. Goodnight, my dear."

I stay on the phone long after the call has disconnected. *Goodnight.* That word lingers in my head: *Goodnight.* It's just like Elias to pick a parting as kind as that.

One that isn't a goodbye.

So I throw myself back into my work. I pour my blood, sweat, and tears into it. I get to the factory earlier than anyone and stay later than everyone. Often, that means bringing along May and her four newly-appointed bodyguards. None of them holds a candle to Buttons, but then again, not everyone can be a perfect protector *and* a perfect pillow.

And just like that, the weeks fly by.

≈

Another thing that's been skyrocketing: my sex life.

"Look at you," Matvey rasps into my ear. He's above me, behind me, inside me. Everywhere, all at once. "So wet for me."

I whine helplessly into the pillow. I'm stuffed to the brim, Matvey's fingers spelling ruin inside me, his free hand locking both of mine into place at the small of my back. "Please," I beg.

"You want my cock that much?"

"I want it," I moan. "Please, Matvey, please—"

He yanks his fingers out of me. I want to cry at the absence— it's so empty now—when I feel them again at my lips. He pushes them rudely in, stuffing me full on that end, too, stifling my moans better than any pillow could.

I can still taste myself on him. "*Blyat*," he groans. "Such a dirty little vixen."

Then he slides inside me.

No, "slides" isn't the right word—it's too gentle. What Matvey's doing to me is nothing less than savage. His cock pushes roughly between the swollen lips of my pussy, and it's all I can do to bite down on the fingers in my mouth to keep quiet.

God help me—I love it.

When I was pregnant, we never got to do anything like this. We were too busy being careful, sticking to positions that wouldn't turn our Nugget into a Pancake.

But after we unlocked hate sex, the possibilities became endless.

There's no hate in it now, not anymore, but the rough edges remain. It's my fault, really: I was never that good at hiding what I like. With my previous boyfriends, it wasn't an issue—and how could it be? As if their fantasies ever extended beyond the mechanical principle of "Tab A inserts into Slot B."

But Matvey's observant. When he saw how wet being manhandled made me, he took notice.

And call me delusional, but I get the feeling I'm not the only one to be... *affected.*

At least judging by how hard he's throbbing inside me.

"God, don't stop," I pant, freeing his fingers from my teeth.

I immediately feel them in my hair. "Stop calling out for God. He's not here."

"Matvey...!" I keen, delicious pain shooting down my spine from my scalp. His fist goes tight, tight, tighter, pulling my curls in a vise grip I could never hope to escape from. I'm trapped, pinned, hopeless—and it feels so good I could cry. "Don't stop, don't sto—*Ahh*!"

His thrusts are ruthless. He fucks me like I'm a thing, a toy. Something that's purely his to ruin whenever he feels like it. Crap, should I be bringing this up in therapy?

"Shameless *kalina*," Matvey growls against the back of my neck, sending tingles all the way down. "Tell me what else you want me to do to you."

"Touch me," I beg. My clit is ready to burst, throbbing neglected between my legs. "Please, need you to touch me, please—"

But Matvey tuts, disappointed. "My cock not enough for you?"

I shake my head frantically. *That's not it*, I want to say. *I just need you everywhere.*

But the second I open my mouth to speak, his fingers dive back into it, smothering all sound. "Filthy little thing. Now, I'm wondering if you deserve to come at all."

His thrusts slow to a punishing halt. I feel tears prickle at the corners of my eyes, the thought of stopping unbearable. Worse—the thought of Matvey painting my insides white without letting me come even once. I mumble incoherently around his fingers, but he refuses to pull them out.

So I use my hips. I start rolling them slowly, pleadingly. Matvey sucks in a harsh breath, and I take it as a sign.

I pick up the pace, all but fucking myself on his throbbing cock. He's so hard, he could easily hurt me. So big, I still can't believe he fits in me. Every time I move, pleasure sparks everywhere inside me, the hot drag of him almost too much to bear.

If I came like this, he'd never forgive me.

I'll be good, I desperately want to promise. *I'll be good, so please...*

Suddenly, his fingers slip out of my mouth. I feel his big, strong hands seize my hips, forcing them to still. "Fuck, *kalina.* Trying to cheat your way out of punishment?"

"N-No!" I gasp. "Never, I—"

THWACK!

I jolt.

Did he just... spank me?

Heat spreads into the rest of my body from the point of impact. My ass tingles, the imprint of Matvey's hand pulsing red and hungry on my cheek. "Don't lie to me."

File under: kinks I didn't know I had. "Matvey, please."

"I'm tempted to do it, you know," he whispers, sandpaper-rough. "Fuck you raw. Put another baby in your belly."

My vision swims. "Matvey…"

"Bet you'd like that, wouldn't you?" he groans between shallow thrusts. "Being stuffed full of my cum?"

"Yes," I moan, too far gone for lies.

"Over and over again. Until you can't take it anymore."

"Give it to me," I gasp. "Fill me up with your babies, fuck me, *breed me—*"

Whatever embarrassing thing I was going to say next, Matvey doesn't let me. "*Blyat*'," he curses between his teeth, and then he's all over me: hands on my hips, mouth on my neck, cock sinking into my sweet spot with every thrust.

I want to touch myself so badly it hurts, but he doesn't let me. The second he sees my hand move, he pins it to the mattress without mercy, five calloused fingers splaying in the gaps left by mine. "You either come on my cock or not at all," he growls.

"Matvey…!"

"Come now, *kalina*. Let me feel it."

I can't say no.

In the end, I can never say no to him.

Afterwards, I bury my face in his chest. "You're the worst," I sigh.

Matvey's fingers come up to stroke my hair. "Am I now?"

"Yeah. I'm pretty sure that violated the Geneva Convention."

The hint of a smirk. "My mistake. I'll be more boring next time."

"S'okay. I can take it."

He presses a kiss on top of my head. "I know."

It's almost better than the sex—this part right after. Just lying here, spent and boneless, and listening to each other breathe. "Mm."

"How's the project coming along?"

"Good," I mumble. "Like, really good. We tested some nanofibers today."

"Anyone I need to fire?"

I smother my laughter in the crook of Matvey's neck. "No, thank you. We need all the hands we can get. By the way, how's your work going?"

He sighs. "It's not. This mole situation is keeping the plan from moving forward."

Lately, Matvey's been way more forthcoming with me—to the point where he can throw around code words like "the plan" and I'll actually know what he's talking about. Dr. Knox would be pleased as punch.

"I'm sorry," I say sincerely. "I wish I could help."

"Oh, believe me, you're helping."

I smack him lightly on the arm. "Not like that. And stop pinching my ass."

"Why? Still too raw?"

This man will be the death of me. "Quit changing the subject."

"But I like this subject more."

"Matvey."

He rolls his eyes, but there's fondness there, too. "I'm serious. You are helping. Your suits will make all the difference in the battles to come."

Battles. I don't like the sound of that, but I know better than to try and dissuade Matvey from his goals. From day one, he's been supportive of mine—it's only fair I return the favor. Even if it's terrifying to think about.

That's why you have to do your best at work: to protect him. It's the only way he'll let you. "But you still can't move forward."

"No," he exhales. "Not until we find the mole. Which is… problematic."

"Why?"

"The *vory*. They're getting restless again. They want the plan."

"And because of the mole, you can't give it to them."

He nods. "Precisely."

I feel my eyelids growing heavy. I can't help it—Matvey's stamina is impossible to keep up with. I barely know what I'm saying when I slur, half-asleep already, "So give them one."

"What?"

"A plan. Just not... *the* plan..."

Matvey doesn't say anything. I force myself to blink one eye open. When I do, I see his expression looks stuck in place, frozen. Like he's had an epiphany or something.

I try to ask, but sleep pulls me under.

Oh, well. We'll talk more in the morning.

37

MATVEY

My strength was never strategy. It was brute, overpowering force. Taking what I wanted, no matter the obstacles in my way. It's how I built the Groza Bratva back up from scratch, how I dragged it across the ocean and made it grow. Force of will, strength of hand: so far, it's the only strategy I've ever needed.

But now, I'm up against an enemy I can't see.

Now, brute force is no longer enough to get me where I want to go.

So I show up at work, gather the *vory*, and make my announcement. "It's time."

Yuri's eyes look ready to bulge out of their sockets. Grisha's, too, though it's less noticeable with him. His poker face has always been better than my brother's.

Neither of them questions me out loud, but I can hear their thoughts clear as day: *What the hell?*

I didn't warn them. That, too, was on purpose. After all, if I want to lure out the rats, I need my bait to look real—and real fucking juicy.

"This is a blueprint of the building we'll acquire."

I lay it out on the conference room table. Everyone stands up, craning their necks to see. "Why this one?" asks Vlad.

"For its position." I spread another roll-up over the first—a map. "This is the Bonaccorsi headquarters. And this is our building. As you can see, it's a straight jump from one rooftop to the other."

"That's how we invade?" Yuri frowns. "From the rooftop?"

"Yes." I continue my explanation. "There's just one problem— the building isn't a single property. It's been split up vertically between two companies. Technically speaking, we're looking at two completely separate entities."

"So which one do we buy?" Stanislav asks.

I grin. "Both."

Ipatiy clears his throat. "Pardon me for the insolence, *pakhan*… but isn't that a waste of resources?"

A few murmurs of agreement follow. I let them pass. My eyes are on the bigger picture now. "It would be," I concede, "if we were *actually* going to purchase both of them."

"We're not?" Gora asks.

"No. We're just going to make a play for both. That way, even if we lose one, we won't end up screwed."

Like last time. No one says it, but it's on everyone's mind: my most recent failure. "Do you have anyone in mind for the job?" Grisha asks, giving me the perfect chance to pivot.

"I do."

"Who?"

"Everyone."

The *vory* frown. "Everyone?" Vlad asks, unconvinced.

I pull out two folders and slide them in opposite directions on the table. "Team Groza. Team Solovyov. Congratulations: you each have a week to get me a building."

"We're... competing?" Stanislav frowns.

"Just a friendly challenge, of course. Put your best men on it: the winning team will get a chance to name our next *vor*."

It's an opportunity no one can afford to pass up. Right now, the Groza and Solovyov *vory* are evenly matched. Whoever wins this will control the board vote-wise.

Not that it'll matter. I've always made my own decisions. I don't intend to change my ways.

But most *vory* don't know that. After the Ivan situation, they've probably been expecting some kind of shift. And if they think this is it, who am I to contradict them?

Stanislav picks up a folder. Vlad snatches away the other. "One week?" he splutters.

"One week."

Then they disperse.

Only Yuri and Grisha stay behind. As soon as the room empties, they both approach me. Then Yuri hisses, "What the hell was that?"

It's a testament to my good mood that I don't punish him. "That, brother, was strategy." He opens his mouth to object, but I cut him off. "Call Petra. Tell her to meet us at my place. The real meeting starts now."

"This better be good," Petra huffs, heel tapping impatiently. "I had to cancel a mani-pedi."

"And we're all grateful for your selfless sacrifice."

"I don't get it," Yuri mutters. "Why did you say all those things at the meeting?"

I don't justify myself. I've never felt the need, and I'm not going to start now. "Grisha. My bag."

Once I have it in my hands, it takes me less than a second to find what I'm looking for. "What I'm about to show you cannot leave this room. Only the four of us will know of it. Understood?"

Everybody nods.

Satisfied, I toss the contents on the table.

"*Another* roll-up?" Yuri cranes his neck to see. "What is it?"

"The plan. The *real* plan."

Petra leans over to inspect it. She slowly unrolls the corners, pinning them with paperweights as she goes. Her eyes trail over every inch of the blueprint. "Whose building is this?"

"Carmine's."

Three pairs of eyes go wide around me. "You've got to be kidding," Yuri says.

"And why's that?"

"Because this looks like… like…"

"Like you want to take the fight to Carmine directly," Grisha fills in. There's none of my brother's shock in his voice, only a vague glint of amusement. "Am I wrong?"

"Not at all." Then I hand over three folders.

"Great," Petra mutters. "More paper."

"Paper is untraceable," I remark. "Like this, the mole can't track us."

"I'm sorry, the what?"

Right. Guess it's time to break that particular glass. After all, this is a war council—and if *that* doesn't count as "in case of emergency"…

Besides, April's right. I need to start trusting the people around me. Even if it's only a handful of them, I can't keep going behind their backs. Either I'm in or I'm out. And Petra's more than proven herself.

"Someone's been spying for Carmine all along," I tell her. "That's how the first deal got blown up. We thought it was just Ivan, but we've started suspecting others."

"Like who?"

"Motya…" Yuri whispers in my ear.

But I press on. "Your father."

Petra's face freezes. For a split second, all movement in her stops. No one would call it "shock," but then again, very few are familiar with Petra's ways of handling emotions.

For better or worse, I've become one of them.

"I see," she rasps.

If this had been anyone else, they might have started screaming in my face—even fainted outright. But this isn't anyone else. This is Petra Solovyova, the Nightingale with wings of ice, and it takes her mere moments to collect herself, forcing her facial muscles to fall back into line. Back under her arctic control.

"I take it you knew?" she asks Yuri, her expression unreadable.

"He was acting under my orders," I cut in. "If you're going to be pissed at anyone, be pissed at me. I forced him not to tell you."

She gives a dry, bitter laugh. "How the tables have turned."

"It's not a given yet," Yuri tries to reassure her. "He might be innocent."

She scoffs. "My father's anything but innocent. But sure, do your worst."

"Petya…"

She rubs her temples and sighs. "Don't get me wrong. I'm not mad that you're investigating my father. I'm mad you thought I was too fragile to take it."

Then she slumps on the chair, the fight drained from her. I used to think pregnancy wouldn't have any effects on Petra— that she was just going to spawn like bacteria—but now, I can spot the signs: the fatigue, the skin-and-bones frailty. I wasn't close to April in her first and second trimesters, but if I had to guess, I'd say this is what taking breakfast hunched over the toilet looks like.

Who knew? My wife's human after all.

"Clearly, you're not."

She gives me a strained smile. "Gee, thanks. Are we gonna hug now?"

"Not a chance in hell."

"Good. I was ready to stab you if you tried."

Yuri sits down next to her. Gingerly, he takes her hand in his. "So are we...?"

She rolls her eyes. "Oh, please. I'm not gonna dump you for keeping one flimsy secret from me. You're not even good at it."

"Hey, what's that supposed to mean?"

"You know, all the sneaking around, the guilty puppy looks. It was like you couldn't keep it in anymore."

"She thought you were either going to drop on one knee or drop off the face of the earth," I whisper jokingly into his ear, not nearly low enough to be subtle. "For God's sake, brother, do better."

Grisha clears his throat. "Hate to ruin the moment for our two lovebirds..."

"Yes, yes, the plan." Petra waves him on. "Let me guess. These are our starring roles?"

"They are," I confirm.

Everyone picks up the folder with their name on it. "Yuri, you'll be first up. I want you to plant a small bomb in the sewers under here."

"The basement?" he frowns. "Why?"

"The mole will expect us to go through the roof."

"Because that's what you told the *vory* you'd do," Grisha realizes.

"Exactly. If there really is a mole, we'll use them to our advantage. No one will be looking at the basement floor."

"How small a bomb are we talking?" Yuri asks.

"Small enough to make it look like the floor caved in on its own. We don't want to draw attention, not yet."

"Sounds reasonable," Grisha says. "What next?"

"Next, you come in. You'll hack into their communication system and intercept their call to the repairmen."

"Let me guess," Petra drawls. "That's where I come in?"

"It is. You'll pretend to be the secretary of a repair company and send in a crew."

"Our men, I take it?"

"Exactly."

Yuri's eyes light up with understanding. "So that other plan..."

"Was to keep the *vory* busy. And smoke out the mole."

"How?"

I smirk. "You'll see. We'll all see, soon enough."

38

MATVEY

After the meeting, I decide to get home early and properly thank my muse. But once again, I'm greeted by a familiar sight: scattered clothes everywhere. "April...?"

"Here!" The voice comes from a pile of black suit jackets. I have no idea how they're different, but one glance tells me where they must come from: the factory.

"Taking a nap in the prototypes?" I ask as I approach cautiously.

"Sleep is for the weak," she replies, a bobby pin between her teeth.

It's ridiculous. Goofy at best. I don't think there's one man alive who'd find it sexy.

And yet, I can't look away.

So I guess there's at least one.

"I take it work has been going well?"

Her face lights up at that. "How 'bout I show you?" She herds me towards an empty spot of floor, in front of a mirror. "Take off your jacket."

"That's awfully forward of you, Ms. Flowers."

She slaps me playfully on the arm. "Unclothe yourself or I'll do it for you. And yes, that is a threat."

In the end, I shrug my jacket off. April's hands help it along, expert and delicate. I want to snatch them out of the air and kiss them, one finger at a time, until she's all red in the face. Then I want to trail my lips up her arm, her shoulder, her smooth and beautiful neck. Until she's breathing hard and begging for more.

"All done!" she claps her hands once, taking a step back to admire her creation.

I look in the mirror. The jacket's fabric is sleek, elegant, with nothing to envy of my usual wardrobe. Its color is a deep charcoal black, reminding me of bulletproof vests. There's the same sense of sturdiness to it, but without the rigidity I'm used to. Experimentally, I start moving around.

April's face lights up like a Christmas tree. "Smooth, right? We think we finally perfected the fabric blend. Kevlar's still the cornerstone, but it was too rigid on its own, so we tried all sorts of…"

I zone out, April's words flying straight over my head. Only her voice remains, passionate enough to put world-class stylists to shame.

Amazing. My woman is amazing.

"… and we think we'll be ready for mass production soon!"

That jolts me out of my reverie. "When?"

"Well, Dr. Reznikov thinks we're there already, but Professor Simmons and I still want to test a few things. There's a couple of kinks to iron out with washability and weather resistance, and then—*mmmph!*"

The kiss swallows the rest.

I don't stop until she's exactly where I want her: face flushed, breaths short, pupils blown to high heaven. "What was that for?" she pants afterwards.

"You."

Her cheeks blush even redder. "I didn't do anything."

"You did. And now, you're going to get a reward."

"Ahh... Matvey...!" Her fingers tangle in my hair, pulling madly. With every lap of my tongue around her clit, her body shakes harder, desperate for a release I'm holding back on purpose. "Please," she gasps, voice breaking.

But she doesn't set the pace here.

I do.

"Please what?"

"Let me come."

It's a convincing plea. A weaker man might even give in. "Not yet," I growl.

I part her thighs wider. My five o'clock shadow grazes against the delicate skin of her inner thighs, an extra layer of sensation she doesn't seem to know how to handle. April's voice cracks as she pants, "You said… this was my… reward…!"

"It is," I answer curtly.

Then I slip my tongue inside.

April's nails dig into my scalp. I can feel the imprints of her touch, sharp crescents of desperation, but it doesn't deter me. If this was enough to break my resolve, I wouldn't be *pakhan*. "Matvey… I need…!"

I fuck her with my tongue, hot and deep. Her pussy spasms around it, threatening to trap me inside. It makes me want to take her right now, bury myself to the hilt in the wet heat of her body, but I restrain myself. *Not yet.*

"Only good girls get to come," I rasp against her flesh. "Have you been good?"

As expected, April makes a noise of protest. "I just… I d-did my job—*ah*!"

"Wrong." I swap out my tongue for my fingers, then start pumping in and out of her roughly. Every time I drag close to her sweet spot, I steer clear of it, missing it on purpose.

April's thighs shudder on either side of me. I can feel her struggling against me, trying to snap them shut and stop the onslaught. Too much pleasure—too much of me inside her. "Matvey, please…!"

"Have you been good?"

When no reply comes, I lick April's clit again. She moans, loud and echoing in the living room, but she still won't say the word.

Just as I expected.

No matter how many sessions with Dr. Knox she's done, this is still her sorest spot of all: accepting praise. For herself, her work, her actions. But no matter how much I torture her with pleasure, she keeps clinging stubbornly to her idea of herself.

That she isn't good enough.

"Alright then." I start to pull away.

"No!" she gasps, voice overflowing with panic. Her hand tightens in my hair, tries to keep me in place with all its strength. "D-Don't stop, just…"

Do it. Unlock your reward. Admit how good you've been.

"You know the rules. Say it."

A shaky exhale. "I… I was…"

I encourage her with a long, deep lap. "Yes?"

"I was… a g-good…"

I pump my fingers in and out, this time faster, deeper. "A good what?"

"A good girl," she breathes at last.

"Mm," I press a kiss to the inside of her thigh, all red from grazing against my beard. "Why?"

"Because… I completed the project."

"And how did you do?" I find her sweet spot again. This time, I don't miss it.

"G-Good…!"

"Just good?" I start torturing it with purpose, rubbing just too lightly for her to come.

She breathes a heavy sigh, eyes squeezed hard against the overstimulation. "N-No, I…"

I add one finger. She takes it beautifully, her pussy lips parting to accept another piece of her reward. "You did great. You were amazing."

"I… I d-did great…"

"Mhmm. Now, ask for your reward."

"I want m-my reward."

I'm almost satisfied, but not yet. There's one more thing I want to hear her say. "What reward?"

"Y-Your cock," she mumbles, too embarrassed to look me in the eye. "I want your cock, I wanna come, Matvey, please…!"

That's it; I can't wait anymore. I grab her thighs and yank her towards me, watching the pain of being left empty flash on her face for just one second before—

"*Ahh!*"

I watch myself sink into her. Slowly, every inch disappears into her body, swallowed up by her wet pussy. No matter how kind she always is, how giving, I know there's another April hidden within: a creature of lust and greed. "Want me to fuck you like this? All spread open for me?"

"Yes!" she screams. "Yes, yes, want you to fuck me—"

"You want it hard?"

"I want it."

"You want it fast?"

A breathless nod. "Yes, I—*yes.*"

"You want it dirty, you little vixen?"

With every "yes," I drive my hips down faster, deeper. April's legs lock at the small of my back, as if she's terrified I'll pull out and leave her like this.

I'll admit, the idea is tempting.

But not today.

Today, April's been a very good girl.

"Yes, yes!"

"Want me to come inside you, *kalina*?"

That's what does her in—the thought of me owning her. Utterly, completely, until there isn't a spot inside her I haven't painted with my cum. "Matvey, Matvey…!"

She comes so violently I can feel it. It's like she's trying to squeeze the life out of me, but I know she's too lost to do anything that intentional. She's too busy coming, coming with my name on her lips, my cock buried all the way inside her, fucking her through it.

Mine.

My orgasm hits, but I still don't stop.

I may never.

39

APRIL

I enter the fashion expo on Matvey's arm, stepping through the doors with jittery feet.

I can't help the nerves. It's not just that the last time I was here, I had a literal gun to my head—it's that this is the Mallard. The hub of New York fashion, the place where history is made.

What am *I* doing here?

"Maybe we should turn back," I mumble.

Matvey raises a skeptical eyebrow. "And miss out on all the hors d'oeuvres?"

"I'm serious. I shouldn't be here."

"April." Matvey leans over. His next words, he speaks directly into my ear. "If you don't stop that right now, I'll be forced to spank you in front of all these good people. Do you want that?"

I swallow. I hate to admit it, but part of me very much wants that. "No, sir."

"Good. Then don't insult my woman's skill in front of me."

I roll my eyes, smiling despite myself. "That's cheating."

We came here on our own. I was too nervous to invite anyone, and the only other people who knew—Petra and Elias—are holding down the fort back home, one for Matvey and one for myself. From what he's told me, things have been tense with his Bratva lately, enough that he needs someone to keep watch at all times. With Yuri busy with some covert mission and Grisha standing guard for Elias and May, there was no one left to ask.

I could've invited June, though. Corey and Rob, too—that's if Rob's firm has finally made peace with giving its lawyers actual vacation days. Either way, I didn't have to be here on my lonesome.

But I just couldn't bring myself to invite anyone. I couldn't bring myself to be humiliated in front of my closest friends. To fail in front of an audience.

Because I'm going to fail, aren't I?

Negative thoughts. Self-loathing spiral. I force myself to snap out of it. This isn't me anymore. This can't be me, not if I want to be a good mother and partner. It's like Dr. Knox says: if you can't love yourself, how in the hell can you love somebody else?

(Though I'm pretty sure she stole that one from a drag show.)

Besides, I'm not actually alone here. In fact, I'm with the person I wanted here the most. "Twelve o'clock. Code purple."

"Wait, what was code purple again? Armani? Or…" I blanch. "Oh."

Definitely not Armani.

I follow Matvey's line of sight to a small group of richly-dressed people. I mean, *everyone* here is oozing fashion, but those specific three clearly spared no expense.

And they're coming straight towards us.

"Crap," I mutter.

"April!" Nora greets with her fakest smile yet. "How odd to see you here."

What, because you stole my dress? "Hi, Nora. Dad."

Off to the side, Dominic stays resolutely quiet. The only sign he heard me at all is a short nod of acknowledgement.

Gee, how heartwarming. Missed you too, Pops.

"Where's May?" Anne asks without even saying hello. "You didn't leave her home alone again, did you?"

"Come now, Anne. I'm sure your sister doesn't do it all the time. Surely she can afford a sitter… somewhere in the Bronx."

Any other time, these comments would have incensed me. They would have driven me crazy with outrage, making me stammer out one weak comeback after the other.

Now, however, all I can feel is a strange sort of calm. Maybe it's all the sessions with Dr. Knox, or Matvey's quiet, solid presence by my side, but their words just… slide off. Like I'm not the same person they knew how to hurt.

"Of course." I smile brightly. "Don't worry, Nora. You didn't take *all* my money."

Nora's jaw nearly falls to the floor. It's quite the sight— almost makes me laugh out loud. "Why, I...!"

Anne clicks her tongue, eyes suddenly cold and sharp. "Say, sister, will we get to see your dress?"

"Sure." I shrug. "Why? Wanna steal that, too?"

"April!" Nora gasps. "Is that any way to talk to your family?"

"Not at all. But I don't see any family of mine here. Do you?"

Next to me, Matvey snorts. It's such a rare thing, I feel my smile turn into a grin.

"That's right!" I clap my hands once. "I haven't introduced you, have I? Dad, this is Matvey Groza. May's father."

Matvey shakes Dominic's trembling hand with a firm grip. Judging by my dad's face, it's just on the wrong side of too tight. "I've heard a lot about you, sir. About you all, actually."

It's enough to make all three shiver on the spot. Jeez, were they always like this? So pathetic and easy to rattle?

They're not the ones who've changed, whispers the voice at the back of my head, sounding proud for once. *You are.*

"Aren't you gonna say anything, Dad?"

Dominic swallows. I spot something in his eyes I've never seen before: fear. "The pleasure's all mine.

"I'm sure."

Those two words light a fire inside me. It's exhilarating enough to see my childhood bullies defeated by a couple of well-placed jabs—but this? Finally having someone on my side?

It's the hottest thing in the world.

"Excuse us."

I don't say anything else.

I take Matvey's hand and drag him to the restrooms.

The second the door to the empty ladies' room slams behind us, I grab Matvey's face in my hands. "Kiss me."

Matvey's never been one to take orders. But tonight, I watch his eyes darken with anticipation as he takes in this new side of me. The side that's done with being polite. "Yeah?"

"Yeah," I breathe. "I want you."

I feel his hot tongue swipe into my mouth. The kiss is savage, brutal, all teeth. It's like being eaten alive.

For once, I want to eat him right back.

"Fuck me," I gasp. "Fuck me right now."

He doesn't make me ask again. With an animalistic growl, he lifts me on the sink counter and pries my legs apart, settling in like he belongs there. I can feel the outline of his already-hard cock grinding against my thigh, bigger and thicker than I've ever had it, and it's making my entire body shiver. God help me, I've never been more turned on.

"Matvey…"

I lock my ankles at the small of his back and dig my nails into his scalp. He hisses in my ear and grabs me back, hands skating down my dress, ripping my panties right off. "Fuck, *kalina.*"

I palm his cock through his suit pants, fumbling for the zipper. I have no patience for undressing, not tonight. I'm drunk on my victory over the ghosts of my past—and now, it's time to claim the spoils.

He fucks me with his fingers first, three sinking in right off the bat. "*Blyat'*. So fucking wet for me."

"Want you inside." I squeeze his throbbing cock in my hand, lining him up between my thighs. "I'm ready, just—"

SLAM.

It happens so fast, I almost come right then and there. In all the time we've been together, Matvey's never taken me like this—so rough and violent. I don't know if my display earlier has worked him up to his limit or if he's just indulging me, but *God.*

"Again."

He pulls all the way out, then slams back in.

"Again," I moan.

Every thrust punches a wild cry from my throat. At this point, it's useless—I can't even remember why I'm supposed to keep quiet anymore.

"Again, again, ahh!"

"You want this?" Matvey snarls, his grip bruising on my hips. "Want me to fuck you in a dirty bathroom like a whore?"

"Yes!" I cry out. "I'm your whore! I'm *yours.*"

"Want them to hear you? Your shitty father, your bitch of a stepmother?"

"I don't care," I moan. "I don't care who hears."

He grins against my throat. "Liar."

That's it: one word and I'm coming. I sink my nails into Matvey's shoulders and bite down into the crook of his neck, stifling my moans. I hear him groan at the sensation, wild and unrestrained, and finally feel the warmth of his release spill inside me.

We catch our breaths against each other. When I turn my head towards the mirror, the person staring back at me isn't the old April anymore.

It's a brand-new me.

~

After fixing ourselves, we slip back into the party. The guests aren't all staring at us, which is good: between the music, the soundproof doors, and the constant buzz of conversation, I doubt anyone truly heard us.

Unless they knew to listen, that is.

"Hi, there."

Nora's face is horrified. "You...!"

I ignore her and turn to Anne. "By the way, here you go. In case you run out of fabric next time you want to steal a design."

I stuff my gift in her bag and sashay away on Matvey's arm. "You didn't," he whispers into my ear as we leave.

"You bet your ass I did."

I'm already halfway across the hall when I hear Anne's scandalized scream. "EW! PANTIES!"

Whatever happens tonight, I've already won.

40

APRIL

At the first glimpse of the runway, all my brazenness goes flying out the proverbial window. "I'm gonna lose this thing so bad."

Matvey shoots me a glare. "What did I just say?"

"'Don't insult my woman's skill'?"

"So you do remember."

Any other day, his concern would be touching. Kind of hot, too, if we're being totally honest. But right now? I'm ready to throw up all over the front row from sheer anxiety.

"What if my dress wasn't even picked for the runway?"

"Impossible."

"I'm serious. There were, like, three hundred submissions this year. The fashion show's only going to feature the top ten. There's no way I made the cut, is there? And I was so smug with Anne, too. God, she will never let me live this down, will she? I—"

"April. Breathe."

I do as instructed. Matvey's commanding voice is a balm: as soon as his words reach me, I feel like I can let myself relax, just a little bit. Like I have no choice but to obey. Did I already mention it's hot as all hell?

"Okay. Breathing."

"Repeat after me: you will do great."

I fumble through a long, shaky inhale. "I will do great."

"You worked hard for this."

"I worked hard for this."

"You deserve this."

"I…" I hesitate.

Luckily, I'm saved by the bell: the lights dim. Everyone falls quiet all at once. The spotlights start revolving all over the crowd, hyping up an already over-excited public.

The music starts, and the first model glides down the runway.

It's a dress I don't recognize, but I'm immediately glad I didn't go for my idea of hand-gluing three million mother of pearl scales to a skirt: the theme is clearly *Little Mermaid*-y. The gown is siren-shaped, shimmering in a thousand shades of blue, purple and green, and the Japanese model's long, black hair complements it perfectly. She's moving like a creature of the deep, flowy gestures and invisible steps, and I wonder if she's barefoot underneath. It'd definitely be a bold choice. As she passes me by, the light catches on her see-through dragonscale sleeves, making them look painted on her skin.

Envy surges through me, but it only fires me up more.

More models come out: a fairycore gown with a forest-green hood; an asymmetrical half-tux, half-dress that screams gender revolution; a gilded Greek-style dress with actual goldwork in the stitching. The fashion-loving part of me is in awe, wanting to track down each designer and squeeze out all their secrets, a thousand questions per minute crowding my mind.

The rest of me thinks, *I'm screwed.*

When the eighth piece finishes its round, I can feel my chances start to dim. But what chances, really? Did I truly think I could measure up to all these amazing people? All these *actual* designers?

Did I think a measly tailor could swoop in at the last minute and win it all?

Maybe with the Daphne dress I might've stood a chance, but...

As if summoned by magic, a familiar silhouette appears: that dress. *My* dress.

The one Anne stole from me.

For a second, I forget this one isn't mine, that it didn't get in this competition with my name on it. All I can feel is a weird sense of exhilaration. Because, while it might not be the exact one I made...

It's still mine. My dress made the cut.

The model is simply stunning: rich ebony skin and gold makeup, complementing the ivory tone of the dress perfectly. She seems to have caught the theme, because her tree bark side keeps stretching upwards, arm reaching up from under a cascade of embroidered leaves. Yearning—for a freedom it might never reach.

It's beautiful.

I feel my eyes grow misty. It's the first time I've thought that about something of mine. The first time I don't have a snide voice at the back of my mind implying otherwise.

Actually, not the first. There was another time that voice was nowhere to be found.

The day May was born.

Silently, Matvey squeezes my hand. I can feel all his support in that gesture, even without words to back it up. *I know this must be hard for you. Keep it together. You're stronger than they think.*

I dry my eyes and focus on the dress. I don't know why, but something's been bothering me about it—the tailor side of me. I concentrate on that, on trying to figure out what's wrong.

Then I see it.

When the model passes me by, she makes a wide bow, as if to spread leaves all over the crowd. Her arm brushes right past me, and *there.*

The stitching is wrong.

When I was making my version of this dress, I made sure to hold the needle at a certain angle, widening my stance with each foot of fabric. I wanted the stitching to reflect Daphne's transformation: the movement, the change. It's the only part that wasn't in the sketches and notes. I came up with it in the moment.

It's not just that, either. Looking at it, I can tell it wasn't the work of one artist, but a hired équipe that didn't fully understand the concept they were bringing to life. When I was crafting my gown, I poured everything I had into it: not just blood, sweat, and tears, but a vision. I wanted whoever wore it to feel seconds away from their own metamorphosis, trapped and freed at the same time. And the spectators—I wanted them to feel it, too.

So I researched sculptors. Not just Bernini, but all the big names: Donatello, Canova, Wildt. Back then, a quote by Michelangelo stuck with me:

"The sculpture is already complete within the marble block."

Now, I'm not so presumptuous to think I've actually managed that. He was freaking Michelangelo—I'm just little old me. Still, I tried. I treated the fabric with respect, working to reveal the potential that was already there. I did it with my own two hands.

Here, it's like thousands of hands passed this piece back and forth between them, treating the fabric as a simple tool. Like an assignment they had to complete. Like...

Like it has no soul.

I feel a pang of pain for my creation. Stolen or not, it deserved better than that.

I'm so caught up in my thoughts, I almost don't notice the tenth model walking out. Gasps rise from the crowd, a thousand murmurs at once.

"Is the dress torn on purpose?"

"What a strange bodice!"

"My God, are those... *guns?*"

I lift my gaze, and there it is.

Ripped hems. Pure white tulle. Pitch black Kevlar.

And two Kalashnikovs poised to strike.

The model is a slim thing, blonde and petite—the closest thing I've seen tonight to a Petra-like figure. It's uncanny—almost like they *knew*.

But they didn't. If I had to guess, I'd say they picked the most innocent-looking model of the bunch to maximize contrast with the veritable armory she's currently carrying. It's a brilliant choice—she has the kind of dollface that wouldn't look out of place in a group of Girl Scouts, like she's never had a single bad thought. Her arms are so delicate, they look like they might break from the strain.

Except that they don't. The model keeps marching on, threatening the crowd with her huge props, as if to say: *Look at me. I'm ready to go to war.*

God, I really hope they're props.

"That's..."

"Your dress," Matvey whispers in my ear. "Good job."

I melt all over. "Can you do me a favor?"

"Name it."

"Pinch me. Like, right n—*ow*!"

Unsurprisingly, the pain sparks from my ass. Of course he'd aim there. "Feeling awake yet?" Matvey teases.

I stare at my dress strutting down a world-class runway, the tenth of ten finalists. I listen to the crowd go wild. I watch the model carry that mountain of torn tulle like a princess answering a call to arms halfway through the happiest day of her life.

"Yeah," I murmur in a daze. "Yeah, I think I am."

And I'm never going back to sleep.

"You realize they also have water, right?"

"Yes," I gasp, then down the third champagne flute in a row. Not because I'm celebrating early—because I'm losing my freaking mind. "Thanks for the tip."

My dress made it to the top ten. *My* dress. Something I made!

In forty-eight hours, my anxiety reminds me. *Good luck making the cut with* that, *champ!*

When I reach for my fourth bubbly, Matvey swipes it right out of my hand. "Hey!" I protest. "I was drinking that."

"Not anymore, you're not."

I make a grab for it, but he's already dumped it in the potted plant behind him. "That was my liquid courage," I pout.

"That was a pounding headache tomorrow morning."

"That's Future April's problem."

He rolls his eyes, but there's unmistakable fondness there. "You can't give your acceptance speech drunk."

"Ha-ha. 'Acceptance speech.' You're hilarious."

"I fail to see what's so funny."

I steal a devilled egg from a passing tray. My stomach's in knots, but I've read somewhere they were good for hangovers. Wait, was that raw eggs? I can't remember. I can barely remember my own name right now.

"Acceptance speeches are for winners."

"You sound awfully confident that you won't win."

"It's not that. It's just that I've already girlbossed too close to the sun. Time to get back down to Earth, Icarus." I tap myself on the head just to make sure the message gets through.

"You're already drunk, aren't you?"

"Yes—*No*. Maybe? You pick."

Honestly, I could get drunker. This is barely taking the edge off. I can still feel my anxiety gnawing at me like some starved squirrel. Which is weird, 'cause I'm pretty sure it's the one emotion I constantly keep fed.

"April."

"It's just..." I sigh. "I don't want to get my hopes up. Isn't it enough that I got this far?"

Even as I'm saying it, I know it's a lie. Of course it's not enough. Whoever says, *"It's an honor just to be nominated"* is a bold-faced Pinocchio.

Who could possibly be happy with second place when first place exists?

When first place gets you a full ride to the Mallard Institute?

"No," Matvey says predictably. "And you don't believe that, either."

He's right, but I'm not going to give him the satisfaction. "Mm." Still, when his hand finds mine, I squeeze it with all I have.

"Everyone, please gather to the main stage," the announcer calls.

"Moment of truth," I murmur.

We gather. Take our seats. The curtain slowly rises. Only three pieces can make it to the podium—and we won't know the placements until the last moment.

"The first piece to make it to the final round is…" the announcer pauses dramatically. "'Mermaid Dream' by Anton Gutierrez!"

No surprises there. I clap along as a young man with gold eyeliner climbs onto the platform, bowing in thanks to the crowd.

"Next up, we have…" *Metaphorical drumroll.* "'Daphne' by Anne Flowers-Le Blanc!"

My nails dig into my palm. I'm prepared to lose tonight, but there's one thing I won't stand for: Anne claiming the grand prize with *my* design. Flawed execution or not, the idea still belongs to me.

If I have to watch my father's replacement family steal another dream right out of my hands…

"Breathe," Matvey whispers, squeezing my hand tight. "There's still one more."

I force myself to do as he says: *Breathe in, breathe out.* "I'm glad you're here," I whisper back, voice almost cracking.

"I'm not going anywhere."

That finally calms me down. Even if tonight ends up a disappointment—even if I lose my dream all over again—I'll still have something I didn't have last time.

My family by my side.

"Thank you," I breathe.

"And finally…"

I resign myself. There's no way he'll say my name. *Oh, well. I had a good run.*

"'The Bulletproof Bride' by April Flowers!"

Wait, what?

"April," Matvey shakes me by the shoulder. "That's you. Go."

"But—"

"Go," he repeats, then pushes me to the front of the crowd.

For a second, I can only blink around. Anne's face is a mask of disgust, as if the idea of sharing the same podium with me repels her.

That's the last push I need: I make my bow and take my place.

My *rightful* place.

Calm down, I tell myself. *You've made it to the top three, but there's still no guarantee. Don't dream too big.*

But what's the point of dreaming small? "And the winner is…"

I can do this, I start chanting in my head for the first time in my life. *I'm here. I can win this. I can be good enough.*

And even if I'm not…

In my anxiety, I see the announcer's lips move, but miss the actual words entirely. It's like all my blood is sloshing around in my ears right now. All I hear is the roar of my racing heart.

Who won?

Then I see it. There, in the crowd, one dot in a sea of clapping hands…

Matvey. *My* Matvey.

And he's grinning.

"Oh my God," I murmur.

The mermaid dress guy pushes me forward with a chuckle. I almost trip and fall, but I manage to right myself at the last second. The crowd's laughing now, but it doesn't feel like they're laughing *at* me.

It feels like they're laughing *with* me.

"Congratulations, Ms. Flowers," someone in a suit says. "We look forward to having you here."

It's like a scene from a movie: just like that, I'm handed a cartoonishly giant check. The crowd's applause is a dull roar, the judges nodding approvingly from their dais. Nora's seething, and I can't imagine Anne's much happier behind me. Admiration, envy, irritation—whatever the emotion behind it, everyone's looking at me now. All of them.

But I only have eyes for one.

41

MATVEY

I couldn't be prouder.

I watch April on the stage, that huge check in her arms, laughing and shaking hands and getting photographed for the contest's yearbook, and I feel my chest swell with something I've never felt before.

When she leaps down from the stage, I catch her in my arms. "Congratulations," I murmur in her hair. "You're about to become a very expensive tailor."

She squeezes me tightly in return. Her cheeks are just the least bit wet, but I pretend I don't notice. "Don't worry," she laughs. "I'll keep giving you the friends and family treatment."

"Just as long as you don't give it to anyone else," I growl as memories of tying April's wrists together with a length of blue silk flash in my head.

Her cheeks burning bright scarlet says she's remembering

the exact same thing. "Hey," she says, "I don't actually have to bring this thing to the bank, do I?"

I ruffle her hair. "Nope. Hand it to a valet. They'll bring it to the car."

"I bet Grisha's gonna be thrilled about having that in his rearview mirror."

"He'll deal. He only uses it to spy on passengers anyway."

Someone coughs behind us. I'm tempted to ignore them, but I have a sneaking suspicion I know who it is. Even the stench of expensive perfume isn't enough to mask how full of shit the wearer is.

I reluctantly let go of April. "Mrs. Le Blanc."

She shoots me a mildly terrified look, but doesn't say anything back. *Probably too scared to talk to me.* "I suppose congratulations are in order," she grumbles to her stepdaughter.

"You really won't have time for that baby now, will you?" Anne fake-sighs.

That's it. I'm about to finally put them in their place when April's hand stops me, landing gently on my shoulder.

"I'll make time." She smiles politely. "That's what family does, after all." Then her face turns serious. "I hope you've learned something from this, Anne."

"Have a quickie in the bathroom for good luck?"

"Cheating gets you nowhere." April's expression goes softer. Kinder. It throws me off—and it seems to throw Anne off, too. "If you're really interested in fashion, I can always give you a few pointers, you know. You can try again with a piece of your own next year."

"And why would you do that?"

"Because I'm still your sister," she replies. "I *can* be your sister. If you'll let me."

I shake my head. Of course she'd say that. It's just like April— to extend a helping hand to someone who's always been an enemy. To try and fix things, even now.

For a second—only a second—something flickers across Anne's eyes. Something like doubt.

But it's gone as quickly as it came. "Oh, please. Don't make me laugh. As if you could ever teach me anything!" She starts cackling maniacally, but it's so forced, everyone can tell. "Did you forget? You lost, too! The shitty dress I stole from you just *lost*!"

It's like watching a train wreck happen. A split second after the words leave Anne's lips, her face goes slack, realization dawning. Of what she just said—and of how loudly she said it.

"I mean… I *mean*…!"

April gives a sad little nod. "Okay. If that's what you want. Goodbye, Anne." Then she turns to leave, my hand firmly in hers.

"You okay?" I whisper as soon as we're out of earshot.

"Yeah, I just… I thought maybe she could still come back to her senses. I know half her act is her mother's doing, so… I don't know." She sighs. "Guess I hadn't given up all hope after all."

I squeeze her hand. I can't blame her for wanting to try to salvage her relationship with her sister. For hoping they could become like her and Charlie: united despite the interference of their parents. "Some people don't change. And it's not your job to change them."

She smiles. "I know. It's gotten me a while to get here, but... now, I know." Her fingers interlace with mine. "Love changes people. And people who don't love anyone but themselves will never change. That's okay, too."

"It is?"

"Yeah. I've already got somebody who loves me."

I pull her closer to me, and we step out under the stars.

My good mood from April's victory carries well into the morning. It's almost a pity I'm going to have to spoil it.

"Well?"

Next to me, Yuri's tapping his foot nervously. I don't blame him. After that meeting at my loft, I still haven't clarified this part of my plan.

But soon, all will become clear.

The two representatives from the Groza and Solovyov teams stand before me. They're two young recruits, messengers sent to the slaughter, to take credit for their bosses if they win and take the fall if they lose. I can't say I envy their positions, but I also don't give a shit. They're Bratva—they knew what they were signing up for. Besides, it's not like they're doing it for free: if the *vory* sent them up, it's because they're the candidates they chose to join their ranks.

But there will be no promotion today. Not that any of these men know that quite yet.

"You." I point to the Solovyov recruit. "Talk."

"Sir…" the recruit begins. His name is Lev, one of Vlad's entourage, still wet behind the ears. "I'm terribly sorry, *pakhan*. The deal for the right half of the building was about to be concluded when…"

"Let me guess," I cut in. "A mystery buyer stole it from under your nose."

His face tells me I'm correct. "If you'll just give me another chance—"

"No need. Get out."

"Sir, please—"

"No." I rise from my seat. "I expected better. Clearly, the Solovyov Bratva wasn't used to winning. That's going to have to change here."

He swallows. "Yes, *pakhan.*"

"Now, go before I change my mind."

I watch him scurry away like a rat, tail tucked between his legs and folders forgotten. "Why did you let him go?" Yuri whispers.

"You'll see," I reply in hushed tones. Then I turn to the Groza recruit—my own man. "Anatoly. What do you have for me?"

He sets the folder on the desk. "The left side was acquired without troubles, sir. Here is the paperwork."

I flip through the file. "Nice work. Flawless, really."

"Thank you, *pakhan.*"

He doesn't see it coming. For some reason, they never do.

I whip out my gun and slam the grip into the back of Anatoly's head. "No, thank *you*."

He goes down like a puppet with strings cut. He's not dead, of course: that would defeat the purpose.

"What the hell?!" Yuri rushes over. "That was *our* man!"

"Yes. And he's a spy."

"How can you know that?"

I lean back against the wall. "Think, Yura. If you were Carmine, would you sabotage another acquisition? Or would you use it to destroy your enemy?"

Realization dawns in my brother's eyes. "So that's why you did this? You set up the one that would 'win'?"

"I did. Whoever's working against us would, naturally, also work against the other team. And now, we know there *is* someone working against us: whatever this is, it didn't die with Ivan. There's a mutiny."

"But... it could've been a coincidence!" he protests. "Just because he lost, it doesn't mean—"

"Really?" I cut in. "You think last-minute mystery buyers come along every other day?" I scoff. "Think again, brother. This is Carmine we're up against. If we want to beat him, we need to be one step ahead of him."

For a long time, he stays silent. "This is crazy," he says finally.

I massage my temples. "Fucking tell me about it."

"What are we gonna do with him?"

I glance at the passed-out recruit on the floor. "Take him to the warehouse. I want him to tell us everything he knows."

Your move, Carmine.

42

APRIL

Ever since I won the contest, I've been walking on air. I still can't believe it: next year, I'll be going to the Mallard Institute of Fashion. *Me.*

I keep pinching myself, but I don't wake up.

On top of that, my work at the factory has been nothing but smooth sailing. Professor Simmons and Dr. Reznikov are amazing at what they do, and the rest of the team seems to have been handpicked with excellency in mind. The best of the best.

Finally, I can count myself among them.

When I came back with the happy news, Elias was ecstatic. He insisted on taking pictures of me with the giant check. "To make memories," he said. I then texted it to Petra, who texted back with the picture of a broken bottle of vodka and the word "POZDRAVLJAJU" in all caps, which was confusing. But Matvey assured me it wasn't a threat, so we're good... I think.

I haven't broken the news to my other friends yet. I want it to be a surprise.

"What are you going to sign your line as, Ms. Flowers?" I ask myself, mimicking the voice of an imaginary interviewer. "Flowers Fashion? April Delight? Clothes A.F.? Wait, on second thought, scratch that. How about—"

I'm interrupted by the doorbell. "Heard that, May? We have visitors."

Lately, I've been trying to talk to her more. Helps with development and all that. I can tell by her inquisitive little face that she's got a lot to say—the sooner she learns how to say it, the better. Though I'm definitely gonna miss Potato Mode.

"Coming!" I put May down in her crib and rush to the door. "Is that you, Grisha? I fixed your jacket last night. It's…" The words die in my throat.

Because that's not Grisha at the door.

"Sweetie! It's been too long!"

It's my mother.

One of the techniques Dr. Knox recommended was mindfulness: closing your eyes, meditating, the whole shebang.

I take a deep breath. Then I take three more, because one lungful of oxygen is not nearly enough to deal with the demonic spawn in front of me. "What are you doing here, Mom?"

Predictably, Eleanor pouts. "Is that any way to greet your mother?"

"My mother I haven't seen for half a year?"

It's not just that, of course. Everything I don't say hovers in the air between us: how our last meeting ended, the vicious fight we had. The fight *she* brought to my doorstep.

It makes me wonder what else she brought this time. I check discreetly for pitchforks, but find none, and the air smells more like lavender than it does sulfur and brimstone.

"Ain't no busier job," she sing-songs. "You know how it is, of course. You're in the Mommy Club now!"

"The Mommy what? Wait—how did you make it past the guards?"

"I have my ways." She then proceeds to push right past me. "Where's my little girl? My cutesy-patootsie grandbaby?"

Here we go. "She's in her crib. Don't wake her."

"Who do you take me for? I've had two, in case you—OW!"

Buttons hisses from the crib, his paw raised like a fluffy scorpion tail, claws in full view. "Mind the cat," I warn belatedly.

"This ugly, mangy thing. I can't believe you'd let it anywhere near the baby!"

"I've let worse things near the baby," I remark. "Mangier *and* uglier."

She pretends not to hear me, which is a pity, because that was really a high-quality burn. "Shoo, shoo!"

With a roll of my eyes, I pick up Buttons from the crib. "Run like the wind, boy," I mutter into his furry little head before setting it free in the living room. He immediately dives under the couch.

I wonder if there's room for two under there. Anywhere, really, to avoid the puppy-eyed look my mother is currently giving me.

I pick up the baby. Eleanor's face goes bright, her arms stretching out immediately.

I settle May against my chest, ignoring her. "What do you want, Mom?"

"Is it so strange I'd want to catch up?" she bristles. "Meet my grandkid, see how my daughter's doing?"

"Yes," I reply immediately. "It is strange."

I've been down this road before. I'm not doing it again: hoping she's changed, seeing only what I want to see, too much wishing and not enough thinking.

I refuse.

Every time I bared my heart to her, I was left bleeding. No more.

"Is this about Charlie?" I ask—the only part of her life I still give a damn about. "Is he okay?"

"Of course he's okay," she says. "This isn't about him, sweetie. This is about you. I just... wanted to see you, that's all. To congratulate you."

"You're six months late for that."

"Not on the baby." She shakes her head. "I mean, yes, of course, the baby's wonderful—but about the contest."

"The contest?" I blink. "How do you know about…?"

"Never mind how I know," she dismisses. "Mothers always know."

Mothers who sneak around sleeping with their exes? I rub my temples and sigh. I really wish Dominic would find a different topic for their pillow talk. Last time we met, he didn't even speak to me. I almost thought he was a puppet. Like in *Weekend at Bernie's.* Or maybe just the twins in a trench coat.

"Thank you," I concede, because there's really no polite way to send this one back to the messenger. Estranged or not, I'm not going to step down into the mud and start accusing my mother of things I have no proof of. Whatever she does with her life is her business, not mine. Same goes for the man who calls himself my father.

Maybe they just work better without you in the way.

I slap that thought away—*No.* I promised Dr. Knox I wouldn't do this, let myself fall down a negative spiral every time my parents came knocking. More than that, I promised Matvey.

Never again.

And it's a promise I intend to keep.

"Look, do you want to hold her or—"

"I heard there was quite the prize, too. For the contest, I mean."

"Yeah," I say cautiously. "Full ride at the Mallard."

"You've always wanted to go there."

"I'm surprised you know that."

"How many times are you going to make me say it?" she laughs, high-pitched and way too nervous to be spontaneous. "Mothers always know."

"Right. Well, now, I'm going."

"Yes, but…" She hesitates. "You don't actually need *all* of it, do you?"

I steady myself. "What do you mean?"

"I mean—you're rich now, aren't you?" She looks around herself as if she's staring at proof of it. "Or at least, your husband is?"

"Partner," I correct. The word leaves a bitter taste on my tongue, but I don't have the time to think about that now. "And yeah, he is. But that's his money."

"But you're together, silly!" she giggles awkwardly. "What's yours is his; what's his is yours—isn't that how it works?"

I narrow my eyes. "Mom, what's going on?"

"Nothing!" she nearly shouts. "I'm just worried here, shortcake. Surely if he truly loves you, then he won't mind sharing? That way, you can keep some of the prize money aside. For a rainy day, or…"

"Is this about Tom?"

Suddenly, it's like the air freezes around us. Eleanor's face turns white, her lips pressed in a tight, angry line. "What are you insinuating?"

"He's been gambling again, hasn't he?" I press. "That's why you're here. You need money."

"That's…!" She goes red as a pepper. "That's preposterous. I came here to see you."

"You came here to scrounge," I bite back, cold as ice. "You didn't even care about the baby. You just wanted a quick payday."

Every time. Every single, goddamn time. Of all the ways to make it clear she doesn't care about me, this has to be the crudest. She didn't even bother to play the long game—she just went straight to bat. Like I'm not even worth the effort.

Worse, it's like she thought I'd actually do it—sacrifice my hard-won scholarship on the altar of Tom's vices. And for what? Five minutes of conversation with my mother? The pretense of caring?

Does she think I'm that starved for affection?

You used to be, the voice inside my head reminds me. *There was a time you'd have given her the world for a crumb of attention. Don't you remember?*

I do. And I'm not gonna go back there.

Never, ever again.

"Careful now," Eleanor hisses, all pleasantries forgotten.

"Maybe it's you who should be careful," I retort. "You're the one who came here wanting something."

"You're always like this," she spits. "Always bitter and ungrateful. Do you have any idea what sacrifices I've had to make to raise you?"

"I'm sure you're about to remind me."

"I had dreams, too, you know!" she snaps. "You're not the only one who wanted to make something of herself!"

Here we go. Nothing like Eleanor's good old guilt-tripping speeches to turn a nice day around.

"Look, Mom," I sigh, trying to defuse the tension. "I'm sorry you had a hard life. I'm sorry you couldn't—"

"Because of you!" she screeches, ignoring my peace offerings completely. "I had a hard life because of *you*! Because I got pregnant with you!"

"That's funny," I say without a trace of laughter. "Because I got pregnant, too, but I never blamed my failings on my daughter."

"Hah! Your *daughter*," she repeats in a mocking tone. "God fucking help her."

"Why? Are you going to try to extort her, too?"

"Because you're a selfish bitch," she seethes. "You can't even be a good daughter. How could you possibly make a good mother?"

Once, her words would've stuck in me like knives.

Once, I would've cared too much for my own good, unable to let go.

But I'm not the person I was. "Once" doesn't apply to me anymore. Thanks to Dr. Knox—and Matvey, and Petra, and Elias, and Yuri, and Grisha, and a million others—I finally started to unravel the mess inside of me—the mess my parents made of me. And my own mess, too, the parts I can't blame on anyone else.

And thanks to my family, I'm no longer looking for crumbs.

"Thanks for coming by, Mom. You can show yourself out."

"So that's it? You don't even care?"

"I care about as much as you do," I say calmly. "If that's not to your liking, you can shout at a mirror next."

"You…!"

"Me," I agree with a smile. "Now, goodbye, you."

She grits her teeth so hard, I hear it. "This isn't over."

"Oh, it is. And you know why?" I take one step forward, then another. With every move, Eleanor's forced to back away. "Because next time, the guards will know not to let you up. They'll know you're not welcome here."

"I'm your family!"

"No, Mom, you're not. And you're no family of May, either. You're just a stranger to both of us."

This time, I don't slam the door in her face.

I shut it with a calm, gentle *click*.

43

APRIL

For the rest of the day, I go about my business like always.

I won't say Eleanor's words didn't touch me at all. I think it's impossible to have your own mother call you a selfish bitch and not have some kind of reaction. So yeah, of course I'm hurt. Of course I wish things hadn't unfolded like they did.

But I'm also used to it.

"Some people don't change. And it's not your job to change them."

I smile to myself. Even in his absence, Matvey's words are keeping me warm.

Which reminds me—we promised we'd keep each other informed. I shoot him a quick text about Eleanor's surprise visit.

The Wicked Bitch of Staten Island was here this morning. We're all fine—I'll tell you more when you get home!

Then, on second thought, I add, **Buttons might need a rabies shot, though. He scratched her. Do you think she's contagious?**

Then, fingers hesitating over the screen, I type a third text: *PS. I love you.*

There. All said.

I pick up my baby and valiant guard cat, one in each arm, and settle on the couch. "What'll it be?" I ask out loud. "Romcom? Action movie? A three-hour long drama about the nihilistic fleetingness of life?"

Before I can decipher May's coos, there's another knock.

I dump Buttons on a pillow and hoist up my growing baby— God, she's gotten big. "Eleanor, if it's you again, I swear…"

I open the door and the words die in my throat.

It's not Eleanor.

It's Charlie.

And he's sporting a nasty black eye.

"How *dare* he?"

"Apes, I'm okay, I swear. It just looks bad."

I move the ice pack around, trying to get all of the swelling. God, how often have I heard those words? *It's not that bad; it looks worse than it is?*

How often have I said those words myself?

I force myself to calm down and swallow my rage. "He shouldn't do these things. He's your father."

"I talked back to him." Charlie shrugs. "I knew what I was getting into."

"What happened?"

He hesitates. "When Mom came back, I heard them fighting. That's how I realized she'd been to visit you. I was almost mad she didn't ask me to come with, and then Dad—he started yelling. About money. He tried to hit her, so I stepped between them... told him off, tried to stop him..." He gives a dry laugh. "Guess I wasn't very good at it."

I feel a stab of guilt. "It's my fault. She came to ask for the prize money."

"From the contest?" He perks up. "You won?!"

A hazy smile spreads on my lips. It's just like Charlie to be happy for someone else's good news when that someone is the reason he got beaten to a pulp in the first place. "Yeah. First place."

"That's amazing, Apes!"

Right now, I feel anything but. That voice I've spent so long trying to silence is back with a vengeance, and for once, I have no good reason to shut it up.

Because it's right.

Charlie got hurt because of me. My brave baby brother, who put himself in the line of fire to save our mother from her deadbeat husband. And why did he have to do that? Because of me.

God help me, Eleanor was right: I am a selfish bitch.

What else was she right about?

Everything, that nasty part of me whispers. And maybe that's not wrong, either. How can I be a good mother when I'm such a shitty daughter? A shitty sister to the only sibling who's ever given a damn about me?

How—

"Apes. Stop. Seriously, I'm okay."

That's when I realize there are tears on my face. "I'm sorry, Charlie. I should've just given her the money."

"No way. Not a chance in hell. That money's yours. You earned it fair and square."

"But Mom's right: I don't need it. Matvey—he'd probably cover the tuition if I asked. And with this new job, maybe I could…"

Charlie's hands squeeze my shoulders. "No," he says with an air of finality that's way beyond his age. "If my dad knows what's good for him, he'll stop gambling. He's not going to do that if someone's footing the bill for him."

"He's not going to do that either way, Char," I murmur. "You know that. We've seen it."

"Maybe," he concedes, smile still bright on his split lips. "But I want to give him a chance."

I pull him into a hug. "You're too good for them," I whisper into his hair. "Way too good."

He chuckles. "Hey, I'm a handful, too."

"No, you're not. You were always the kindest kid in the room."

"I doubt that," he replies. "You were there for a good while, too."

I pull away before I can start bawling on my teenage brother's shoulder. "Are you sure you don't want the money?"

"I'm sure," he says. "I want to be like you. I want to earn my keep. And my dream—I want to earn that, too."

I think back to his one thousand hobbies and laugh. "Oh? Have we decided, then?"

"No." He shrugs. "But isn't that half the fun? Finding out what it is?"

That's it: I hug him again. "I'm so proud of you."

He makes a choking sound in response. Am I squeezing too hard? Oh, whatever. I already checked his ribs and they're fine. He can take a little more of this.

"Apes—"

"Shh. We're having a moment."

"Sis, I can't breathe."

Right then, the door opens: it's Matvey. "April?" His appearance is a bit ruffled, as if he rushed all the way here. "You weren't answering my texts, so I—"

Then his eyes find Charlie.

For a second, I panic. I remember how pissed he was last time Charlie dropped by unannounced, telling me I'd broken the rules. I scramble to my feet, rushing to explain. "Sorry, I wasn't checking my phone! There was kind of an emergency back home, so Charlie—"

But Matvey passes right by me. He tips Charlie's head up without a word, those keen blue eyes assessing the damage.

No doubt he's done a lot of this in his line of work. "Anything broken?"

I realize he's asking me. "Oh! No, no, we don't think so. It's probably just the eye."

"It looks worse than it is," Charlie adds helpfully.

"I doubt that," Matvey comments. Then he moves his hand to the top of Charlie's head…

And *pats it.*

I'm speechless. It's such a one-eighty from what the old Matvey would've done. Sure, he was good to Charlie back then, too, but not before he took his pound of flesh out of me. And now…

Now, it's like watching someone else entirely.

"You did the right thing coming here," he says. "I'll have the guest room made up for you."

"Th-That's okay!" Charlie waves his hands. "Things have probably calmed down at home. I should—"

"Stay."

They both turn to me.

"Stay," I repeat. "Seriously. I'd feel much better if I knew you were here tonight."

I glance at Matvey for confirmation. The corner of his lips curves upwards, imperceptible to anyone else.

But not to me.

I know *Matvey,* I remind myself. *I don't have to be afraid of him anymore.* Because this is the new Matvey, the one who's been changing for my sake only. And *this* Matvey—

This Matvey, I'd trust with my life.

Just like that, my anxiety melts away. "I'll throw in pizza and a movie to seal the deal?" I offer.

Charlie's eyes light up. "Is that really okay?"

"Of course," Matvey answers. "You're family."

Family. Once, that six-letter word meant nothing to me. Not in the way it usually meant something to other people. But now...

Now, it's something I have. The side I chose and the side I didn't—two halves of my heart, now beating in unison.

I couldn't be more grateful.

44

MATVEY

That morning, I leave April and Charlie snoozing on the couch and head down to the lobby.

Yuri and Grisha are already waiting for me. I told them to meet here—I didn't want to be away from the penthouse any more than I had to. Not after yesterday's pop-up visit by April's harpy of a mother.

"Who was on guard duty yesterday?" I ask first thing.

"Taras and Shura," Grisha replies.

"Fire them. I want someone more capable next time."

We head to the restaurant area. The waiter's eyes go wide at the sight of me. "S-Sir! If I'd known you'd be here, I would have—"

"Are you telling me I need a reservation to have breakfast in my own hotel's restaurant?"

He goes white as a sheet. "N-No, sir, of course not!"

"Good. I didn't think so."

He leads us to a table with jittery steps, the menus practically vibrating in his hands. I can see the pencil crack as he takes our orders. Anyone else would probably feel bad for the poor guy.

But I'm not anyone else.

"Where are we on the interrogation?" I ask Yuri as soon as the waiter's out of sight.

"Fine," he sighs. "Anatoly isn't saying a word. Doesn't matter what I use, his answer's the same: 'I don't know anything.'"

"Do you believe him?"

"I don't know. He might be innocent."

I give a bitter laugh. "No one's innocent in the Bratva. What about Vlad?"

"I kept on his tail. Nothing suspicious yet."

"Maybe you're overextended, Yurochka," Grisha suggests. "I could take over tailing Vlad. Or extracting information from the suspect."

"Sure. You wanna kiss my ass, too?"

"Stop it," I growl. "He's right, Yura. I've been asking a lot of you."

"No, you haven't," he insists, that old desperation to prove himself shining right out of his eyes.

"Yes, I have. You can't be in two places at once."

"I can deal with Anatoly when Vlad's in a meeting," he protests. "I've done it before. It's not hard."

"Yuri—"

"Please," he murmurs. "Let me do this."

That's when it finally clicks.

Of course. There's a reason he doesn't want to give up the Vlad investigation, and a damn good one at that: Petra. He probably wants to be certain of Vlad's guilt—wants to see it with his own two eyes.

And he's too conflicted to tell me.

"Fine," I concede. "But you can't use this as an excuse to shirk your other duties. I'll expect you to fulfill those, too."

"I will," Yuri promises. "Thank you."

Conflict. I've been seeing a lot of that in my brother's eyes lately. I can't say I envy his position. He's got blood on either side of the equation.

No, not blood—*family.*

I used to think those two were the same thing. But if April's taught me anything, it's that you can't paint the world in black and white like that. Not when there are so many shades in between. April's blood did nothing but stab her in the back, time and time again, with the sharpest knives it could find. Still does, if given the chance. In her family by blood, everyone but Charlie is an enemy.

Charlie and April. In a way, I see us in them—Yuri and myself. After our father's betrayal, we were all we had. Just each other, the endless snow, and an unquenchable thirst for revenge. Those two half-siblings I left snoozing on the couch… they don't have anyone else, either.

Wrong. They have you.

Yes. They have me.

And like fuck am I going to abandon them. That promise I forced April to make wasn't just one-way; I intend to honor it, too. *Never again.*

Never again will I leave April to deal with her ghosts alone.

Clearly, Yuri's dealing with ghosts of his own, too, no matter what he says. He can refuse help all he wants, but that doesn't mean it's not needed. I've known my brother long enough to know what the circles under his eyes mean: he's exhausted, physically and mentally.

And I can't let that go on any longer.

"Stay on Vlad today. Let's give our suspect a break."

"A break?"

"Make him think we've abandoned him."

Yuri nods. "That makes sense. He'd be more willing to talk after that."

"What about me?" Grisha asks.

"You'll stay on April. After what happened yesterday, I want you with the other guards as often as possible. Keep them in line. Remind them it's not just Carmine they have to protect her from."

"Yes, *pakhan.*"

We break it off there. Our coffees have long since gone cold, but I swallow mine anyway. The bitterness helps. Grounds me in a way nothing else can.

I watch Yuri leave, then stop Grisha from going up. "I've changed my mind. I need you to drive me somewhere first."

"What about April?"

I hesitate. I want her to be safe, but this is important. "Have your men call if anyone comes," I decide. "And I do mean *anyone*, Grisha. I don't care if it's the fucking Tooth Fairy—I want to know about it."

"Noted." He types a quick text, then turns back to me. "Where to?"

The warehouse is exactly as I left it: rust-eaten, rank with the smell of blood and disinfectant. Half-hospital, half-prison.

Only, there's no chance of getting out of here.

I find Anatoly in Room A, as expected. He's been roughed up. Half his face is swollen, almost unrecognizable. If he'd been able to escape like that, I'm not sure I could have found him.

"Hello, Anatoly."

His head snaps up. "*Pakhan*. What… are you doing here?"

"I'm here to get answers."

I glance at the tools. Either they're untouched, or they've been cleaned spotless, because there isn't a speck of blood on them. I wonder if this is why Yuri couldn't get this guy to talk —if he didn't go hard enough on Anatoly for one reason and one reason only.

Kindness.

"Please, wait—"

I land the first punch in his gut. "Who are you spying for?"

This thing with Vlad must've been getting to Yuri more than I thought. He doesn't want to ruin that man's life—Petra's life—

without hard proof. That must be why he's been going soft on Anatoly. Subconsciously, he's been linking the two together.

I should've known it would be too much for him. This isn't just his mess—it's mine as well. And now, I'm going to clean it up.

Anatoly spits out a mouthful of blood. It's a while before he stops choking enough to answer, so I grow impatient. I land another blow, this time with the back of my hand to his face. "Who put you up to it? Who's been working with the enemy?"

"I already told him!"

I blink. "What?"

"That guy..." he heaves. "H-He was here before. I told him... everything..."

Sirens start blaring in my head. "What guy?" I shake Anatoly by the shoulders. "Who was here before me?"

"You know him... you, y-you..."

Shit. I shouldn't have called Yuri away this morning. "Talk to me, Anatoly. Talk to me and you're free: who came here?"

"He's your... h-he's..."

Suddenly, he starts foaming at the mouth. Blood mixes with it, coming down his chin in rivers. Fucking hell, did I hit him too hard?

A seizure, I realize. That's why Yuri was going easy: he must've known Anatoly was sick.

And, like an idiot, I stepped right into it.

"Call our doctor," I bark at Grisha. "Hurry!"

But he's barely dialed two digits when Anatoly's head rolls back, his tremors stopping.

I check his eyes: glassy, lifeless.

Dead.

"Shit!" I kick the tool cart over. "Fucking HELL!"

It takes me a minute to calm down. By the time I'm done trashing the room, I'm breathing hard and heavy. Cautiously, Grisha approaches me. "Did he say who he's been talking to?"

"He didn't have to. He said enough."

You know him. Those words are lodged into my brain like splinters. And then the other thing he was trying to get out. *He's your...*

"My father," I growl.

All this time, I've been following Vlad around like a fool, but he never had anything to do with it. The spy was on the Groza side—*my* side.

And my father was the one pulling the strings.

Again, Carmine's been one step ahead of me.

Again, he's taken away my only witness.

And again, I let him.

"FUCK!"

"Matvey," Grisha calls urgently, "there's something you need to know."

"What?"

He lifts his phone. "The bodyguards just texted me. Someone's at the penthouse. He said he was family, so they let him up."

I feel the blood drain from me. "Who?"

"They took a picture."

I stare at the screen. *It can't be. Not now, not today.*

Why the fuck is this happening now?!

"Stay here," I order him. "Call cleanup. Handle this mess. I'll take the car."

I don't have time to call Yuri and update him. I don't have time to think about anything else but the family I left at the penthouse, thinking foolishly they'd be safe without me.

But they're not.

They're in danger—all of them.

45

APRIL

When I wake up, there's a note from Matvey on the table.

Business meeting over breakfast downstairs. Will bring muffins back.

PS. Your cat is a menace.

I shake my head and laugh. "What did you do this time, Buttons?"

A furry little head pops up from the crib, the picture of innocence. It would almost work, except for the blue tie in its mouth.

"You little plunderer!" I scold without any real heat. "Always looking for treasures to hoard. I swear, it's like you're an actual pirate."

"Mrowr."

I swipe the tie and check on my baby. May's sound asleep, her tiny hands holding tightly onto Buttons's tail. To his credit, Buttons hasn't complained yet. "Fine. I'll let it slide, but only this once."

I give him a scratch behind the ears, then go wake up Charlie. "Rise and shine, sleepyhead."

He groans. "Five m're minutes…"

It's such a domestic scene, I can't help the stupid grin on my face. My cat's antics, my brother's complaints. My baby, sleeping the morning away just because. And then Matvey's note, sweet and ordinary, like we're just any other normal couple.

No Bratva, no fake marriages—just us.

I poke Charlie some more. When that doesn't work, I pull out my secret weapon. "I heard there's muffins on the way."

His head immediately pops up from the blanket. "Chocolate or blueberry?"

"Knowing Matvey, probably both."

"Can I have coffee, too?"

"Nope. You're way too young."

We're interrupted by knocking on the door. "I'll get it," I tell him.

Then, once I'm there, I stop. My hand is on the doorknob, but something tells me to be careful. Call it a sixth sense, a mother's instinct—whatever.

"Forgot your keys?" I ask through the door, putting on a carefree tone.

No reply.

"Matvey?" I try again.

The knocking resumes, more insistent. *BoomBOOMboomBOOM.*

"Sis?" Charlie calls over from the couch. "Something wrong?"

Yes. I don't tell him that, though. Instead, I lean quietly down and look through the peephole.

I freeze.

What is he doing here? How did he know where...?

I force my voice to sound calm. "Hey, can you take May to your room for a bit?"

Charlie frowns. "Apes, are you...?"

"It's okay," I cut him off. "I'll only be a second. But this is really important: no matter what you hear, I want you to stay with her. Can you do that for me?"

"You're scaring me."

"I know." I give him the best smile I can muster. "Don't worry. This'll be over in a second."

With a tight nod, Charlie obeys.

I can tell he doesn't want to. Even when we were kids, he was always throwing himself between me and danger. He was younger than me, but he still tried to save me every time.

Now, it's my turn to save him.

You could just keep the door shut, the rational part of me whispers. *Call Matvey, tell him what's happening. He'd come rushing at your side.*

But I don't call him. I'm done hiding behind other people's backs. I'm done running away.

I fight my own battles now.

So I take a deep breath, steel myself, and open the door.

"Hi, April," says the man on the other side.

I offer him a tight smile. "Hi, Tom."

The last time I saw my stepfather, I was seventeen.

It was the day I decided to stick it out at Dominic's until my eighteenth birthday. Not that I had any control over that: back then, I was being shipped back and forth like an unwanted parcel. But I knew how it worked, and I knew how to beg.

So I begged. I begged my father to take me back. I begged Nora, too, and my stepsisters. I apologized for all the imagined slights they'd cooked up against me and promised to be good from then on. I'd do all the chores, stay out of sight, be as quiet as a mouse.

Because I couldn't bear to see Charlie hurt again.

No—I couldn't bear to see him hurt *because of me.*

And I'm not going to let it happen now.

"Where's my son, April?"

I swallow hard. "I don't know what you mean."

"Oh, but you do. That's his backpack right there." He points to the corner of the couch.

Crap. "It's a common brand," I try.

"Sure, and I'm fucking Santa Claus. Now, where is he?"

I have to force myself not to gag or reel back. The stench of alcohol on his breath is enough to make anyone in a range of fifty feet test positive to a breathalyzer by osmosis. "I don't think this is a good idea, Tom. You've clearly had a few."

"And I'll have a few more after I get the kid back. Teach him some respect, while I'm at it."

"And give him another black eye?"

"I've got nothing to do with that."

"Right. I'm sure he just tripped."

"Why not? The boy's clumsy." He shrugs. His face is lobster-red, like just spent a week straight in the sun. I know better, of course. If there's anything Tom hates more than staying sober, it's waking up before dark. "Could trip over his own two feet. You remember, don't you? How distracted he can be?"

I grit my teeth. "I remember you helping him with that. And I'm not letting you do that anymore."

"For fuck's sake, he's a minor," he barks back. "You can't keep him from his parents. You'd be breaking the law."

"So let's call the police," I retort. "See what they think about that black eye. See what *he* tells them."

Unexpectedly, Tom bursts out laughing. "Oh, please! He won't say a goddamn thing, and you know it. After all, I still have his mom at home. Yours, too, not that you'd care."

I care enough not to want her in the hospital. I keep the words sealed tightly behind my lips. It wouldn't do me any good now to give Tom another weakness to exploit.

But he sees right through me. "Aw, isn't that sweet? Someone's got a heart after all. Thought all that money was turning you into a snob like your daddy."

"Tom, I will call the cops."

"Nah, see, I don't think you will. I mean, do you really want the police here?" He gestures broadly at the hotel. "Your *boyfriend* certainly wouldn't appreciate it."

"Partner," I correct icily.

"Sure, whatever. You think I don't read the papers? You think I don't know you hooked up with a mob boss? By all means, let's call the cops. See what they think of *that.*"

"Conspiracy blogs aren't 'papers'—"

"Whatever you sheeple say."

"—and if you think I'm going to just hand over Charlie, you're even stupider than I remembered."

That gets a reaction. "I'd be careful if I were you, April."

"Right back at you, Tom."

He laughs, dry and deranged. "What, you think I want the kid back? It's a hassle! But his mother won't stop fuckin' crying. It's like she's depressed or something. Won't even put out anymore."

"You're the worst, you know that?"

"I do my best."

"I can see that."

"How 'bout this, then?" He grins, showing a row of rotten teeth. "Step up and I'll let you keep him."

I frown. "'Step up' as in…?"

"Put out. Cross an item off your dear mommy's to-do list. I'm sure you remember how it goes? I mean, you've had a kid, so clearly you've finally learned what that shit between your legs is for. Or do you need a reminder?"

It takes me a moment to fully process what I'm hearing.

Then the rage sets in.

"You're disgusting," I spit.

"And you're not?" he guffaws. "Look who thinks she's hot shit just because she's fuckin' the gangster boss. Lemme tell you something, sweetheart: you're a whore."

"You—"

"A pathetic little side piece to some rich, married guy," he cuts me off without ceremony. "It's all over the papers, you know? Him with that blonde wife of his. Wouldn't mind getting a piece of *that*, but I guess everyone has to make do sometimes."

Suddenly, his hand shoots towards me. I pull away, but I'm not fast enough—his sweaty fingers close around my wrist, trapping me in the doorway.

"Let go of me," I rasp.

"What? You don't like married men anymore?" he mocks. His stale breath is right against me now, so close I could retch from the stench alone.

But what worries me the most is his other hand. It finds my hip and squeezes, hard enough to leave a bruise. I try to shake it off, but it's useless. I'm useless.

Come on, react. For God's sake, react! You're not a kid anymore! You're not young like you were when he last tried... when he...

I cast the memories off. They're no good to me now. Charlie was there last time. He didn't understand what was going on —only that his father wanted to hurt me. Back then, he saved me.

Now, there's no one.

Before long, Tom's hand starts sliding down, down, *down.* I'm paralyzed, a deer in the headlights. For a second, I forget everything: my brother in the next room, Matvey downstairs. All I can think is, *This is it. This is gonna happen.*

"You want it, don't you?"

"No," I croak.

"Fuck yeah, you do. You've always wanted it. That's what all those skimpy dresses were about, huh? You wanted me to rip them off of ya?"

"They weren't skimpy!" I cry out. "They were just dresses! I was seventeen, Tom!"

"And with a rack like a porn star. C'mon, be honest: you wanted to pull one over on Mommy, didn't ya? Steal her man and then brag about it?"

He keeps pouring filth into my ear. I can't do anything to stop it. Everything I say, he ignores; every denial, he mocks; and with every move I make to free myself, he only grips me harder.

React.

Fucking hell, react!

What if this was happening to your daughter?

That's what snaps me out of it. Of all things, it's May. May, who was born a girl in a world like this—a world I'm going to have to protect her from.

How the hell can I do that if I can't even protect myself?

"Guess I can make the sacrifice." Tom sneers as he feels up my thigh. "Fuck a couple cobwebs away since I'm at it. Maybe even put another bastard in ya."

"I doubt it," I force out. "You'd have to get it up for that."

I watch the lust drain from his face. Fury replaces it instead. "You little...!"

He pries his hand off my thigh and raises it high. I squeeze my eyes shut and brace myself: it's not the first slap I've ever gotten from Tom, but it's the first in a long time. I don't know how used to it I am anymore.

But before the blow can land, I hear a voice.

His voice.

"Get the fuck away from my woman."

46

MATVEY

I see red.

My fist meets Tom's face and something goes *crack*, sharp and sickening. I don't register the spray of blood, only the mounting rage in my chest. The beast inside me, howling, *That's not enough. Make him pay.*

It isn't just everything I've overheard during my walk down that long, long hallway. Words, I could still answer with words of my own. But the second I saw Tom's filthy hands on April, I fucking lost it.

"You piece of shit," I snarl as I throw him to the floor. "You stupid, miserable piece of—"

I hit him again, and again, and again. It's all I can see: my fist diving down, coming back redder each time. I can't even tell if he's begging—the ringing in my ears drowns out all else.

I knew Tom was violent. I knew he'd likely hit April in the time she was forced to live under his roof.

But *this*?

I can't even think straight. Is this the kind of attention she had to suffer? The humiliation she had to endure? Fucking hell, she was seventeen. Seventeen, and still, this scumbag would try...

Who says he only tried? whispers the darkest, ugliest part of me. *Who says he didn't succeed?*

I let out a roar and start pummeling him full-force. "I'll kill you. I'll fucking kill you, you fillthy—"

"MATVEY, STOP!"

The second I feel April's hands on me, my vision clears. The ringing fades. I can hear echoes of screams—a woman and a young boy. Eleanor, I realize, rushing over from the elevator.

And then...

Charlie.

I see him now, trembling in the doorway. His face is white, drained of all blood. He looks terrified.

He looks terrified of *me*.

"Dad...?"

I finally glance down. Tom's face is a red pulp, barely recognizable, like a bruised fruit squished under my heel. For a second, I think I've killed him.

Then I hear a rattling breath. "M-Mercy..."

I heave a sigh of relief. *He's alive.* I turn my attention back to the siblings, tuning out Eleanor's wails. "Charlie, I didn't mean—"

But when I stretch out my hand, he flinches away.

"Charlie?" I frown, but someone steps between us.

April.

"Don't talk to him," she says in the iciest voice I've ever heard.

"April, I didn't want…"

"He needs an ambulance," Eleanor sobs. "He's g-gonna die!"

"He's not gonna die, Mom." April rolls her eyes, but still whips out her phone. "It looks worse than it is. Right, Tom?"

I watch the family spring into action—or rather, April. Out of everyone here, she seems to be the only one keeping a cool head.

But the fury in her gaze is unmistakable.

I fucked up.

I fucked up again.

~

Before the ambulance arrives, I make myself scarce.

It's not exactly my choice, but April's firm: Right now, Charlie needs his space. And it wouldn't be good for me to be there when the paramedics arrived. Not with the state of my knuckles being a dead giveaway.

So I leave.

I spend that time wandering the streets. I wash my hands in a water fountain, the first I can find. The blood rushes down and melts with the dark gray of the sidewalk, leaving me with purple bruises only. I wash my face, too, letting the icy water ground me.

By the time I make it back, it's already dark. "Where's Charlie?"

"He went home," April replies curtly. "He might be still at the hospital, though."

"So he isn't coming back?"

She gives a dry laugh. "What do you think?"

"What do *I* think?" I growl, rage suddenly bubbling back to the surface. "I think Tom deserved it."

"Oh, yeah?" She takes an angry step towards me. "So that's why you almost killed him? You decided he deserved to die?"

"He was touching you!" I roar. "He was grabbing you. He was trying to—"

"So stop him!" April yells. "Punch him once and be done with it! But you don't beat him within an inch of death in front of his goddamn son!"

Even as I grind my teeth, the rational part of me knows April's right: I crossed a line. But right now, I'm too furious to listen to that part. Every time I close my eyes, that scene starts playing again on a loop, and it's driving me fucking insane.

Tom's hands.

April's terrified face.

"He was threatening my family," I snarl. "I'll protect my family in any way I see fit."

"No, actually, you won't." April's jaw sets. "Believe it or not, Matvey, this isn't how it works. This isn't your Bratva. In this home, we don't repay slights with death."

"'Slights'?" I hiss back. "You call those 'slights'? He called you a side piece!"

"Well, he was right, wasn't he?"

That stuns me into silence. "Excuse me?"

"You heard me."

Suddenly, it's like the world is spinning on its head. "The fuck does that mean?"

"What am I, Matvey?" she asks. "I'm not your girlfriend; I'm not your fiancée. I'm certainly not your wife. So what am I to you?"

"You're my woman," I rasp.

"I'm your side piece." Her voice starts to crack. "As far as the world is concerned, that's what I am."

"Who gives a shit about the world?"

"*I* do!" she screams. "I do, Matvey! If someone like Tom Hill can be right about me, then I care!"

"He wasn't right about—"

"You're married to another woman," she cuts in. "So how was he wrong?"

"That's different," I protest. "That's necessary."

"Yes, and for how long?"

That question catches me off-guard. "What does that mean?"

"What else can it mean?" she half-sobs. "Do you even plan to marry me, Matvey? Or is this all we're ever going to be?"

Of course I'm going to marry you. The words are halfway out already, but at the last possible second, they get stuck in my throat.

I can see the conversation playing out in my mind: *When?*

I don't know.

Where?

I don't know.

How?

I don't fucking know.

That's the simple truth of it: I do not know. "April…"

"Don't," she orders. I can tell she's biting back tears, trying hard not to break down in front of me. To be strong.

"I want nothing more than to be married to you," I tell her.

But she just gives me a sad, watery smile in return. "That's not true."

"It is."

"No. You have your dreams, Matvey: yours and Petra's. You want to conquer D.C., cut off the head of Carmine's operation, get your prizes. Your revenge. Her recognition."

"I thought you supported that," I say bitterly. "I thought you agreed."

"I do support you!" she says. "I support you both so much, you have no idea. But that's just it, Matvey: These are *your* dreams—yours and hers. Not yours and mine." Her voice drops to a whisper. "Will there ever be room for those?"

I don't know what to say. For the first time in my life, I'm left completely speechless. My rage has long ebbed away, leaving me empty as a shell.

Our dreams. All this time, I never even thought of that. Not with everything else I've got on my plate.

But if I start, what will happen to mine? My war? My revenge? No matter what, they're the most important things. That's what I've always told myself.

But do you still believe it?

Faced with my silence, April lifts her head high. "Go away. I need to be alone right now."

"April—"

"Please," she begs. "Just go."

I don't want to. Every cell inside me, every atom, is screaming at me not to do it. *Don't leave her. She's yours.*

But I do.

God help me, I do.

47

MATVEY

"You really fucked up this time, huh?"

I roll my eyes. "Go away, Petra."

Predictably, Petra ignores me. She sets down her copy of the keys and heads to the loft kitchenette. "Where's all your food?"

"Gone."

The truth is, I haven't stocked the pantry in a while. Haven't had a reason to. These past few months, I've only ever been here once or twice, to pick up stuff or check that no one was squatting.

Now, I can't remember what it was like to live here. I've been staring at the ceiling for God knows how long, and all I can think of is how unfamiliar this suddenly feels: the exposed brick walls, the industrial atmosphere, the steel-and-wood furnishings.

The silence.

The fucking *silence.*

Which is immediately broken again by Petra's rummaging. "How can you not have a single box of cereal?"

"I'm not five years old, that's how."

"Boring." She pulls an old bag of chips from the bottom of a cabinet and starts snacking. I almost miss when she was throwing up all the time from morning sickness—at least she wasn't raiding my kitchen. "Guess this'll do."

"Good. Now, get out."

"Is that any way to talk to your pregnant wife?"

"If she's being a bitch, then yeah."

"Ouch. I might just tell April you said that."

"See, this is what I don't get," I snap. "You're the reason I'm married. Why isn't April mad at you?"

"Who says she isn't?"

"You're here. I didn't call you here. In fact, I'd rather cut off both my balls with a butter knife."

Petra sighs. "Alright, fine. She told me. Happy?"

"No."

It's the height of insanity: Petra forced me to marry her. She needed this more than I did. So why isn't April tearing *her* a new one? Why am I getting kicked out while Petra's getting invitations to tea parties?

"God, you're such a man." She shakes her head.

"What's that supposed to mean?"

"That you're an incurable idiot," she clarifies. "You think April doesn't resent me? Wake up, Matvey: she does. She's just too kind to say it."

"Wasn't too kind to say it to me," I growl.

"Because you're the one who was supposed to put a ring on her finger," she retorts. "Have you done that yet?"

"Sure. Let's all go to Saudi Arabia. Then we can live happily ever after as a married triad."

"Matvey, look at me." She leans over the back of the couch with her elbows. "I'm safe now. My child is safe. If you were to divorce me, no one would blame me."

"Right. They'd blame *me.*"

"Yes. And you'd lose your army."

I let out a bitter laugh. "So what? You get what you wanted, but I don't get what I wanted?" I pull myself up from the couch, back turned to her. "Sure sounds like one hell of a deal."

"I wanted to be *vor*, Matvey. That hasn't happened yet."

"Forgive me for only saving your life, then."

"You're not listening." It's weird, hearing her like this: not angry, but resigned. Like she's aged ten years while I wasn't looking. "I'm telling you that I'm fine with that. I'm willing to make the sacrifice if it means my friend will be happy."

I stop. For a second, I wonder if I've heard wrong.

Because there's no fucking way, right?

There's no way Petra Solovyova just said she'll give up her power for the sake of someone else.

But she did. No matter how many times I replay her words in my head, they're still the same. "You're saying being *vor* doesn't matter to you anymore?"

"Are you kidding me?" she bristles. "Of course it does. But April matters more." She hesitates, words stuck somewhere between her lips and her heart. "I don't want my happiness to come at the cost of hers. I'm just… not that person anymore." She walks around the room and plants her feet right in front of me. "What about you?"

"What about me?"

"Are you willing to sacrifice?"

My vengeance. My dream. All my life, that's all that mattered to me. And now…

Now, I'm being asked to make an impossible choice. "I…"

When nothing else comes out, Petra nods. "See now why April will talk to me and not you?"

Fucking hell. She's so lucky she's pregnant. If anyone else had talked to me like that, they wouldn't have a tongue to clarify what they meant. "I get the feeling you're about to enlighten me."

"It's because you've still got one foot out the door," she explains. "You want to be with April, but you won't commit. It's all on your terms—never hers."

"I *am* committed."

"Right. So when are you going to marry her?"

I feel the rage mounting. "I already said—"

"That now is not a good time," Petra fills in. "Yes. I heard you. So what's the plan? Six months from now? A year? Until my father wakes up cold in his bed and yours is buried six feet under? Until May's going to college?"

"How am I supposed to know?!" I yell.

"Then how is April?!" she yells right back. "How is *she* supposed to know, Matvey?"

I open my mouth to answer, but no words come out.

In my mind, the dominoes start falling. One by one, like a fallen pebble slowly turning into an avalanche. Everything starts clicking then: April's melancholy, her reaction to Tom's insinuation, her anger. Her tears, stubbornly unshed.

"Good." Petra nods, watching me like a hawk. "I see the light bulb's gone off."

"I despise you."

"I know." She smirks. "Doesn't mean I'm wrong, though."

Unfortunately, it doesn't.

"*Blyat'*," I massage my temples against a raging headache. "Can't believe Yuri wants to marry you."

"Says the man who married me first."

"I think we've established that I deeply regret it."

Petra shrugs. "Maybe we were always meant to be something else."

"Like what?" I frown.

"Siblings-in-law?" she offers. "We certainly bicker enough."

Siblings. The idea should be ridiculous. I don't share a single drop of blood with Petra—how could I possibly put her in the same place as Yuri?

And yet, when she says it like that, it doesn't sound ridiculous at all. It sounds… factual.

It sounds right.

"Have I told you I despise you?"

"Only every day," she says wearily. "Now, go make things right with April. I don't want to be poked full of holes again next time she needs a living mannequin."

"She poked you full of holes?"

"'Accidentally.' Didn't I tell you she was mad at me, too?"

I shake my head. If there's one thing I'll never understand, it's this weird friendship of theirs. It would have been much easier to hate each other.

But hate is exhausting. Like love, it takes constant energy.

And, unlike love, it never gives back.

"Thank you."

"For my sacrifice?"

"Among other things."

Petra crumples the empty chip bag and dunks it in the trash. Then she turns to me from the doorway. "By the way, if you want to pay me back, you can do one thing."

"Which is?"

"Stop sending my boyfriend on errands. I haven't seen him in two days. I'm starting to forget what he looks like."

I frown. Why would Yuri…?

Oh. Right. In all the chaos, I forgot to call off the surveillance on Vlad. "My mistake. I'll make sure he comes back to you in one piece."

"That's all a girl can ask for."

She starts to leave, but I stop her. "Petra."

"Yeah?"

"Your father's in the clear. I thought you should know."

I watch her shoulders drop imperceptibly. With her back turned, I can't see her face, but maybe it's better that way. I have a feeling she wouldn't want me to see. Some things aren't for the eyes of others.

"Is that all?"

"That's all."

She climbs down the stairs without another word.

Once she's left, so do I.

~

"Yura, it's me. The suspect's dead. Report back to me as soon as you get this."

I finish my voice note just as my destination comes into view. Yuri hasn't been picking up, but that's nothing new. Lately, he's been in the middle of a hundred different assignments.

That's going to change.

When I get to the penthouse, April opens the door with a blank face. "I wasn't expecting you."

"I came to see May."

I don't know why I say that. The second the words are out of my mouth, I regret them. The last time I gave a proper apology, it was in the heat of the moment; now, under April's cold stare, it's like my ego's rebelling against me. That part of me that doesn't ask, only demands, is proving to be a lot harder to overcome than I thought.

"Of course," April replies, sounding disappointed. "She's in her crib."

I walk to the middle of the living room. May's having a rare moment of wakefulness. She's mesmerized by her mobile, pulling on the colorful toys one by one. When she sees me, her face breaks into a grin. "Da!"

I shake my head and smile. I'm not sure if she's trying to say "Dad" or if it's just a random sound of acknowledgement, but either way, it's meant for me. Or so I'll choose to believe.

"Hey there, *malyshka*."

She brightens even more. "Da! Da!"

At her request, I pick her up. It's amazing how big she's gotten in six short months. "Where's your friend, huh?"

Something shifts under the blankets. "Mrowr."

As expected. "Sounds like you're in good company."

"Buh, Buh!"

"That means 'Buttons,'" April informs me. "She only says it when he's near."

"Which is always."

"More or less, yeah."

NICOLE FOX

Silence descends back between us. "You haven't eaten yet." I nod towards the untouched tray.

"I wasn't hungry."

Let's have dinner. Three simple words, and yet I can't get them out. Something's still blocking me—something ugly and entitled rowing against my every move. My pride.

"Look—"

"Since you're here," April interrupts, grabbing a folder from the table, "I need you to sign this."

I frown. "And this is…?"

"Medical bills. For Tom."

My old rage immediately bubbles back up. "I'm not paying for that shithead's treatment."

"Yes, you are," April counters. "You put him there, Matvey. It's the least you can do."

"He put his hands on you."

"And you put your hands on him," she bites back. "So I guess you're even."

"Like hell we are."

Suddenly, a shriek pierces my ears. I remember May in my arms. Shit, did I grip her too tight? "Hey—"

"I've got this." She holds out her hands and the baby goes willingly, hiding her crying face in her mother's chest. "It's nothing you did," she reassures me as if reading my mind. "She's just sensitive to moods."

"I didn't mean to upset her."

"Yeah." She presses her lips tight. "Lots of things you didn't mean to do lately."

"That's not fair."

"Right. Because you've been nothing but fair to me."

I clench my fists at my sides. "April—"

"I'm tired," she says. "If there's nothing else you need, I'm going to bed."

"I came here to talk," I say. "I came here to—"

"To show me the divorce papers?"

I set my jaw. "It's complicated."

"No, Matvey. Actually, it's not complicated at all."

Shit. This isn't how this was supposed to go. "April…"

But she's already heading to the bedroom with the baby. The cat jumps after them. He watches me just long enough to give me the stink eye, then disappears behind the door seconds before it closes.

… Fuck.

48

MATVEY

Change is never easy. But sometimes, it's necessary. Sometimes, it's all we have.

So I'm going to do what I have to.

I make my way to Staten Island first thing in the morning. Finding the address is easy: the background check Grisha put together all those months ago still holds true.

It takes me to a trailer park. Again, no surprises.

I step around a heap of trash on the unkempt lawn. It's a far cry from my five-star hotel, but it isn't enough to move me to pity, either. I've seen worse. I've *been* worse.

Compared to the snows of Russia, this is paradise.

I stop in front of the right trailer and raise my fist to knock. For a second, though, I hesitate. The old me would never do something like this. No—he'd never even consider it. Matvey Groza, come to apologize? Please. He would find it humiliating, beneath him in every way possible.

But the old me didn't have April.

There used to be something comfortable in that: having nothing to lose. Having no one. If you're alone, you can't be called out, can't be pushed into a corner by anything or anyone. Can't be made to look in a mirror and risk hating what you see.

Once, I would have sworn by that life. I thought it was the only kind of life worth having. No one to answer to, no responsibilities to anyone but yourself. No one to come home to.

Now, I can't bear the thought of it.

I don't care how many advantages there are—I'm not going back to that. I'm not going back to a life of emptiness and misery. I've been in my own company long enough. Back then, I thought it meant strength: being alone.

But it doesn't. It just means loneliness.

And I've never been stronger than now that I have a family to protect.

I fucked things up with them. I know I did. And now, I have to make it right. So I take a breath and force myself to knock.

At first, I don't hear anything. *Maybe they aren't home.*

Then the shouting begins. "GET THE DOOR!"

"I'M ON CRUTCHES! YOU GET IT!"

"WELL, I'M COOKING *YOUR* LUNCH, YOU UNGRATEFUL FREELOADER!"

"Stop yelling! I'll do it!" comes a younger voice from the bottom of the trailer. Seconds later, the door cracks open. "Yes…?" The second he sees me, his eyes go wide. "Matvey."

"Charlie," I whisper back. "I was hoping I could talk to you for a second. In private."

Hesitation flashes across his face. I can't blame him—he's got every right to be afraid. Last time we saw each other, I was a beast. I lost sight of myself and everyone around me. Why should he trust me now?

From inside, Tom bellows, "WHO IS IT, BRAT?"

"IF IT'S THE LANDLORD, TELL HIM WE'LL PAY AS SOON AS HE FIXES THE WATER HEATER!" Eleanor adds.

"STARTING NEXT MONTH, THOUGH!"

"It's not the landlord!" Charlie shouts back. "It's just…" He pauses, uncertain. "Girl Scouts."

"TELL THEM WE DON'T WANT THEIR SHITTY COOKIES!" Eleanor screeches.

"OHH, GET ME NOUGAT!" Tom chimes in.

"NOT WITH MY MONEY, YOU DON'T!"

"AND TWO BOXES OF CARAMEL!"

"Okay! I'll just be a minute!" He shuts the door behind his back and sighs. "Sorry."

"No need to apologize." I nod towards the trailer. "Are they always like this?"

"No. Usually, they're worse." A weak laugh. "So, what did you…?"

"Right." God, this is awkward. "Is there anywhere we could…?"

At first, Charlie hesitates. Just for a second, but there's no way I'd miss it. That's my fault, too: that single heartbeat of fear. I despise myself for putting it there.

"I know a place," he says eventually. "Follow me."

Behind the trailer park, there's an actual park. It's a small, jungle-looking thing that doesn't show up on any map, probably because no one's taken care of it since the war ended. The *Civil* War.

"Here," Charlie says, hopping up a moss-covered garden wall to sit. "No one will hear us."

I remain standing. "Good."

Then I don't say anything else.

Charlie peers up at me, uncertain. He has the same nervous habit April has: wringing his hands when uncomfortable. Silence, it seems, has a way of making both siblings uneasy.

So I break it the only way I can. "I'm sorry. For what happened the other day."

Charlie swallows. "I-I know. April said you didn't mean to..."

April. Even when she's not present, here she is, defending the worst of me. "I didn't mean to put him in the hospital," I agree. "I did mean to punch him, though. I won't apologize for that. But I never wanted you to see it, Charlie. Never."

He gives a weak nod. "It was scary, seeing you like that. It was like you weren't there. I thought you were gonna..." He doesn't finish that sentence, but I can damn well fill in the rest. *Kill him.* "It reminded me of him a little bit. My dad."

That cuts deep. Not just because of my pride, but because of my family. Did I really show April such an ugly side of me? Did I remind her of Tom, too?

No wonder she was so furious with me. So heartbroken.

"It was one of my worst moments," I say. "I wasn't always a good man. Even now, I'm not sure you'd call me that. But since I met your sister... I've been trying to do better. I *want* to do better. And I want to be better for you, too." I look him straight in the eye. "Will you give me another chance?"

Charlie blinks. He seems surprised by my words. The rawness of them. It must be a new experience for him, seeing an adult own up to his mistakes. "Okay."

"Okay," I repeat.

"Can I ask you something?"

"Of course. Shoot."

"What happened the other day?" he asks. "Why did you guys start fighting like that?"

Ah. There it is.

"What did April tell you?"

"Not much," he mumbles. "Just that things got out of hand. But I still don't understand what was going on."

"Your dad..." I start. "He was saying some things. *Doing* some things that..." Just the memory's enough to make my blood boil again, but I force myself to push through it. Charlie's blameless in this. I won't taint his father's image in his eyes. "They were inexcusable. But so was I."

"What things?" he presses. "I only caught a few words, but I couldn't really tell what April and Dad were talking about. It sounded like they were arguing."

"They were," I confirm. "I didn't get there myself until the very end, but by the time I got there, it wasn't just an argument anymore. Your father was calling your sister some very nasty names. And then..." I grit my teeth. I don't want to ruin whatever scrap of relationship this boy has with his dad, but like fuck am I going to cover for Tom of all people. And yet, at the same time, the thought of shoving the worst of his dad—the worst any man is capable of—in Charlie's face is more than I can bear. Out of anyone in this situation, he's the one true innocent. "He had his hands on her," I say in the end. "And I wasn't going to stand for that."

Charlie's eyes widen in understanding. "He was trying to beat her up again?"

Among other things. "Yes."

His face darkens. "She didn't tell me that."

"She probably didn't want to get between you and your dad," I suggest. "She was trying to protect you. Him, too, I suppose."

"Yeah, she's always doing that," he mutters. "Trying to protect all of us. Even the ones who don't deserve it."

"*You* deserve it," I cut in. "Of all people, you deserved to be kept safe from him. He gave you a black eye, Charlie."

"You gave him two."

I grimace. Of course a simple apology wasn't going to make up for putting his father in the goddamn hospital. That's just the first step in earning a person's forgiveness. Unless I follow it up with action, it will mean nothing.

"That's fair. I deserved that."

"Sorry," he winces. "I didn't mean to get snappy."

"You have every right to." I put my hand on his shoulder. There's a slight flinch in his frame as I draw near, and it breaks my goddamn heart.

I did this. I made him afraid of me.

But in the end, he lets me. In the end, he chooses to trust me. Even if I haven't earned it back yet.

In that, too, he's so much like his sister.

"But Charlie, I need you to understand something: I hit a grown man. I didn't hit a kid—*my* kid. Doing that to your own child... that's not okay. Never."

He nods grimly. "Apes used to say the same thing. Back when she lived here."

"Your sister's wise. You should listen to her."

His lips twitch, the ghost of a smile. "Yeah, I know. You should, too, by the way."

"Believe me, I know."

"I'm glad she found someone like you," Charlie says, surprising me. "April's never... She didn't have much growing up. Even though her dad's rich, he never gave her a cent. Never took her anywhere, never came to visit... I'm not saying mine's better, but at least I got to know him. For better or worse, he's around. Dominic's just... some stranger."

I feel a stab straight through my chest. That's why April doesn't want to come clean, isn't it? She knows the pain of not having her dad around. How could she possibly inflict that on her brother?

"And Mom always played favorites. She would spoil me all the time and treat April as a second-rate kid. It was unfair, but she never said anything. She just took it."

"She loved you," I say. "Sometimes, we eat shit for the people we love."

"She had every right to hate me," Charlie says. "But she never did. She was more of a parent to me than either of mine. All while both of hers treated her as the second choice."

Second choice. I didn't realize until now, but Charlie's words have finally opened my eyes: that's what I've been doing, too. It wasn't intentional, but I still did it.

By marrying Petra, I treated April as a second choice, too.

It's no wonder she reacted the way she did. No wonder she finally gave me an ultimatum. Would I ever have noticed if she hadn't? Or would I have kept going on like this, blind to all her suffering?

"Matvey? Did I say something?"

I shake myself out of my thoughts. "No, no. I just realized I have to be somewhere."

"I'll walk you back."

As we make our way out of the jungle-park, I give Charlie my number. "Not just for emergencies—for anything. I can't promise I'll pick up all the time, what with work and everything, but I'll always call back. Always."

"Thanks," he says. Then: "Hey, is it true that you're with the mob? Dad was yelling about that yesterday in the hospital."

I give him a sideways glance. "I could tell you, but then I'd have to kill you."

"Too soon."

"Right. Sorry."

He breaks into a big grin. "Nah, I'm just messing with you. I'll visit, okay?"

I nod. "Anytime."

Then I'm back on the road.

～

"*Krasiviy!* One more of these!" Vlad punctuates his request by slapping the waitress on the ass.

I clench my fist under the table, forcing myself not to create another diplomatic incident. "Tip her generously," I mutter under my breath, then realize there's no one at my side.

Right. Yuri's still MIA.

I type a quick text under the table. *You don't need to follow Vlad anymore. Call me back.*

P.S. Your girlfriend's been camping out in my kitchen. Come get her before I have to call security.

There. Maybe this time, he'll deign to pop out of the bushes or something.

"Am I boring you, son?"

"Not at all," I lie. When April asked me for space, I took the chance to indulge Vlad's demands for a night out. Now, I'm regretting every single thought that led me to that decision. "Your way of bonding with the servers is enlightening."

He gives a boisterous laugh. "Oh, loosen up! Girls are meant to be sampled."

"And here I thought that was the wine."

"Like you're such a saint," he harrumphs. "Though I can't say I blame you. I know we've had our differences on the subject, but now that the ax is buried, I've got to tell you I almost envy you."

"I have no idea what you're talking about."

"That woman," he waves. "The one you keep around to warm your bed."

My knuckles go white. "I beg your pardon?"

"I'm just saying, I wish *my* wife had been so understanding. Then I wouldn't have had to spend a fortune in hotel rooms every time I wanted a good fuck."

"If you're talking about April, I suggest you shut your—"

"Oh, let's not beat around the bush," he cackles. "A wife is to make a family with. But every man needs a whore."

That's it: I rise from my chair and knock it to the floor. My fists slam on the table, sending the glasses toppling every which way.

"Oy!" Vlad shouts. "What's gotten into you?!"

"I have to go."

Wife. Whore. In the world's eyes, it's always one or the other. That's how it's always going to be, isn't it?

Because I already have a wife.

So what does that make April?

It's the last straw. I ditch Vlad in his red-faced stupor and get back to my car. Then I race to the penthouse.

Time to make things right.

49

APRIL

I've already put May to bed when I hear him knocking.

I know it's him. Of course it is. No kidnapper in their right mind would even think of knocking, and it's way too late for any of the other usual suspects: Grisha, Yuri, Petra. Only one person remains.

Only him.

I make my way to the door with trudging steps. I'm exhausted. These past few days have been harrowing in more ways than one. Right now, I just want to sink into a dreamless sleep.

"April? Are you still up?"

I place my palm on the door. "It's late, Matvey. If you're here for May—"

"I'm here for you."

My heart skips a beat. My stupid, stupid heart, still holding onto every crumb it can find: affection, love, hope. A future in paling grays. "I'm tired. Can we do this another time?"

"No."

I sigh. "Matvey—"

"You don't have to let me in," he adds. "I'll talk from here. You just have to listen."

Listen. It's what I begged of him all those months ago. How can I deny him now? How can I deny him anything?

"Fine. But I don't want to fight."

"Neither do I."

With a slow exhale, I turn my back to the door and let myself lean against it. My palm finds a spot to rest on, fingers slightly curled, as if looking for a hand on the other side.

I wonder if there is one. If, right now, Matvey's doing the same thing I am: putting all the weight of the past few days on this impersonal slab of wood, the only physical thing separating us. The door he used to come through every night for dinner. The door I used to open for him, after a knock just like tonight's.

The door I might never open again.

I've already made up my mind. He doesn't know, but I have. This is the last chance I'm going to give him. If he keeps missing the point—if he keeps trying to shove me in a penthouse-shaped box for him to come and go as he likes, in the dark, while he steps out into the light with Petra on his arm—then I'll pack my things and leave. I'll go back to my old apartment with June. I'll go back to my old life, the life I would have led if that fateful kidnapping had never happened. If I'd never had to seek out the stranger I met that day at the tailor shop.

If I never got to know him in the first place.

And if he wants to see May, of course I'll let him. Of course I'll open another door for him, treat him like the father of my daughter, treat him as a friend. Maybe we could get there, in time.

And maybe, in time, I could forget him.

It's the hardest decision I've ever had to make. Even thinking about it is enough to bring tears to my eyes, tightness to my throat, and how lucky is it that I don't have to talk tonight? That I can hide behind this wall we've built?

All I have to do is listen. For two words that will never, ever come.

Because this is Matvey Groza we're talking about. He's already apologized for a lifetime; he's not going to do it again.

He's just *not*.

He's—

"I'm sorry."

I blink through the tears. "Huh?"

He doesn't hear me. It was such a small sound, so of course he doesn't hear me. But he does one thing: he keeps talking. "I'm sorry," he repeats, like a mantra he hasn't quite mastered yet. "For everything."

I find my voice again. Weak, and small, but there. "What's 'everything'?"

"My choices," he replies. "From the start, I've been making the wrong ones. When you came to me at the wedding, I should've called it off. I didn't know what you'd become to me, but I should have. I should have known. Maybe part of me always knew, deep down."

"Matvey...?"

"And everything after that, too," he continues, oblivious to the way I'm shaking. The way *he's* making me shake, one word at a time. "The coldness. The silence. I was so cruel to you. I literally pushed you to the edge."

"That wasn't you." I shake my head in the dark. "That was a lot of things. That was *me.*"

"But it was me, too. And I should've seen it coming." He takes a deep, ragged breath, like he's in pain. Like the words are splinters and he's prying them out one by one. "I promised I'd listen after that, but I didn't. Not really."

"You did," I protest.

"No, I didn't. I missed the most important part. The part you weren't saying out loud."

I laugh, dark and bitter. "How is that your fault?"

"Because it was obvious. Because all I had to do was listen to everything else. The way your family treated you, the way you expected to be treated—that's the way I treated you, too. I didn't mean to, but I did. I treated you as a second choice. And for that, there is no excuse."

I feel like I'm dreaming. Like I'm passed out somewhere and hallucinating, letting my subconscious pour every word I've ever wanted to hear out of Matvey's mouth into my sleeping ears.

If so, then it's the cruelest dream I've ever had.

"You mean that?"

"I do," he rasps. "Do you remember the letter you left me? When you went away?"

"How could I forget?"

"You said our baby deserved better than me. Better than a divided heart."

"And I was wrong!"

"Yes, you were. But not the way you think."

I clutch the door with all I have. I sink my nails into the wood, hoping something, anything will come from the other side. A single trace of warmth will do. A hint of his cologne. Proof that he's real. That this is all real.

"How, then?"

"Because you deserved that, too. You also deserved better than a divided heart, April, not just our daughter. And you deserve it still."

A divided heart. For so long, those words have haunted me, reminding me of my worst mistake. Our worst misunderstanding.

And yet, deep down, I felt them to be true. I didn't know how, or why, but I felt them. Deep down, I wasn't ready to let them go.

Now, I finally know why. "What are you saying?"

"That you'll always be first for me, April. You'll always be first in my heart."

My head spins. I'm forced to brace against the door, brace with all I have. My other hand rises to cover my mouth, to keep my sobs at bay for just a little longer.

Because no one has ever said that to me. All my life, no one has ever called me "first."

No one.

"I can't change what I've done," Matvey says. "I can't change the way I made you feel. And I can't... I can't break things off with Petra. Not yet."

The whiplash almost knocks me to my knees. "But you said..."

"I know, and I mean it. But I have responsibilities, too. To my Bratva... and to myself. So I can't divorce Petra right now."

I knew it. Here I am, getting all my hopes up like some schoolgirl, and now... Now, we're back where we started.

"I can't accept that, Matvey." I harden myself. "Either I'm first or I'm not. There's no middle ground for—"

"One month."

I blink. "What?"

"One month," he growls. "Give me one month to go through with the D.C. plan. That way, I can attack Carmine with the full force of my army."

"And if you lose?"

"Then I'm done."

It feels like my ears are playing tricks on me. "Done...?"

"Done with this life. Done with all of it."

I can't believe it. *Is he really saying...?* "You'd give up on your revenge? For me?"

"I'd give up everything for you."

"Don't say that," I warn. "Don't say it if you don't mean it."

"Win or lose, I will stop living a lie. I *want* to stop living a lie. Because you're the only truth that matters."

"Matvey..."

"I will get down on one knee and I will put the biggest, gaudiest rock I can find on your finger," he says, and I'm a mess of tears now, because how else can I react to that? How else does anyone react when being told that... that...

That they're the most important thing in the world?

"You're serious?"

"I'm serious," he insists. "All this time, I've been chasing after the shadows of my past—but you're my future, April. And I want it all with you."

"I... I... I don't know what to say."

"You don't have to say anything. You just have to let me in."

I look back at the dark penthouse. At the things I was ready to pack, the life I was ready to leave.

Then I turn and unlock the door.

50

APRIL

I crash into Matvey's chest before I can even think about it. "You really mean it? You'll marry me?"

"Yes." He holds me close for a moment, then lets out a low chuckle. "But if you want me to do this properly, you'll have to let me go."

Reluctantly, I oblige. I don't want to let him go—I never want to let him go again—but part of me is too curious to resist.

"Fine. Be quick?"

"Promise."

Then he gets down on one knee.

My heart jumps. It's like all the breath has been knocked out of my lungs. My mouth is hanging open like a goldfish's, because this can't be what he meant, can it? He can't be...

Proposing.

"Actually, this isn't proper at all," Matvey corrects himself. "I've got no ring, no roses, not even a glass of champagne."

"I'm in my pajamas," I blurt back. "I look like a mess."

"You look beautiful." His eyes lock with mine, so blue and deep I could lose myself in them. Maybe I already have. "And I promise I will do this properly—"

"When my hair is done."

"When your hair is done," he concedes. "But I couldn't wait a moment longer."

Then he pulls something out of his pocket.

I squint. Despite the dim lights, I manage to make out a piece of fabric, long and sleek and gray. No, blue.

No—*cornflower blue.*

It's a hair ribbon. *My* hair ribbon. From when we first met.

"You kept it all this time?"

"Always," he replies, and it sounds like the truth. Like a vow.

Wordlessly, he ties it to my finger. *I have no ring*, he said, but this is better than a ring, better than any diamond.

This is *us*.

And it's all I ever wanted.

"April Esther Flowers…"

"I never told you my middle name," I sniffle, but there's no stopping the smile spreading on my cheeks.

"I have my sources." He winks. "Now, can I please pop the question?"

I look at the ribbon around my finger. At his tie, his suit—the same one from the shop. I didn't notice until now, but it's the very same, down to the gray shirt and blue tie. *Ours.* "Do it."

"April Esther Flowers, will you marry me?"

Will I? After you've made me fall in love with you in every possible way, will I marry you?

"Yes." I nod, crying and laughing at the same time. "Yes, Matvey Groza, I'll marry you."

The second he stands back up, I fly into his arms. He twirls me like I'm weightless, the curve of his smile pressed against my skin. It's such a rare thing, I want to burn it there forever.

Forever. Maybe we can have that after all.

I'm expecting my feet to touch the ground, but they don't. "Matvey?"

"I'm sorry."

I blink. "You already apologized."

"No, I'm sorry for this." He carries me to the bedroom, then presses me down on the mattress. "I can't wait anymore," he rasps, voice filled with desire. "I want you now."

My eyes go dark and hooded. "Then take me."

And he does.

He takes me every way he can, any way he wants me. He takes me with his mouth first, capturing my lips like a hunter with his prey, like he wants to eat me whole.

When his teeth graze my throat, I sigh. "Matvey."

When his beard scratches my inner thigh, I keen. "*Matvey.*"

When his tongue plunges deep inside me, hot and rough and beautiful, all I can do is hold on for dear life. "Matvey!"

"*Blyat*," he curses against my flesh. "Say it again. Let me hear you, *kalina*."

So I do. I say his name like a prayer, letting it echo in the four walls of our bedroom. I say it like a vow. It's sacred, it's obscene. It's both, because that's what we are: a mix of the best and worst of us.

"Fuck me," I gasp. "I need you."

I'm so wet I could come from his gaze alone, but he doesn't let me. Instead, he parts my legs ferociously and yanks me forward until our hips are flush together. Until there can't possibly be a distinction between us.

Then he sinks into me.

I grab the sheets and twist them in my hands. I know this isn't our wedding night, but it feels like it is. All the ingredients are here: a vow, a kiss, a bed. His rough palms on my breasts, his hard cock pushing its way into me. I lock my ankles at the small of his back, refusing to let go.

"April," he groans. "Fuck, *April.* I can't… I need to—"

"Do it," I rasp. "I'm yours."

That's all it takes to convince him.

He throws one leg around his shoulder and starts fucking me in earnest, spearing me open with every thrust. There's no self-control in it, no restraint—only raw, selfish need.

"Just like that," I moan. "Just like that, Matvey, I—*ahh*—"

He finds my hand and covers it with his. I can feel his warm fingers fill the gaps between mine. His mouth descends on me: hungry, primal, possessive. Like he can't bear to have a single inch of empty space between us. His cock keeps pistoning inside me, trying to reach the deepest part of me.

"Matvey, I'm gonna—"

"Come for me," he snarls. "Come for me, *kalina*. Only for me."

"For you," I promise. "Only for you."

Then I see white.

It's the most intense orgasm I've ever had. For a second, it's like my body doesn't belong to me at all; like it belongs to *him*. Pleasure sparks so hot, I'm afraid I'm going to pass out, but Matvey doesn't let me. He just keeps going.

So I come again. And again, and again, until I lose track of it all: my pleas, my cries, my prayers. Night turning into day. Into everything.

Everything for *us*.

~

By the time I manage to grab a shower, it's well into the day. "Morning." I smile as I step out.

"Morning," Matvey greets, even though it's almost noon. "Slept well?"

"No," I laugh. "Not a wink. You made sure of that."

"That I did." He presses a kiss to my ring finger, the one with the ribbon still tied. Even under the spray, I refused to take it off. "My future wife deserves nothing less."

Wife. It still seems so unreal, so dreamlike. "Maybe we should just elope. Next month, I mean."

"Mhmm."

"Planning weddings is expensive."

"I can do expensive."

"And time-consuming."

"Someone's in a rush to lock me down."

"Can you blame me?"

I say it jokingly, but Matvey's eyes turn intense, his hand coming to hold mine. "No," he says. "Anything you want."

For a second, words fail me. I don't think I'll ever get used to it: being on the other side of that look. The sheer adoration in it.

"Even if it's a shotgun wedding?"

"Even if it's a shotgun wedding."

"No literal shotguns, though."

"I'll be sure to clear that with the guests." He presses one last kiss to my knuckles, then rises from the bed. "I have to go now."

"I know." I press a kiss right back. "Wars don't win themselves."

"No, they don't. And little brothers who won't pick up the phone need to be scolded back into line."

"Yuri's ghosting you?" I laugh. Talk about attitude.

"Apparently. To think, I wanted to give him *less* work. Serves me right."

"I'm sure he'll appreciate it once he finds out." Matvey goes to pick up his jacket, but I stop him. "Wait. I have something you can change into."

I walk up to the mannequin and take off the sheet.

Matvey shakes his head, but there's a hint of a smile there. "How come you've always got a suit jacket waiting for me?"

"That's kinda my whole thing." I wink. "Try it on?" He obligingly turns his back to me. I slip it around his shoulders, letting him get a feel for it. "Good? Not too rigid?"

He grins. "It's perfect."

Of course it is. I made it with him in mind. Everything, from the sleek black fabric to the lining, was picked for one person.

My person.

I steal one more kiss at the door. "Call me later?"

"I will."

The next hour goes by in a giddy flurry of activity. I get dressed, fix some of the mess around the house, take care of May. "Rise and shine, sleepyhead." I swear, if I hadn't gone to wake her, she might've just slept the day away.

My stomach's growling for lunch when I hear the doorbell. "Room service?" I wonder out loud. Maybe Matvey sent them for me?

Or maybe he decided to come back early?

But when I open the door, it's not room service. Or Matvey.

"Yuri!" I jump up to hug him. "It's been so long. I feel like I haven't seen you in forever!"

"Hi," he replies, taken aback.

To his immense relief, I let him go. "Been busy with work?"

"Yeah," he says. "Kind of. Is Matvey around?"

"You just missed him," I tell him. "He took Grisha and went to work. He was looking for you, actually."

"Really?" he asks. "Did he say why?"

"Nope." I shrug. "Just that you were ghosting him."

I turn my back and lean down to fix the last of the mess in the living room. I mean, it's Yuri, but still—can't show him I've been living in a pigsty.

"Hey, are you hungry?" I ask. "I was just about to call up room service. Why don't you stop for lunch? You can spend a little time with May, and we can—"

"I'm sorry."

I blink. "Oh, that's okay! I understand if you can't stay. We can catch up some other time, or—"

"I'm really sorry, April."

"It's fine! You shouldn't—"

BAM!

Pain explodes behind my head. Suddenly, everything starts spinning. "—apolo... gize... huh...?"

I fall on my back, but someone catches me.

I try desperately not to blink. It's like the world is fading, pulsing in and out of focus. "Yu... ri...?"

It's the last thing I see: Yuri's eyes, hard and cold, unlike any other time I've seen them. Like they belong to an entirely different person.

And his face, overflowing with heartbreak.

"I'm sorry. I had no choice."

My head swims, and the world goes black.

51

APRIL

It's the cold that wakes me up.

I blink my bleary eyes open with effort, the back of my head pounding. "Wh...what... h-happened?" I rasp. "Where am I...?"

I try to look around. This is a place I don't recognize. The light is dim, too dim to see properly. Which is strange, because I can hear birds outside.

What was I doing before this? I was at the penthouse. I was alone with May. Matvey had just gone to work.

Then I remember.

I *wasn't* alone. Someone came by.

I let him in, but that was okay, because I knew him. Because I trusted him.

And then...

I'm sorry. I had no choice.

I scramble upright. I squint, willing my eyes to adjust to the semi-darkness around me. It's like being in a damp hole in the ground. For a second, I wonder if I've been shoved into a well.

"May?" I call. "Baby, are you there?"

I feel around on the floor, but she isn't anywhere.

Panic sets in. "My daughter," I gasp. "Where's my daughter?"

I try to find purchase on the wall, but when I stretch out my hand, it isn't concrete I find.

It's iron bars.

Not a well, then.

Somehow, the thought isn't all that comforting.

I grab the bars with both hands and start tugging. It's useless —they're too heavy—but the mama bear in me won't hear it. I keep trying to pry the ugly things off the ground, screaming my lungs off in the process. "WHERE'S MY DAUGHTER?"

"Ma! Ma!"

I stop.

May. I'd recognize her voice anywhere. "Who's there?" I snarl. "Show yourself!"

Then I see her.

But she isn't alone. There's a man holding her, and as he steps out of the shadows, I give a huge sigh of relief. My baby's docile in his arms, the tiniest frown on her little face from the distress in my tone. But otherwise, she looks perfectly content where she is. And why wouldn't she be?

After all, she's in her uncle's arms.

"Yuri." It's such a familiar sight that, for a second, the prison bars disappear. Like we're back at the motel in Jersey. "What's going on?"

But something's wrong. Not just with the situation— with *him*.

Yuri's face is dark, guarded. Miles away from the honest young man I've come to know. "April. How are you feeling?"

I don't like the way he asks me that. Like he knows way more than I do about how we ended up here, and why. Normally, that would be a weight off my shoulders, but every single piece of this puzzle feels crooked.

Like it doesn't really fit with the picture in my mind.

Like it's a part of a different picture entirely.

"How am I feeling?" I echo. I blink in disbelief. "I'm in a cell. I woke up on the floor. How do you think I'm feeling?"

He grimaces. "Yeah. Sorry. That must've been uncomfortable."

"Uncomf—" I stop and collect myself before I try again. "Yuri, what the hell? What is this? Why am I in here? And why are you holding my kid over *there*?"

"Here," a second man says, stepping out of the shadows. "I'll take her."

I freeze.

That voice.

The first time I heard it, I was in my motel room. The second time, I was in a cabin. Now, I have no idea where I am.

But if *he's* here, it can't be anywhere good.

"Carmine," I hiss.

A hand descends on Yuri's shoulder. His eyes widen, a spark of irritation flaring in the dark. For a fraction of a second, it looks like he might bite the whole thing off.

But then Yuri swallows, just once, and obediently hands over my daughter to the devil himself. "Careful. She doesn't like strangers."

"Strangers?" the man chuckles. "My, my, you wound me. We actually have a lot in common, this little one and I. After all, am I not her grandpa?"

"Get your hands off of her."

He finally looks at me. "April," he greets with a polite, everyday smile. "Are you quite sure? Because I can do that, but then she'll fall."

Then, with the most natural shrug in the world, he starts to loosen his grip.

"NO!" I scream.

I stretch out both hands through the bars, but I'm too far away.

Yuri isn't, though. His palms immediately shoot forward, ready to break my baby's fall, ready to...

"Just kidding." Carmine smirks, grip growing firm again. "Oh, loosen up, you two. I wasn't going to actually drop her."

With a snarl, Yuri's arms fall back to his sides. "Quit fucking around," he snaps. "No harm must come to them. That was the deal."

"And I'm a man of my word," Carmine agrees, his cheerful lilt suddenly sharpening at the edges. "So why don't we watch that tone, *consigliere?*"

Yuri's face drains. It's just for a heartbeat, but the fear there is unmistakable. And yet, instead of reaching for his gun, all he does is hang his head in defeat. "Yes, boss."

Boss. No. It can't be.

"Yuri?" I murmur. "That's... that's not true, is it?"

His lips press into a tight line, but he stays quiet.

"Tell me it's not true."

Nothing.

"You wouldn't do this to us," I stammer, hands tight around the bars. "You wouldn't do this to Matv—"

"Don't," he barks. "Don't say his name."

"Why?" I ask. "Why can't I say his name, Yuri? Why are you doing this?"

But he doesn't answer.

This is a nightmare. It has to be. Because there's no way Yuri would turn traitor, right? There's no way he'd ally with Carmine. That he'd kidnap me and my kid, bring us into the den of the enemy, and then...

I'm sorry. I had no choice.

"The mole," I realize, pieces finally falling into place. "That was you. All along, you've been working with *him?*"

Again, silence.

This can't be real. This is Yuri we're talking about—*our* Yuri. The same Yuri who's always had my back, who helped me hide when I needed to… Who brought us food, sang lullabies to my daughter when I was too tired to do it…

Matvey's little brother, the person he trusts most in the world…

I can't believe this. I don't *want* to believe this.

"Say something," I beg, voice breaking. "For God's sake, just say something!"

But his silence is more damning than any excuse.

"Does Petra know?" I ask finally. "Does she know you betrayed everyone? That you betrayed your own *family*?"

"I didn't betray my family!"

His outburst catches me by surprise. He steps forward and I reel back on instinct.

For the first time in my life, I'm afraid of the person in front of me.

"I didn't betray my family," he repeats, lower. "They're the ones I'm doing this for. So don't come for me, April. Not when I know you'd do anything to protect yours."

"Yuri…"

What happened? I want to ask again. *What forced you to do this? What made you think you had no choice?*

Why didn't you just talk *to us?*

I try to reach for him through the bars, but he slips away in an instant.

"I take it you haven't told her?" Carmine inquires.

"Told me what?"

"Shut up," Yuri seethes, but not at me. "There's nothing to tell. She has nothing to do with it. There's no need to involve her."

"I'd say she's already involved," Carmine counters with a shrug and a pointed look at my cage. "But sure. Whatever you want."

"Would everyone please stop talking as if I'm not here?" I snap.

That seems to amuse Carmine. "I love nothing more than a dramatic reveal, Ms. Flowers, but I'm afraid this isn't my story to tell."

Then they start walking away.

"Wait!" I yell. "Where are you taking her?! Give me back my daughter!" I start rattling my bars again. "May! MAY!"

"April, ENOUGH!" Yuri yells back. "Seriously, just... stop. This isn't helping anyone."

"How can you ask me that?" I croak. "How can you ask me to just give her up like this?"

"I'm not," he says. "But until this is over, you need to trust me."

"I did trust you. And look where that got me."

Pain flashes across Yuri's face. Agony, deep and raw and true. "I'm sorry," he says, and for the first time, I believe him. "I wish it didn't have to be like this."

Then he's turning away again, walking back into the dark tunnel at Carmine's heel.

"Wait!" I call after him. "Whatever he said to you, whatever he promised you—he's lying! He's a liar, Yuri! He may be your father, but he's—"

"Oh, will you just shut the fuck up, you *shlyukha*?"

If he hadn't spoken, I never would've seen him. A third man, hiding in the shadows behind them. Neither Yuri nor Carmine seems surprised by his presence, probably because he's exactly where he's supposed to be.

The second I recognize him, my eyes go wide. "You…!"

52

MATVEY

Meet me here.

"Fucking finally," I mutter under my breath. *So my brother isn't dead after all.*

My eyes scan the location attached to Yuri's unusually cryptic text: a café in the smack-middle of Times Square. "What the hell is he thinking?"

I start to type a reply, but another text from him comes right after.

It's important.

Goddammit. "Grisha, change of plans. We're stopping here first."

He cranes his neck at the first red light and squints at my phone. "Busy place to be. Probably won't be able to find parking."

"No matter. I'll bring the earpiece so you can stay looped in."

"Meeting someone, then?"

"Yes," I sigh, irritated. "My ghost of a brother. He finally deigned to return my texts. Now, he wants to meet."

"In the most inconvenient place in the city?"

"Apparently. But he says it's important, so we're going."

"Roger that, boss."

I have Grisha drop me off on a side street, then walk the rest of the way there. The café is crowded, exactly the kind of place I'd never choose to have a sensitive meeting in. I hope my brother has a damn good reason to drag me out here, because otherwise, there'll be hell to pay.

I spot Yuri at a table outside. "Where the fuck have you been?" I growl.

"Sit."

What's with the attitude? I try to hook his gaze, but he keeps evading me. With no other choice, I drop down in the opposite chair. "I've been trying to reach you for days, Yuri."

"I know. I've been busy."

"Too busy to let your pregnant girlfriend know?"

That seems to have an effect. He finally lifts his eyes from the table, a trace of guilt in them. "Petra was…?"

"Worried sick? Yeah," I grunt. "She didn't say it in so many words, but I could tell."

He bites his lip and nods. "Thank you. For taking care of her."

Weird. Ever since I got here, that's all I can think of: everything about Yuri seems weird today. Something's just… off.

"What's going on, brother? If you found the mole—"

"Shut up."

I raise my eyebrows. "Ex-fucking-scuse me?"

"I said shut up," Yuri repeats with icy calm. "You're not the one in charge here, Matvey. I am. And I'm the one speaking."

"I have no idea what's gotten into you," I growl, all concern forgotten in a heartbeat, "but you'd do well to remember I'm your *pakhan*, Yuri."

"No, you're not. Not anymore."

Then he slides something my way.

I'm so livid I can barely fucking think. What the hell is going on with my brother? Why is he acting like this all of a sudden?

And then, through the fog of rage, I see it.

A picture.

It's April, handcuffed and behind the bars of some damp warehouse cell. She's lying on the dirty floor, eyes shut, passed out cold. On the other side of the bars, a faceless man holds a bundle in his arms.

No, not just a bundle.

Our daughter.

For a long moment, I can't even process it. I tell myself I must be seeing things. Because this can't be real. It *can't.*

It has to be a nightmare.

But no matter how hard I stare, the image doesn't change. No matter how hard I bite my tongue, I don't wake up.

And no matter how hard I wish I was wrong, Yuri's eyes don't change.

"It was you," I rasp. "All along, it was you."

I've been so blind. So, so fucking blind.

The mole was someone from the inner circle. Someone who knew our every move, who could keep Carmine one step ahead of us at every turn. Someone who could access the logs, manipulate the reports, keep the search off-course.

Someone who had my full trust.

I kick back my chair and grab him by the collar. "Tell me it's not true." Because even now, with all this damning evidence in front of me, a part of me wants to believe in him. My little brother—my family. My blood.

Yuri kills that hope with two words. "It's true."

BAM!

I watch him reel from my punch. I'm breathing heavily now, nostrils flared, my vision red. Blood trickles from Yuri's cheekbone, and all I can think is that I should've picked a better spot to hit: snapped his nose in half, blinded him in one eye.

"You betrayed me," I spit.

He wipes the blood away calmly. "I'm gonna let you have that one because you're upset. But if you don't get your hands off me in the next five seconds, we're gonna have a problem. Or rather, *they* are." His eyes flit to the picture to make his point.

"You'd do this to them? To *me*?!" I yell, uncaring of all the other guests staring at us. "Your own blood?!"

Unexpectedly, Yuri laughs. It's a crazed, manic sound, clashing with his personality like nails on a chalkboard. "Blood?" he scoffs. "We're not blood, Matvey. We've never been blood."

I fall silent.

What does that even mean? If there's one thing I'm sure of, it's the tie that binds us: *blood.* Thicker than water, thicker than anything.

"Explain yourself," I order.

"Gladly."

And he begins.

~

It was the day of the DNA test.

Back then, you didn't trust April as far as you could throw her. You didn't know her, didn't know what she wanted from you. So you entrusted me with the most important task you'd ever given me.

Determining if the child was truly yours.

I don't think you realize how much I looked up to you then. I don't think you ever did. You were this big, strong pakhan *who could conquer every country he set foot in. Russia killed so many of us. If it hadn't been for you, it would've killed me, too.*

I wanted to prove myself so badly.

But something went wrong. The hair sample you gave me—by the time I got to the lab, I realized I'd lost it. It wasn't the end of the world, but it was the end of the world to me. Because I'd made a mistake, and you didn't tolerate mistakes.

So I improvised. I took a few strands of my own hair and gave them to the technician. I thought, why not? The match wouldn't be as high, but it would still be there. If the kid was yours, that is.

Then the test came back negative.

I didn't even think to question it, you know? I was so sure April had lied to you. I was about to tell you as much.

Then I got a call.

I don't know how he found me. My guess is the same way he found April: he was keeping tabs on lab reports, anything tied to your name or hers. Maybe he was always going to call.

When he told me who he was, I was ready to hang up. I told him to stay the fuck away from me. From us.

But there was no "us."

See, your research was right... up to a point. Carmine did have a relationship with my mother.

But by then, she already had a child.

Her husband had died, she said, of sickness. The same sickness that took everyone back then: cold, hunger, poverty. She needed protection, and he needed somewhere to lay low.

Then they parted ways.

I don't know if it was before the sickness or after. My memories are fuzzy, and I doubt he'd tell me the truth if it didn't serve his purposes. I'm not stupid.

But he was telling the truth on one thing.

I didn't believe him, of course, so I sought the answer for myself. I swiped a few strands of hair from one of your jackets, ran the test again, then ran a new one. Not between you and April's child— between you and me.

Can you guess what it said?

All my life, I'd thought I had one thing: a brother. A brother who was my hero, who saved me from the snow and helped me make something of myself. Who gave me a real shot at life.

But I didn't.

At first, I didn't care. So what if we weren't actually related? We were brothers in everything that mattered. We grew up together, came here together, built our empire together. Surely one piece of paper couldn't change that?

And yet, I knew it would.

Because there was nothing you trusted more than blood.

So when Carmine called again, I answered.

He told me what would happen to me if you found out. That you'd be disgusted with me, get rid of me the first chance you got. I argued viciously, but I couldn't bury my head in the sand forever. The more I denied them, the more Carmine's grim words made sense.

You trusted me because I was your brother. And now, I wasn't. I was just a nobody who knew too much.

I was so scared you'd kill me.

But Carmine said he didn't mind that I wasn't his biological son. He was in the market for a successor. As long as I played my part, he would welcome me with open arms.

I felt so sick, I threw up then and there.

I hung up without giving him an answer. He said it was fine; he could wait. He'd need a favor soon. I could give him my answer then.

I was torn up inside. I didn't know what to do. I wanted to tell you, but I was terrified. What if I lost you? What if I lost more than you?

I hoped you'd change your mind. That April would change it.

But your mind wasn't changing at all. Even with her in the mix, you were adamant: blood was the only thing that mattered. Without that, there was nothing.

Then Carmine called in that favor. You were planning a war against him, and he wanted to know where you'd strike. To cut off your legs before the start of the race.

He wanted the D.C. acquisition.

So I gave it to him.

I had no other choice. I was terrified out of my mind. I wanted to be loyal, but I didn't want to die.

I didn't join him then. I thought I could sweep this under the rug and still stay by your side. Instead, I asked for only one thing in return: Do not tell him.

How naïve I was.

The lie caught up to me. I didn't cover my tracks well enough: soon, Ivan realized something was wrong with the logs. That someone from the inner circle was selling information to the enemy. He asked me to tell you. He thought it'd be better coming from me. Maybe this would finally push you into action.

He didn't know he was signing his death sentence.

I never wanted to lie to you, Matvey. Until then, I hadn't. I was guilty of omission, but that was where it ended. Even when I hid April away, I did my best to avoid it.

That day, I lied.

I lied to your face. I brought you the information because Ivan gave me no other choice, but I couldn't tell you it was me. Instead, I let you suspect everyone around you.

And then Ivan lost his patience.

When you killed him, I hoped the truth would die with him. But you kept searching. You found Anatoly. And I knew it was only a matter of time before he talked.

I should have killed him while I had the chance.

When you sent me off that last day, I didn't follow Vlad. I followed you. I needed to know what you knew.

Then you went to the warehouse.

I knew then I had to make a choice. And this time, it wasn't just my life on the line.

It was my family's.

So I don't care what you think of me. I don't care if I've become a monster. I don't care if you understand why I did it.

Because the truth is, I did.

Every word out of Yuri's mouth fills me with horror. The past few months come flashing in front of my eyes: the lies, the betrayals, the changes.

That's when I realize something else.

I can't remember the last time Yuri called me "brother."

When did it stop? When? I rack my brain for an answer and come up short. When did this nightmare begin? When did my *Yura* become this stranger in front of me?

After the failed wedding, something inside me whispers. *Think back. Remember.*

Yes. It all started then.

It's uncanny how quickly the dominoes fall into place. All it needs is the right push—and Yuri just gave a giant fucking shove.

Once. Only once did he call me his brother after that: the day he begged me to save Petra.

To use you. To manipulate you.

I slam my fist on the table and hear the wood crack. "You filthy traitor."

"Don't make a scene," Yuri warns me. "We're not done talking."

"Yes, we are."

"No, we're not. So stay put or I'm gonna have to make you."

The worst of it, though? I fucking *knew* it. I knew he was acting strangely. The guilty looks, the sneaking around, the reluctance to so much as meet my eyes. I chalked it all up to his clandestine relationship with Petra because it was convenient, but fuck me, I should've kept looking.

You wouldn't have seen it. You didn't want to see it.

That's right: I didn't want to see it.

And now, April and May are in danger because of it.

"You're threatening me?" I hiss. "*You?* When I'm the one who taught you how to hold a fucking gun in the first place?"

"Yes. And you taught me well, so don't make me take it out."

"We both know I'm the faster draw."

"And we both know I'm not dumb enough to come alone."

I grit my teeth. He has me. *God fucking dammit.* Of course I didn't think to bring reinforcements—I thought I was meeting my *brother.* My own flesh and blood.

But it turns out I didn't know who I was meeting at all.

"Fine. If you're gonna talk, then talk."

I dig my nails into my thigh until I can feel them through the fabric of my suit. All I want right now is to grab him again and punch him until he sees sense. But I can't. No matter how badly I want to teach him a lesson, I can't do it while cornered.

And I certainly can't do it at the expense of my family.

He has them hostage: my woman, my daughter. And my hands are tied. If there's even the slightest chance we're being watched, I have to play by the rules.

His rules.

For now.

"Release my family," I growl. "Do that and I'll spare your worthless life."

He clicks his tongue in distaste. "'Family.' How quickly you crossed me out of that. So I was right all along."

"After what you did? You're lucky you're still fucking breathing." I glare at him with all the hatred I feel. "You lied to me. You manipulated me. You made me kill a friend and now, you *kidnapped* my woman and my daughter!"

"I didn't make you do anything," he replies curtly. "And the girls will be fine if you do as I say."

Carmine is here. Finally, the true meaning of Ivan's last words dawns on me. It wasn't a threat—it was a warning.

He knew. During our fight, he must've realized what truly happened. He used his final breath to warn me.

And I killed him.

"You have three days to surrender yourself," Yuri says. "If you do, no harm will come to your family. They will be released and provided for."

"I can damn well provide for my own family."

"No, you can't," the traitor replies. "But you have my word. They will lack for nothing."

"Some fucking word that is."

"And yet, it's all you have. So take it or leave it."

He rises. I immediately regret not punching him harder when I had the chance to. But there's something else I regret, deeper and sharper, buried under the fire of my rage.

The fact that it had to come to this.

"Here's the address." Yuri slides over a business card. "In three days' time, at dawn. After that, I can't protect your family anymore."

"You never protected them," I spit. "You sold them out."

For a moment, Yuri's eyes cloud over with emotion. It's too

quick to grasp, but in that split-second, he almost looks like he's back to his old self again. Almost.

"I did what I had to do."

Then it's gone.

"Three days," he repeats as he fixes his shirt. "Don't forget."

"You're dead to me."

"I know."

When he passes me by, he hesitates. Just for a second. Just enough to make me wonder if his hands are really shaking. "Goodbye, Matvey."

Then he walks away.

I wait for his steps to fade. For his presence to disappear. Afterwards, I tap my earpiece. "Did you get all that, Grisha?"

"… Yes. I did."

"Good." I rise. "Gather the *vory*. This ends now."

53

APRIL

Ever since I saw the third man, I've been pacing like a lion in a cage. Not just because they took my daughter—the thought alone is unbearable—but because of what they're using her to do. *Who* they're using her to get.

Which is why I have to warn him.

Matvey will never see it coming. I have to get to him before they do—before they manage to blindside him. This conspiracy runs so deep, he'll have no idea what hit him.

Not until it's too late.

Think. I force myself to breathe, to calm down my body and mind. Right now, I can't afford to lose my head. I need to focus, to find a way out of this.

For my family.

So I think. I take in my surroundings. The cell isn't too small, but there's nothing in it. Certainly nowhere to hide. It's a smart move on their part, I'll give them that.

That just means I have to be smarter.

What can I use? I rack my brain to find something, anything I can turn into a tool.

Then my eyes meet my guard's.

A young man, no older than eighteen. Probably a fresh recruit. He's leaning on the opposite wall, stealing glances at me as he plays on his phone, engrossed in some kind of game. I can tell he's nervous: the way his gaze darts between me and the screen gives it all away. It's also clear that he's bored out of his mind, but that he doesn't want to mess this up. Maybe it's even his first assignment.

Too fucking bad.

"AHH, IT HURTS!"

I throw myself down to the floor and curl into a ball. I keep my eyes shut, pointedly ignoring any reaction, because I know it'll give me away. I only get one shot at this—better make it count.

Three, two, one...

"M-Miss?"

Bingo.

"Help," I croak. "M-My stomach… It hurts so much."

He rushes over, fumbling with the keys. I crack one eye open and see a full-blown battle on his face: the urge to obey fighting against the fear of letting me die. Who knows what they might do to him then?

"Where does it hurt?" he asks, one hand on the keys, the other on the bars.

"Low," I grunt. "I think it might be my appendix. Oh, God, what if it burst?"

"It can do that?!"

Jesus, where do they get these people? "Yeah, it can do that. Please, just... help me check."

Conflict flashes across the man's face again, so I cry out again, squeezing my eyes against the imaginary pain.

Then I hear it: the keys, jingling against the iron lock.

Gotcha.

The guard kneels by my side. "H-How do I check? How— *fuck—*"

"Don't panic," I tell him. The irony's almost too much: here I am, hand-holding the guy I'm about to screw over through a completely fake medical emergency. Not exactly Girl Scout behavior. "Just feel around here. Press a little. I can't do it myself; I'm too scared."

"Okay, um..." He lays me down on the floor, then flushes bright red. "H-Here?"

"Bit higher, thanks."

"Sorry."

As he cops a feel and then some, I keep my eyes from rolling to the back of my head and sneak my hand into his back pocket.

God, I bet this looks so bad. "L-Like this?"

"Harder."

I close my fingers around something smooth and flat.

There.

I slide it into my sleeve, then pull myself back up. "Actually, you know what? I feel better now. It's probably just my period coming."

The guy's face blanches. "R-Right. I'm just gonna, uhh…"

He slinks out, still looking queasy. *Gee, isn't this kid supposed to be mafia or something?* I watch him lock the door and put at least ten feet between us. I almost feel bad—did I scar him that much?

Oh, well. Whatever. He shouldn't have sided with the man who took my daughter.

Before he can notice something's missing, I jump to the next part of my plan. "Listen, could you do me a favor?"

"A favor?"

"I'm really thirsty. Could I have a glass of water?"

The guard looks around uneasily. "I'm really not supposed to leave."

"I understand. It's your—*cough*—job. Sorry, I shouldn't—*COUGH*—have asked, I…"

"Okay, okay, look," he breaks eventually, "I'll do it. But you stay right there, you hear me?"

I join my hands in a prayer position, his phone squeezed between my hands. I kneel, too, thighs pressed together to hide the part that sticks out. "Of course. I won't move an inch." Then I give him my best puppy-dog eyes.

Satisfied, the guard leaves the room. The second he's gone, I slip out the phone and dial.

Time to save my future husband.

He doesn't answer right away. I listen to the call ring out, head bowed, phone hidden in my hands. For a second, I feel like I'm really praying.

Pick up. Please, pick up.

Please, please, please...

"You have five seconds to tell me who you are, how you got this number, and why I shouldn't have you killed."

"Only five seconds for all that?"

"April," he rasps. "You're okay."

"Kind of?" I whisper back. "I'm in mafia jail."

"In what?" he asks. "Wait—how are you calling me? Where are they keeping you?"

"We don't have time," I cut in. "Matvey, it's Yuri. He's the mole. He's working with Carmine, and they..." I swallow. "They have our daughter."

"I know," he grits. "I swear to you, April, I won't let anyone harm either of you. Not Carmine, and not... Not Yuri," he spits, full of disdain. But I can hear other feelings buried underneath: shock, hurt, betrayal. Sometimes, even the *pakhan* of the Groza Bratva has no choice but to be human. "He'll pay for what he's done. Grisha's gathering the *vory* as we speak."

I freeze. "He's what? No, Matvey, you can't."

"Can't what?"

"Don't let him gather the *vory*. Yuri and Carmine aren't working alone. Someone else is in on it! It's—"

I manage to blurt out my warning. By a split-second, but I manage.

Then my cage bursts open.

Yuri's face is a mask of fury as he strides towards me. He yanks the phone out of my grip, not fooled for a second by my efforts to mask it, and throws it violently on the floor. Then, for good measure, he crushes it with his heel.

"I told you not to let her out of your sight," he barks at the returning guard.

"I—" he babbles, but Yuri cuts him off.

"Give me that." Without mercy, he swipes the glass of water from his hands. "I take it you were going to use this as a weapon?"

Dammit. Right on the freaking money. "Yuri, please, let's talk."

"No."

He hurls the glass at the opposite wall, missing the guard by a hair's breadth. It shatters, sending shards flying. "B-Boss, I'm sorry! I didn't mean—"

"I don't give a shit," he snarls. "You had your orders. You chose to ignore them."

"She's sick! She asked for water, she—"

"She's *dangerous*!" he roars back. "She's ten times smarter than you. Maybe more. So when I say, 'Don't go anywhere near her,' it's for a good fucking reason."

Then he takes out his gun.

"Stop!" I cry out. "He didn't do anything, it was me! I tricked him!"

"I know," he replies, voice icy. "And if you so much as think of trying anything else, I won't punish you—I'll punish *him*."

"Why?" I start sobbing. "Why are you doing all this? We're family, aren't we?"

"Family?" another voice laughs. "I'm afraid not."

Carmine.

He steps out of the shadows, again, one hand landing on Yuri's raised arm. "He has his mother's eyes; did you know that? Of course, he couldn't have mine. After all, when I met Irina... Well, she already had a son."

My head's spinning. *This can't be real.* Because if it is, then that would imply...

"You're lying," I murmur. "He's lying, Yuri. Don't listen to him, don't—"

"He's not," Yuri cuts in. "I verified it myself. Carmine's not my father. Which means that Matvey isn't..." He clenches his teeth, like it's painful to say it. Like it's painful to even think it. "We were never really family, April. Not me and you, and not... me and him. Never."

"You're wrong."

He frowns. "What?"

"You're wrong," I repeat. I don't care how badly my voice is shaking—I will say it as many times as he needs to hear it. Until my last goddamn breath. "You may not be related, but you're still family. All this time, you've been family. You think that just goes away? You think it doesn't matter?"

For a second, he hesitates.

But that's all it is—a second.

"It doesn't," he rasps. "Not to him. Because I'm not blood."

My heart breaks for him. For both of them, two brothers on opposite sides of a war. "Have you tried asking him that?"

"I don't need to. He's made it clear over and over."

"He's changed," I whisper. "He isn't the same person he was."

"He's changed for *you*," he replies, voice hoarse. "He will never change for me."

He puts the gun away, turns on his heel, and disappears in the tunnel.

"Too bad you couldn't talk him out of it," Carmine remarks as soon as he's gone. "I guess that son of mine did too much damage. All that talk of 'blood.' Obsessive, wouldn't you agree?"

"Only because of you."

"Maybe. But now, I have his blood. And once I'm done with him, I'll make sure to wipe away every trace."

My heart drops. "You'd hurt our daughter?"

"Oh, no, sweetheart. She won't feel a thing." He gives me a cruel, sinister smile, all shark teeth and broken promises. "And neither will you."

54

MATVEY

"You knew."

Grisha doesn't reply right away, just takes a long drag out of his cigarette. "I suspected."

"How long?"

"Since April was taken from the motel." The smoke rises, curling into spirals. "How did he know where to find her? How did he know she was missing at all?"

I clench my fists. Great. So everyone realized *something* didn't add up—everyone but me. "You should've told me."

"I didn't have any proof. Besides..." His usual poker face morphs into something rare: a smile. "Would you have listened?"

It's the saddest smile I've ever seen.

Goddammit. He's right. I wouldn't have listened at all. One word from Yuri, one denial, and I would've considered the matter closed. Worse, I might've turned my fangs against the one accusing my brother in the first place.

My brother.

If only we were that.

A memory bubbles up: Yuri and I, storming out of Ipatiy's club. No—*me* storming out, Yuri rushing to catch up at my heels. He was warning me about something, but I didn't want to hear it. That I couldn't alienate the *vory* just because they weren't blood. That it was wrong of me to treat them as "glorified attack dogs," as I'd so elegantly put it.

He told me, *"Even the most loyal dog will bite if backed into a corner."*

What did I say in return?

Try as I might, I just can't remember.

"Who's coming?" I ask Grisha instead, determined to put my —*Yuri*—out of my mind.

"Vlad's men," he replies. "Our *vory* are gathering at the HQ right now. They want to discuss the implications of moving against Carmine before they lend their support."

"Fucking cowards," I spit. "They're Bratva, not a bunch of shareholders. Why the hell can't they remember that?"

"My guess is they have no one to keep them in line now," Grisha remarks. "Not after…"

Ivan.

"I see."

It's not a good feeling, when your mistakes catch up to you.

It's even worse when they do it all at once, one after the other. An avalanche of wrong choices.

If I'm not careful, they will be the dirt on my grave.

"Go to them," I tell Grisha. "Remind them what it means to be Bratva. By any means necessary."

"Do I have the authority to do that?" he asks.

"You do now, *brigadir*."

I shake his hand and seal the deal. It's firm, refreshingly real. Grisha's face is lacking any of the joy that usually comes with a promotion, showing instead the grim expression of a soldier on the battlefield.

Good. I need men who understand duty around me.

Duty… and loyalty.

"Be careful," I tell him.

He nods. "You, too, *pakhan*."

I watch him go, the car speeding off into New York traffic. Any time now, Vlad should be here with half my army. The irony doesn't escape me: I spent so long suspecting the wrong man, and now, here I am, waiting for him to bring the cavalry.

Some leader I turned out to be.

I spy a long line of black cars. One by one, they crowd the alley next to the warehouse and start spitting out men in suits. *Vlad's* men.

Then another car speeds into the alley, nearly crashing into the last one. "What's the meaning of this?!"

Petra.

I steel myself. With everything that's happened in the past few hours, there was one question I was forced to table for later. Because I didn't have the bandwidth. Because there were other priorities.

Is Petra working against me, too?

"Petya!" Vlad bellows. "I told you to go home."

But she ignores him. Instead, she makes a beeline for me, elbowing her father's men left and right to get there. "Tell me it's not true," she demands. "Say it."

I turn to Vlad. "What the hell is she doing here?"

"She was with me when you called."

"And you let her listen?"

"How was I supposed to know you were going to drop a bomb like that?!" he scoffs. "I tried to keep her away, but you know women. Long legs, even longer ears."

"Quit talking like I'm not here!" she cries out. "Especially you, Matvey. You've never done that to me before. Don't you dare start now."

I clench my jaw. Petra's face is a mask of heartbreak, hurt and confusion swirling together in the pools of her eyes.

But is that all it is? A mask?

Just then, my phone rings.

"Ignore it," she growls. "Look at me, Matvey. Tell me I heard wrong. Tell me that Yuri didn't…" She swallows a sob.

Fucking hell. If she's acting, she's doing a damn good job of it.

And if she's not…

If she's not, I can't tell her what she wants to hear.

So I pick up the phone. "You have five seconds to tell me who you are, how you got this number, and why I shouldn't have you killed," I snarl.

"Only five seconds for all that?"

The voice on the other side of the line hits me like a sucker punch.

It can't be. It's not possible.

But it is. Because there's no one else that voice could possibly belong to. "April," I rasp. "You're okay."

"Kind of?" She laughs awkwardly. All this hell breaking loose, and she *laughs.* My woman was always the strongest soldier among us. "I'm in mafia jail."

"In what?" A thousand questions crowd my mind. "Wait— how are you calling me? Where are they keeping you?"

"We don't have time," she cuts me off. Suddenly, her voice fills with urgency. "Matvey, it's Yuri. He's the mole. He's working with Carmine, and they... They have our daughter."

I grit my teeth. Somehow, April got hold of a phone. She went to God knows what pains to secure that, to dial my number and warn me...

And it's too late.

"I know. I swear to you, April, I won't let anyone harm either of you. Not Carmine, and not..." My mouth fills with bitterness. "Not Yuri. He'll pay for what he's done."

"No," Petra whispers. Her face fills with the kind of heartbreak you can't find on TV, the kind that destroys empires.

"Grisha's gathering the *vory* as we speak," I tell April, forcing my gaze away from her grief.

April's response is the last thing I expect. "He's what?" she stammers. "No, Matvey, you can't."

I frown. "Can't what?"

"Don't let him gather the *vory*," she rushes to say. "Yuri and Carmine aren't working alone. Someone else is in on it!"

Her words turn me to stone.

Someone else.

Another betrayal.

Possibilities flash through my mind. Where is the kiss of Judas going to come from next?

Grisha and his loyalty?

Petra and her grief?

Before I can go any further, April answers the question for me. "It's—"

A name slips out of her lips. One name, and then the line is brutally cut, the sound of crushed circuits echoing in my ear.

I can't even be properly furious about that—the fact that they discovered her, that she must be in danger right now—because the name she gave me demands my immediate attention.

Because the owner of that name is right in front of me.

I reach for my gun, but another one's safety clicks off before I can draw. "I wouldn't do that if I were you, son."

55

MATVEY

It happens in an instant: one second, I'm on the phone with April, and the next…

The next, Vladimir Solovyov is pointing a gun at my head.

"So it was you."

"Of course it was me," he spits. "You didn't think I'd let you live after what you've done, did you?"

Blyat'. I've been a fool until the end. Again, the answer was right in front of me.

Why did I cross Vlad out of my list of suspects? Why did I think he had nothing to do with this? Who did I send to spy on him in the first place?

Yuri.

Once more, my subconscious betrayed me. Because, even after he stabbed me in the back…

Part of me still trusted the man he was.

"Even the most loyal dog will bite if backed into a corner."

Why the fuck can't I remember my answer?

"Dad...?" Petra murmurs. "What are you...?"

"Stay back," he barks at her. "I told you this was no place for you."

"You were planning this?" she asks. "All along, you've been planning this?"

But he doesn't deign to give her a reply. "Go wait in the car," he orders instead.

"Have you lost your mind?" Shock fades from her face, giving way to a much more familiar expression: fury. "You think I'll let you do this? That I'll let you gun down my husband?!"

"Husband!" he scoffs. "You think I'm an idiot, don't you? Tell me, girl: why don't you tell everyone here who the father of your bastard truly is?"

Her eyes go wide. "You knew?"

"Of course I fucking knew!" he bellows. "Everybody knew! It was goddamn obvious!" He jabs the gun in my direction to make a point. "This one only had eyes for that freckled bitch, and you..." A sneer mars his face. "You, *solnyshka*, had already set your sights elsewhere. Though at least you had the decency to keep your affair behind closed doors."

"All this time, you forced me to keep that secret..."

"Oh, please. I didn't force you to do a damn thing. You were just too dumb to keep your legs closed."

"Enough," I croak. "Petra, go. I can handle it here."

It's a lie. I've painted myself into a corner, and everyone here knows it. The second I sent Grisha away, my fate was sealed.

But that doesn't mean hers has to be.

I've loathed this woman. I've wanted her out of my life more times than I can count, resented her for every sacrifice I've had to make to keep this pretense alive. I've blamed her, over and over again, for tearing me and April apart.

But, God help me, I've never wanted her dead.

"No."

"For fuck's sake, Petra, will you just listen to me for once?!"

"Do as he says," her father demands. "Or else you'll be the next one with a gun to your head."

Her face falls. "You wouldn't."

"Why not? You're no good to me as an heir. And now, you're no good as a broodmare either. You're lucky that lover of yours came to me for a deal, or else I would've had you gunned down long ago. But if you test me now…"

Petra's face hardens. With a single step, she places herself between me and her father's gun. "Then fucking come and get me."

"Stop that," I hiss.

She doesn't look at me as she hisses back, "Shut up and let me save your goddamn life."

"Like hell," I snarl. "You're a pregnant fucking woman."

"And if I die, Yuri's child dies with me," she declares. "So let's see if he's got the balls to blow up his alliance."

"You stupid girl," Vlad mutters. "You're always getting in my way. Even when I sent those assassins to that whore's place, you just had to be there and foil my plan."

"That was you?!"

"How many times are you gonna make me say it?" With his free hand, he gives his men a signal. Slowly, they start to surround us. "Of fucking course it was me."

"The kidnappers who took April," I realize. "One of them was Italian, but the other wasn't. He was Russian." My face twists into a snarl. "All along, you've been in bed with Carmine."

"Why else would your little brother come to me?" he cackles. "Oh, wait. Guess I should stop calling him that, should I?"

"What does that mean?" Petra demands.

"Nothing you need to concern yourself with, girl."

We're completely surrounded now. Unfriendly guns bristling in every direction. "Stand the fuck down," I repeat to her. "I've got this."

"You really suck at lying, you know that?"

"Petra."

"No!" she insists. "Whatever happens, we're family. I'm not going to abandon my family."

I should tell her that she's wrong. That we aren't family, not in any way that matters. She isn't my real wife; she isn't my brother's girlfriend; and to that child inside of her, I'm no one.

So why can't I do it?

"Take them," Vlad commands.

We don't resist. We can't—if I fight, he'll shoot her; if she fights, he'll shoot me. It's a catch-22, and for the first time in my life, I'm forced to let the enemy put me in cuffs willingly.

But there's another reason I let it happen. Another reason I let some nameless minion of Vlad's bash my head in with the grip of their gun, painting my vision with black, dancing spots.

If they're not killing us, they can only be taking us to them. And wherever they *are...*

That's where my family will be.

56

APRIL

"… the hell were they thinking?!"

My ears perk up at the sound of shouting in the tunnel.

"… really need to relax, Yuri. It's no…"

I recognize the voices: Yuri and Carmine, arguing about—well, something.

"… wrong! Why even offer the three-day deal if we weren't going to honor…"

Deal? I wasn't trying to listen in, but sue me: now, I'm interested.

"… getting what we want now instead of later… not a bad outcome, is it? Besides…"

Man, someone should really teach the home team a thing or two about acoustics. If they don't want the sound to carry, they shouldn't be having secret meetings in a freaking tunnel of all places.

Without hesitation, I press myself closer to the bars.

"I gave him my word," Yuri growls. "Now, I need to know: did Vlad go rogue or did you?"

"Does that matter?" Carmine asks.

"Yes. Because then I'd have to worry."

"About what?"

"How much your word is really worth."

Damn. Hope Carmine's got aloe vera on hand, because that was one hell of a burn.

But when he speaks next, his voice is ice: cold, smooth, and dangerously sharp. "Are we going to have a problem, Yuri?"

"You tell me. Did you break the deal or not?"

Fear seeps back into my heart. Not for myself, or even for my daughter: for *Yuri.*

Speaking to Carmine like that is as good as a death sentence.

But it seems that, whatever understanding they have, it's too valuable to throw away. So Carmine lets out a long sigh and says, his tone much calmer, "It was the girl. She gave away our last inside man. He had to make a call on the spot."

Me?

"Don't look so put-out. You were in charge of her surveillance, weren't you?" Carmine sneers. "If you're going to point fingers for this, then by all means, I'll find you a mirror."

Wow. Gaslighting much?

I can't help the guilt that grips me. I'm not sorry for stealing that phone—I did what I had to do. But now, I'm wondering if I didn't set off a chain reaction of consequences. Not only for me, but for others, too.

I just hope Matvey's okay.

"Haul 'em in!"

I startle. Quickly, I push myself as far away from the bars as I can, pretending I didn't just eavesdrop on a mafia war council.

Then new men swarm the room.

"Toss them in the cell," someone says.

"The one with the girl?"

"Do you see another?" the first man snaps. "C'mon, we don't have all day."

Two men come forward, dragging a third one between them. His head is hanging forward, as if he was knocked unconscious, which means I can't make out his face.

But I don't need to. His suit, his frame, his cologne—I'd recognize those anywhere. "Matvey!"

"Stay back!" one of them barks. "One wrong move and I'll feed you a bullet myself."

And they say chivalry is dead. Still, I do as I'm told. The panic I'd worked so hard to chase from my heart is mounting again, full stereo.

Ta-thump, ta-thump, ta-fucking-thump.

When they toss Matvey inside, I spring up and catch him. His dead weight is almost too much. But what truly makes my legs buckle is that thought: *dead* weight.

Is he…?

God, please don't be dead. Please, I'll do anything.

Please, please, please…

But then I feel it: a heartbeat. Faint, and distant, but there. "Thank goodness," I sob into his shirt as we both fall to our knees. "Thank goodness you're okay."

Then I hear screaming.

"Let me go!" snarls a very familiar voice. "I will cut off your balls and feed them to your mothers if you don't let me go this *fucking* instant!"

I never thought I'd be so glad to hear it. "Petra!"

"April?" she calls to me. Her eyes meet mine, then rage sets them ablaze again. "You put her in a *cell*? How fucking dare— GET YOUR HANDS OFF OF ME! I'll eat your fucking eyes!"

Yep. Good ol' Petra.

In the end, all her kicking and screaming is useless. Carmine's henchmen throw her in as well, though all of them are looking worse for the wear than she is. Rule number one of doing crime: don't fuck with the pregnant ones. Just don't.

The second she's behind bars, she throws herself down at my side. "Are you okay?"

"I mean…" I glance towards the four men limping out of the room. "Better than them for sure."

"Bastards," she bites out. "I had no idea—I…"

"I know," I quickly reassure her. "This isn't your style. Say what you will, but you'd have gotten me a suite."

Her eyes flit guiltily to Matvey. "Is he...?"

"Just knocked out." I exhale. "Let me guess: they were afraid he'd put up a fight?"

"Yeah," she hisses. "Fucking cowards."

Bet they regretted they didn't knock her *out, too.* "I'm so sorry," I murmur. "This must be hell for you. Your dad, and then..."

I still can't say it. Despite all I've seen, I still can't say it.

"Is it true?" she whispers. "Is Yuri really...?"

Luckily, I'm spared from having to answer that.

Because the man himself answers for me. "Petra..."

She whirls around like lightning. "*You.*"

"I'm sorry," Yuri murmurs. "You weren't supposed to be dragged into this. Are you okay?"

"Am I okay?" She laughs hysterically. "Do I look fucking okay to you?"

"I already told them off for—"

"Is it true?" she cuts him off without mercy. "Did you betray your own brother?"

Short and to the point. Some things never change.

"I..."

"It's a yes-or-no question, Yuri."

"It's not so simple."

"Looks simple enough to me."

"Petya…"

"Don't," she snarls. "Don't you fucking dare call me that."

"I did this for us!" he objects. "I did this for—"

"Are you here to let us go?"

He blinks. "I… I can't do that. If you'll cooperate, then yes, but…"

"But not April?"

Silence.

Petra scoffs. "Go. Get out of my sight."

"Please, just listen—"

"I LOVED YOU!"

It's worse than a scream—it's a howl. Like there's nothing human left there. Just a broken beast with a bleeding heart.

"I loved you," Petra exhales when the echoes of her wail die down. "And you betrayed me. You betrayed *us*."

"I saved us," Yuri whispers, his pain just as real.

"No, you killed us. Now go."

"Petra—"

"GO!" she screams. "Or I swear I will kill myself with the first sharp thing I find."

It's as good a threat as Yuri used with me. With us. He took Matvey's family hostage, and now…

Now, Petra holds hostage his.

With a silent nod, Yuri obeys. He turns around, fists

clenching and unclenching at his sides, and leaves the same way he came.

The second his steps fade, Petra slumps against the bars. She takes one deep breath, then another. "Okay." She turns to me, eyes blazing. "Time to get the fuck out of here."

For once, we are in perfect agreement.

57

MATVEY

At first, I think I'm dreaming.

There's a hand combing through my hair. There aren't many people I would give that privilege to, either in this world or the next, and right now, I'm unsure which one I'm in.

But then her scent reaches me. Not like snow and crackling firewood, but like flowers. Battered and bruised, but still stubbornly growing out of the cracks in the concrete.

April.

Her fingers skirt around the edges of my wound carefully, a nasty bump at the back of my head. I can't have bled much, but I can still feel a matted clump of hair there, even as she does her best to avoid it. Her warmth surrounds me. When I move, my cheekbone grazes the exposed part of her knees.

If this is heaven, you can leave me right here.

"Dummy," April snorts. "Heaven can wait. I still need you on planet Earth."

It's the one request I can't deny.

I drag myself upright, already mourning the warmth of April's lap, and scan my surroundings. It's not very bright, but I'm used to the darkness by now. In a handful of seconds, my eyes have adjusted, and I can make out the place I've been tossed into.

A cold, damp cell.

"Rise and shine, *solnyshko.*"

Yep. Definitely not heaven. "I take it our fathers couldn't splurge on separate cells?" I mutter, head pounding like crazy.

"Nope. Stingy motherfuckers."

"How are you feeling?" April asks me, all concern. I finally take in her face: soot-stained, hair sticking to the sweat on her brow, her smudged makeup turning her into a raccoon.

She's never been more beautiful to me.

"I should be asking that." I take her hands in mine and squeeze. Her fingers are cold as ice, as if she'd been holding on to the iron bars for hours before I joined her. Guilt pierces me at the thought: once again, I've done too little, too late. "If they did something to you, I swear—"

"They didn't," she quickly reassures me. "Well, except give me a nasty bump to the head. But that just makes us twinsies, right?"

How can she crack jokes at a time like this? Any other civilian would be screaming their head off in this situation. Taken by the mafia *and* the Bratva? Even on the best of days, that's not something ordinary people can handle. It's just not.

But April's always been different: a soldier in everything but name. A fighter. And today, we're going to need that more than ever.

I pull her into my arms. Once we're close enough, I whisper in her ear, "Guards?"

"Two," April murmurs back. "Both at the entrance of the tunnel."

Hm. That's fewer than I expected. Guess Carmine's feeling a little too confident, then. "May?"

"Carmine has her," she rasps. "We can't fail, Matvey. If we do…"

There's no telling what he'll do to her.

"I know."

It's taking everything I have to keep my boiling blood at bay. The old me would've started pounding the bars the second he woke up, barking threats for everyone to hear. He would've yanked the fucking things off their hinges, then gotten shot for his trouble.

Or maybe he'd have died surrounded by Vlad's men, with no one to take his side.

But now, after everything that's happened… I finally understand.

What it truly means to be a leader.

Until now, I thought going it alone was the only way. Getting angry, getting even: that was my creed. As *pakhan* and as a man.

But that's not it. "Angry" doesn't equal "right"; "alone" doesn't equal "strong." That recipe for misery and an untimely death

—I'm done following its instructions. I'm done fighting for the sake of fighting.

Now, I finally have something worth fighting for. *Someone* worth fighting for. Someone who will fight with me, for me, in return.

My family.

"Okay," I say. "Let's make a plan."

A grin blooms on April's face. "Yes, *pakhan.*"

"Look at you. You finally learned how to say it."

She flips her hair, preening at the praise. "Of course I did. I'm your future piranha."

"*Pakhansha.*"

"Details."

God, I love her. It's absurd how often the thought keeps blindsiding me. In the smallest of things, the most insignificant moments: *I love her. I never want to let her go.*

Once this nightmare is over, I'm putting a ring on her finger. I don't care if I have to drag her to the courthouse in her pajamas—I'm not waiting a fucking month. I'm not waiting another minute.

But first, we have to get out of here.

"We need to do something about the cuffs."

"I might have a solution to that," April murmurs. "But we'll need a distraction."

"Excuse me?" Petra interjects, irritated. "Care to loop me in?"

We both turn to look at her at the same time. I'm no psychic. I don't even believe that shit. But when I lock eyes with April again, I can practically see her thoughts.

Because they're exactly like mine.

"Uhh…" Petra says, uncomfortable. "Why are you looking at me like that?"

"Petra…" April pipes up, her pitch an octave higher. "How would you feel about another heist?"

"This is stupid," Petra mutters.

"No, it's not," April retorts. "It's our only play."

"They're never gonna fall for it."

"You're seriously overestimating these guys' IQ."

"But—"

"Stop fucking around," I hiss through my teeth from my position on the floor, trying to move my lips as little as possible. "You wanna be *vor*? This is your audition."

"That's discriminatory," she grumbles. "I was gonna make *vor* before I got pregnant. I didn't need an audition."

"I'll be sure to let HR know of your complaints."

"Alright, enough sass," April whispers. "Let's get this show on the road."

With one final huff, Petra obeys. "AAAAAHHHHH!!! MY BABY!!!"

I grimace. When we said for her to "scream like a gutted pig," I wasn't expecting *this* level of a performance.

Oh, well. The louder the better.

"Help!" April rushes to the bars. "She's bleeding!"

I crack an eye open just in time to catch the guards exchanging a look. If it were me, I'd have told them not to get close for any reason, especially after April managed to dupe the previous shift exactly like this.

But this isn't April. This is a different hostage.

A hostage who matters to their boss.

"Hurry!" April insists. "What are you waiting for?!"

"W-we…" one of the guards stutters. His eyes clearly fix on me. But like this, bathed in darkness as I am, he can only glimpse my frame.

"He's knocked out; he can't do anything!" April sighs in frustration. "Look, if it's me you're worried about, you can cuff me to the bars. Just—"

"AAAHHH! IT HURTS TOO MUCH! JUST KILL ME, PLEASE!"

"Tone it down, Cameron Diaz," I mumble out of the side of my mouth. "There's no Oscar on the table for you."

She gives me a half-shrug as if to say, *You never know.*

Then she proceeds to mimic a seizure.

"Cuff her!" the second guard shouts to his colleague before rushing to the door. "I'll get the other one out!"

April obediently sticks out her already-cuffed hands. Her guard fumbles with the keys for a second, trying to figure out how to uncuff her and cuff her back around the bars with the smallest delay possible. He's been warned; he thinks he needs to worry about her.

He's wrong.

He needs to worry about *me*.

While the first guard's busy with April, the second one kneels by Petra's side. He has his gun drawn, seemingly under some mistaken notion that it's going to save his ass.

It's not.

"*BLYAT*!"

Petra gives the signal, and I sprint into action.

I launch myself out of the shadows and kick the guard's gun out of his grip. The second he's disarmed, Petra stops screaming and elbows him right in the ribs, then at the back of the head.

One down, one to go.

I steal the gun and glance up to see how April's doing...

"OW! YOU BITCH!"

... just in time to watch her yank her target face-first into the bars.

~

"Well," April comments. "That was easy."

"That was awful," Petra complains. "My throat's gonna be sore for days."

"I'm sure the company will sponsor your honey and tea," I deadpan.

We put our handcuffs on the guards. It'll take a while for them to come to, but one can never be too careful.

Speaking of...

I take off my socks, ball them up, and stuff them in the first guy's mouth. "That's for disrespecting my fiancée, *mudak.*"

If it were up to me, I'd have kicked him *and* shot him, risks be damned. But we've already made too much noise—a gunshot would summon Carmine's entire army in a heartbeat.

Besides, April's here. And I don't want to expose her to any more bloodshed than she needs to see.

Petra frowns. "Fiancée?"

I toss her the second gun. "Right," I reply. "I forgot to tell you."

She catches it out of the air. "Tell me what?"

I grin. "I want a divorce."

58

APRIL

On the list of *Top Three Hottest Things Matvey's Ever Done*:

- Disarm a guard with a flying round kick straight out of a kung fu movie;
- Finger-fuck me in the Mallard's bathroom, within earshot of half my family;
- Claim me in a damp, dirty cell.

Verbally, that is.

"You sly *koshka*," Petra punches me on the shoulder as we make our way down the tunnel. "You didn't tell me you got engaged!"

I laugh awkwardly. "It all happened so fast. Also, I wasn't sure how to... um..."

"What, you thought I'd be jealous?" she scoffs. "Please. I can't wait to be rid of this ball and chain."

"This ball and chain is right here, you know," Matvey remarks dryly.

Petra ignores him. "Besides, the whole thing's pointless now anyway. My father knows. Apparently, he's always known."

Her voice tells me she's trying to be strong, but I can only imagine the betrayal she must feel. "I'm sorry," I murmur. "First, your dad, and then…"

I leave it unspoken. There's no need to say it. We all know who we're talking about.

Petra clicks her tongue in disdain. "That *mudak*'s dead to me. He can be Carmine's puppet for the rest of his miserable life."

I place my hand on her arm. She's angry right now, and she has every right to be. I don't think she means what she's saying—or maybe she does. What do I know?

All I know is the look I saw on Yuri's face.

"I don't think he's been told everything," I whisper. "When I woke up, he promised me we wouldn't be harmed if Matvey surrendered, but when I was alone with Carmine…"

"You were alone with him?" Matvey growls, hackles rising instantly. "Did that piece of shit—?"

"He didn't do anything," I quickly promise him. "But he didn't sound like he was intending to keep that promise. I think Yuri's being lied to."

"That's his own fucking problem," Matvey snarls. "He's the one who threw his lot in with Carmine. He can handle the consequences."

"Maybe," I concede. "But I still think it's odd."

"What's odd?"

"That he's the one acting betrayed. The way he spoke to

me..." I feel a pang of sympathy in my chest. "It's like he didn't think he had a choice. Like it was him or you."

Matvey falls silent. Again, I can't blame him, either. Yuri's betrayal—it hit deep. Deeper than any of us was prepared to handle.

But then why did he look so sad?

Petra purses her lips, lost in thought. "He said something earlier. When I accused him of having betrayed his brother."

"What?" Matvey asks, irritated.

"He said, 'It's not so simple.'" Petra's eyes lock with his. "Do you know what he meant by that? Did you...?"

"If you're going to ask, just ask."

"Did you do something to him, Matvey?"

He clenches his fists at his sides. "The only thing I'm guilty of is my blood."

"What does that even mean?"

But Matvey doesn't stay to answer. He just strides ahead.

"Petra," I murmur, "there's something you should know."

After listening to my explanation, Petra spends five full minutes staring into space. "That's why he did all this?" she asks finally. "Because he found out that Matvey wasn't...?"

"His biological brother," I fill in. "Yeah. I guess it must've been quite a shock."

"But that doesn't change anything," she retorts. "They have history. They have a bond. Why would he think that didn't matter?"

"Maybe he didn't." I wring my hands. "Maybe he just thought it wouldn't matter to…"

I steal a glance at Matvey's back. I have no doubt our voices carry far enough for him to hear, but he's not saying anything. Just marching straight ahead, like a soldier on the battlefield. It probably helps—to focus on the here and now.

"Motherfucker," Petra curses. "Why didn't he just talk to me?"

"Because he's a man?"

Petra just huffs. "*Blyat*. Ever think we should just run away together?"

"Who, us?"

"Yup. Raise our kids like Amazon queens."

I bite back a laugh. "What if you have a boy?"

"He can fetch our arrows."

My eyes turn back to Matvey. "That's tempting," I say. "But I have too many reasons to stay."

She follows my gaze. "Looks like one, from where I'm sitting."

"Yeah, well, it's an important one." I let my chest fill with warmth. "Maybe the most important reason of all."

"Christ, get a room."

I laugh and catch up with Matvey. When I slip my hand into his, he doesn't move away. Only throws me a sideways glance and mutters, "Amazons? Really?"

"Hey, it was your wife's idea."

"You gonna teach May how to ride a horse?"

My smile wavers. "If I can, I want to teach her everything."

He squeezes my hand, firm and sure, as if trying to share his strength with me. To tell me, in his language of a man of few words: *I am here. I'm not going anywhere.*

I squeeze back, then step into the light at the end of the tunnel.

~

"Do you think we took a wrong turn?" Petra asks after five minutes of searching the empty room.

"We didn't take any turns," Matvey says. "It was a straight path."

"Maybe you missed something."

"Maybe you should shut the fuck up."

"Guys?" I tremble. "Maybe you should both look here."

I point with a shaking finger to a section of the wall across from us. It's like a sci-fi movie: one second there was nothing there, and the next, the outline of a door appears.

And from that door…

"Carmine," Matvey growls.

When I see the bundle in his arms, my heart drops. "May."

Petra bares her teeth. "*You.*"

I'm not sure if she's snarling at Vlad or Yuri, but both of them take their places at Carmine's sides.

"Nice touch, isn't it?" Carmine muses. "Impenetrable room. Nothing gets in or out without my say."

"Makes the cells a bit useless, then," Petra comments dryly.

"Call it a design choice." He shrugs. "You know, I'd applaud you for getting this far, but…" He points at the child in his arms. *My* child. "I don't think the little one would approve."

I watch the rise and fall of her chest, but something feels… off. "Why isn't she waking up?" I ask.

"What do you mean?" Yuri frowns. "She's always sleeping, isn't she?"

"Not like this." I can hear the panic leaching into my voice now, like a dam slowly breaking. "What did you give her?"

It's just a hunch, but Carmine's smirk confirms it. "Just a little something to help her doze. After all, who wants a final showdown with a crying baby as background music?"

I knew it. We've been apart for hours now. Even if they'd fed her—which I highly doubt—she would still wake up at the sound of my voice. She would still want to be with me.

"You did *what*?" Yuri balks.

But his indignation is drowned out by Matvey's low rumble. "You're dead," he sneers, straight at Carmine.

"No, son." He smiles benevolently. "You are."

Then he points a gun at May's head.

It's like the ground crumbles right under my feet. I've never felt so weak and so dangerous at the same time. My knees are buckling, legs shaking like they're suddenly made of pudding, and yet…

And yet, I could kill him with my bare hands.

"The hell?!" Yuri snaps. "Put that down!"

"I think I told you already I don't appreciate that tone."

"You just pointed a gun at a baby!"

"I pointed a gun at a hostage," Carmine gently corrects. "And if you looked at your brother instead of me, you'd know why it's the smart move." He pretends to wince. "Sorry. *Former* brother."

He's right. God help me, he's right. I tear my gaze off my daughter and Matvey's just... stone. Frozen. A statue carved out of marble.

"*Yebanyi podonok*," Petra spits. I have no idea what it means, but I'll go out on a limb and guess it's not a compliment.

"Hah!" Carmine's booming laugh fills the room. "You've got a mouth on you, young lady. I do hope you'll come around and join our side."

"Over my dead fucking body."

"Petra..." Yuri murmurs. "Please. Don't make this all be for nothing."

Conflict crosses Petra's eyes. And how could it not? She knows the full story now. She understands what brought him there: the road to hell and all its good intentions.

But then she sets her jaw and steps back towards us. "It already is."

"Let them go," Matvey grits. "It's me you want. Let the girls go and I'll surrender."

"Nah, I don't think so." Carmine snaps his fingers. Immediately, the room fills with henchmen. "Kill them all," he commands.

It's over.

It's truly over.

I squeeze Matvey's hand tight. "I love you," I whisper.

Goodbye, May.

"NO!"

It's Yuri's voice. He's standing between us and Carmine, uselessly trying to shield Petra from the guns.

Carmine's hand rises to stop his men. "What gives, Yuri? Having a change of heart?"

"No," he bites out. "I have a request."

"Let's hear it then."

"Let me have him."

Carmine raises a skeptical eyebrow. "Come again?"

"My brother," he grits. "My *fake* brother. Over the years, he's been horrible to me. Always ordering me around, kicking me like a dog. Treating me like a weakling."

"Yura…" Matvey whispers, but Yuri doesn't turn.

"I always wanted to teach him a lesson," he insists. "Please. Let me prove I'm stronger."

For one endless minute, I'm terrified Carmine won't allow it. That he'll drop his hand again and shower us with bullets, without so much as an instant to say goodbye.

But then his face breaks into a grin. "Sounds fun," he declares. "Alright then. Go for it."

"Matvey Groza," Yuri says solemnly, "in the name of the code of honor, I challenge you to a duel."

59

MATVEY

I never thought we'd end up here. But life has a way of making you pay. For mistakes, pride, arrogance, all of it. Every single misstep I made has brought me here.

This place.

This moment.

"The rules are simple," Carmine announces. "If Yuri wins, he gets to decide the fate of the hostages. If Matvey wins, he gets the same honor. If no one wins, I get to shoot whoever I want, wherever I want, however many times I want. How's that for incentive?"

The irony doesn't escape me. Not long ago, I killed Ivan in a duel just like this, albeit with much fairer rules.

But that hardly matters now. Whatever machinations steered my hand, ultimately, I was the one who plunged the knife. He was my most loyal *vor*—my most loyal friend—and I repaid him with death.

If this is my punishment, it's a fitting one.

Carmine's men frisk us. The gun I stole from the guard is unceremoniously taken away. Petra's, too, even though she has nothing to do with the duel itself.

They don't frisk Yuri, but he hands over his weapon all the same.

Carmine motions for one of his men to approach. He obeys the unspoken order and pulls out two combat knives from his belt.

"Here you go." My father smiles as he tosses one to each of us. "Play nice."

This is all a game to him. If I ever thought there might be something left there—a stray crumb of affection for the man who was once his son—that face tells me all I need to know.

Whoever dies tonight, he's already won.

Yuri waits for me to pick my weapon. His expression is unreadable. If I weren't furious with him for everything he's done, I'd acknowledge the honor in his gesture: these knives come from Carmine. One of them might easily have been tampered with. By giving me first pick, he's ensuring a fair fight.

But there's nothing honorable in what he's done.

And this fight will be anything but fair.

Because I'm the one who trained Yuri. I know his strengths, his weaknesses, which moves he can execute confidently and which he still struggles with. Even if he's been training in secret, he's no match for me. And while that might be true in reverse—because if I know his style, then he damn well knows mine—there's still one problem.

He has never once defeated me.

If I didn't know better, I'd say he's being suicidal. The same crawling feeling I got against Ivan makes its way under my skin. That this doesn't make sense—that I'm missing something.

And that, if I don't figure it out, I'm going to regret it for the rest of my life.

Why did you have to ask for this? I clench my fists until my knuckles turn white. *You know you can't possibly win, so why?*

Why do I have to be the one to kill you?

I grab my knife. Yuri grabs his.

"You should have taken the deal," he whispers when no one can hear us.

"I don't make deals with cowards," I growl, my anger still getting the better of me.

We split in the middle of the room, then walk to the opposite ends. The Bonaccorsi men make up the perimeter of our makeshift arena, leaving just enough room to let four other people through: on Yuri's side, Carmine and Vlad.

And on mine…

"Don't look," I warn April. Whatever happens, I don't want her to see this.

But she just shakes her head, as stubborn as the day I met her, and fixes her eyes on mine. "Don't die," she whispers back.

I don't get a chance to say anything else.

"FIGHT!"

As soon as the referee shoots his gun into the air, Yuri charges.

Our knives clash. The screech of metal echoes through the air as my blade parries his. "Stop fighting this!" Yuri grits. "If you surrender yourself, we can still—"

"There's no 'we,'" I spit. "And if you're pissing yourself that bad, you can just say so."

His eyes harden. "Fine. If you won't save our family, I will."

Then he slashes downwards.

Pain explodes across my knuckles. We both jump back at the same time, my hand the same shade of red as his blade. It's a superficial cut, but it's enough to turn my grip slick if I'm not careful.

I lick the blood off, then roll the knife in my palm.

We circle each other like wolves. Carmine's men are whooping behind us, launching into raucous stadium chants. Like this is a fucking football game instead of a duel to the death.

When we clash again, it's Yuri who pulls back bleeding. "That all you can do?"

He's trying to provoke me. "You know exactly what I can do."

"Then fucking come and do it."

Once, I would've fallen for the taunt. But now, I listen—*truly* listen—to the words, and the intent behind them becomes obvious.

Pressing the one advantage he has.

I've always had strength on my side. I'm bigger, taller, with thicker muscle and a heavier blow. When I strike, bones snap like twigs.

But there's a drawback to that, and it surfaces when I face off against opponents like Yuri.

Speed.

"Why the rush?" I taunt back. "You got somewhere better to be?"

If I fall for his tricks—if I let myself lose my cool and charge blindly—I'll be signing my own death sentence. It's the one scenario where I'm vulnerable. It almost makes me wonder why he never used it against me before. If he had, he might've won a sparring match or two.

He respected you too much, whispers the voice at the back of my head. *No matter what, you were still his big brother.*

And he never wanted to see you fall.

I'm snapped out of my thoughts by Yuri charging again. He feints to the right, but I see right through it: with one swift move, I slam my elbow into his forearm and knock him back.

He almost drops the knife—almost. "You're going to get them killed," he snarls, barely audible.

"Carmine's never going to honor the terms, Yuri." I lunge, but he side-steps. "You might have been blinded by his promises, but I never was."

"He will," he counters with a slash aimed at my throat. "If he's got nothing to gain and everything to lose, he will."

"He's a snake." I dodge just in time, earning another superficial cut across my cheekbone. Any higher, and my eye would've been gouged out. "He left both our mothers to die. You really think that's a coincidence? That wherever he goes, whatever ties he has, they all meet bloody ends?"

"He didn't make them sick, Matvey."

"No. But he sure as hell didn't save them."

I sweep his leg out from under him, sending him sprawled on his back on the dirty floor. He cries out in pain, the breath knocked right out of his lungs.

I could end it right here, but I don't. "Get up," I order. "I'm not done talking to you."

He does as he's told. "You'll regret this," he warns, wiping a bloody streak across his mouth.

I look at him. The man who was my brother. The boy who was alone, just him and snow and death.

"I know."

Then we clash again in the middle of the arena.

"Think," I hiss. "Think of everything he's done." I twist my knife to disarm him, but he holds on tight.

"This is pointless," Yuri says. "What's done is done."

"This is the truth! He didn't kill me then, and he regretted that. Do you really believe he'll stop at me? That he won't clean up all loose ends? April. May—"

"Shut up."

"—Petra—"

"Shut *up*."

"—*You*."

"THEN WHAT AM I SUPPOSED TO DO?!"

It's the roar of a wounded animal. It's a howl, desperate and raw, a lone wolf's last breath.

It's also the best chance I'm going to get.

I grab his wrist, twist the knife out of his grip, and press my blade against his neck. "Don't move," I warn the room loudly. "Or else I'll slit his throat."

But Carmine's men have already raised their guns.

"Are you trying to get them killed?" Yuri hisses. He tries to struggle free, but my headlock's too strong.

"I'm trying to finish this."

He exhales against the knife. I can feel the fight draining from him, every muscle in his body giving in. No—giving *up*. "Fine," he mutters. "Do it then. Put me down."

That's when I remember.

"Even the most loyal dog will bite if backed into a corner." Yuri's voice rings clear in my memories, a ghost from a lifetime ago.

Before, I couldn't recall my answer. But now…

"Will it?"

Now, I can hear nothing else.

"Then I'll just have to put it down."

My own voice echoes in my head. Haughty, arrogant—the face of pride itself.

I close my eyes.

And, finally, I listen.

"Blood is the only tie I need. The only tie we can trust."

∽

"Did you mean what you said? That if the child hadn't been yours..."

"Of course. Who in their right mind would keep around someone who's nobody to them?"

"I'm just saying, the vory matter."

"They're not blood. That's what matters."

"Matvey, there's something I need to—"

"You don't need to say anything. You're forgiven. After all, we're blood."

"That's... why you're forgiving me?"

"You're my blood. No one else can say that. No one in the whole world. Do you understand?"

"... I understand."

"Blood is everything to me."

"I'm sorry," I murmur.

Then I let the knife clatter to the ground.

"Motya...?" Yuri whispers, confused. "What are you doing?"

"The right thing."

He looks at me like I've gone insane. Maybe I have. Or maybe I just remember what it's like to be sane after decades of obsession.

Blood.

What a stupid thing to die for.

I didn't want to avenge my mother because she was blood—I wanted it because I loved her. Because she was important to me.

My crusade against my father was never because he betrayed some abstract primal concept—it was because he betrayed her. Because he betrayed me.

A family who used to love him.

Family. If only I'd understood before what that word truly meant.

I throw one last glance at April. The woman who changed my life—the woman who changed me.

If this has to be goodbye, let her see me go like this. Like a man and not a monster. Let her see the good in me until the end.

"*Bravo!*" Carmine claps. "Truly an outstanding performance. But I'm afraid it's time for curtain call."

I ignore him. There's nothing he can say that will be of any worth to me now. Maybe there never was.

Instead, I turn to Yuri. "Take care of them," I whisper. "When he kills me, take them and run. Hide them somewhere safe. Don't you ever let him get to them, you hear me?"

"No," Yuri stammers. "You can't—no. Not like this."

"Promise me, Yura."

"Kill me! He might honor the terms then. Or—or just give me the knife! It won't be honorable, but—"

"I can't do that. I've already bested you."

"But if you do this, then no one has won! Don't you get it? He'll get to decide, he—"

"That's why I need you to promise."

"What was that?" Carmine goes. "Sorry, can you speak up? I feel like we're missing the end of the play here. That's not very nice, you know."

"Promise me," I insist.

Yuri stares at me with wide eyes. Finally, I can see the truth in them: pain, heartbreak, guilt. All the bent and broken things I never wanted to look for.

But I was the one who put them there.

And now, it's time to pay my debts.

"I promise," he rasps.

It's all I can ask for.

"Hellooo?" Carmine calls. "Mind sharing that with the rest of the audience? Seriously, this is the grand finale. Do we have to get a mic in here?" He taps his foot impatiently on the floor. "Care to loop me in, Yuri?"

I roll my eyes. This man never fucking shuts up, does he? "I said—"

"HE SURRENDERS!"

We all turn to Yuri. "The hell?" I whisper.

"You asked me to save them," Yuri hisses. "So let me fucking save them." Then he turns back to Carmine. "He says he surrenders. He accepts your deal."

"My deal?" Carmine frowns.

"Yes. Your original deal."

Finally, I realize what he's up to.

You have three days to surrender yourself. If you do, no harm will come to your family. That's the deal Yuri came to me with earlier. The *original* deal.

The room erupts in murmurs: disbelief, outrage, the whole shebang.

"That deal's no longer on the table, *consigliere*," Carmine tuts, his eye twitching with barely suppressed anger.

"The three days haven't expired."

He's pushing it. If he keeps this up, he's gonna get himself killed too. "Yuri—"

"It's what you wanted, isn't it?" he insists. "Matvey will be dead. His Bratva will be yours. What good will three dead girls do to you?"

"He's got a point," Vlad grumbles. "My idiot daughter can still be of use. And the Groza runt—her whore of a mother can raise her for us, preserve the bloodline. We can marry her off when it suits our needs."

"No!" April screams.

I lock eyes with April at the edge of the arena. I can tell she wants to wring Vlad's neck with her own bare hands, and Petra certainly isn't looking any happier, but I need them to understand. To push their emotions aside and let me do this.

If they don't, they will be killed. *May* will be killed.

This way, only one of us has to die.

"April…" Her hazel eyes look just like they did when I first met her: big, bright, beautiful—and filled with all the hope in the world. "Trust me."

Wordlessly, she nods.

"Fine," Carmine finally concedes, though not happily. "Then I guess we'd better make it official."

He gives Yuri a signal. Immediately, he twists my arms behind my back. He isn't using any strength at all, but he doesn't need to: I let him.

"Matvey Groza…" My father grins. "I accept your surrender."

60

APRIL

This is a nightmare.

It has to be. There's no way this can be happening. There's no way that Matvey…

He's going to die.

He's going to sacrifice himself for us.

I watch the man I love walk past me, hands twisted behind his back, and something inside me just snaps. My reason, my logic—it all goes flying out the window.

Because I can't lose him.

"Matvey…" I whisper brokenly. "Matvey! MATVEY!"

Carmine's men hold me back. I barely even feel them—like a banshee, I keep throwing myself forward and screaming. Wailing with a kind of pain they cannot possibly understand.

Until two seconds ago, I didn't think I could, either.

"Will someone keep that bitch quiet?" Vlad spits from his podium of traitors.

"April," Petra murmurs, "you need to calm down. There's nothing we can do. He made his choice."

But her words fall on deaf ears. "No," I keep chanting over and over. "No, no, Matvey, you can't—YOU CAN'T!"

With one last push, I free myself from the guards. I run like a woman possessed. Yuri looks at me like I've gone crazy, but it's not me who's done that. It's *him*. "How could you do this?!" I yell. "He's your brother! You're killing him! HOW COULD YOU DO THIS?!"

I can hear the symphony of guns clicking all around me, bullets waiting in their chambers, ready to strike me down. But for once, I don't care. I keep yelling, clawing at Yuri like he's the only thing standing between me and Matvey, even though I know it's not that simple. Even though he isn't lifting a single finger to defend himself.

Even though—

He's the one who just saved your life.

But what good is my life if Matvey can't be a part of it?

"Traitor!" I scream, oblivious to Carmine's hand slowly rising to signal his men. Nothing can snap me out of my frenzy— nothing, *nothing*. "Traitor, traitor, TRAITOR—"

"Let me."

Except that voice.

The guns go still. Carmine's palm, too, one move shy from spelling my doom. "Fine. But make it quick."

Then he motions for Yuri to step aside.

"April." Matvey kneels down with me. His hands are free now, but he isn't making a single move to run. Why? "Thank you. But you need to stand down now."

"No," I croak.

"Yes," he insists, though gently. Without a single trace of force in his voice. It's like, for the first time, I'm speaking to a version of Matvey who's at peace.

Problem is, *I'm* not. I'm at war with the world. I am hatred and fury and a single selfish wish: *Take me with you.*

"I can't."

"Yes, you can. You will."

"I won't—"

"For our daughter."

Our daughter. That's right. I have a daughter. I…

I lift up my gaze. The bundle in Carmine's arms is stirring, trying to fight whatever potion he's given her. Trying to reach me.

Finally, the fog clears. "For our daughter," I murmur back.

"Yes. She'll need you," Matvey continues to speak into my ear, low and gentle. "More than ever now."

"It's not fair," I sob.

"Nothing's fair," he rasps, catching a falling tear with his thumb, "in love and war."

Then he stands up again. "Yuri."

Like old times, Yuri obeys the unspoken command in an instant. He secures Matvey's hands behind his back one more time and curses, low enough that only he and I can hear, in a Russian dialect I can't understand.

"You should've just killed me," he whispers to Matvey in English. "Why didn't you kill me?"

Matvey doesn't reply in English. When his words come, they come in his native idiom. *"Potomu chto ty moy brat."*

And this time, I don't need to speak the language to know what they mean.

Because you're my brother.

Then Carmine forces him down to his knees. "You played a valiant game," he commends. "But in the end, you just can't beat the house."

Then he points a gun at Matvey's head.

Matvey sets his jaw. In the crook of Carmine's spare arm, our daughter is still sleeping. Is he going to do it like this? Kill his own son and let his blood cover his daughter?

"Monster."

He glances towards me. "Sorry, what was that?"

"I said you're a monster," I growl. "You don't deserve your family."

"Let me tell you a secret." He smiles cruelly. "There's no such thing as 'family.' And we're all monsters in the end."

"Like fuck we are," Yuri snarls.

"Huh?"

It happens in a heartbeat. One second, Carmine's giving his evil villain speech, and the next—

The next, Yuri's kicking the legs out from under him.

Matvey reacts instantly. The second Carmine's down, he uses both hands to block the gun while Yuri lunges to break May's fall.

"I got you," he exhales as he catches my baby girl. Then he rushes to my side and gives her back to me.

"Thank you," I whisper.

"Take cover," Yuri ushers me towards the exit. "We'll talk later."

"What about Matvey? Wait, what about Pet—"

"IDI NA HUI, PERHOT' PODZALUPNAYA!"

Petra's battle cry cuts me off. I twist my head around as we run, and there she is, a stolen gun in each hand, shooting and roundhouse-kicking her way to freedom.

No need to worry about her, I guess. "What, uhh—what does that mean?"

Yuri winces. "'Fuck you, peehole dandruff.' More or less."

"Sorry, pee-*what?*"

"GET THEM!" Carmine yells over the chaos. "THE HELL ARE YOU WAITING FOR?!"

"But boss, you didn't give the signal—"

"I HAVE NO HANDS, IN CASE YOU DIDN'T FUCKING NOTICE!"

True to his word, Carmine's still locked in a struggle against Matvey. His men are trying to reach him, but Petra's like a one-woman army: the second one of them raises his gun, they lose the gun *and* the hand holding it.

Like I said: never fuck with the pregnant ones.

"Go to her," I urge, sensing Yuri's conflict. "I'll be okay. I can—"

"Not so fast, *suka*."

My blood freezes. "Vlad."

"I'm not going to monologue," he spits. "Die, bitch."

BANG!

I squeeze my eyes shut. It's all I have the time for—that and wrapping my arms tight around my baby. I brace for pain, but it doesn't come.

When I open them again, I see why.

Yuri's standing in front of me. He's dressed all in black, so I don't see it immediately: the reason I'm still breathing.

But then he stumbles.

"Yuri!" I catch him with my free arm and lay him on the floor, then put a hand to his chest.

It comes away soaked in red.

Petra hears my scream and twists around. "NO!"

Out of the corner of my eye, I see her fly past the crowd of enemies, gunning down everyone who's stupid enough to stand between her and her new target.

Her father.

"You're dead, Otets."

Vlad sneers. "You stupid girl. Your mother didn't know her place, either. I should've put you down the same way I did with her."

Petra allows herself exactly one second of shock before her rage comes back tenfold. "You can fucking try, old man."

Then she pulls out her knives and charges.

I can't spare any attention for their fight. I wish I could: she's pregnant and surrounded and fighting against her *father—* who, unless I heard wrong, just admitted to murdering her mother. The same mother Petra grew up believing *she'd* killed.

But there's only one way I can be there for her now.

"Yuri. Look at me."

Yuri's gaze is hazy, unfocused. "I'm sorry," he rasps.

"None of that now. Here, just—" I shrug off my jacket. "Press this to the wound. Don't let up, okay?"

"I'm so sorry."

"You have nothing to be sorry for. You did the right thing in the end. You—you saved my life, you—" I try to find something else to plug the wound, but there's just so much blood... "Yuri. Stay with me."

"C-Call—"

BANG!

For a second, I think it's Vlad again, trying to take another shot at me. But when I glance back, I see Petra standing over his body, one bloody knife in each hand. And her eyes, wide and terrified, are staring somewhere else entirely.

No...

It can't be...

"MATVEY!"

I watch the man I love fall backwards, pushed by the tip of Carmine's gun, still smoking with the bullet that got him.

A bullet straight through the heart.

61

APRIL

No.

No, no, no...

"Whew!" Carmine goes. "Thought he had me for a second there." He gives Matvey a cursory glance, then steps over him.

I want to kill him. I've never felt like this before. Never in all my life. If I didn't have a baby in my arms right now, I'd be wringing his neck with my own two hands.

"But like I said..." He gives a light kick backwards, jostling Matvey's limp arm in the process. "—can't beat the house. Right, Miss?"

It's like watching a kid gloat over the flightless torso of a butterfly. Like nothing could make him happier than plucking those wings right off. Not because he hates it—just because he's *curious*. Because he wants to see what will happen.

"You're a child," I realize.

Carmine's face hardens imperceptibly. "Come again?"

"You're a child," I repeat, rising to my full height. "That's why you left, over and over. Because you couldn't possibly handle the responsibility of being the adult in the room."

"I understand you're upset—"

"You understand nothing," I laugh. It's the last thing I expected to do in a moment like this, but here I am: lips curling into a half-snarl, half-grin. All the mockery I was always on the receiving end of, ready to overflow towards the other side. "You didn't go after Matvey because he was after you—you went after him because he knew the truth. That you, the great Don Carmine Bonaccorsi, were nothing but an overgrown toddler."

Carmine's smile freezes on his face. "Interesting choice of words for someone on the wrong side of the barrel."

"Then use it," I drawl, taking another step forward. "Make me disappear. And prove me right while you're at it."

Finally, there it is: conflict. Such a big man, hemmed into a corner by a measly seamstress. "No, no," he sneers. "You don't get the easy way out, Miss. Not after this enlightening conversation. And, I'm sorry to say, neither does your daughter."

If anything could make me freeze, it's that.

In any other circumstances, I might have forced myself to eat my own words. To fall to my knees and beg for forgiveness, for mercy. Not because I believed any of it, but because it was the smart thing to do. For my daughter—*our* daughter.

Except that I see movement.

It's the barest twitch out of the corner of my eye. For a second, I wonder if I've imagined it. I'm certainly desperate enough.

But then it happens again.

And suddenly, I know exactly what to do.

"You'd take it out on a baby?" I scoff. "Wow. What a big, bad man you are."

"I was under the impression you were the clever one. Now, did I get that wrong?"

"And I was under the impression you had a goddamn mafia at your beck and call." I take a step forward. "But I guess all the good ones left you."

"No one leaves me," he growls.

"Right. You just do it before they can."

"You know, I'm getting real tired of this," he says. "Don't get me wrong—I feel for you. It's never easy to fall for the wrong man. But allow me to give you one final piece of advice. For your next life, shall we say."

"Can't wait," I mutter.

He gives a deranged smile. "Next time, make sure you pick the winning side."

Then he cocks his gun.

I should be afraid. No, scratch that—I should be goddamn terrified. But I'm not. All I feel is a strange sort of calm. "I've got some advice as well."

"Oh?" he asks. "Let's hear it then."

"Next time, check for a pulse."

NICOLE FOX

I see the color drain from his face. It's immensely satisfying, bringing a giant to his knees.

It all happens in slow motion.

I watch him turn, eyes wide, and meet the gaze of his son. "But you're dead," he blurts out.

"No," Matvey replies evenly, showing off the tattered lapel of his jacket. His *bulletproof* jacket—the one I gave him to wear. The one I made for him, one careful stitch at a time. "You are."

Then he fires.

I don't avert my eyes. I don't brace myself. I don't even try to step out of the way.

I just cover up my baby.

Blood sprays me from head to toe. *Carmine* blood—talk about irony. I let it shower over me, disgust giving way to something stronger and far more intoxicating.

Power.

The second the body drops, Matvey rushes to my side. "Are you okay?" He pulls out a pocket handkerchief—also shot straight through the middle—and starts cleaning me up.

"Me? Sure." I shrug. "I'm a future *pakhansha*. What's a little blood?"

He grins. "You learned how to say that one, too."

"Took longer than I would've liked, but we got there in the end."

"I'll say." He grabs my face and kisses me. I'm gross from

head to toe, but it's like he couldn't care less. Like I'm all he needs and then some.

Lucky for him, he's all I need, too.

"YURI!"

Our heads snap back in unison. Petra's just dropped the last of Carmine's henchmen to the floor—and she's running straight towards the back of the room.

Oh, no. With everything that was happening, I completely forgot.

We both run after Petra. She's kneeling in a pool of blood, her pristine cream clothes stained beyond repair, her fingers trembling as she drops her knives to the ground and grabs Yuri's face with both hands. "Yuri. Wake up."

Nothing.

"I said wake up!" she shrieks. "I'm not done with you! I haven't forgiven you yet!"

I want to tell her there's hope, but I'm not sure that's true. I try to find a pulse, but I'm not a nurse, so I have no idea if I'm doing it right. All I know is that I can't feel anything under my fingers, nothing except...

Cold.

I glance at Yuri's hand. It's clutching his phone, something it wasn't doing before, when I was here by his side. The screen's covered in blood, but it looks like he'd been trying to text someone.

He was trying to save us. With his last breath, he was still...

Matvey's gaze follows mine, and I can tell he's come to my same conclusion. His face is a complicated tangle of emotions. Strong, conflicting emotions, all warring in the icy pools of his eyes.

"Give me that," he rasps. "We need to call—"

BOOM!

One of the walls bursts open, revealing another hidden door. And from that door…

"Vlad's men," Matvey growls. "Looks like the fight isn't over yet."

"Like hell it isn't," Petra spits. She tries to stand up, but—

"Easy," I murmur. "You've been fighting all this time. You're in no condition."

"You're right. So help me up."

I blink. It's the last request I expected from Petra: *help me.* "Okay."

We both hold her up, me on one side, Matvey on the other. "Petra…"

"Carry me to my father's corpse."

We do.

The Solovyov traitors surround us. I glance back at Yuri, but we don't need to walk too far before Petra shrugs us both off.

Then she plants her foot on her father's chest. "The king is dead. You have ten seconds to say, 'Long live the queen' or end up like him."

"What's she trying to do?" I whisper.

"Rule by consensus," Matvey whispers back. "But it won't work. Not with Vlad's men."

He's right. I realize it immediately: for every recruit who moves over to our side, there are ten who don't. Who sneer and spit out insults: *suka* here, *shlyukha* there.

Funnily enough, I don't feel like I need a dictionary for these ones.

"What are we gonna do?"

Matvey steps in front of me. "Fight."

It's so unfair. Yuri's still lying there; Petra's tears haven't even dried yet; and *Matvey.* He escaped death twice for me today. Will we really be lucky enough for a third time?

"I want a gun, too," I decide.

"No fucking way."

"Matvey, I need to protect May, I need—"

"So you know how to shoot one?"

"I…" I pause. *Dammit, he's got me there.* "I'm a quick study?"

The last man comes over. We're still ridiculously outnumbered, but at least like this we have a fighting chance. Right?

Right…?

"I love you," I whisper to Matvey.

"I love you, too."

"I don't hate you," Petra mutters. "Either of you."

Well, *now,* we're really going to die.

Vlad's men take aim. I squeeze my eyes shut, preparing myself for the inevitable bloody end.

I'm sorry, May. I'm sorry I couldn't be a good mother to you.

I'm sorry I...

"Evening, gentlemen. Care to drop those guns?"

I blink.

Grisha?

I must be hallucinating. This has to be a stress reaction of some kind. An illusion conjured by my subconscious to make my last moments bearable.

But if it is, why am I seeing *Grisha* of all people?

And yet, one quick glance at the room tells me it's not my imagination's doing. Not Grisha, not the army he's brought with him—and not the hundreds of guns aimed at the Solovyov traitors.

It's the cavalry.

62

MATVEY

After Grisha's grand entrance, getting rid of the traitors is a quick affair. "Care to do the honors, boss?"

As a matter of fact, I do.

"Kill them all."

In less than a minute, it's over. Lena and Julia seem to take particular pleasure in teaching whoever dared disrespect their mistress a swift, brutal lesson.

"Yuri!" Petra rushes back to him. "Did you...? Were you the one who...?" She wipes the blood from his phone.

There it is: a text. To Grisha.

With our location.

"You idiot," she sobs, and there's no holding back the flood now. Not with no one left to fight. "You stupid, careless idiot, *svoloch—*"

"He took that bullet for me." April trembles. "I'm so sorry, Petra, Matvey— This is all—"

But I don't let her finish. "Hush." I pull her close. "It was his choice."

Choice. That's what all this comes down to, isn't it? Not who we are—but who we *choose* to be.

"I wish—"

"I know. Me, too."

Petra doesn't seem to be paying attention to our conversation. She just bends over on Yuri's chest, smothering her cries in the crook of his neck. One last hug, one last time.

"… dandruff…"

Wait, what?

Petra's head shoots up. "Yuri?!"

There's no mistaking it: that's his voice. Rough and breathless, but still, it's *him*.

"As long…" He coughs, blood splattering all over his front. "… as you don't call me… dandruff…"

"He's alive…?" April sniffles. "I'm not imagining this? He's really…?"

"Oh my God," Petra exhales. "Someone! Anyone!"

"I've got him."

I put all my *pakhan* authority in my voice. At the sound of it, both Petra and April make way automatically.

Then I crouch down and scoop Yuri up.

"Motya…"

"Don't speak," I order.

"I'm s-sorry… I'm really, really…"

"I said shut up. Or did the blood loss make you deaf as well as stupid?"

A weak laugh. "You're always… such an ass…"

Of course I am. How else am I going to cope? "Grisha, call an ambulance. We'll figure out a cover story later."

"Yes, boss."

I lift my brother up and carry him out of the room. There's another tunnel, one that leads to the surface. With April holding down the fort and Petra stuck handling business with her new men, we're finally alone.

For a while, neither one of us speaks. It leaves me with time to think—about the past twenty-four hours. About everything. About the betrayal.

And about the one part that doesn't add up.

"Is…" Yuri coughs as I carry him out. "Is Petra… okay…?"

"She took out damn near fifty guys. She's just peachy."

Another coughing fit shakes him, but he still manages to croak out, "What about April…? And May…?"

"They're both fine." My throat goes tight. "You saved them."

"I didn't. I put them in danger."

"No, *I* did. And I put you in danger, too."

"Motya…"

But I cut him off. "You left out something when you confessed to me."

"I did?"

"Yes. You covered everything from the beginning to the end, but you deliberately avoided one part."

"Which part…?"

"That night in the woods. When April was taken by Carmine."

Realization dawns on him. "I…"

"You wanted me to hate you. So why leave out the one part that was guaranteed to make me do that?" He doesn't answer, but he doesn't need to. I already know why. "It's because you had nothing to do with it, isn't it?"

"Why are you—"

"Carmine knew you had her. He couldn't not know. But you still held him off for a month. So when his patience snapped, he acted on his own. And you came to me."

He presses his lips tight. "It was the right thing to do."

"Not for a traitor, it wasn't."

He falls silent for a long time. "Matvey, I…"

"I didn't mean it," I say before he can finish. He's had his time to confess—now, it's my turn. "All that talk of blood. I was lashing out. I was in pain and I hurt everyone around me because of it. I was just too stupid to see it."

"But I betrayed you," he whispers.

"I betrayed you first. I should've seen what was going on with you."

"You couldn't—"

"Yes, I damn well could." Because it's the truth, isn't it? There were signs everywhere. And if I'd just been a little less self-absorbed...

Then maybe I could've saved us.

"I'm sorry, Yuri. I'm sorry it took me this long to see you."

His eyes are wet now. Christ, when did we become a bunch of schoolgirls? "I still betrayed the Bratva," he shakes his head. "I betrayed my *pakhan.*"

"And you'll be punished for that," I declare. "So don't you dare quit on me before I can give you the beating you deserve."

"Is that an order?"

I feel the corner of my lips twitch. "No, smartass. It's a request from your brother."

He smiles in return. "Okay, then." It's weak and wavering, but there. "Brother."

63

MATVEY

24 HOURS LATER

I blink awake to an odd combination of smells: antiseptic wound dressing and croissants.

Specifically, *fresh* croissants. Straight from the French bakery around the corner.

It wouldn't usually be enough to rouse me, but I've had one hell of a weekend. "Save me a plain one," I grumble.

"Trust me, no one's lining up to steal that."

Petra. What a celestial voice to wake up to. "Where's April?"

"*Hwen pho geph mophee.*"

"Right. Thanks for clarifying."

She swallows her gigantic bite. Grisha hasn't been here fifty seconds, and she's already wolfed down one—no, *two* chocolate croissants. "I said she went to get coffee," she clarifies. Then she reaches for a third pastry.

"Enough, you jackal. Leave some for my girlfriend."

Petra arches a brow. "That depends on how long she's planning to be gone."

"I'm here!" April rushes in, May in tow. "Any cream puffs?"

"I wouldn't hang you out to dry." Grisha smiles, handing over a separate paper bag. Talk about preferential treatment.

I snatch my breakfast before the Cookie Monster can inhale that, too. "How long was I asleep?"

"Not long," April answers. "Just under an hour. You should grab some more rest."

"I'm fine."

"You're not. Also, stop scratching your arm."

I scowl, but I let my hand fall to my side. "Don't you have a baby to fuss over?"

"Actually," she sighs, "sometimes, I think I have two."

"What's that supposed to mean?" I ask with a frown.

"Nothing. Nothing at all."

"Really? 'Cause it sounded a lot like sarcasm."

"I don't know what you're talking ab—"

"Is there any left for me?"

Our heads turn in unison.

"Yuri!" Petra rushes over to the bed. "How are you feeling?"

Yuri stirs. He squeezes his eyes against the fluorescent hospital lights. Between surgery and recovery, he's been out a whole day. "Hungry," he replies.

"Nice try," she deadpans. "You're on a hospital food diet for the next three weeks, you fuckhead."

"It's good to see you, too."

She punches him on the shoulder. His *good* shoulder, but I can't imagine it doesn't still hurt. "Stop wasting your breath on fucking jokes of all things. Your left lung almost collapsed."

"What if it wasn't a joke?" His voice dips lower, softer. "I am glad to see you. I didn't think I'd get the chance again."

"Oh, shut up," Petra growls, but her eyes are shiny now. "And don't you ever scare me like that again. You almost lost two pints of blood! They wouldn't even let me donate!"

"Because you're pregnant," April points out.

"So what? It's my choice!"

"Now, now," Grisha tries to placate her. "It all turned out fine in the end, didn't it?"

"No thanks to *him*," she hisses in Yuri's direction. "I swear, it's like he was trying to make me into a single mother."

"Is her bedside manner always like this?" April whispers to me.

"I wouldn't know," I mutter back. "Never had the misfortune."

"I'll clear my calendar if you get shot," Petra offers.

My lips twitch. Truth is, I *did* get shot, but it didn't matter. Because I had someone looking out for me.

I glance down at my jacket. I haven't had time to change—we all came straight here. The bullet hole is still there, blinking back at me from the special fabric April's team created. An invisible, everyday armor.

Well, everyday for me. I doubt shop clerks out there are spending their days in three-piece suits, especially ones with this price tag. But I understand April's been thinking of expanding the scope. Already, her mind is on the next big thing. So who knows what the future might hold?

"Matvey." Yuri's voice snaps me out of my thoughts. "Can we talk?"

"You shouldn't be exerting yourself right now. Rest. We'll talk later."

"No, I…" he shakes his head. "I need to say this. I feel like I won't be able to sleep until I do."

I look at him. Once, he wouldn't have dared to contradict a direct order from me. But this isn't the same Yuri I met two days ago, a week ago, or even a year ago. This is someone else—someone new. And this someone isn't going to take no for an answer.

"Alright. Speak."

He gives a small, grateful nod. "When I found out we weren't…" He trails off. He doesn't need to finish that sentence—we all know what lies at the end. "I was scared. I thought that would be the end of us. That if it came out, we would… that you would…"

"I know," I say. "I know."

"But in the end, I just turned it into a self-fulfilling prophecy. My fears, my guilt—it all got away from me so fast. I wanted to dig myself out and didn't know how to do it. So I just kept digging myself deeper down."

"You thought it was necessary."

"No. I *told* myself it was." He looks at me then, eyes bright and open. For a second, he's the scrawny kid I found in the snow. "But I should've talked to you. I should've risked it. If I had, then maybe…"

The worst part is, I can't fill in the rest of that sentence, because I just don't know. If he'd told me, what would I have done?

I know I wouldn't have had him killed. I know I probably would've kept him in the higher-ups of my Bratva on his practical value alone. What I don't know is everything else.

Would I have kept thinking of him as a brother? As *family*?

Would I have trusted him again?

I don't know. Because the truth is, Yuri isn't the only one who walked out of that warehouse a different man. And if I'm being honest, I was already someone else when I walked in.

Because the woman I love deserved better than that man.

She deserved the world.

And she deserves it still.

"Can you ever forgive me?" Yuri asks in the end. "Can we ever go back to the way things were?"

I sit on the edge of the bed. "You lied to me, Yura."

"I know."

"For months."

"I know. I'm sorry."

"You kidnapped my woman and child and almost cost them their lives. You trusted the wrong person because you couldn't bring yourself to trust me. Hell, you didn't even trust Petra with the truth."

"I'm so sorry," he croaks. "I understand if you don't want anything to do with me after this. I'll accept any punishment. I'll—"

"I'm not done."

Yuri falls silent. Everyone in the room has their gazes fixed on me, even May.

"You lied, kidnapped, deceived. You did that to the people closest to you."

"Motya…"

"And then you saved them."

He blinks. "What?"

"You saved them," I repeat. "You looked after them. You protected them from Carmine's overreach, made sure their safety was part of the deal. And then you ate a bullet for them." I finally let my expression thaw. "You chose wrong at first. But when you had to choose again, you chose them. You chose *us*."

"But is that really okay?" Yuri protests. "Shouldn't I pay for what I've done?"

"Of course," I reply. "Effective immediately, you are no longer part of the Groza Bratva."

He nods, like he'd been expecting this. "The *vory* voted?"

"On the phone. Like you said, I can't keep stiffing them. Their voices matter, whether I like it or not."

"But I didn't just betray the Bratva. I betrayed *you*. I betrayed everyone."

"Yes. Blood betrayals are paid in blood." I tap my finger on the bandages, just shy of the bullet wound. "And it seems to me, you've already done that. So we're good."

"B-But…" Yuri stammers in disbelief. "But I'm not blood."

"Actually…"

I lift up my sleeve and show off a piece of gauze. It still itches like hell, but April's right: if I keep scratching it, it will just keep bleeding. "They didn't have enough blood bags for your type. They asked for a donor. Turns out we're a match."

"You… you gave your blood for me?" Yuri whispers. "Even after all I've done?"

"Yes. And now, we're blood again. In a way." I shake my head. "Not that it matters."

"What does that mean?"

Here we are. The million-dollar question: *What does "blood" mean to me?* I've had a lot of time to think about the answer. Before this all started, I'd already reached a new one. I just didn't know it yet.

"I won't pretend blood isn't important," I start. "It is. But it's not the only way to make a family. Being there for each other, protecting each other—that's what family truly is. Someone very special showed me that."

I turn to April. Her eyes are glistening, a watery smile on her lips. "Took you long enough," she mumbles.

Yeah. Too long. "I've had a very patient teacher."

Then I take her hand in mine.

"Any other questions, brother?"

"You really mean it?" he asks, voice unsteady. "You'll take me back?"

"If everyone else agrees."

April is the first to raise her hand. "I second the motion." Then May starts laughing, imitating her as if she's done something particularly funny. Her tiny hands reach for her uncle, almost out of habit, and Yuri's eyes get just a little bit shinier.

"You don't actually have to say it like that, you know."

"Killjoy."

Grisha shakes his head at our antics. "Well, let's see. I'm not particularly thrilled with the way this all went down. Loyalty isn't something you choose. It's something you either have or don't."

Yuri starts nodding. "I understand."

"And laying down your life for your comrades is exactly what being loyal means." Grisha smiles. "You're not a big, bad traitor, Yurochka. You're just way too goddamn dense."

"Ass!"

Here they go again. It's nice to see some things never change.

"Petra?"

All eyes turn to her. She's been quiet the longest, and also hurt the deepest. I can't begin to imagine what her answer will be. If this has been too much for her, I'd understand.

"I have a condition," she says eventually.

"Name it," Yuri whispers.

"Marry me." She grabs his hand before any of us can get over the shock, Yuri included. "Give me the wedding of my dreams. Or I swear, Yuri Romanov, you will see your kid grow up exclusively through postcards for as long as you live."

It's a weird proposal, to be sure.

It's also very much Petra's style.

And while any sane man would run in the other direction, IV drips be damned, my brother just cracks the biggest, stupidest grin in the world. "Third time's the charm, right?"

"You bet your ass it is."

Then she kisses him. If it can even be called a kiss. I feel like I'm watching a wildlife documentary about lions and gazelles —and Petra sure as fuck isn't the gazelle.

"We should probably give them some space," April mutters in my ear while blocking May's view.

"Yeah. And find some acid for my eyes, while we're at it."

"I'm sure the hospital staff will have something."

We head out of the room. "Grisha," I call.

"What?" he huffs. "I was enjoying the show."

"More like stacking up blackmail material."

"I'm only human, boss."

We ditch him to stand guard—*far* away from the door—and walk out into the parking lot. "So weird," April muses. "This is where I was kidnapped the first time."

"Here?" I frown.

"Yeah. Right between those two spots. There was a black van and it just swallowed me up."

"But you escaped."

"Of course." She flashes the cheekiest grin in the world. "Never mess with the pregnant ones."

"Do you regret it?" I ask. "Being snatched that day?"

It's a fair question. Even though so much has happened between us since then, I can't let myself forget how we got here. Originally, April wanted nothing to do with me. If Carmine hadn't gotten in the way, I might have never known I had a daughter.

I might have never known a lot of things.

For a second, April doesn't answer. She just looks up at me with her impossibly wide eyes, until a warm smile slowly spreads on her lips. "No," she answers, and I can hear the truth in her voice. "Because then I'd have never crashed your wedding."

"That's a weird reason."

"Is it?" she laughs. "It brought me here. It brought me to you. I don't think I need a better reason than that."

She finds my hand and interlaces our fingers. There's no ring, no material promise of what's to come, but there is something else I only notice now. Bruised and battered and blackened by dirt, but it's there.

The ribbon I gave her.

"You said, 'Don't mess with the pregnant ones,'" I echo, drawing close. "Does that mean I can mess with you now?"

"That depends," she murmurs against my lips. "Are you going to kiss me half as good as that?"

"April Flowers," I drawl, her chin already between my fingers, "I will kiss you until my last breath."

Her cheeks dust with red. "Good answer," she whispers. "Now, prove it."

So I do. But when I kiss her this time, it's different from all the others.

Because, for the first time, I kiss her in the light of day.

EPILOGUE: APRIL

I burst out of the limo in full wedding gear. "Sorry! I think I'll walk after all!"

I don't stick around to hear the driver's apologies—I just run. Like the motherfricking wind. Which isn't a simple feat, considering the five-inch stiletto heels June shoved my feet into, but I've beaten worse odds.

After all, what's one more wedding to crash?

I leave behind the traffic jam and hoist up my white skirts. Some dudes wolf-whistle at me from the sidewalk, but I don't have the time to give them a piece of my mind. New York traffic has already robbed me of half my prep hour— I'm not sacrificing any more.

Besides—if there was ever a day to run, it's this.

Thank God we did hair and makeup at home.

I get to the venue with my heels in one hand and my skirts in the other. My feet look like I've been walking on coals, and frankly, the sensation isn't all that different.

"There you are!" Petra scolds me as soon as she sees me running up the stone steps. "What took you so long?"

"Sorry," I heave. "There was a last-minute hold-up."

"See, Nugget?" June croons to the bundle in her arms. A very *big* bundle, but a bundle nonetheless. The tulle certainly doesn't help. "Your mommy's a total sleepyhead, too."

"I wasn't sleeping!" I say. "I just forgot something, that's all. I had to go back home and grab it."

"What could possibly be that important?!" Petra hisses, her own white dress puffing around her like an angry prairie chicken.

I fish around my pockets—because if there's one advantage to designing my own wedding dress, it's that I get to have those, thank you very much—until I find the offending object. It isn't much to look at: a simple piece of blue satin. Cornflower blue, to be exact.

"Can you tie it to my wrist?" I ask.

"Now?!"

"I know, I know! It's just that I can't do it on my own and we're already—"

"Allow me."

Oh.

Oh my.

I feel rough fingers slip the ribbon from mine. "I thought it was bad luck to see the bride before the wedding," I murmur.

"So don't turn around," that husky voice replies. "Give me your hand."

Stunned, I obey. I keep my eyes fixed on some distant spot, somewhere between Petra tapping her heel and June smirking behind her hand.

Maid of honor, my ass.

The fabric grazes my inner wrist. It's a soft, gentle touch, almost too light to feel. But I could never overlook the heat of that hand, not in a hundred lifetimes. It's the hand that brought me here, the hand that saved me.

The hand that reached out to me when no one else would.

"Done," he whispers against my ear.

To say I'm blushing is an understatement. I could stop traffic just by stepping off the sidewalk. "Thank you," I breathe.

Before he releases my hand, I feel the press of his lips on my knuckles. Just once—just enough to drive me crazy.

"I almost forgot," he says. "I have a gift for you."

"Me?" I blink.

"No. For the other bride."

Petra frowns. "What are you talking about?"

That's when I see his hand reach between us. I'm still not looking at him—call me superstitious, but I'm not going to invite any more bad luck on myself—so I'm even more surprised when I see what it is.

A folder.

"That's a weird gift," June comments as Petra takes the folder from Matvey's grasp. "I mean, dude, no offense, but I'd have gone with jewelry at the very least."

"I'll leave that to Yuri," he says. "This is from me only."

Well, now, I'm starting to get jealous. "Where's my special gift?" I grumble.

"*Your* special gift isn't something I can give you in public."

"Ew!" Petra says. "Double ew, triple ew—just get a room already!"

"Let them tie the knot first," June pipes up. "God knows these two have sinned enough."

"Jay!"

While I'm busy bickering with my maid of *dis*honor, Petra's eyebrows rise. "Huh. I thought these weren't going to be ready in time for the ceremony."

"What are they?" I prod.

"Our divorce papers."

Oh.

Oh.

Matvey mentioned that it was taking longer than expected. Since we'd already booked everything, we thought we'd go ahead with the ceremony anyway and formalize later, but…

This is real. This is happening.

"How did you get the lawyers to speed this up?" Petra flips through the pages with efficiency.

"Threatened mine," he says with a low chuckle.

"That's such bullshit," she mutters. "I threatened mine, too. What, they're taking you seriously but not me?"

"Simple math. *Pakhan* trumps *vor*. Nothing personal."

"Yeah, yeah, tell that to those dudebros you hired."

I feel exhilarated. I want to laugh and cry at the same time. "So we can sign?" I ask. "We can really sign today?"

"As soon as she signs," he confirms.

I take a glance at the papers. They've already been signed and initialed by him, every single page. "Got a pen?" Petra asks.

"Right here."

Once everything's in order, she hands the folder back over. "You'll send me a copy?"

"Sure. Consider it your honeymoon gift."

"You stingy bastard."

Despite Petra's words, this might just be the most amicable divorce I've ever witnessed. "So we're good?" I ask, still incredulous. "We can get married? For real?"

"For real," Matvey replies. He presses a kiss to the back of my head, and I can feel all his affection there. The love that already binds us, more than any contract ever could.

But still, the ring's pretty nice.

"I'd better go look for my brother," he sighs. "Make sure he isn't breathing in a paper bag."

Petra's eyes narrow. "He's not getting cold feet, is he?"

"I've blocked the exits just in case."

"Double check the locks."

I roll my eyes. *Freaking Bratva.* Some things never change. "See you at the altar, then."

"See you at the altar, Ms. Flowers."

He speaks those words right against my ear, low and gravelly as sin. It reminds me of the day we met, back when he still did call me that. *'Ms. Flowers.'*

How far we've come from that changing room.

Then again, some things never change. Like the heat crawling down my spine, so strong I can barely breathe. I want to rip this dress right off and let him sweep me off my feet, carry me where no one can see us. Declare his love for me in all the ways he knows how.

But first, we've got a wedding to attend.

After Matvey leaves, June spirits me away to the prep room. She touches up my hair and makeup—not without some choice swearing at the damage I did during my mad dash for the silk ribbon—and turns me once again into my fairytale self. Then she does the same to Petra.

"I have bridesmaids, you know," she protests.

"Sure. And they're both in the kitchens, making sure no tart goes untasted."

Petra mutters something about poison, but June's already moved on to her dress. "Jeez, did someone shoot at you on the way here?"

"Ask *your* bride. It's her design."

Indeed it is. Once the Mallard's exhibit was done, they reluctantly agreed to hand over my "Bulletproof Bride" piece. They even asked if I was interested in selling, but I told them no. This piece was made with one person in mind—it's only fair that she gets to wear it on her big day.

Well. *Third* big day.

"Swiss cheese effect aside, it's definitely a good choice. You don't even look pregnant in this one."

"Say that again, I dare you."

"What? It was a compliment!"

It's kind of true: the skirt starts high and puffs wide, so even if she's close to popping, you'd be hard-pressed to tell. Especially to her face.

I tune out their banter and look in the mirror. My own dress is familiar, but at the same time, it isn't. It has the same ivory color, the same draping, the same shape on my body. But on the left sleeve, where embroidered leaves once were, something else has taken their place.

Blossoms.

"Girls!" Corey comes knocking. "It's time."

I close my eyes and take a deep breath. In and out, like my grandmother taught me. Then I step out.

The nave is big, brightly lit, with white flowers cascading from every wall. I let Petra go first—I'm way too nervous to take the first step down the aisle. Everything still feels so surreal. Like I might wake up at any moment.

But when I pinch myself, it stings like a motherfucker.

Good. I spent all my life dreaming. I'm ready to wake the hell up. I'm ready to make my dreams a reality.

I take my first step. Then another. As I advance, I spy everyone I've ever loved in this room: Corey and Rob, their eyes wet already. Charlie, beaming like a kid on Christmas. Elias, looking at me with pride, carrying the memory of my grandmother here for me. Through us, Maia is here, too.

And then June, leading my daughter by her tiny little hands, helping her scatter flower petals all the way down the nave. She's stumbling with every step, not even one year old yet, but that's okay. That's how we all start.

Buttons trails after her, showing off the classiest bow tie in the room.

And then, on the altar, the rest of my family: Petra, the sister I never thought I'd find. Yuri, a brother beyond blood. Grisha, best man and loyal friend. And at the center, waiting for me...

Matvey.

The love of my life.

"Ready?" He holds out a hand.

For better and for worse. For richer and for poorer. In sickness and in health. Until death do us part—and it can damn well try.

"Ready," I answer.

Then I take his hand in mine.

~

Admittedly, I haven't been to many weddings in my life. And while I'm sure this has been the best, most kick-ass wedding on the planet, I can't help but wonder one thing...

How long before it's socially acceptable to drag your new husband to bed?

Husband. Such an unfamiliar word.

I try it on for size. *Husband. Hus-band.* I mouth it silently to myself while the guests party to their hearts' content. Rivers of champagne are flowing, and the cake's still receiving visits, especially from two hulking Russian bridesmaids in matching suits.

Out in the garden, I take in the villa in all its glory. It's gigantic—I can't even begin to imagine how much it cost to reserve it for one night. But we wanted our guests to have the best time without having to worry about getting home safe in the middle of the night, and this seemed like the ideal way to go.

It also meant we wouldn't have to wait for our wedding night.

God, I can't believe I'm so nervous. Matvey's seen all there is to see—surely there's no point getting shy now?

And yet, the butterflies won't stop butterflying.

It doesn't help that Matvey's never looked this handsome before. It's unfair, honestly: *I* should've seen all there was to see, too. Where did this glow-up come from? And how is it even possible in the first place? He was already the hottest guy I'd ever seen!

Like I said: unfair.

We've danced half the night away already, our hands roaming in all the appropriate ways. Now, nursing a drink as my husband—*hus-band;* nope, still weird—entertains his guests, I'm thinking of all the other ways. The not-so-appropriate ways.

Maybe another hour? I chew on my bottom lip, throwing cautious glances around the room. *Maybe until the guests go to sleep? Or until Petra drags Yuri into the bushes?*

Luckily, I don't have to wonder for long. "Come with me."

I almost jump at the sudden voice behind my ear. "Where?"

"I don't care," Matvey growls. "But if you're not somewhere else in the next fifty seconds, I'm going to take you right here, right now, in front of every single guest."

I swallow. He's definitely capable of doing that. "B-But the wedding—"

"We've had our wedding. Now, come be my wife."

Wife. Goddammit, he just had to play that card. It sounds way too hot coming out of his mouth—how in the hell am I going to say no?

Then don't say it.

That's right. This is our night. If we don't make the rules, who will?

"Fine," I drawl. "But if *you're* not in our room in the next fifty seconds, I'm starting without you."

I can feel his gaze on me, hot and molten. I feel it every step of the way as I glide out of the garden. The villa interior greets me in marble and gold, a place fit for royalty.

Isn't that what you are now? the voice inside me whispers. *A crowned queen?*

If I am, then my king better not keep me waiting.

I stride towards our suite, my dress trailing after me like a carpet of flowers. Maybe the champagne's gone to my head, but I've never felt more powerful. More in control. Like I could take on the world and everyone in it.

And then, just as I'm about to step inside, my feet are swept out from under me. "Matvey!" I protest.

"You didn't think I was going to let you cross that threshold on your own, did you?"

"Yes? No? I don't know. I was having a cool moment."

"Ah, so I interrupted, did I?" He sucks my earlobe between his teeth, but only for a second. Enough to drive me wild with the promise of more. "I can leave. Let you get back to it."

Not a chance in hell. "Eh, the moment's passed."

"Pity. Guess I'll just have to carry you inside then."

"It's not even our house!" I laugh, too exhilarated to do anything else. Other people don't get to see this: Matvey's playful side. That's a privilege reserved for family only.

And his playful side in bed…

Well, let's just say I've got that under contract now.

"Then lead the way, *husband.*"

He groans against me. "Fuck, *kalina.*"

"What? Did I say something wrong?"

He doesn't even let me gawk at the expensive décor of the suite. Just presses me up against the nearest flat surface. "No. But if you keep saying that, I can't promise I'll stick to my plan."

"Which is?"

"To worship every inch of your body."

A shiver runs down my spine. "Better get to it then. Before you change your mind."

He smirks, wolfish and hungry. "As you wish, *moya pakhansha.*"

Then he's sealing his lips over mine.

It's a deep, devouring kiss. It leaves me stranded against the wall, drowning in pleasure and heat, with not a single second to catch my breath. *I'm going to die*, I think helplessly as Matvey steals my oxygen again, and again, and again. *This kiss will be the death of me.*

But when we break apart, I just dive back for more.

I feel his hands on my dress, fighting off layers and layers of tulle to get to my bare skin. But this dress is mermaid-shaped, which means there's very little space to maneuver anything down there.

"Wait," I gasp. "Let me."

I reach for a clasp at my side. It's a hellish endeavor, trying to connect my last two functioning brain cells enough to work it loose. But the second I do…

My skirts flare, open and ready.

"*Blyat',*" he curses against my neck. "Had that ready for me, didn't you?"

"Actually, I had it ready for the dance," I breathe under an assault of kisses. "But then it wasn't really necess—*ah!*"

Pleasure sparks through me. With a single, swift move, Matvey frees my breasts from their cups and dives between them, biting each nipple in turn. His tongue is a hot, molten thing.

"M-Matvey…"

"Mine," he growls against my skin. "Only mine."

Yours, I want to gasp back. *Only yours.*

Then he drops to his knees.

I understand what he's about to do a split second before he actually does it. "Matvey, that's...!"

Embarrassing. Ridiculous. Corny.

None of those words make it halfway past my throat.

Because the truth is, it's also hot as sin.

Matvey's teeth clamp the lace garter around my thigh. I can feel his beard graze me all the way down, his canines scraping the sensitive skin of my inner thigh.

When he emerges with the piece of lace in his mouth, I almost lose it. "What am I going to do with you?" I exhale.

He spits out the lace. "That's the wrong question to ask."

"What's the right one?"

His eyes go dark, hooded. Hungry in a million different ways. "What am *I* going to do with *you?*"

Then he dives back under my skirts.

At the first lap of his tongue, I bite my lip so hard I draw blood. But I can't afford anything less—if I don't, everyone out there will hear me.

Except that Matvey seems determined to accomplish just that. "Don't hide," he rasps. "Let me hear your pretty little voice sing."

So I do. I throw my head back against the wall and moan as Matvey's tongue spells doom inside of me. With one leg hooked around his neck and five manicured nails digging into his scalp, I feel like the dirtiest bride who's ever lived.

I don't know how long he goes on: minutes, hours, days. Like he's eating me alive.

"Matvey," I gasp. I'm so close I can taste it, but it scares me, too. How good it feels—this rising wave of pure pleasure. How strong it'll hit when it finally crests and crashes. "I can't…!"

"Then don't."

That's all it takes. I push his mouth fully on me, shameless in my undone bridal gown, and ride out my orgasm.

When Matvey rises back to me, I hook both arms around his shoulders. "Bed," I demand. "Now."

He doesn't make me ask twice.

My feet lose solid ground again. He carries me all the way across the room, to the giant four-poster bed at the end. It looks lavish—fit for a king.

And his queen, I remind myself.

He lays me down gently, but there's no mistaking the hunger in his eyes. "I am going to keep you up all night."

He slips off my shoes and presses a reverent kiss to the side of my foot, then my ankle. With every kiss upward, I shiver a little more. Matvey's lips graze all the most forgettable parts of me, the ones that even I forget I have: the underside of my calf, the dip in my knee, the birthmark under my belly button. Places that should be worth nothing in a situation like this, and yet he makes them feel so precious.

He makes *me* feel precious.

And suddenly, the same hunger flares up in me: the burning

urge to *consume.* To show Matvey just how much I want him, too.

"Lie back," I whisper.

He arches one eyebrow at me, but doesn't protest. He doesn't exactly go full starfish, but strips off his clothes and sits up against the headboard, which is about as submissive as he's ever going to get. *Pakhan* pride and all that.

But that's okay. I don't need him to submit. I just need him exactly where he is.

I shed my wedding dress and crawl into his lap. My panties have already been unceremoniously ripped off—not that I'd expected any different. In fact, it just makes my job easier.

"What's this?" he smirks.

When I take him in hand, he's already dripping. "Me being a good wife."

Then I sink.

"Fuck," he swears as I pop the tip in. *"Fuck."*

Honestly, I'm right there with him.

I savor the drag of his length inside me, inch by torturous inch. I take him slowly, my gaze fixed on Matvey's hooded eyes, determined to catch every fleeting expression.

If I'm his, then he's mine, too.

I start moving. "Husband," I breathe.

Matvey bites back a curse. "Say it again."

"Husband."

"Again."

He thrusts up inside me as I ride him, the rhythm merciless. "Husband, husband, husb—*ahh*!"

It happens in a blink. One second, I'm the one on top, and the next—

The next, my back hits the mattress. "I warned you."

"Ma—!" He drives into me. This time, it's so deep I can't even breathe. "*Matvey.*"

"I'm going to fuck you until the sun comes up," he growls against my pulse point. "Until you're begging for me to let you go."

"Ahh—"

"Until you're fucking *stuffed*."

My eyes roll back. I *just* came—why am I feeling like I could come again in seconds? "Is that so?"

"Yes."

"You're going to put another baby into me?"

It's a half-joke, but the look Matvey gives me is dead serious. "Yes. And then another."

"I—"

"And another, and another, until not a day goes by when you aren't filled with my babies."

God help me. I know it's just dirty talking, and yet...

And yet, part of me wants nothing else. Not in the literal *stuffed-with-babies-until-you-die* sense, but in the only sense that matters.

May's going to be one soon. And really, I've always wanted a big family. Three kids at least, maybe more. Perhaps it isn't such a bad idea to start right away.

"Okay," I breathe.

"Yeah?" Matvey rasps into my ear.

"Yes." I take his face in my hands. "Fill me with your baby."

Whatever else I have to say to that, it gets swallowed up by his lips.

He hooks my leg behind his shoulder and makes good on his promise: he fucks me until I'm begging. Until I can't tell if I'm still coming from a previous orgasm or if I'm being tipped over the edge again, over and over.

"Ready?" he teases.

"Yes," I babble incoherently. "Put your baby in me. I'm ready, I'm—*ahh!*"

He bites down on my shoulder and spills inside me. I can feel it everywhere, filling me up just like he promised, so much that I have to squeeze my legs around his hips to keep it from overflowing. And yet, I still can't get enough: of this, of him. Of us.

So I keep chanting it to him. Every time he starts thrusting into me again, I sink my nails into his scalp and moan, *I'm ready, I'm ready, I'm ready.*

I'm ready for your baby.

The best part, though?

This time, I really am.

EXTENDED EPILOGUE: MATVEY
TEN YEARS LATER

Check out the exclusive Extended Epilogue to Cashmere Ruin!
Download here: https://dl.bookfunnel.com/o7x8hux1jk

ALSO BY NICOLE FOX

Kuznetsov Bratva
Emerald Malice
Emerald Vices

Novikov Bratva
Ivory Ashes
Ivory Oath

Egorov Bratva
Tangled Innocence
Tangled Decadence

Zakrevsky Bratva
Requiem of Sin
Sonata of Lies
Rhapsody of Pain

Bugrov Bratva
Midnight Purgatory
Midnight Sanctuary

Oryolov Bratva
Cruel Paradise
Cruel Promise

Pushkin Bratva
Cognac Villain
Cognac Vixen

Viktorov Bratva

Whiskey Poison

Whiskey Pain

Orlov Bratva

Champagne Venom

Champagne Wrath

Uvarov Bratva

Sapphire Scars

Sapphire Tears

Vlasov Bratva

Arrogant Monster

Arrogant Mistake

Zhukova Bratva

Tarnished Tyrant

Tarnished Queen

Stepanov Bratva

Satin Sinner

Satin Princess

Makarova Bratva

Shattered Altar

Shattered Cradle

Solovev Bratva

Ravaged Crown

Ravaged Throne

Vorobev Bratva

Velvet Devil

Velvet Angel

Romanoff Bratva

Immaculate Deception

Immaculate Corruption

Kovalyov Bratva

Gilded Cage

Gilded Tears

Jaded Soul

Jaded Devil

Ripped Veil

Ripped Lace

Mazzeo Mafia Duet

Liar's Lullaby (Book 1)

Sinner's Lullaby (Book 2)

Bratva Crime Syndicate

Can be read in any order!

Lies He Told Me

Scars He Gave Me

Sins He Taught Me

Belluci Mafia Trilogy

Corrupted Angel (Book 1)

Corrupted Queen (Book 2)

Corrupted Empire (Book 3)

De Maggio Mafia Duet

Devil in a Suit (Book 1)

Devil at the Altar (Book 2)

Kornilov Bratva Duet
Married to the Don (Book 1)

Til Death Do Us Part (Book 2)

Heirs to the Bratva Empire
Can be read in any order!

Kostya

Maksim

Andrei

Princes of Ravenlake Academy (Bully Romance)
Can be read as standalones!

Cruel Prep

Cruel Academy

Cruel Elite

Tsezar Bratva
Nightfall (Book 1)

Daybreak (Book 2)

Russian Crime Brotherhood
Can be read in any order!

Owned by the Mob Boss

Unprotected with the Mob Boss

Knocked Up by the Mob Boss

Sold to the Mob Boss

Stolen by the Mob Boss

Trapped with the Mob Boss

Volkov Bratva

Broken Vows (Book 1)

Broken Hope (Book 2)

Broken Sins *(standalone)*

Other Standalones

Vin: A Mafia Romance

Box Sets

Bratva Mob Bosses (Russian Crime Brotherhood Books 1-6)

Tsezar Bratva (Tsezar Bratva Duet Books 1-2)

Heirs to the Bratva Empire

The Mafia Dons Collection

The Don's Corruption